# STAR-SPANGLED REJECTS

## THE HEAVENLY GRILLE CAFÉ: BOOK III

*Star-Spangled Rejects*
*The Heavenly Grille Café Book Three*
Copyright © 2016 by Joyce T. Livingston

Cover art: Shutterstock/Rachata Sinthopachakul

Published by Piscataqua Press
An imprint of RiverRun Bookstore Inc.
142 Fleet Street | Portsmouth, NH | 03801
www.riverrunbookstore.com
www.piscaaquapress.com

Printed in the United States of America

ISBN: 978-1-939739-22-9

# STAR-SPANGLED REJECTS

## THE HEAVENLY GRILLE CAFÉ: BOOK III

By

## J.T. Livingston

This last book in the Heavenly Grille Café series is dedicated to my nephew, TYLER GENE JONES, who died from a drug overdose, on April 30, 2016. He was only 24 years old and his life was just beginning for him. He chose the wrong friends, and he made some bad decisions—something we all do throughout our life time—but, God's timing is never our own, and there are no guarantees that our lives will be without trials and tribulations. I know you will be playing your guitar in Heaven, Tyler…maybe even as you sit beside your dad at the Golden Falls.

For all the young people out there who have fallen prey to the illegal drugs manufactured and sold throughout our country, my prayer for you is that you wake up in time to make a change in your life—before it is too late. For all the parents of the young people who have fallen prey, my prayer for you is that you, too, wake up in time—know who your children's friends are, and stay involved in their lives. Don't ever think that it will never happen to you or your family.

Let's all wake up before it's too late. Let's push for legislation that results in murder charges for anyone convicted of selling illegal drugs that end up killing someone's child—someone's spouse—someone's mother or father. Wake up…

The first book in The Heavenly Grille Café series began in the summer of 2011 and introduced the reader to three special angels: Maximus, a former Gladiator; Bertie, whose boisterous personality had earned her the proprietary title of Heaven's naughty angel; and, Doug, a young soldier who died in battle in 1953. These three angels run the Heavenly Grille Café, located in the middle of nowhere, in the small town of Monticello, Florida. The café is famous for the golden halo that seems to float miraculously above it. The first book also introduced us to Amanda Turner, a young girl from Tampa, Florida who found refuge, and a new family, at the Heavenly Grille Café. Amanda returned to Tampa at the end of Book I to pursue a career in law enforcement, and the angels decided to remain in Monticello, FL for the time being.

Book II of the series began in October 2013 and introduced the reader to a different kind of angel—a four-footed angel. His name was Sam, and he was Amanda's dog for 10 years before he died. Sam and his human angels at the cafe were on a mission to do what they could do to help those who could not help themselves—bait and fighter dogs. If you have ever wondered whether or not we will be reunited in Heaven with our four-legged companions, then Book II provides some heavenly—albeit fictional—insight to that question.

Book III of the series begins in January 2016, in a new location—Rome, GA—and introduces the reader and our angels to two characters that are part of a growing section of America's population: the homeless Veterans who proudly served their country, only to feel rejected and abandoned upon their return from battle. One of the characters is a Vietnam Veteran, while the other one is an Iraq War Veteran—a generation apart—yet, they share so much in common. Book III, like the other two books in the series, is a book of fiction, but it is based on a very real problem that many Veterans face on a daily basis—their struggle with Post-Traumatic Stress Disorder (PTSD). One of these two Veterans will be charged for a murder he did not commit. Will the angels be able to save either of these fragile men in time?

Book III is, also, dedicated to ALL Veterans who have proudly served and protected the United States of America. The poetry throughout Book III was written by MAJ (Retired U.S. Army, Special Forces) Edwin C. Livingston, who proudly served his country from January 24, 1957 until his retirement on June 30, 1977, and knows first-hand, the daily frustration and agony of living with PTSD.

# CHAPTER 1

## Midnight Under the Bridge

It was almost midnight on Friday, January 22, 2016. The temperature had recently dropped below freezing, but the small group of homeless people that lived beneath the underpass barely noticed. They had all endured colder winters than this one and, God-willing, they would live to endure many more. They were all just thankful that this particular winter was being spent in the warmer climate of Rome, GA instead of previous ones that had been spent farther north.

There were seven of them on this night—five men and two women—who claimed the area around the underpass as their temporary home. The area was surrounded on all sides with a thick fusion of pine trees, needle palms, and wild azaleas, all of which helped to keep the cold wind from being as intrusive as it would have been without the presence of the native plants and trees.

The old man, known to the group as "Skipper", stood away from the others and stared at the large golden halo that seemed to miraculously float above the diner across the street. He had watched the building go up in a matter of days, but had not been there whenever the halo had been erected above the diner. A large, flashing marquee stood in the parking lot: THE HEAVENLY GRILLE CAFÉ, OPEN MONDAY – SATURDAY, 7 AM – 11 PM, GOD LOVES YOU & SO DO WE! He took a last drag of the cigarette he was smoking, flicked it, and grinded it firmly into the dirt. He shook his head in wonderment at the floating halo that lit up the entire parking lot and surrounding grounds. Not much surprised him these days, but, the halo certainly did.

Skipper looked down at the old wristwatch he had worn since he returned home from his final tour in Vietnam, back in April 1970. It was 11:45 PM when the young man, who worked at the diner, walked out of the front door carrying two large sacks. Skipper guessed the sacks would be filled with sandwiches, hot coffee, and whatever dessert that might have been served that day. "Right on time," he muttered beneath his breath. He thought about leaving the group in order to avoid any conversation the young man might try to start with him again, but the temptation of a sandwich and hot cup of coffee left him teetering on the edge of indecision. He had to admit that whoever the cook was at the diner certainly knew his trade, because the food was the best he had tasted in more years than he could remember.

Three male members of this homeless clan climbed slowly from beneath their cardboard boxes; two senior women emerged from makeshift tents that had been pitched about 50 feet away from the men. Skipper and a young man in his thirties always slept out in the open, in their sleeping bags, at opposite ends from each other. Both men were loners and had no desire to mingle with their fellow, homeless comrades, or with each other.

Stella Sieber was 82 years old and had been homeless, by choice, for the past 27 years. She came from a small town in Michigan, and had been 55 years old when her abusive, alcoholic husband had died under—what the local police deemed—"mysterious" circumstances. Stella had been on the move ever since then, relocating herself farther south every few months. She was as much a loner as the old man they called Skipper, but she considered herself to be a lot more amiable than was he. "Ain't it about time for that young fella to be bringing us something to eat?" she snarled at no one in particular.

Skipper turned to look at the mangy old woman who constantly grated on his last nerve. He turned back toward the café without proffering a response.

"Cat got your tongue, does he?" Stella crackled after spitting out a large clump of phlegm from her smoke-ridden lungs. She removed the remnant of a cigarette, from her coat pocket, and lit it up. She managed to get two tokes from the cigarette butt before the red ash burned her calloused thumb. She cursed under her breath and threw the butt on the ground behind her, not bothering to grind it out.

"You should be more careful, Stella," the middle-aged black woman spoke softly as she moved to stand behind the older, white woman. "The last thing we need is a brush fire to draw attention to us. I like this place...I feel safe here..." Peggy Jensen dropped her head and kicked dirt on Stella's cigarette butt.

"Aw, why don't you just shut up, PJ; ain't nobody talking to you. Go on back inside your tent," Stella shouted. She didn't like mealy-minded women who were afraid to speak up for themselves. She had been one of those women for 37 years, but "mysterious" circumstances had provided her the opportunity she so desperately desired, and she had finally escaped the matrimonial prison in which she had been ensconced.

PJ kicked at the dirt again and muttered under her breath, "But, I'm so hungry..." She was startled when she felt a firm hand squeeze her left shoulder. She jerked her head around sharply and saw the young man who had joined their group just a couple of weeks ago. PJ thought he was a handsome-enough white man—one that she might have fancied for herself in her younger years. She always had a preference for white men over those of her own race, and this personal preference had driven a solid wedge between her and other family members, who still lived in Selma, Alabama. She had walked away from all of them 5 years ago, but found herself wondering more and more if she shouldn't have been more placating of their opinions.

The young white man, known to the group as Jason, looked down at PJ and shook his head. "She's not worth it; don't pay any attention to what she says." His voice was a blended mixture of gruff deepness, yet soothingly mellow at the same time. He wore a black, knitted cap over his dark, short-shaven hair.

PJ caught a slight glimpse of strong, white teeth beneath his timid grin. That was the most she had ever heard him speak during the short time he had been there. She lowered her head and simply nodded.

Three men in their sixties ambled slowly and clumsily toward the small campfire at the center of their sheltered hideaway. They could easily have been mistaken for the Three Stooges—Larry, Curly, and Moe—as they comically bumped into one another due to their varying degrees of soberness. Larry was a former real estate broker who had lost everything during the housing bubble crash that ended in 2009; he was 62 years old and his real name was Norman Weissman. Curly was a bald-headed, former college football coach, whose wife had left him for one of his best tight ends; he was 60 years old and his real name was Joe Sanders. Moe was the unofficial leader of this comical trio, and was a retired pharmacist who had grown tired of the rat race, as well as the wife and kids that went along with it, and whom he thought wanted nothing from him except his money. He had left them all his money and walked away one night with just the clothes on his back; he was 67 years old and his real name was Bernard Cartwright.

None of these seven people, excluding Stella, were the stereotypical homeless persons depicted on television and in newspapers. They maintained their appearances as best as they possibly could, and worked odd jobs whenever they could be found. None of them had truly bonded with the others in the group, but they all felt a sense of limited safety and security within their temporary family.

Joe Sanders belched loudly and squinted his eyes. "Hey, look!" he said as he pointed in the direction of the Heavenly Grille Café. "Here comes our midnight snack." He stumbled and grinned at Bernard, who caught him by the elbow. "Thanks, Moe," he winked, acknowledging the group's constant reference to them as the Three Stooges.

"Ahhh...think nothing of it, my good Curly!" Bernard winked back at him.

"I sure hope there's some more of that buttermilk cake," Norman yawned. "Guess a cup of coffee wouldn't hurt any of us none, huh?"

The group began to spread out when the young man from the diner across the street stepped through the bushes and into the clearing that was their common area.

Doug was one of the three angels who operated the Heavenly Grille Café. Their assignment was to help as many people as they could, without interfering with destiny in any form or fashion. He grinned at all of them and made his way toward their campfire. He sat the bag that held seven large cups of strong, black coffee on the ground in front of him. Angels have a remarkable sense of hearing and he had listened in to all their conversations, both verbal and unspoken, on his way across the street. "Good evening, everyone," his deep voice was unassuming and non-confrontational. "I hope you're all hungry because Max had lots of grilled meatloaf sandwiches left over tonight. There are plenty of home fries, too, and buttermilk cake—enough for everyone to have seconds if they want. There is coffee in the other bag," he offered as he began passing around the sandwiches and fries. "Do you mind if I sit with all of you for a little while?"

Nobody acknowledged his question.

PJ kept her eyes downward as she took the offered food. "Thank you very much," she whispered shyly and walked over to get a coffee from the other bag.

Stella gave her a dirty look and deliberately bumped into PJ, causing her to spill some of the hot coffee. "Who said you could go first!" she hissed into PJs ear, low enough so nobody could hear.

Doug heard but decided not to say anything to Stella. "How are you tonight, Stella? You're looking beautiful, as always."

Stella grabbed the sandwich and fries from Doug's fingers and looked up at him. "I don't need your lying sweet talk, pretty boy. Just give me the food and leave me alone, why don't you? I don't need to hear any preachin' from you either, and if that's part of the deal, then you can just keep your food!"

Doug smiled back at the old woman. He knew about her "mysterious" secret, and hoped and prayed for her salvation and repentance before it was too late. He held out another piece of wrapped food. "Don't forget your cake, Stella."

Larry, Curly, and Moe moved as one toward Doug. "We'll be glad to take her share if she doesn't want it," Norman, the former real estate broker, grinned. "I hope that coffee is decaf...we don't need anything that will interfere with our beauty sleep, you know!"

Doug laughed at the good-natured man who he had grown to like so much since the café opened on New Year's Day. He had never met anyone that was better suited to the homeless life than Norman Weissman. Norman had told him his story more than once—how he had been in the real estate business for 30 years and had made millions of dollars before numerous bad investments had sent his empire crumbling before his very eyes. His partner of 15 years had left him and taken whatever the bank had not pilfered. "Yes, Norman...I definitely have decaf for you!" Doug grinned.

Norman closed his eyes and sighed when he felt Doug's firm hand upon his shoulder. The calmness and serenity that came over him every time Doug touched him was beyond anything he had ever before experienced. If Doug's touch didn't sober him up, the strong decaf coffee surely would.

Doug handed sandwiches and fries to Joe and Bernard. "Here you go, gentlemen. How was your day?"

Curly, AKA: Joe Sanders, shuffled from side to side, mimicking his favorite touchdown dance. "Couldn't be better, Doug, my boy...couldn't be better. Tomorrow is going to be a wonderful day; I can feel it in these old bones." He winked at Doug and made his way to the coffee.

Bernard Cartwright pulled his knitted cap over his ears and smiled at Doug. "It's a bit on the cool side tonight. We certainly do appreciate your kindness."

Doug touched Bernard's shoulder. "Would you like to pray, Bernard?" He knew that Bernard had been having second thoughts lately about having abandoned his family five years ago. He had been sensing a quiet need in Bernard since they first met three weeks ago.

Bernard stiffened under Doug's touch. He did not feel the same calmness and serenity that Norman had felt. He shook his head. "No...thank you, no. I don't deserve your prayers..." He took his food and joined his friends who sat cross-legged in front of the campfire. "If we sit like this for too long, fellas," he joked, "We may never be able to get up again!"

Doug sighed as he watched Bernard join the two men and two women at the campfire. His assignment, as an angel, was never to interfere with destiny. He was simply there to offer an ear and a prayer to anyone who might want or need it. He felt that Bernard was at a crossroads of sorts; but he, also, knew that he had to be careful in the part he played in any decision Bernard might eventually make. He sighed again and looked around the area that was home to seven very different people; the only thing they had in common was that neither of them felt they could return to their real homes...to their real lives. He spotted the remaining two men, standing at opposite ends of the shelter site. They had more in common with each other than either of them realized, but Doug knew that it was up to them to discover what that might be.

Doug walked over to where Jason leaned against a tall pine tree. He glanced down and saw a sleeping bag neatly rolled up beneath it. "This is your bed?" Doug asked.

Jason stared at the man who appeared to be near his own age. He resisted the urge to converse, and simply nodded. He held out his hand for the offered sandwiches, fries, and cake. He raised his eyes and stared directly into Doug's emerald-green ones. "Thanks," he nodded again and walked toward the campfire for coffee.

Doug watched him leave and exhaled softly. "You're welcome." He looked into the bag at the remaining food. His eyes scanned the entire camp area, but he did not see the older man they called Skipper. He had been there just moments before, and Doug sensed that he was still close by. He strolled toward the opposite end of the camp and sat the bag down on top of another rolled-up sleeping bag. "This is for you, Skipper," he spoke softly.

He looked toward the strange group of comrades who sat in front of the campfire, eating sandwiches and drinking coffee. Larry, Curly, and Moe were laughing and enjoying one another's companionship. PJ smiled at their antics, but kept quiet and to herself; Stella scratched at old scabs on her scalp and grunted at how ridiculous she thought they all were, all the while, using her few remaining teeth to stuff the sandwiches and cake down her throat as fast as she could.

"I'll be back in the morning!" Doug shouted to the group as he walked slowly through the dense brush and back toward the golden hue that glowed from the floating halo above the café.

The other two angels that operated the Heavenly Grille Café had listened in on Doug's conversations with the homeless group across the street. Max, a former Gladiator, and owner of the café, was a huge black man with an even huger heart, filled with his love of God. His co-hort on earth was Bertie; everyone always remarked on her resemblance to the late actress, Shirley Booth, and the character — Hazel — that she played on television from 1961 to 1966. Bertie, also, had the reputation in Heaven as being the "Naughty Angel" due to her inability, from time to time, to control her foul language.

Bertie punched Max against his hard-as-rock shoulder. "Did you listen to them, Max? Did you? Whatever are we going to do with that bunch? Every single one of them could go back to their homes and their lives, if they wanted to; but, NOOOO…they would all rather stay outside in below-freezing weather and act like they don't have a care in the world."

Max grinned as he crossed the floor and opened the door for Doug.

"Thanks," Doug said as he walked toward the counter where Bertie was already pouring him a cup of black coffee. "I don't know either, Bertie. I've been over there every night, and every morning, for three weeks now, and I don't feel like I've gotten any closer to any of them. Three of the men are pretty friendly, but careful not to express any real feelings; PJ is scared to death of being homeless, but too proud to return to her family; Stella is a time bomb set to explode at any moment; and, the other two men — the Veterans — they are extremely unapproachable and unresponsive. The older one only accepts the food every few days, but he never lets me see him do that. Those are the two that I worry the most about; they are lost souls searching for a reason…any reason…to go on living. I'm afraid they may be running low on inspiration for doing that."

Max joined them at the counter and the three of them sat together for another 45 minutes talking, and praying, about the group of seven that God had sent for them to watch over.

Bertie finally stood up and straightened her apron and

halo headband. She punched Max on the shoulder again and barked, "You know, big fella...when you said it was time for us to move the café again, I clearly remember you saying that our next move would be to Rome."

Max grinned and nodded. "I did indeed, Bertie." He flinched when Bertie punched him again.

"Well, Hells-Bells, why didn't you tell me you meant Rome, GEORGIA! I'm pretty sure that I won't be getting the opportunity to ever meet the Pope here!"

Three hours later, Bertie and Max had long gone their separate ways to the rooms they rented a few miles down the road. Doug lived in one of the two upstairs apartments above the café. Even though angels do not require sleep, the three of them often rested in prayer during the late-evening-to-early-morning hours.

Doug was in such prayer when the night was suddenly shattered with the sound of Stella's piercing screams from across the road. He flung open his apartment door and flew down the stairs to the paved parking lot. He was across the road and standing in the center of the homeless camp ground in less than two minutes. His eyes quickly took in the scene before him. Stella was leaning against the concrete underpass wall, pulling at her hair with both hands and screaming as loud as her 82-year old, air-starved lungs would allow. PJ's head poked out from her makeshift tent and she stared, dumbfounded, at the screaming Stella. Curly and Moe stumbled from beneath their cardboard boxes and crashed into each other. Jason and Skipper were nowhere to be found.

A small puddle of blood pooled at Stella's feet, and Doug's eyes travelled slowly from the puddle to the bloody splatters on the concrete wall, just above Stella's head.

The Three Stooges were no more.

Norman Weissman lay dead at Stella's feet. A piece of his favorite buttermilk cake was still clasped between his calloused fingers.

The remaining group of four gathered what belongings they could, scattered, and ran in different directions before Doug could stop them.

# CHAPTER 2

## Getting the Story Straight

Fourteen-year old Jimmy Crennan slumped down in the booth he shared with his mother, Cheryl, at nine o'clock Saturday morning. He tried his best to avoid looking toward the woods across the road from the Heavenly Grille Café. He wanted to forget what had happened there just a few hours earlier.

"Did you hear what I said, Jimmy?" Cheryl smiled at her slumping son.

"What?" Jimmy stared at her with a dazed expression.

Cheryl picked up her cup of coffee. "I said…I can tell something is bothering you. Do you want to talk about it?" She saw him turn to look at the area across the street, which had been cordoned off with yellow crime tape.

Jimmy shook his head. "No, Mom…nothing's wrong. I'm just tired."

"That's another thing," Cheryl spoke softly. "You missed your curfew last night by several hours. "I didn't hear you come in until almost four o'clock this morning."

Jimmy stared at his mother and marveled at how young she looked. Nobody ever believed him when he told them she was his mother; she looked more like an older sister. He shared her dark, auburn hair and green eyes, but, he assumed he inherited the rest of his looks from the father that he had never known. His mother had been born in Columbus, Georgia—an only child—and gotten pregnant at sixteen; she had gone to live with her paternal grandmother in Hogansville, Georgia after her mother had kicked her out and disowned her. Jimmy knew the story of how life had unfolded for her, how she and his father had hooked up at a party one weekend, had too much to drink, and she had lost her virginity to a total stranger. She had been embarrassed, but she had told him that she didn't even know his father's name—he really had been a total stranger—and, she had drank too much, in order to forget an argument she had had earlier that evening with her overbearing mother. She never saw that young boy again, and he never knew that he had gotten her pregnant.

Jimmy sipped at his own coffee, loaded down with lots of cream and sugar to mask the bitter taste that he did not particularly like. "I know, Mom. I'm really sorry about that...it won't happen again, I promise. Kirk ran out of gas and it took us a while to find a station that was open that late. I didn't mean to worry you."

Bertie ambled over to their table, loaded down with stacks of pancakes for the teenager, and a sausage-and-cheese omelet for the pretty woman who sat across from him. "I don't believe I've seen you two in here before," she grinned. "You're gonna love these pancakes, young man. Max, our cook, likes to call them hoe-cakes, but they're really just extra-large, buttermilk pancakes if you ask me. I put some extra bacon on your plate, too."

"Thank you, ma'am," Jimmy replied. "They look good, but I'm not sure if I'm all that hungry, to tell you the truth."

Bertie studied the young man for a quick moment. Something was definitely bothering him, but the woman sitting across from him did not seem overly concerned. She placed the omelet in front of the woman. "I'm guessing you must be the sister, huh? You two look amazingly alike, you know? Of course, you probably hear that all the time."

Cheryl inhaled the wonderful aroma that came from the steaming omelet. "It all smells so good, and, don't worry, if he can't eat all of his food, I'll help him out." She smiled up at the middle-aged waitress. It was strange, but she felt like she had known the woman all of her life; she shook her head at the thought. "Actually, we are told that all the time, but...I am his mother, not his sister. I'm Cheryl Crennan, and this is my son, Jimmy—the best thing that's ever happened to me."

"Mom..." Jimmy blushed with embarrassment.

Bertie punched the young man against his shoulder and laughed out loud. "It's nice to meet you both. I'm Bertie." She stared intently at the young man. "There's nothing to be embarrassed about, Jimmy; it's your mom's right to be proud of you. I'm sure you would never do anything to rattle that pride, now would you?"

Jimmy jerked involuntarily when the boisterous waitress punched his shoulder. It didn't hurt, but his nerves jumped to attention at her question. He looked up to stare into intense blue eyes that seemed to be boring straight through him, before they darted discreetly to the woods across the street. There was no way she could know about his involvement in the incident that had happened in the wee hours of this morning. His mouth went dry and he couldn't swallow.

Cheryl saw Bertie's eyes move in the direction of the wood line adjacent to the café. "We noticed the crime tape over there. Do you know what happened?"

Bertie never lost eye contact with Jimmy. "A homeless man, by the name of Norman Weissman, was found dead there early this morning."

Cheryl gasped. "Oh, no...that's awful."

Bertie nodded. "Yeah, it is pretty awful. Norman was a nice man, never bothered anybody. The police stopped by a couple of hours ago to see if we heard anything."

The lump in Jimmy's throat almost prohibited him from

speaking. "But...you close at eleven...I mean, that's what the sign out front says. How could anybody here have heard anything?"

Bertie took her time responding to Jimmy's question. She waited until she saw Doug walk through the front door. She nodded in his direction. "That's Doug. He works here, and, he sleeps in the apartment above the café. He heard the screams last night, and was the first one on the scene. He spent most of the morning talking to the police about the group of homeless people that live over there."

The color drained from Jimmy's face.

"Shucks, I didn't mean to put a damper on your morning, folks," Bertie grinned. "Y'all go ahead and enjoy your breakfast, and let me know if I can get anything else for you."

Jimmy watched while the waitress spoke briefly with the man she called Doug. He flinched when Doug raised his head and looked directly at him. *"Oh, God...oh, God...they know what happened...they know I was involved in what happened...oh, God..."* his thoughts terrified him and he fought to retain control of his facial expression and emotions.

Jimmy's cell phone rang and he glanced down to see Kirk Blankenship's number lit up. He had felt special when Kirk and his friends decided to include him in last night's shenanigans—filled with booze, girls, weed, and, a small murder on the side for good measure. "I've got to take this, Mom. I'll be right back. Help yourself to some pancakes..." He pushed himself up and out of the booth before his mom could object, and rushed outside to the crowded parking lot.

"Jimmy, wait!" Cheryl cried out. She started to follow her son outside, but sat back down when she noticed several customers staring at her. She was never one to cause a scene; it wasn't in her nature. She sat back down and sipped at the black coffee. She had an uneasy feeling in the pit of her stomach, and had suddenly lost her appetite. Something felt off with Jimmy, but she couldn't put her finger on it. She sensed that he might be in some kind of trouble; he was a good kid – he had never, ever been in any trouble.

The Crennans were new residents in Rome, Georgia. They had moved there in late August of 2015, just in time for the new school year to start. Cheryl had no immediate family left. Her beloved grandmother, who had been her life support after Jimmy had been born, had passed away in her sleep just two years earlier. She had kept in touch with her father as best she could, and knew that he had sold his mother's house when she died, took the money, and moved out west to California — as far away from his ex-wife as he could possibly get. Her father had tried to talk her in to moving to California with him, but Cheryl loved Georgia and could not imagine living anywhere else. She and her father never talked about her mother, so Cheryl had no idea where the woman had ended up; and, she didn't care. She had hoped she could get through the rest of her life without ever having to lay eyes on Olivia Crennan again. Cheryl's best friends, a married couple from Hogansville, had moved to Rome, Georgia after the husband had been offered a job there as a criminal defense attorney for the county. They had convinced Cheryl that it would be a good place for Jimmy to complete high school and go to college. She had discussed it with Jimmy, and he was game, so the two of them packed up everything they owned, rented a U-Haul truck, and prepared for a fresh start in Rome, Georgia.

"Is there something wrong with the food?" Doug's deep voice cut through Cheryl's memories. "I'll be glad to get you something else."

Cheryl blinked and stared up into the greenest eyes she had ever seen, not to mention, the most handsome man she had ever seen. "What..." she stammered, before exhaling and shaking her head. "No, everything is fine...better than fine; I'm just not as hungry as I thought I was. I will take a refill on coffee, though."

"I'll be right back with a fresh pot," Doug smiled down at her. "That was your son who went outside, right?"

Cheryl nodded. "Yes. His name is Jimmy. He should be right back; he just had to make a quick phone call."

Doug grinned. "I'll bring him a refill, too. Be right back."

Cheryl watched the manly merchandise make his way back behind the counter. He said something to the matronly waitress, and looked back at Cheryl, who promptly dropped her eyes and placed both hands on top of the table. *"Oh, my goodness...he saw me watching him!"*


Jimmy paced back and forth in the parking lot, waiting impatiently for Kirk to answer his call. "Come on, Kirk...pick up!"

Kirk Blankenship answered on the fourth ring. "Hey, Crennan, where the devil are you? We were all supposed to meet at the Clocktower an hour ago. Everyone showed up, except for you, so you can imagine what the others are thinking."

"I couldn't get away," Jimmy offered in explanation. "My mom insisted on taking me to breakfast at a new café she heard about..."

"I don't give a crap about where you're eating breakfast, Crennan! I think there are more important things for you to be thinking about, don't you?"

Jimmy was quiet for a long minute. "I told you I wouldn't say anything, and I won't."

"You better not...because if you do, something just might happen to that hot mama of yours..."

Jimmy cut Kirk off abruptly. "Leave my mother out of this, Kirk. If you want me to keep silent about what happened—about what you did—then, you just keep my mother out of it."

"There's no need to worry about what happened last night, Crennan. I took care of it. Nobody will ever connect us to that. He was just some old homeless freak, anyway. Nobody will even miss him."

Jimmy broke the connection. He wished he could break

his relationship with Kirk and his friends as easily as he broke the phone connection. He wished he had never met the group of three rich friends. "You don't know that," he spoke out loud. "He could have a family somewhere, someone who loved him, someone who missed him...you don't know..."

He cast a quick glance behind him to make sure his mother wasn't watching him from the window. She wasn't, so Jimmy made a spontaneous decision that he hoped he would not regret. He quickly sprinted across the parking lot to the taped off wooded area, across the street. He lifted the crime-scene tape and pushed through some bushes until he came to the campground clearing. He saw a few cardboard boxes propped up, side-side-by side. He wondered if people actually lived inside those boxes. He saw the darkened ashes from a campfire and went over to squat down beside it. "Is this where you ate your meals?" he whispered. He walked over to one of the large, cardboard boxes and peeked inside at the old newspapers that covered the bottom of the box, maybe as a blanket against the cold, hard ground. "Is this where you slept?"

He stood up and closed his eyes. He lowered his head and said, "Oh, God...I am so sorry...so very sorry that this happened to you. Nobody was supposed to get hurt..."

Jimmy felt the hairs on the back of his neck stiffen and he knew that he was no longer alone in the clearing. He was almost afraid to open his eyes—he was afraid that he would see the smiling face of the old man they had encountered last night; instead, when he opened his eyes, he saw another old man standing behind a bush, watching him. The man leaned casually against a tree, and appeared to be in his late sixties, but his physique was not that of an old man. He was tall and lean, with black and silver hair; his mustache and beard were both solid white. He wore an old denim jacket and a black, non-descript baseball cap that covered most of his bushy brows; his jeans were well-worn but clean, and his boots showed signs that he had walked more than a mile through the Georgia red mud. Jimmy took it all in, but he was unable to speak. His tongue felt like it had swollen to three times its normal size inside his mouth.

Skipper walked slowly from behind the bush; he never took his eyes off the young kid that stood nervously, twenty feet away. "You're one of them."

Jimmy tried to swallow, but found that he had no spit to assist him with that endeavor. "What?"

Skipper was within ten feet of the boy now. "Yeah, you're one of them, alright. I was in the bushes over there when you and your buddies stumbled over each other, laughing and egging one another on. They wanted you to kick over the boxes, tear down the tents..."

Jimmy shook his head. "Mister, I don't know who you are, or what you're talking about. You need to back off...stay away from me..." He was close to hyperventilating.

Skipper continued a forward motion. He shook his head. "No...I don't think so. You and your friends killed an innocent man last night. The only thing poor Norman was guilty of, was waking up in the middle of the night, and wanting an extra piece of cake. That's the only reason he was even awake when you and your gang crept into our area. All of you thought it was fun to push him around, watch an old man fall and try to get up again and again. He never stood a chance against the four of you. So...where's the rest of your gang? Did you come back to make sure you didn't leave any evidence behind? You're too late. The cops have already gathered all the evidence they need."

Jimmy shook his head again. "No, it wasn't like that — we didn't mean to hurt anybody..." He stopped short and realized, too late, that he had said too much. He clinched his fists and looked up, ready to defend himself against the old man, but, the old man was gone. Jimmy spun around, looking in all directions, but the old man had disappeared as suddenly as he had appeared.

A slight rustling of leaves brought Jimmy back around to the spot where the old man had recently stood.

Stella Sieber wrinkled her nose and stared hard at Jimmy Crennan. She shook her head vehemently from side to side and began to back away. "No!" she screamed. "You can't have it back. He gave it to ME! The money is mine and I'm gonna keep it...you can't have it back! I told him I would keep quiet about what y'all done to old Norman, and I will." She checked the spot inside her bra where she had tucked the hundred dollar bill that Kirk Blankenship had given her while she stood next to the concrete overpass, staring down into the lifeless eyes of Norman Weissman. "You can't have it back!" she screamed as she turned and ran back into the woods.

Jimmy brought both hands to his face and pushed his cheeks together. He walked backwards a few feet before he turned and ran away from the campsite, and rushed back to the café's parking lot. He stopped beside his mom's car to catch his breath before he went back inside. "Oh, God, I am so, so sorry..." he inhaled deeply, opened his eyes, and stood erect. He turned to look back at the woods across the street, and saw the old man standing on the side of the road, staring back at him.

Jimmy turned and ran inside the café. He made his way back to the booth where his mother waited for him. He cast a sideways-glance out the window, into the woods across the street.

The old man was gone.

# CHAPTER 3

## Skipper's and Jason's Stories

The temperature had warmed to a pleasant 52 degrees by noon, and Skipper stretched out his long legs in front of him, closed his eyes, and enjoyed the warmth of the sun upon his tired eyelids. He could not remember the last time he had slept through the night, or the last time he had closed his eyes and not had the horrifying nightmares invade his sleep.

He sighed deeply and thought about the young boy from the diner. He never intended to say anything to the boy; and, he never intended to get involved in what happened to Norman Weissman. It had been a long time since he had spoken that many consecutive words, and he was surprised that his voice still functioned.

He sat up straighter and removed a weathered, black-and-white composition book from his backpack. The war poems that he had written over the years rested within those pages; they had been his salvation — they had kept him relatively sane. Writing them had been therapeutic — had saved him from doing what so many other Veterans had done after the horrors they had witnessed in battle. He still wanted to do it—to die—every day, but he was still here. He opened the composition book to a poem that summed up life for him. He had titled it, "Flight 341", his returning flight number home from his last battle in 1970:

*Crossing the great Pacific waters one last time*
*Mighty ships collide with the setting sun;*
*In the wake of tomorrow, there will always be sorrow*
*For those of us aboard Flight 341.*

*Soaring above the jungles of pain and despair*
*Heaven descends to meet the darkened sea;*
*Sounds of war fade away, except for those who stay*
*To pay for the cost of being free.*

*There was angry silence as we flew through the clouds*
*Knowing we fought a war that was never won;*
*To the guys left below, we hope they all know*
*Our prayers were with them on Flight 341.*

*No one would greet us with flowers and cheer*
*They would cuss us and spit in our face;*
*With San Francisco in view, all of us knew*
*We'd be like lepers of the human race.*

*We were neither villains of terror, nor demons from Hell*
*Just someone's American son;*
*We only hope and pray, that maybe some day*
*Homecomings will be different for Flight 341.*

Skipper closed his eyes and remembered his homecoming flights from his three tours in Vietnam. There had never been a "Welcome Home" for him or his fellow soldiers. Each homecoming had been worse than the one before, and he felt less and less significant with each one. Each homecoming, also, brought more nightmares into his life. So many young soldiers died in that thankless war, and he had never been able to fully understand why he hadn't—

why he was still here.

Skipper never heard the approaching footsteps.

The policeman nudged Skipper's muddy boat. "Okay, Buddy, you need to move along now. There's no loitering in the parks."

Skipper's muscles tensed automatically, and he fought the insatiable urge to inflict bodily harm upon the police officer. He hated being around people in general, but especially the young, arrogant members of the police force who appeared to be more impressed with the power and authority their uniforms provided them, than they were in actually serving and protecting. He held up his composition book for visual inspection. "I'm not loitering, officer. I'm just enjoying the peace and quiet while writing some poetry."

"Is that so?" the officer replied.

Skipper took a closer look at the officer, who had sat down on the bench beside him and removed his cap. He wasn't as young as Skipper had first thought him to be, but that didn't mean that he wasn't still arrogant and self-serving. "Yeah, that is so," Skipper replied. "But, if it's a problem, I'll be glad to find another bench, in another park."

The officer nodded toward the composition book. "Mind if I look at that?"

Skipper surprised himself; he never allowed anyone to read his poetry. They were his private thoughts, and they belonged to only him. He shrugged and handed the book to the officer. "Knock yourself out, but opinions are a dime a dozen, and I've had a life time of them, so kindly keep yours to yourself, okay?"

The two men sat in silence for the next fifteen minutes while Officer Thomas O'Brady scanned through the old composition book that held at least a hundred poems written over one man's life time.

Officer O'Brady cleared his throat and handed the book back to Skipper. "I wish I had time to read all of these. I'm certainly no expert at poetry, and, I know you don't want or need my opinion, but...these are very good. Am I right in guessing that you served in Viet Nam?"

Skipper's brows pulled inward and he nodded.

"I thought so," Officer O'Brady smiled. "I never knew my father. My mother was pregnant with me when he was shipped to Nam in 1973. He never made it back."

Skipper looked more closely at the officer. "You don't look old enough to have had a father who served in Nam."

"Baby-face O'Brady — that's what they all call me. I'll be forty-four in a few months. Dad was only twenty-four when most of his company got hit." He looked at Skipper for a long moment. "He'd probably be about your age, if he had lived."

Skipper shook his head. "I'm a bit older than I look, too." He paused slightly before he did something that he had not done in many years. He reached out to shake hands with the man sitting beside him. "They call me Skipper. My last tour in Nam was in 1970. I retired from the Army in 1977, and I was seventy-six years old last month." He had no idea why he was revealing so much about himself to a total stranger, and to a cop at that.

Thomas shook his head and grinned. "Wow, you're pretty well-preserved."

Skipper pursed his lips together and did something else he had not done in years. He smiled. "Yeah, alcohol preserves old fossils like me."

Officer O'Brady stood up and Skipper followed suit. He began to pack his book into his backpack when the officer stopped him. "Take your time, Skipper. Stay as long as you like. It's a nice day right now, but the night will be cold again. There's a men's shelter just a few blocks down..."

Skipper held up his hand. "Thanks, I know the place, but, I'll be fine."

The officer nodded and turned to leave, but stopped and turned back around to face Skipper. "One more thing, sir...welcome home, and, thank you for your service!"

Skipper raised his brows. It took a lot these days to surprise him, but Officer Thomas O'Brady had certainly done that. He took a deep breath and nodded. "Thanks." He watched the officer walk away and sat back down on the bench. He removed the grilled meatloaf sandwich from his backpack and stared at it for a long moment. He knew that Norman had left the sandwich but taken Skipper's piece of buttermilk cake from his sleeping bag the night before.

He ate the sandwich in silence and threw the crumbs in the direction of some visiting pigeons. He chased it with some bottled water that he always kept in his backpack. He wished he had the piece of cake to eat—the buttermilk cake that Norman Weissman loved so much—and, a lump stuck in his throat. He took out his composition book again, closed his eyes, and leaned his head back against the steel bench. "Rest in peace, Norman; you're in a much better place than the rest of us now."

Jason Benton sat on his own bench about a half-mile north of where Skipper sat. He had not been back to the camp site since Norman Weissman had been killed. He had not seen what happened, and he did not know who was to blame. He had awakened around 2:30 AM, unable to sleep due to the constant nightmares and flashbacks that invaded his mind—one flashback in particular—so he had gone for one of his many late-night walks.

He had just turned twenty-three years old when he received his orders for Iraq. It was his first of two tours in that God-forsaken country. He had only been there for thirty-seven days when he got up close and personal with his first taste of death. He had become friends with another young soldier who was, also, serving his first tour away from family and friends—a strong, muscular Italian from Queens, New York — Dante Fiorello. Their squad was on a routine patrol, and he and Dante had been comparing notes about the girls waiting for them back home. They were walking down a dirt path, with nothing but trees and brush on either side, when Jason had stopped to re-tie his boot lace, and fallen a few feet behind his friend. One minute, Dante was using his cupped hands to describe the best feature of Miss Bambi Constanza, and the next minute he had simply vaporized after having stepped on a buried improvised explosive device (IED). The explosion blew Jason fifteen feet backward, and when he tried to open his eyes, something warm and gooey prevented him from being able to do so—his friend's brains and entrails were splattered all over him. He was extremely lucky that the noise-induced hearing loss he experienced was only temporary. He only wished that he could say the same about the flashbacks and nightmares he continued to have, almost eight years later, about that day.

"Hey there, handsome, you got any boom?" the southern, female voice shook Jason out of his reverie.

Jason stood up to see a teenage girl, probably around sixteen years old staring at him. She was with three male teenagers; and, judging from their clothing and manner, they all appeared to be from better-to-well-off families. "No...that stuff will kill you."

Kirk Blankenship was leading the group back to his 2016, black Toyota Land Cruiser. It was definitely advantageous to have a father who owned the three highest profitable car dealerships in the tri-county area. He usually had his choice of wheels to drive at any given time. "Get away from that loser, Kristy. You might catch something," he snickered as he deliberately brushed against Jason's brown, cracked-leather jacket.

Kristy pouted and stomped her foot. "But I need a hit of something...anything!"

Kirk jerked her by the forearm and pulled her along the path that led to the parking lot. "I'll give you a hit of something if you don't get moving. Now! Get going—or I'll leave you here with your new plaything."

Jason took three steps forward and grabbed Kirk by the wrist. "Let her go. Let her go now."

Kirk pursed his lips together and was about to deliver a

punch to the gut of the loser that had dared to interfere with his afternoon delight. He swung his right fist back, but stopped when he saw a police officer walking in their direction. He stared defiantly at the man in the leather jacket and grinned. "You just got lucky…real lucky." He dropped Kristy's arm and commanded his group. "Come on, let's get out of here."

The two male friends in his group had seen the cop walking in their direction. "Yeah, that's probably a good idea," one of them agreed.

Officer Thomas O'Brady was at the tail end of his daily route, and he suspected trouble when he saw the group of teenagers up ahead. He recognized Kirk Blankenship, who had been in trouble with the local police more times than he could count. He stopped when he reached the man wearing a worn leather jacket, even more worn-out jeans, and a black, knit cap pulled over his ears. "Any trouble here?" he queried.

Jason walked back to the bench and retrieved his backpack. He looked at the police officer and thought, not for the first time, that that could be him. He had always wanted to go into law enforcement, but after his military discharge four years ago, he had decided that it was probably too late. He doubted if he could pass the required psychological testing. "No."

"Are you sure?" Officer O'Brady grinned. "I recognize one in that bunch, and he is trouble with a capital T. It wouldn't be the first time that his group has ganged up on someone, just for fun."

Jason continued to stare at Officer O'Brady. "No, no trouble. They were just being typical teenagers." He began to walk in the direction from which the police officer had come.

"Okay, if you say so. Have a good day."

Jason looked back at the officer and nodded.

He continued to walk for the next two hours until he found himself standing at the wood line across from the

Heavenly Grille Café. He looked at the yellow crime tape that sectioned off a city block, and slipped beneath it. He walked closer to their burned-out camp fire and remembered Larry, Curly, and Moe cracking jokes the night before. He walked about another thirty feet to where he had bedded down beneath two giant pine trees. He turned left and walked another fifty feet to the concrete overpass wall. He stared down at the brown, circular blob in the dirt that had been Norman Weissman's blood. He stared at the wall where the blood spatters obviously began.

"What happened to you, Norman?" he spoke softly. "You didn't deserve this. Nobody deserves to die this way." He was startled by a noise that came from behind him. He turned around quickly and saw PJ crawling out of her make-shift tent. "PJ?"

PJ looked back and forth from Jason to her make-shift tent. "I...I had to come back for the rest of my stuff, but...it's all gone. Someone took all my stuff. I knew I should have grabbed it all when I ran, but, I just wasn't thinking straight."

Jason thought that she looked like a lost child in a busy mall. "PJ? Did you see what happened here last night?"

PJ's eyes grew round with fright and she shook her head vigorously from side to side. She had seen some of what happened, but she knew better than to admit that to anyone, not even to Jason. "No," she whispered as she began to back away. "No! I didn't see anything. Not anything!" She turned and ran toward the busy highway that separated their camp ground from the diner across the street.

"PJ! Wait!" Jason called after her. He stopped in his tracks when he heard the blowing horn and screeching tires. "Oh, dear God...no!"

Peggy Jensen lay upon the black asphalt, one leg and one arm splayed in unnatural positions. Blood oozed from her nose and ears. She wouldn't have to worry about a place to stay that night.

# CHAPTER 4

## Meeting the Past

It was five-fifteen when the ambulance driver turned on the siren and rushed the middle-aged, black woman to Floyd Medical Center—the primary medical facility that provided care for indigent patients in Floyd County, Georgia.

Doug had, once again, been one of the first people on the scene. He ran outside the moment he heard the blaring horn and the screaming tires outside the café. He knew, immediately, that it was PJ who lay sprawled out on the pavement; one arm and one leg were bent into odd positions. Doug prayed that the splintered bones had not hit any major blood vessels. He recognized Jason right away, too, who was kneeling on the pavement, holding PJ's head in his lap.

Jason and Doug had stayed with PJ until the Emergency Medical Technicians had stabilized her enough for transport. The police were interviewing the nine-teen year old driver who had not seen the black woman until it was too late; she had been so inconsolable that the police had moved her car to the parking lot of the Heavenly Grille Café and driven her home.

Doug placed a hand on Jason's shoulder as the ambulance rushed off. "Jason? Why don't you come inside the café and have some coffee? It's going to be dark soon..."

Jason shrugged off Doug's hand and shook his head. "No. No, thanks." He removed the black, knit cap and ran his fingers through his short hair. He stared at Doug for a long moment and shook his head. "It's my fault."

"What do you mean?"

Jason closed his eyes and blew out a breath that felt like it had been trapped inside since he first heard the loud horn and squealing tires. "It's my fault she got hurt. She was running from me."

"I don't understand," Doug shook his head. "What do you mean? Why was PJ running from you?"

Jason shrugged again and took a backward step, away from Doug's touch. "I just wanted to know if she knew what happened last night...to Norman." He shook his head again. "I can't believe it—two of us in less than twenty-four hours. What are the odds of that happening?"

Doug took a step forward and placed a firm hand on Jason's shoulder. The touch did not allow for any possible disconnection on Jason's part. "We don't know that PJ is going to die, Jason. Her injuries look bad, I will admit, but she's a lot stronger than people give her credit for being."

Jason initially tensed at Doug's firm grasp upon his shoulder, but quickly began to relax as his breathing became less labored and a sense of mental and physical restoration slowly came upon him. "I think she knows what happened to Norman, but, like the rest of us, she doesn't want to get involved in any of it. I shouldn't have asked her anything about it..."

"It's not your fault, Jason. You couldn't have known she would run from you like that. Please...will you reconsider that cup of coffee? Let's give them time to get PJ settled and we'll call later to check on her condition."

Jason wanted to decline Doug's invitation, but he needed to know that PJ was going to make it, too. He nodded and moved forward. "Okay."

"That's great," Doug smiled back at him.

Anyone who saw them together might have thought that the two men were brothers. They were the same height and had the same muscular build and stance.

Doug walked beside Jason and placed his hand upon the man's back as they entered the café. "I know that food is probably the last thing on your mind, but Max has a huge pot of Brunswick stew on the stove, and his famous jalapeno cornbread is in the oven now. Once we check on PJ, maybe I can talk you into trying it out."

Jason felt a comforting shiver that started at the nape of his neck and travelled slowly down his spine, through his legs, and ended in his feet. Once the sensation ceased, he felt like the weight of the world had been lifted off his shoulders. He felt something that he had not experienced in more years than he could remember — he felt — *hope*. "Yeah," he nodded. "Maybe."

Cheryl had rented a furnished, two-bedroom, two-bath, 1950s bungalow located a couple of blocks from the high school. It was similar to other homes in the older, but well-established and quaint neighborhood, with its hardwood floors throughout, vaulted ceilings, fireplace, and, stacked-stone exterior. Cheryl's master suite came complete with a garden tub and a massive walk-in closet. There was a small bonus room off the master suite that Cheryl and Jimmy shared as a computer room. They both, also, enjoyed the small, screened-in patio where they could look out over a tiny, yet well-manicured and fenced back yard.

Cheryl had dropped out of high school so that she could take care of Jimmy when he was small, but her grandmother made sure that she had obtained her GED. She had worked mostly waitressing and retail sales jobs until her grandmother died, and, had managed to get one year of community college under her belt before she and Jimmy had made the decision to move to Rome. She was currently working two, part-time jobs until she could find a more permanent one; and, she still had all of the ten-thousand dollars she had received as beneficiary of a small life insurance policy her grandmother had taken out without her knowledge.

It was after five o'clock when she knocked on her son's bedroom door, and found him sprawled, on his stomach, upon his single twin bed. She stared in awe for a moment as she realized that he wasn't her little boy any more. He was at least five inches taller than she was and outweighed her by forty pounds. She cleared her throat and said, "Hey, kiddo. It's going to be dark soon and I was able to pick up a shift tonight at that pancake house that is open 24/7. I thought I'd swing by that little café we ate breakfast at this morning. Bertie, that waitress, told me that the cook was making Brunswick stew tonight, and — get this — *your* favorite, jalapeno cornbread."

Jimmy had ear phones plugged in, listening to one of his favorite country singers — a fairly new singer by the name of Mo Pitney. Jimmy especially liked Pitney's style because he did not practice a lot of the vocal acrobatics that some singers felt the need to exhibit. His sound was much more of a traditional-country sound, and Jimmy's favorite song on the singer's debut disc was, "I Didn't Go To Sleep Last Night." Jimmy could, most certainly, relate to that particular song today.

He sensed, more than he heard, his mother's presence. He turned on his side and looked back at her. He removed the ear phones and said, "Sorry, Mom...did you say something?"

Cheryl grinned and sat on the edge of the small bed. "Let me guess...Mo Pitney, again?"

Jimmy nodded. "He's the best thing since the one that you're so crazy about."

"Tim McGraw? Yes, he is still my favorite country male singer. Anyway, I was just saying that I'm going to run by that café we were at this morning and get something for dinner. I have to work the midnight-to-eight shift tonight at that pancake restaurant."

"You don't have to do that, Mom. I can find something here to eat."

"I know, but that cook is making Brunswick stew and I know how much you love that."

Jimmy smiled. "It's been a while since we've had that…since Gigi died."

"I know," Cheryl closed her eyes, thinking of her grandmother. "She did make the best Brunswick stew, didn't she?"

"Sure did. Hey, do you want me to ride with you?"

"You're not going out with your friends again tonight?" Cheryl asked.

Jimmy shook his head. "No, I don't think so. I, uh, I doubt if I'll be hanging out with them anymore."

There was clearly a story there, but Cheryl knew her son well enough to know that he would talk to her about it when he was ready. She trusted him and his judgment; he must have a good reason for wanting to end the friendship with Kirk Blankenship. She would have been lying to herself if she admitted that it upset her that Jimmy would end that particular relationship. There was something about the Blankenship boy that always put Cheryl on edge. She never felt completely at ease around him and his friends. "Well, in that case, kiddo—I would love the company. Come on; if we leave now, we can get there before dark. We could even eat there if you'd like, and you could bring some leftovers home to snack on later, while I'm at work."

Jimmy grabbed his Mo Pitney disc and grinned. "Something to listen to on the way…you are going to let me drive, aren't you?"

"I probably shouldn't," Cheryl laughed. "I know we'll be breaking the law, but you'll be getting your learner's permit at the end of April, and you've been practicing for months already. I know you're a safe driver, but, just please be careful and don't get pulled over for any reason!"


Even though the Heavenly Grille Café had only been in operation for three weeks at its latest location, word-of-mouth advertising had more than done its job. People from every walk of life had stopped in to sample the soulful, comfort food for which the café was becoming known; construction workers, city employees, attorneys, nurses, truck drivers, day care workers, and even a couple of CEOs had quickly become regulars. Fortunately, for the angels, the truckers who visited them now worked for different companies and had different routes than did the truckers who had gotten to know the café staff so well back in Monticello, Florida. No doubt, some of the old truckers might find the café again, and wonder how the angels maintained their "youthful" appearance, but Max would handle that problem when and if it occurred.

It was almost six o'clock when Jason followed Doug inside the café. All twelve tables and booths were filled to the brim, but there were a few empty seats available at the counter.

"Grab yourself a seat, Jason," Doug patted the counter. "Let me wash my hands and I'll get you that coffee."

"Thanks," Jason acknowledged. "I probably need to wash up, too. Is there a rest room?"

Doug nodded to the left. "Just around the corner there...should be plenty of hand towels in there. Just toss the dirty ones in the hamper and come back out when you're ready."

Max was stirring two five-gallon pots of Brunswick stew when Doug made his way back to the kitchen. Bertie was trying to reach the cabinet that held the large, ceramic bowls with angel wings painted on them.

Doug came up behind her and reached easily above her. "Here you go, Bertie."

"Thanks, handsome. Old Max over there wasn't thinking

about me when he built these dang cabinets so high and out of my reach."

"That's because the kitchen is my domain, Bertie…the tables and customers are yours," Max grinned mischievously. His baritone voice seemed to echo throughout the room. He waited until Doug had retrieved at least a dozen more bowls. "We've been listening, Doug. Was it bad? Is PJ going to make it?"

Doug walked over to the sink and washed his hands in steaming hot water. He shook his head. "I'll be honest, Max…I just don't know. She was hit pretty hard. The trooper said that the driver was going under the speed limit, but estimated impact at close to forty-five miles per hour. I don't think PJ ever knew what hit her."

"We've already started praying," Bertie said. "I sure wish we had some insight as to how things like this are going to turn out. If I wasn't already turning gray, all this worrying about these mortals would surely make me completely white-headed."

"Well, that would be better than bald, I suppose," Max grinned as he ran a hand over his perfectly shaped bald head. "Are you going to be with her, Doug?"

Doug dried his hands and leaned back against the counter. "I talked Jason into coming inside for a cup of coffee. I'll call the hospital for an update in a little bit to see if they can tell me anything about PJ. I was hoping I could talk Jason into riding to the hospital with me to see her, if they'll allow visitors."

"That's a fine idea," Bertie chimed in. "We heard him when he said he feels guilty, and that he's to blame for her getting hit."

Doug nodded. "Yeah, he does. I don't know what went down in their camp ground last night, but I have a feeling that someone in their group knows more than what they've told the police. I was hoping to find Stella, but she's nowhere to found."

"She's probably going to keep a low profile for the next

few days, like all the others," Max said.

"Maybe," Doug agreed. "But, I think I'll make my regular visit over there tonight, just in case. The temperature is already dropping outside. I worry about the others, especially Joe and Bernard. They were pretty tight with Norman."

"What will happen to Norman?" Bertie asked. "I mean, if nobody claims his body."

"The state has procedures in place if that happens, Bertie," Doug explained. "I don't know how hard the police will actually work to find the person that killed Norman, but they will need to do something with the body within a 10-day time frame. If they can't locate any next of kin, and if Norman's body is usable, then it could be donated to a medical school. They even have body farms that are used by law enforcement and medical school students; these are areas where the human bodies are left untreated by chemicals so that they can be studied at various stages of decomposition."

"Oh, that is just sick!" Bertie turned and punched Doug against the shoulder. "That poor man deserves a proper burial. There has to be somebody out there who misses him."

Max placed a hand on Bertie's shoulder. "Maybe we can ask Martin to do some checking when we go Home to visit tomorrow."

"That's a great idea!" Bertie nodded. "Martin has information on everybody. He can tell us all about Norman."

Max shook his head. "He can tell us all about Norman, that is true, Bertie; however, you know as well as I do that we cannot interfere by using any of the information we might discover."

"Come on, Bertie," Doug offered her his arm. "We have a house full of customers out there, and I don't see it thinning out any time soon."

"I know, handsome, I know. Lead the way," she pushed

Doug ahead of her. "But, I still think it's a sick, sick idea...body farms!" She was still shaking her head when she walked through the open doorway and saw Jason sitting at the counter. She punched him on the shoulder as she walked by and said, "I'll be back in a jiffy."

Jason rubbed his shoulder. That waitress had a pretty good punch for such a little person. "Yes, ma'am."

Doug moved behind the counter and poured two cups of coffee. He sat one down in front of Jason. "She won't take no for an answer either, trust me. When she comes back by, you had best be prepared to say yes to a bowl of stew." He saw the embarrassed, uneasy look come upon Jason's face. "Don't worry, my friend. After all you have been through in the last few hours, the meal is on the house."

"I don't need charity," Jason said, defensively. "I have enough for a cup of coffee."

Doug held up his hand. "Your money is no good in here, Jason. Please...let us do this for you."

Jason was about to offer up an objection when a blast of cool air hit him as the café door opened and the angel chimes above it sounded. He turned when he heard the waitress welcome two new customers.

"Y'all just have a seat at the counter!" Bertie grinned when she saw Cheryl and Jimmy come through the door. "I knew you would be back to try Max's Brunswick stew."

Cheryl stood at the front door and spoke with Bertie for a moment, while Jimmy made his way to the counter. He stopped at the vacant seat next to Jason and asked politely, "Is this seat taken, sir?"

Jason turned to look at the young man standing behind him. The kid was almost as tall as he was, but was obviously still a minor. "No. Help yourself, kid," he said as he turned back to his coffee. He stared straight ahead and held the cup between both his hands.

Jimmy scooted over to the next vacant seat so that his mother would be sitting between him and the man who sat at the end of the counter. "Thanks," Jimmy smiled. "Over here, Mom," he motioned to Cheryl, who was still talking to the waitress.

Cheryl made her way to the counter, removed her jacket, and hung it on the back of the stool. "Thanks, sweetie. That waitress—Bertie—is so nice. I feel like I've known her all my life."

Doug poured two more cups of coffee and placed them in front of the Crennans. "That's our Bertie, alright. She has a no-nonsense way of making folks feel right at home."

Jason smiled when he heard the woman's soft laughter in response. It had been a while since he had heard a woman's laughter.

"She certainly does," Cheryl laughed again. She squeezed in to lift herself up on the twisting stool and accidentally bumped the man beside her just as he was about to take a sip of hot coffee.

"Oh! Please forgive me! I am so, so sorry..." She was unable to complete her sentence.

Jason managed to keep the cup from spilling over entirely and turned to look at the woman, whose laughter had warmed his soul for a few moments. He stood up and stared down into green eyes—green eyes that he never thought he would see again in this life time.

Cheryl's words caught in her throat as she stared back at the tall, muscular man looking down at her. It had been fifteen years, and she had never known his name; but, she knew that she would never forget his eyes.

She was the only thing that now separated Jimmy Crennan and his biological father.

# CHAPTER 5

## - Heaven -
## Martin Does Some Research

*T* *wo of the three Heavenly Grille Café angels always visited Home on Sundays, while one usually remained behind to watch over things and people close to their given assignment. On this next to the last Sunday in January, Doug had offered to stay behind while Max and Bertie visited with Martin and their families in Heaven.*

*Martin was Max's primary assistant in Heaven. He was a tall, thin black man who many often described as being perspicuous and introverted. He served as mentor to a lot of the senior angels, and, to some new recruits. It was his responsibility to oversee the main data base that contained information on every living and dead soul in the universe. It was a job he took very seriously.*

*Martin stood before the large screen and scanned the information he had on Norman Weissman. His thumb pushed upward under his chin while his index finger tapped rapidly against his full, pursed lips. He sighed softly as he looked over Norman's history:*

*Angel was born on September 04, 1953 to parents, William and Victoria (both deceased).*

*Angel was older brother to one sister, Lynn.*

*Angel was bullied as a youth, but maintained a good-natured and friendly spirit.*

*Angel was well-educated.*

*Angel was respected by his peers as a successful businessman.*

*Angel was a confirmed homosexual until he became a born-again Christian in 2009, after he lost everything he owned when the housing market bubble burst. His former partner left him when angel acknowledged that he believed that homosexuality was a sin, and took everything that the banks had not taken from him.*

*Angel abandoned his former life and began travelling around the southern states in late 2009, making many friends and living a Christian-filled life along with way, but never putting down any roots.*

*Angel lost all contact with his only living relative, his sister, Lynn; Angel unaware that he was an uncle.*

*Angel was homeless when he died in the early hours on Saturday, January 17, 2016.*

*"Martin! You 'ole buzzard, how are ya!"*

*Martin squeezed his eyes closed and tensed in anticipation of the punch he knew was coming.*

*"Hello, Bertie," he exhaled, taking the punch to the back of his left shoulder. He turned around and accepted Max's bear hug. "It's so good to see you, my friend."*

*Max smiled down at the thin, weak-looking man who had been his friend for as long as he could remember. He hugged Martin tighter against him. "It's really good to see you, too."*

*Bertie squeezed between the two men and shouted, "Hey! What about me? Aren't you glad to see me, too?" She punched Martin again for good measure.*

*Martin glanced at Max, who simply smiled back at him. "Yes, Bertie; of course, I'm glad to see you, too."*

*Bertie glanced at the screen that highlighted information about Norman Weissman. "You must've known we were going to ask about him. It's good to see you're on the ball, Martin. Maybe you'll get to keep your job, after all."*

*Martin's spine stiffened. "What do mean, keep my job? Of course, I'm going to keep my job."*

*Bertie continued to tease the angel who always took life, and* death, much too seriously. *"Oh, don't go getting your gown in a knot, Martin. I was just kidding. Besides, I can't imagine that anyone else would want all this responsibility."* She waved her hand at the large screen behind them. *"So, did you find anything out that might help us find Martin's relatives?"*

*"You are not to interfere with any of that, Bertie..."* Martin began.

Bertie held up her hand to hush him. *"I know, I know, but...there has to be someone out there who is missing him. Did you know that his body could end up in one of those godforsaken BODY FARMS?"*

Max draped an arm over Bertie's shoulder. *"Calm down, Bertie."* He looked at Martin and explained. *"Doug gave Bertie a quick course on what happens to unclaimed bodies down on earth. The body farm scenario did not go over well, as you can see."*

Martin shivered. *"Ewww...body farms...what an absolutely disgusting development!"*

*"I agree one-hundred percent!"* Bertie chimed in. *"So, who does he have in his past that can stop that from happening?"*

Martin turned back to the screen. *"He only has two living relatives – a younger sister – her name is Lynn, and her daughter. Actually, the sister has been searching for Norman since he disappeared in 2009. She has become quite ill, herself, the last couple of years and has had to curtail her search for her brother."*

*"Oh, no..."* Max sighed.

*"Well, that just sucks!"* Bertie pouted. *"How sick is she?"*

Martin shook his head. *"She's terminal, but she has good days and bad days. She has a daughter who has promised her that she will continue to search for her Uncle Norman. Such a shame, to die like that, separated from one's family and loved ones."*

*"Norman wasn't alone,"* Bertie said. *"He was part of a homeless group. I don't know how close any of them really were, but they were a group who tried to look after one another."*

*"Well, they obviously didn't do too good a job, now did they?"* Martin replied. *"Oh, I'm sorry, forgive me. I should not have said that. It wasn't the group's fault that Norman died."*

Max stared hard at his old friend. *"You know who killed Norman, don't you, my friend?"* Sometimes, this information was revealed to the angels on earth, and sometimes not; but, Max knew that Martin had access to that information.

Martin nodded. "I do, yes, but please understand that I cannot reveal that information to even you, Max. There is more to be played out down there than you might realize."

"Obviously," Max nodded. "Don't worry, Martin, I understand your predicament, and will not press you for more answers on that subject."

"Well, Hells-Bells! I sure will!" Bertie bellowed. "How can we help any of them if we don't know what's really going on down there?"

Max pulled Bertie to him. "Let it go for now, Bertie. Martin will tell us what we need to know when he can, and not before. So, what do you say we go visit our families for a spell?"

Bertie pulled away from Max and pouted. "I'm going, I'm going. I can take a hint, you know. You two want to be alone to talk in private, so go right ahead."

She vanished before their eyes.

Martin shook his head. "She's so melodramatic. I do not envy you having to keep a reign on her, Maximus." He sighed. "So what about you? Are you going to visit your family today?"

Max nodded. "In a little bit. I wanted to speak with you, privately, about Doug."

"I already know what you're thinking," Martin said, as he waved his hand and the words on the large screen disappeared. "Do you think he suspects?"

Max shook his head. "No, I don't think so. I don't think he's made the connection yet, and I have to admit that I'm a little concerned about how he may react when he does make it."

"Well," Martin winked. "There's only one person who has a definitive answer to that!"

"That is true, my friend, that is true." Max turned to leave. "It would be nice to have a heads-up on the end result, though, wouldn't it?"


Bertie had delayed her visitation with her family and made a quick detour to the Receiving Station — one of two transition *stations in Heaven. She nodded to the dozens of people wandering around, and even punched a few of them on their shoulders. "Welcome, Home!" she grinned at them, all the while, scanning the area for one in particular.*

*She was almost ready to think that Norman Weissman may not have asked for repentance quick enough, when she finally spotted him in the middle of a small group of men and women. She listened while he laughed with them and, apparently, relished the fact that he had indeed made it to Heaven, after all.*

*Norman laughed good-naturedly with his fellow, recent transients. He spotted Bertie coming toward them and pointed. "Hey! I know you. You're that waitress that works in the diner that has the halo floating over it!"*

*Bertie weaved her way inside the group and punched Norman against the shoulder. "Yep, that would be me, alright. How are you, Norman?"*

*Norman did a little penquin-waddle and laughed. "How am I? Well, not bad for being a dead man, I guess. I am dead, aren't I?" He looked around at all the transients in their white robes before glancing down at his own. "Just look at me – finally – in a dress!"*

*Bertie couldn't help but laugh along with him. She pulled him away from the crowd and said, "Walk with me, Norman."*

*"But, I don't want to miss anything here," Norman worried. "What if they call my name or something, and I don't hear them?"*

*Bertie shook her head. "That's not how it works. Don't worry, you're not going to miss anything, and you're not going anywhere you don't want to be. You made it! You're in Heaven, and you are going to know a peace that you've never experienced before."*

*Norman tagged along behind her but looked back at the group of transients. "I already feel it, and it feels wonderful. I, uh, kind of had my doubts that I would be let in here...I mean, with my past sins and all."*

*"You're talking about the whole homosexual thing, huh?" Bertie queried. "Yeah, well, I try not to get too involved in all that. The way I figure it, that's something really, really personal between you and God. It isn't my place to judge you or anyone else. Trust me, we've all done things that we aren't too proud about."*

*"Well, that's good to know, but I still feel awkward being here. I was forty-one years old before I had my first sexual experience, and it was with the man that was my partner for almost fifteen years. After I lost everything in 2009, I began to question a lot of things. Somehow, along the way, I turned to the Bible. That's where I first read the words that I was living in sin. I didn't want to believe it. I mean, I truly loved the man I was with, and we were totally devoted to each other; but, after learning more about what the Bible and church had to say about homosexuality, I began to question our relationship. It hurt him – a lot – and, after I lost my real estate business, I lost him, too. He took everything that the bank forgot to take. I never even said good-bye to him; I just packed a few clothes in a duffel bag, took a few hundred dollars I had managed to hide, and walked away from my life."*

Bertie shook her head. *"None of that is important anymore, Norman. You'll see that in time. You'll never move on to the second station, though, if you keep hanging on to all these doubts you have about yourself."*

Norman looked around him at the calming, white serenity that surrounded them. *"You mean there's more to Heaven that this?"* he asked, incredulously.

*"Oh, honey, you have no idea what's in store for you up here!"* Bertie laughed and punched him again. She looked around to make sure no one was within hearing distance. *"But, listen,"* she whispered as she pulled him closer to her. *"I want to know what you remember about who did this to you. Who killed you, Norman?"*

**"B-E-R-T-I-E!!"**

Bertie cringed. *"Oh, Hells-Bells…"* She knew that voice all too well. How could she have forgotten about the one person that heard absolutely *EVERYTHING*?

**"The fear of the Lord is the beginning of knowledge, but fools despise wisdom and instruction." Proverbs 1:7 (NKJV)**

# CHAPTER 6

## Returning Memories

Doug entered the clearing to the campground around seven-thirty on Monday morning. He noticed that the crime scene tape had been removed, probably by either the police or by teenagers, and, the only evidence that anything sinister had happened there was the dark splatter of Norman's blood on the overpass's concrete wall.

He didn't know what to expect when he pushed through the brush, but it certainly was not the sight that greeted him. Joe Sanders and Bernard Cartwright—alias, Curly and Moe—were sitting shoulder-to-shoulder close to the camp fire, warming their hands. Doug glanced quickly around and saw Jason rolling up his sleeping bag. He looked to his right and saw Skipper coming out of the woods.

Doug walked over to the two makeshift tents and peered inside, hoping to see Stella in one of them. She wasn't there, and it pained him to see PJ's empty tent.

"Good morning, Douglas," Bernard nodded. "I hope there's hot coffee in one of those bags."

Doug nodded to Jason and Skipper before turning back to the camp fire. "You bet there is—two cups for each of you, plus two extra—I was hoping Stella might be here, too. It got pretty cold out last night. Is everyone okay?" He began passing around the coffee, as well as sausage and egg biscuits that Max had cooked up, especially for the homeless group.

"Nobody has seen Stella, and, I haven't had much of an appetite since..." Bernard began. "Well, since Norman left us. I have to admit it...I really miss him."

"Me, too," Joe agreed, "But, old Norman wouldn't want us passing up free food, now would he? If you don't want your biscuits, I'll be more than glad to take them off your hands!" He took a big bite of the huge buttermilk biscuit, filled with smoked sausage and a fried egg. "Norman would want us to keep up our strength."

Skipper walked closer to the camp fire and bent down. He held out his hand and said, "I'll take a cup of that coffee. You can give my share of the biscuits to Joe."

Doug was more than a little surprised that Skipper had emerged from the woods and asked for the coffee. He usually just left the food on top of Skipper's bed roll, and hoped that the man got to it before the bugs, or Joe, did. "You bet, Skipper." He looked toward Jason. "How about you, Jason...want to join us?"

Something had happened to Jason on Saturday evening, and Doug had no idea what had caused the change. One minute, he had been sitting there drinking coffee and waiting until they could get an update from the hospital about PJ's condition...and, the next minute, he had stood up and walked out of the café, saying that he would be back later to check on PJ. He never returned.

Jason released a deep breath and rubbed his gloveless hands together. "Yeah, I think I will. Thanks," he said as he joined the group and took the coffee and biscuit. "I, uh, didn't get to eat anything last night. This smells good." He took a bite of the biscuit and chased it down with the hot coffee. He looked over at Doug and asked, "What about PJ? Did you hear anything?"

The other three men looked up from their own coffee; apparently, none of them had noticed PJ's absence. Skipper was the first to ask, "What's happened to PJ?"

"Oh, no!" Joe exclaimed. "Don't tell me she's dead, too!"

Doug glanced at Jason. "Do you want to tell them, or should I?"

Jason finished his biscuit and held his coffee in one hand. He finally nodded and addressed the group. "PJ was hit by a car late Saturday afternoon. I saw her here, looking in her tent. She said she came to get the rest of her stuff, but it was all gone."

"Yes," Bernard said. "The cops took everything that we left behind—for evidence, I presume. What else happened, Jason?"

Jason rubbed the back of his neck, clearly uneasy at being the center of attention. "We were standing here talking, and I asked her if she saw what happened with Norman. She just...panicked...yelled that she didn't know anything, and then took off running through the bushes, toward the highway. I...I don't think she ever saw the car that hit her."

"She's dead, isn't she?" Joe asked, his eyes tearing up.

Doug placed a hand on Joe's shoulder and looked deep into his eyes. "No, she isn't dead, Joe, but she was badly hurt. I checked with the hospital Saturday night, and they took her in to surgery to repair broken bones in her pelvis, leg and arm. The head nurse said she had a severe concussion from her head hitting the pavement, but that all tests indicate that she should be okay, once she wakes up."

Skipper scoffed. "I'm surprised they would tell you anything about her. You're not family."

"No, I'm not," Doug agreed. "However, they would not even had known her name if I had not told them. I told them that she was homeless and that we did not have any information on her next of kin."

Jason lowered his head and closed his eyes. When he looked back up at Doug, he smiled. "So, she's really going to be okay? She's going to make it?"

Doug nodded. "They couldn't guarantee that, and it's important that she wake up today, but, I have a strong feeling and belief that PJ is going to be just fine."

"What about when she's released from the hospital?" Skipper asked. "Where will she go? She sure can't come back here to home, sweet home." He waved his arms around their camp site. "She's going to need someone to help her until she heals."

"Do you know anything about her background, her family?" Doug asked Skipper.

Skipper grabbed a second cup of coffee and turned to leave. "No, and I don't want to know." He walked over to the pine tree he had slept beneath the night before, and grabbed his backpack and sleeping bag. He never looked back at the group of men sitting around the camp fire.

Joe and Bernard both stood and brushed the pine needles off their clothes. Doug stood with them and offered them more coffee and biscuits from the large bag. "Thanks," Joe grinned. "Keep us posted on PJ, okay? She's a good gal."

"I'll do that," Doug nodded. "So…none of you have seen Stella since all this went down?"

Bernard shook his head. "No, but we all make some of the same daily rounds, so we'll keep an eye out for her. I wouldn't worry too much about Stella, though. Something tells me that she's more than capable of taking care of herself."

Jason waited until Curly and Moe had ambled off toward town. He sat back down and began eating a second biscuit. "This is really good. Thanks for the food. We all appreciate it, you know, but, you don't have to keep bringing it to us."

Doug squatted down beside Jason. "I know, but, Max and I hold a special place in our hearts for Veterans."

Jason turned his head sharply in Doug's direction. "What makes you think any of us are Veterans?"

"I know more than you think, Jason, but that's not important right now. I really wanted a chance to talk to you alone this morning, to find out why you left the café so abruptly on Saturday. Max wanted to meet you. I mean, one minute you were there, and the next..."

Jason interrupted Doug's line of questioning. "I said...thanks for the food. That doesn't mean that you, or your friend, Max, has any right to know anything about any of us. We don't bother anyone, and we don't want anyone bothering us." He stood up to leave.

"I'm sorry, Jason," Doug answered back. "We don't mean to pry. We just want to help, if we can."

"You can't help with the demons that keep us awake at night," Jason looked back. "You're right. I am a Veteran, and I'm pretty sure that Skipper is, too; but, unless you've seen and been through the things we have, then there's no way you can relate to us — to understand why we are who we are today. Anyway...thanks for the update on PJ."

Doug watched with sadness as Jason walked away from him. He rubbed the bridge of his nose between his thumb and index finger, and sighed deeply. "I understand more than you'll ever know, my friend."


It was nine o'clock Monday morning by the time Cheryl finished another night shift and collapsed at her kitchen table. She glanced over to the coffee maker and was grateful that Jimmy had made a pot of coffee before he left for school. She got up and poured coffee into a large ceramic mug that Jimmy had made for her when he was eight years old. She stood at the kitchen sink and looked out the small window that provided a view of her driveway. "This cannot be happening..." she shook her head and sat back down at the table.

*"It can't be him. It's not possible. How could it be him? No, no...it's not him..."* her wrestling thoughts scrambled for a plausible explanation. *"The eyes — his eyes — that's the only thing I really remember about him...such unbelievably, beautiful eyes."* She closed her own eyes and allowed her memories to take her back in time to almost sixteen years ago.

✦

The summer of 2000 had been as historically hot as any other summer in Columbus, Georgia; Saturday, July 29 was no different. The high temperature had reached ninety-four degrees by noon, and the squelching humidity threatened to encroach the night as well.

Cheryl Crennan was fifteen years old at the time, the only child of Olivia and James Crennan. She was a daddy's girl, and because of that, she often found herself the object of her mother's ire, sour moods and disposition.

Olivia constantly criticized her daughter, about the way she dressed, the way she talked, the way she walked, the way she ate her food, the way she laughed. Cheryl grew up feeling like she would never be able to do anything to please her mother, so she took the criticism and bottled it up inside her. However, by early evening July 29, she had taken as much belittling from her mother as she could handle in one day. "Just leave me alone!" she screamed at her, slamming the screen door behind her.

"You get back here right this instant, Cheryl Renae Crennan!" Olivia yelled.

Cheryl jumped on her bike and took off down their residential street that was lined on both sides by huge, blossoming crepe myrtle trees. She rode for a couple of miles before she stopped and parked her bike outside a Sonic Drive-In. She sat down at one of the outside tables and ordered a large sweet tea, with extra ice, doubting there could be enough ice in Georgia to cool her down at the moment.

She was sipping her tea when a car load of teenaged boys drove up and parked behind her table. She cast a quick look at them and recognized a couple of the older boys from her high school. There were four of them all together; two of them she had never seen before. She assumed those two must have attended a different school.

"Hey! Don't you go to my school?" the driver asked as he leaned out the window.

Cheryl ignored him.

"What's the matter, beautiful? Are you too good to talk to us?"

"*Not according to my mother,*" Cheryl thought. She could not explain what came over her, but she suddenly felt very rebellious, and did something that she had never thought she was capable of doing—she began to flirt with the boy. By the time everyone had eaten their food, the older boy had talked Cheryl into riding with them to a party. He told her they would bring her back to get her bike.

She never saw that bike again.

She was one of the youngest girls at the party, and she knew the minute she walked into the dark living room, that she had made a hasty, wrong decision. The loud music, the empty beer bottles, and, the smell of what she thought might be marijuana filled every room. She turned to walk out, but the older boy who went to her school cornered her and placed both hands against the wall, above her shoulders, pinning her in place. "You don't want to leave; you just got here. We haven't had any fun yet."

"I really should go," Cheryl mumbled.

Someone walked past them and handed the boy a lit joint. He took a long toke and handed it to Cheryl. "Go ahead, it'll relax you, and, trust me...*you* definitely need to relax."

It only took two tokes for the marijuana to hit Cheryl's brain. The sensation was something she had never before experienced, and, she *liked* it! She took two more hits off the joint before another girl wrapped her arms around the boy's waist and pulled him away into another room.

Cheryl felt a little light-headed and swayed against the wall.

"Whoa, there—easy now—I've got you," Jason Benton laughed as he tried to keep the pretty girl, they had picked up at Sonic, upright. "Come on, maybe you should sit down."

"Oh, I'm fine, just fine..." Cheryl grinned with her eyes half-closed. "In fact, I've never felt so fine in all my life."

Jason laughed. "Something tells me you've never smoked pot before in your life, either."

Cheryl shook her head from side to side. "Nope, no pot, no beer, no cigarettes, nope...I've never even been...*kissed!*" She tapped her finger against pursed lips, indicating that he should keep her secret.

This was fifteen-year old Jason Benton's last night in Columbus, Georgia. His father had been stationed at Fort Benning for two years and had recently received orders for Korea. It was just a one-year tour, but his parents had agreed that it would be best for the family if they moved back to North Carolina, to be closer to his maternal grandparents. Part of the reason for this party was to be a going-away present from some of the friends he had made. His friends had taken it upon themselves to ensure that Jason lost his virginity before he left Georgia.

"You've never been kissed?" Jason asked with disbelief. "Wow, I find that really hard to believe."

Cheryl scrunched up her nose and squeezed her eyes to get a closer look at the boy holding her up. He really was cute, but his eyes were stunning. She had never seen eyes the shade of light blue that his were; they seemed to sparkle like cut crystal. She puckered up her lips and closed her eyes all the way.

Jason cleared his throat and looked around them to make sure nobody was watching them. They weren't; they were all too engrossed in their own lustful encounters. He lowered his head and shared his first kiss with the girl with the long, auburn pony-tail and mesmerizing green eyes.

Cheryl opened her eyes and stared at the boy. "I've had pot for the first time, I've been kissed for the first time, and, now, I think I want to taste my first beer."

"You may not like it," the boy laughed, "But, come on, I'll get us some."

One hour and three beers later, Jason and Cheryl found their way to one of the back bedrooms, stripped down to their birthday suits, and clumsily lost their virginity to each other—it took less than ten minutes; after which, they both passed out upon the bed.

Four hours later, the older boy dropped Cheryl off in front of her house. Her mother was waiting on the porch, arms crossed and foot tapping. The boy sped off in a hurry, and Cheryl stumbled on the steps leading up to the porch.

Olivia took one look at her daughter and suspected what she had been doing. "You filthy slut—get out of my sight!" She turned and went back inside the house, leaving Cheryl puking in the bushes.


Cheryl's thoughts slowly returned to the present where she sat slumped at the kitchen table, her coffee now cold. She shook her head in disbelief. "How is this possible? What kind of joke is God trying to play on me?" She shook her head again. "No, no...this simply is not happening. That could not have been him on Saturday night. There must be other men out there with eyes as blue and as mesmerizing as his."

If there was another explanation for what she was thinking, Cheryl Crennan knew she wouldn't find it sitting at her kitchen table. As tired as she was from working an eight-hour night shift, she pulled her jacket back on, locked the door, and pointed her 2006 Beetle Bug in the direction of the Heavenly Grille Café.

# CHAPTER 7

## Breakfast at the Blankenship's

Ernest Blankenship sat at the marble-topped kitchen table, enjoying his cream-cheese Danish and reading the morning paper. He checked the automobile section to make sure his weekly, two-page ad was listed, before he switched to the local news section. "Hmm...there was a murder over the weekend...some homeless person was killed."

Rae Blankenship looked up from her Kindle and glanced at her fourth husband. She grimaced inwardly at the sight of his balding head and unattractive pot belly, and wondered if the money and security were really worth having to sleep next to this snoring pig for the rest of her life. A quick glance at the ten thousand dollar wedding ring on her finger solidified her decision, for the time being, anyway. "And, you care about this...why?" she sighed.

Ernest Blankenship was a good man who had made at least one wrong, personal decision since his first wife, Elizabeth, had passed away from cervical cancer, four years ago. Their only child, Kirk, had been twelve years old when Elizabeth died, and friends had introduced him to Rae Sanchez at a cookout. Marriage was, most certainly, the last thing on his mind, but it only took a few months for the attractive red-head to get under his skin. They were married before the year ended, and that was the beginning of the end of his relationship with his only child.

"Well, I just think it's sad that someone was killed, and it's possible that his family, if he has one, may never know what happened to him. He's listed as a John Doe."

Rae closed the cover of her Kindle and walked to stand behind her husband. She massaged his shoulders and tried not to think of the soft flesh beneath his business suit. She was only forty-nine years old, the same age as her current husband, but she had definitely taken better care of herself than had he. "Well," she sighed again. "It's not likely that he could have afforded one of your cars, and I doubt if anyone will really miss him..."

"That's a cold thing to say, Rae. Surely you don't mean that?"

Rae took her cue from his critical tone. "Of course not, dear. I'm sure the police will find out who he is and who committed this horrible crime. What does it say happened to him?" She did her best to feign some interest in the story her husband was reading.

"They found his body lying beneath the underpass near the edge of town. I think it's the underpass near that new café that some of my employees are talking about. They said he suffered severe head trauma and probably died instantly."

"Well, I really do doubt the police will spend much time investigating the death of a homeless man," Rae replied.

"Again, Rae...that's a really cruel thing to say." Ernest pushed away from the table and stared down at his petite and shapely wife. "Sometimes, your opinions...shock and appall me."

Rae moved closer to him and wrapped her arms around his huge mid-section. She closed her eyes and tried to imagine him as a younger, firmer man. "I think we both know that you didn't marry me for my *opinions*," she murmured coyly. "Why don't you come back upstairs with me for a few minutes before you leave?"

Ernest left the paper open on the article he had been reading about the murder of the homeless man. He reached around his wife for his coffee mug and answered, "I've got a busy day." He turned to straighten his tie and walked out the back door without kissing his wife good-bye.

Rae watched from the enormous bay kitchen window until her husband's Mercedes had backed down the long drive-way and turned toward town. "Well, thank God for small miracles," she snickered. She grabbed her Kindle and made her way slowly up the back staircase to the master suite. She had a lot of shopping to do today and wanted to soak in the tub for an hour before she left.

Kirk had skipped school and was on the back staircase when he heard the conversation between his father and step-mother. He had slipped into the downstairs den while Rae massaged his father's shoulders, and, now he waited until he heard the door to the master suite close and the bath water running. He moved slowly into the kitchen and saw the open paper on the kitchen table. It didn't take him long to find the article about the death of the homeless man. "Nice," he grinned. "They have no clues, nothing to go on, and I don't think we have to worry about anyone coming forward with information about the case." He folded the newspaper and took it with him. "But, just in case, maybe I should try to find that homeless woman and make sure she doesn't remember anything."

Cheryl pulled into the parking lot of the Heavenly Grille Café at nine-thirty. There were only a few empty parking spaces available, and she pulled her Beetle Bug into one closest to the front door. She didn't notice the black, Toyota Land Cruiser pull in behind her and take the parking space closest to the main road. She took a deep breath, pulled her jacket tight against her, and walked inside the café. *"What if he's here? Oh, my goodness, what if he's here? What do I say to him, or do I say anything at all to him? I'm sure he wouldn't remember me, anyway. Maybe he won't be here at all."* Her rambling thoughts consumed her as she stood inside the warm, inviting café before finally making her way to an empty stool at the counter.

The handsome man who had served her and Jimmy coffee on Saturday night was behind the counter, talking to a couple of men who looked like they might be lumberjacks or long-distance truckers. Cheryl smiled at him as she slid onto the stool. "Good morning. Could I have some coffee, please?"

Bertie brushed behind Cheryl and punched her lightly against the shoulder. "Hey, you! It's good to see you in here again. Where's that handsome son of yours? Oh, wait, never mind. I forgot that it's Monday. He's probably in school, huh?"

Cheryl warmed at Bertie's chatter. "Good morning, Bertie. Yes, Jimmy's in school, or at least, he'd better be!"

"I don't think you have to worry too much about that young man," Bertie grinned. "He's one of the good ones. You should be very proud of him."

"Oh, I am...I am," Cheryl nodded. "Thank you," she looked at Doug when he placed a large mug of hot, steaming black coffee in front of her.

"I've got a house full of hungry customers, so I've gotta get busy," Bertie said. "Come on back sometime when we're not so crowded, and we can have more time to talk about that young man of yours."

"I'd like that," Cheryl smiled. "Maybe I'll bring him with me the next time." She waved at Bertie and looked back at Doug. "There's something very special about Bertie. Why is it that I feel like I've known her all my life, yet, I've only spoken to her a couple of times?"

Doug stared at Cheryl and grinned. "Bertie has that effect on a lot of people. She's easy to talk to, but more importantly, she listens to what people have to say."

Cheryl stared into Doug's emerald-green eyes. They were almost hypnotizing and she felt herself being pulled into a calming sensation of warmth and relaxation. She shook her head and smiled. What was it about some men's mesmerizing eyes that turned her to utter mush? "I love talking to her," she hesitated slightly, "But, it was really you I was hoping to talk to this morning. I'm sorry, but I don't remember your name."

"It's Doug. I met you and Jimmy Saturday evening; I believe it was Brunswick stew night here."

Cheryl nodded. "Yes, it was, and please let the cook know that my son and I have not had Brunswick stew that good in a long, long time."

"Max will be happy to hear that. May I get you some breakfast to go along with that coffee?"

"No, thanks—just coffee this morning. Actually…" Cheryl paused, not sure of how much information she needed to share with a complete stranger. "I was wondering if you could tell me anything about the man I was sitting next to Saturday night." She held her hands up and shook her head. "Oh, never mind. You get so many customers in here, I'm sure you couldn't possibly remember who sat next to me on Saturday night…"

Doug waited for Cheryl to take a much-needed breath before answering. "I remember every customer that comes in here; in fact, all of us who work here remember every customer—it's just something we strive to do. You're talking about Jason…"

"He had on an old, brown-leather jacket, and…he had light-blue eyes, a black knit cap…"

Doug nodded his confirmation. "Jason Benton."

Cheryl allowed the name to roll around inside her head for a moment. "Jason Benton?"

"He doesn't come in very often," Doug offered. "I see him every day, but I usually go to him, rather than him coming to me."

"I don't understand," Cheryl looked perplexed.

Doug pointed toward the parking lot. "See the woods across the highway? Well, behind those bushes is where you'll find Jason most mornings and evenings. I don't know where he goes during the day, but I take him coffee and food every morning and late at night after we close up."

The look of perplexity on Cheryl's face deepened as the reality of what Doug said seeped in. Her hand flew to her mouth and she whispered, "You mean, he's...homeless?"

Doug nodded. "By choice, I'd say. I don't know his story, but you can bet he has one to tell. Why are you so curious about Jason? Do you know him?"

Cheryl nodded as she stood to leave. "Yes, I think I do." She looked back at Doug and shrugged. "Can you keep a secret?"

Doug smiled. "What do you think?"

Cheryl returned his smile. "I think that being in this café is the safest I've felt in many years, and I think I could trust you and Bertie with every secret I've ever had." She turned back and walked closer to Doug so that she could whisper in his ear. "I think your friend, Jason Benton, is the father of my son." She took another sip of coffee, turned, and walked out of the café.

Angels do not get taken by surprise easily, but Doug had not seen this revelation coming. His mouth dropped open and Bertie punched him when she walked by.

"Heh, heh! You really didn't see that one coming, did you, handsome!" she whispered and laughed out loud as she passed by Doug. She moved into the kitchen to confirm that Max had heard the conversation, too.

Cheryl took a deep breath of the cool, refreshing air when she stepped outside the café. The previous tension inside her had evaporated, and she closed her eyes. She didn't know why this was happening now, but she knew she had to find out more about Jason Benton. She stood by her car for several minutes and stared at the woods across the road—the woods that Jason Benton called home. She zipped up her jacket and began a slow walk across the parking lot, across the highway, and through the bushes to a camp ground of sorts. She saw three, large cardboard boxes and two makeshift tents. She walked closer to each of them and peered inside. "I wonder if one of these is where you sleep, Jason Benton."

She saw a slight movement out of the corner of her eye and glanced toward the concrete overpass about fifty feet away. She watched while a young man seemed to be inspecting the ground before he stood and rubbed his fingers against the concrete wall. He was too far away for her to identify, and she wondered if it might be Jason Benton. A longer inspection of the man's silhouette proved her wrong; the body was smaller than the man she remembered sitting next to on Saturday night. No, it wasn't Jason Benton, but something about him seemed vaguely familiar to her. The young man turned toward her, and Cheryl sensed a moment of hesitation on the young man's part. No, it definitely was not Jason Benton, but she was certain that she had seen him before. She raised her hand and started to call out to him, but the young man took off running through the woods.

"Well, that was strange," Cheryl muddled. She turned to walk past the smoldering camp fire and back through the brush that would lead her across the road and back to her car. She never saw the other man who had been watching her and Kirk Blankenship.

Jason walked slowly from where he had hidden in the woods when he first heard the teenager scavenging through their camp site. He recognized the boy as being the same one he had confronted in the park Saturday afternoon. He also recognized the beautiful, auburn-haired woman with the green eyes; the same green eyes he had dreamed about time and time again over the years. "No," he shook his head. "It's not possible. She couldn't have remembered me. It's just not possible..."

# CHAPTER 8

## Finding Stella

Kirk jerked open the car door and quickly slipped down in the driver seat. He pushed the START button and only sat upright after glancing toward the woods across the street to make sure that Jimmy Crennan's mother had not followed him. He had recognized her immediately; not many of his friends had mothers who were as hot-looking as Cheryl Crennan. "That was too close," he whispered hoarsely as he sped out of the café's parking lot. "What the hell was *she* doing there? If Crennan said anything to his mom..."

He knew he should report to school, no matter how late he was, but there was something more important than school on his mind at the moment. He had to find the homeless woman who saw them at the underpass Friday night; she was the only one who could positively identify them. He felt confident that the hundred-dollar bill he gave her, along with the chilling warning that he would come back for her if she told anyone what she had seen, was enough to ensure her silence; however, he had too much to lose if she did decide to speak to anyone. He had to find her, to talk to her, and, if he had to, silence her permanently. His entire future depended on the old hag keeping her mouth shut.

Kirk drove all over south Rome, searching every park bench, every underpass, any place he thought a homeless person might hide out during the day. He knew absolutely nothing about being homeless, but he knew that he had no use for these people who did little more than occupy space, and did nothing to better themselves. His cell phone beeped, indicating a new text message. It was from his best friend, David Mizen, wanting to know why he wasn't in school.

Kirk turned his car around and fumbled on the keyboard while he was driving. *"Tkg care of bzness,"* he texted back. David had been one of the three other people who had been with him the night that the old man died. Kirk drove slowly up and down the main streets of Rome. *"She has to be around here somewhere..."* he mused. He rubbed at his right temple as he allowed the memory of what had happened Friday night to bounce around inside his brain.

Kirk and his two best friends had decided to invite the younger, new kid in town to Kristy's party. Her parents were out of town for the weekend, and that always resulted in one hell of a good time for Kirk and his friends. Kirk had a college friend who had provided them plenty of beer for the party, and they had all taken advantage of that friendship. The new kid had stopped drinking after a couple of beers and had tried to leave the party, but Kirk had persuaded Jimmy Crennan to stay and hang out with them. He promised to get him home before his mom got off work from her night shift job—not that the kid had any other choice—he was a long way from home.

Kirk and Kristy had disappeared upstairs for a couple of hours; by the time he stumbled back downstairs, Jimmy Crennan was waiting for him—insisting that they take him home. Kirk pulled away from him. "Get your hands off me,

Crennan. I told the others you were too young to hang out with us, but they thought it would be fun to show you the ropes. If you want to go home, little boy, there's the front door. Start walking. "

Jimmy backed away. "I live a good twenty miles from here, Kirk. You promised that you would take me home when I needed to go."

"Too bad you don't know me any better than you do," Kirk smirked. "I rarely keep promises. You could learn from that." He watched while Jimmy turned toward the front door, ready to leave on his own, no doubt. He shook his head. "Oh, what the hell. Wait up, Crennan. It's too late for you to be out walking now, not to mention that it's colder than a witch's tit out there — my Dad says that all the time. Give me a few more minutes, and then we'll go. Why don't you go round up David and Mike?"

Jimmy looked at him with justifiable uncertainty.

"Go on!" Kirk smirked. "I *promise* I'll take you home."


It was almost two-thirty in the morning when Kirk pulled Kristy to him for one last kiss and touch. "Okay, everyone, pile in the car. We've got to get Crennan home before he turns into a pumpkin.

David Mizen and Michael Bozeman snickered as they walked ahead of Jimmy. Kirk followed behind all of them. Once they were all situated inside the car, Kirk rolled down his window to let the cold air hit his face. "We can't go straight home, guys. I need to drive around for a little while, until I sober up some. If my Dad sees me like this, I can forget this month's, and next month's, allowance."

"But, you said..." Jimmy stammered.

"Shut the hell up, Crennan," Kirk stared hard into the rear-view mirror to where Jimmy sat next to Michael in the back seat. "I told you that I would get you home, and I will. Quit acting like a baby."

"Yeah," David snickered from the front passenger seat.

"You were right, Kirk; it was a mistake to invite someone as young as him to hang out with us. Hell, we'll be seniors after this summer, and he's only a freshman, who doesn't even know how to drink, much less, anything else."

"You can shut up, too, David," Kirk warned. "I have one hell of a headache and none of you are helping it any. I just need to sober up a little."

They drove in silence for the next fifteen minutes until Kirk pulled sharply off the road. He glanced over at the empty parking lot of the diner that had recently opened. The café was closed, but the golden halo that floated—literally, floated—above it provided sufficient light for what he needed to do. "I've got to piss. Come with me, all of you."

"Why do we need to come with you, man? I don't need to piss," Michael swayed in the back seat. "I just want to sleep."

"Get out, NOW!" Kirk shouted. I want to lock the doors and I don't want to leave any of you in my car without me being in it, so get out!"

The three young men reluctantly followed Kirk into the bushes. Kirk turned away from them and unzipped his pants. David and Michael ambled slowly around what appeared to be a camp site, while Jimmy remained standing near the edge of the wood line.

"I think someone must live here," Jimmy whispered. "We need to get out of here."

David and Michael kicked dirt onto the dying embers of the fire that had, hours ago, been the center of jovial conversation and good food among a group of homeless comrades. David pointed toward the concrete underpass, to a lone figure moving about. "We're not alone," he laughed. "Come on, let's go say hello. I've never met a homeless person before."

Norman Weissman had awakened several minutes before the group of teenagers arrived. Nature called and he had taken care of business in the woods behind their camp. He stopped at Skipper's rolled-up sleeping bag, on his way back into camp, and saw the bag of food sitting on top of it. "Such a waste of good food," he sighed as he bent down and sorted through the contents. He left the meatloaf sandwich for Skipper, but couldn't resist the piece of buttermilk cake that he loved so much. He removed the cake from its wrapping and walked over to the under pass, where the silvery glow of the moon offered a little more light. He reasoned that there was, also, less chance of him waking his fellow comrades if he ate his late-night snack away from the main sleeping area. He had only taken one bite of the delicious cake when someone shoved him from behind. His hand tightened reflexively around the piece of cake.

"Well, well...what do we have here?" Kirk snorted. "What are you doing, old man? Who told you that you could sleep here in my woods?"

Norman swallowed the bite of cake and turned around slowly. He saw three young boys surrounding him, and he noticed another one standing alone, close to the main highway, maybe acting as a lookout. "I'm not bothering anyone—I'm just having myself a late-night snack before turning in for the night." He smiled at them and shook his head. "No, no, I'm not bothering anyone. If you want me to leave, I will be more than happy to leave. I was not aware these were your woods."

Kirk took two steps closer to the old man and shoved him again, this time in Michael's direction. "Now, you're just being a smart-ass, old man."

Michael giggled drunkenly and took his turn by shoving Norman directly into David.

"Get off me, you filthy buzzard!" David shrieked. He quickly shoved the old man back to Kirk.

"Please!" Norman spoke softly, trying to maintain his balance. "Please, don't hurt me. I'll leave, I promise..." He tried to turn around toward the camp fire, but a loose boot string entangled his feet and tripped him up.

Kirk shoved him away from him—hard—toward the concrete wall, just as Norman's feet twisted against each other.

The sound of a man's head bouncing off a solid concrete wall was more than enough to ensure instant sobriety. They heard the man gasp at impact with the wall, and they watched in horror as blood spurted from the crack in his skull. Nobody moved—nobody except Norman—who took one final gasp of air before falling to his knees and, then, face-first onto the frozen ground. The group watched as the old man's hand closed tightly around the cake that he held, his eyes rolled back in his head, and, he took his last breath.

"Ooohhh..." a cracked voice came from the woods behind them.

Kirk, David, and Michael quickly turned to see a really old woman standing behind them. Her wrinkled face showcased eyes that were wide with fear. They stood dumbfounded while she stumbled forward, toward the body of the homeless man. They watched on with disbelief when the old woman kneeled down and felt for a pulse at the old man's neck. They gaped in horror when the old woman looked up at them and began shaking her head.

"You killed him—you killed Norman."

Kirk was the first to re-gather his wits, and he quickly jerked the old woman up by her bony arms. He wasn't thinking—he was simply reacting to the situation. He fumbled in his pants pocket for the first bill that came out, and stuffed it down the front of the old woman's shirt. He stared into her cataract-filled eyes and shook her hard. "You didn't see anything, do you understand me, old woman?"

Stella shook all over and closed her eyes tight. She shook her head from side-to-side. "I didn't see nothing—nothing at all—I didn't..."

Kirk pulled her close to him and whispered into her ear. "I will find you—you can be sure of that. If you say anything, to anyone, I will find you, and personally slit your throat. Now, you take this money, and get the hell out of here. Remember what I said...I *will* find you."

Stella fell backward when the boy released her abruptly.

She pushed herself up and continued backing away from the group of boys. "I didn't see nothing..." She backed up until she could touch the concrete wall of the overpass. She wanted to run away, but her eighty-two year old legs felt like lead-weight and the ground was a magnet for them. She waited until the boys ran off before she started screaming.

It was almost lunch time, and Kirk was ready to give up his search for the old woman. If he showed up for half a day at school, there was a chance they might not notify his father of his tardiness. "Where are you, old woman?" he muttered. By now he was back where he started from, sitting in the parking lot of the Heavenly Grille Café. He leaned his head back against the head rest and closed his eyes. When he opened them, he glanced at the woods across the street. "Whatever! I may as well have one more look."

He waited for a break in traffic and darted across the street. A sense of déjà vu quickly came over him when he stepped into the clearing. He would never admit it to his friends, but he would have given anything if he could have turned back time and prevented what happened to the old man Friday night. It had never been his intention to hurt anyone, but he had an image to maintain—his tough-guy image that began to develop the day his father married Rae Sanchez.

He scanned the area to make sure nobody was around before he entered. He walked past the burned ashes of a camp fire and peered inside the three cardboard boxes. He was ready to turn around and leave when he saw her—the old woman was there, crawling out backwards from one of the makeshift tents, on her knees. Kirk moved quickly toward the tent and stood still, until the old woman backed directly into him.

Stella gasped and shouted, "Who's here?" She pushed herself, shakily, to a standing position and slowly turned around. She was prepared to confront PJ, Bernard, or Joe.

She wasn't afraid of them; however, she hoped it wasn't either of the other two men who shared the camp site.

The last person Stella expected to see standing behind her, with his arms crossed against his chest, was the boy from Friday night—the one who had shoved the hundred-dollar bill down her shirt. The temperature was in the low fifties, but Stella Sieber began to sweat profusely. "What? What are you doing here? What do want? Don't come near me, or I'll scream!"

Kirk stood still and smiled. "Oh, please—do it. Give me a reason to slit your wrinkled throat right here and now." He pulled a three-inch Spyderco Embassy Automatic Knife from his jean pocket. The expensive switch blade had been a Christmas present from his father, who was an avid collector of guns and hunting knives. "Come on, old woman, give me a reason." When the old woman began to tremble and shake her head, Kirk shoved her back onto the ground. He knelt in front of her, reached into another pocket, and pulled out five, one-hundred dollar bills, and waved the money in front of her face. "You and I are going to have a little talk. If you listen to me, and do as I say, this money is yours."

Stella was still shaking her head and clutching a large paper bag against her chest. Everything she owned was in that paper bag and she was not going to release her grasp on it. "Leave me alone. I already told you I wasn't going to say anything. I still have your money." She fumbled inside her shirt and threw the wrinkled, hundred-dollar bill on the ground. "Take it, and leave me alone. I don't want your money. I mind my own business."

Kirk picked up the money and shoved it back inside her old, flannel shirt. "Keep it. Like I said, if you do what I tell you to do, there's another five-hundred in it for you."

"You want me to leave town, don't you?" Stella blurted and shook her head. "I don't want to leave town."

Kirk squeezed her chin between his thumb and forefinger and jerked her head up, forcing her to look at him. "It's not a request, old woman. You will do as I tell you to do, and you will do it before Friday. I'll know when you've done it, and I'll find you and give you the other five hundred. You *will* leave this city before the weekend is up, or I will slit your throat while you sleep. Do you understand what I'm saying?" He squeezed harder, until tears formed at the corners of the old woman's tightly closed eyes. "Open your eyes and look at me, old woman!"

Stella had a sudden flashback to a time when another man had beat her, and threatened her. That man had died under "mysterious" circumstances. She knew that if she was even twenty years younger, she could probably do the same to the young punk who was currently crushing her jaw. However, she wasn't twenty years younger; she was an eighty-two year old woman who didn't see many options lying in wait for her. She could make six hundred dollars last a while; she could even get off the street for a couple of months, until the weather began to warm up. She opened her eyes and nodded assent. "I understand. I'll do whatever you tell me to do..."

# CHAPTER 9

## Between the Rivers

One of Skipper's favorite places to rest during the day hours was the "Between the Rivers" Historic District in downtown Rome, Georgia. The area, which was situated between the Etowah and Oostanaula Rivers, was also the site of Rome's founding in 1834. It was the same area where early business and industry served the residents of the new town. Most of the original district was severely ravaged and burned during the Civil War; however, the spirit of the survivors burned stronger than the fires that destroyed their beloved town, and that same spirit eventually rebuilt the community into the thriving town it was today.

Skipper had a special, out-of-the-way, bench that allowed him the privacy to sit, think, read, write his poetry, and, to ponder the possibilities for his next destination. He had made it a point never to spend more than a couple of months at any location, and, ever since Norman's death, he had felt the need to move on. He was seventy-six years old and the cold weather was taking a toll on his old bones—bones that had been through more pain and trauma than one person should ever have to endure in one life time.

Skipper laid his notebook on the bench beside him and stretched out his long legs. He closed his eyes and thought about all the places he had travelled to in his life time, and all the strange/beautiful things he had seen: the northern lights over the Rocky Mountains from Canada; a phenomenon in the skies of Himalaya—an iridescent spiral cloud—in 2009; Heaven's Gate in Zhangjiajie in Tianmen Mountain, China; the Road to Heaven in Ireland, that occurred every two years when the stars aligned perfectly with the road; and, the northern lights again—this time, from Alaska. There were many other places that filled Skipper's memory, but those were some of his absolute favorites.

"We've got to quit meeting like this," the masculine voice with just the slightest hint of an Irish brogue said. Officer Thomas O'Brady was dressed in civilian clothes—jeans and a black leather jacket—on this late Monday afternoon. He didn't wait for an invitation to join Skipper on the bench.

Skipper pulled his legs in before he opened his eyes. He already recognized the voice. "Isn't this a little off your beaten path, Officer O'Brady?" He reached for his notebook, but the rosy-cheeked officer smiled and beat him to it.

"I was going to ask you the same thing," Thomas O'Brady grinned. "Actually, it's my day off. I was at the library most of the day, doing some research. I always like to stop by this area before I head home; it's very peaceful here."

Skipper nodded and closed his eyes again. "Well, it was..."

Thomas laughed and disregarded the ornery criticism. He doubted Skipper would offer, so he took the liberty and opened the notebook. "I haven't been able to get these poems off my mind. It's Skipper, right?"

Skipper opened his eyes. It was five o'clock and would be dark within the next thirty to forty-five minutes. It would take him almost two hours to make the walk back to the old camp site, and he wasn't one to sit around and chit-chat, especially with cops. He nodded affirmation of his name, but did not want to encourage conversation, so he didn't say anything in response.

Officer O'Brady was flipping through the book of war poems and tapped his finger on a page, titled, "Oh Withered Rose." He looked at Skipper and said, "I especially like this one. If I knew you better, I would swear you wrote it just for me." He cleared his throat and began to read the poem aloud:

*A child of sorrow with deep set eyes*
*Kneeling by a granite marker stone;*
*Gazing at a single flower on the ground*
*Lying there all alone.*

*The child's tiny frame begins to fade*
*When the quarter moon appeared;*
*Descending stars helped light the field*
*As the child disappeared.*

*Withered rose, oh withered rose*
*Time has robbed you of your scent;*
*You and my Daddy had so much life*
*I wonder where it went.*

*Thunder roared from up above*
*A star-bright sky turned solid black;*
*Then a timber fell from a lightning bolt*
*With a deathly frightening crack.*

*Seconds passed, then all was calm*
*It wasn't clear what had occurred;*
*There was silence in the still of night*
*When the child's fading voice was heard.*

*Withered rose, oh withered rose*
*You once graced my father's mound;*

*His body rots but his soul's now free*
*Of all sorrow above the ground.*

Thomas looked at the homeless Veteran sitting beside him, and felt ashamed that his country had failed him and other Veterans like him, adding to the pain and torment that lay buried deep inside them. Skipper's anger and resentment resonated throughout his poetry; even Thomas could see that. When it was obvious to him that Skipper wasn't going to participate in conversation, he cleared his throat again and looked upward. "It will be dark soon, Skipper. May I give you a ride somewhere?"

Skipper stood and held out his hand for the notebook. "No thanks. I can walk. I've been doing it for a long, long time now."

"The temperature is already dropping. The weatherman said it could drop near freezing tonight. Please let me drop you at one of the men's shelters."

Skipper tucked his notebook inside his backpack and looked at the baby-faced man with the red buzz-cut hair and twinkling blue eyes. "Why do you care?"

Thomas stuffed his hands inside his jean pockets and grinned. "I honestly don't know. There's just something about you—I don't know—I just feel compelled to try to help you."

Skipper shook his head. "I don't need your help. I don't need anyone's help for that matter. I've been travelling every road imaginable since I retired in 1977. I think I've walked down most of them by now. In all that time, I've never come across a cop who really cared where I spent the night, as long as it wasn't out on a public bench."

"You retired from the Army, so that must mean you receive a pension, right?"

Skipper's brows rose in skepticism. "Your point being, Officer?"

"Well," Thomas shook his head. "I don't know what rank you retired as, but if you receive a monthly check, why in

God's name are you living on the streets?"

Skipper turned to walk away but stopped to look back at Thomas O'Brady. "Because living on the streets usually ensures that I don't have to be around people. I detest the human race, especially politicians—and, police. If I thought I could get away with it, I'd bomb all of Washington and try to get rid of all of them at one time. You're right, I do receive a monthly pension, and I use what I need to use when I have to. I'm on the streets *by choice*; I don't really expect you, or anyone else, to care or begin to understand why."

Thomas shook his head. "I absolutely do not understand that; but, it's not any of my business how you spend your money or where you spend your nights. I just keep thinking..."

All was quiet for a couple of minutes, and when it was obvious to Skipper that the Officer was not going to complete his sentence he said, "You see me and you can't help but think of your own father—the father you never got a chance to know—and, you would never want to think of your father living on the streets, nobody offering to lend a helping hand. Am I close?"

"Close enough, I guess," Thomas replied with a crack to his voice. "Well, I won't bother you any longer. It was good to see you again, Skipper. Try to keep warm out there tonight." He turned and walked toward a parking lot off in the distance.

Skipper rubbed the back of his neck and chewed on the inside of his cheek. *"Hell..."* he thought before grumbling out loud. "Officer O'Brady? Wait a minute. I've changed my mind about that ride."


It was pitch-dark outside by six o'clock. Cheryl was standing in the kitchen, staring blankly into the food pantry, when Jimmy burst through the back door.

"Hey, Mom! What's for dinner? I'm starving."

Cheryl closed the pantry door and smiled. "You're

always starving. I swear, I don't know where you put all the food you eat." She pulled him toward her and kissed his cheek. "I wasn't sure if you were coming straight home from basketball practice or not, so I haven't started supper yet. I thought you might grab a bite to eat with your friends."

Jimmy sighed and flopped down on one of the kitchen stools. "I told you...I don't think I'll be hanging out with Kirk Blankenship and his friends anymore."

"Yes, you did mention that possibility before, but you never said why. Did something happen?"

Jimmy wanted, more than anything, to confide in his mother, but he didn't want to get her involved. He, also, did not want to see the disappointment that he was sure he would see in her face, if he confided to her what had happened Friday night. He really just wanted it all to go away. He decided that the best way to make that happen would be by cutting ties with Kirk and his friends; and, he had managed to avoid all of them at school today. "No, not really. I think it has more to do with the age gap between me and all of them. I think I need to find more friends my own age to hang out with," he shrugged.

Cheryl came up behind him and wrapped her arms around him. "I think that's probably a smart decision on your part. Kirk and his friends drive, don't they? So, I assume they must be at least 16 years old, right?"

"Yeah—plus—they're all rich, spoiled kids."

Cheryl rested her chin on top of her son's head. "Totally different from you, that's for sure; there's definitely nothing spoiled about you."

Jimmy laughed. "There's nothing rich about me either!"

"Yep, there is that, alright," Cheryl agreed. "Hey, I don't have to work tonight, so tell me what you'd like for dinner and I'll whip it up. We can watch a movie or something after you get your homework done."

Something about his mom felt off to Jimmy, but he wasn't quite sure what it could be. "What's going on, Mom?

We never watch movies during the week." He pushed the chair beside him out and patted it. "Have a seat and tell me what's up. You seem—I don't know—distracted tonight."

Cheryl sat down in the chair next to Jimmy and looked at him for a long moment. "You are so intuitive, you know that?" She had not planned on saying anything to her son until she knew for sure that Jason Benton really was who she thought he was, but, she couldn't get the man off her mind.

Jimmy stretched his neck from side to side. "Yeah, I hear the girls really like sensitive guys, so it helps me to practice my technique on you. Seriously, though, what's going on? Anything you want to talk about?"

Cheryl exhaled and shrugged her shoulders. "Okay. So, don't freak out on me or anything, but...what would you say if I told you that I think I saw...your...*father*?"

The grin faded from Jimmy's handsome face. "I would say that was pretty much impossible."

Cheryl raised her hands, palms forward, in front of her face. "Yeah, that's pretty much what I would have thought, too; but, Jimmy, I'm like seventy-five percent sure that we were sitting next to him Saturday night at the café we went to for Brunswick stew, remember..."

Jimmy's mind began to race backward, trying to think back to Saturday night, trying to remember who had been inside the café that night. Who had they been sitting next to? He couldn't remember anyone specifically. "Mom?"

"I know, I know," Cheryl blew out a burst of air she wasn't aware that she had been holding inside. "It's crazy, right? I mean, I've told you all about the night you were conceived. I never knew the boy's name, where he lived, nothing...I knew absolutely nothing about him."

"Why do I have the feeling that you know more about him now?" Jimmy asked slowly.

Cheryl nodded. "It's true. I haven't been able to get him off my mind, so I went back to that café this morning and talked with Doug—that nice man who works there with

Bertie. Anyway, I found out the name of the man who was sitting beside me that night."

A few moments of silence followed before Jimmy burst, "Well? Are you going to tell me? What's my father's name?"

Cheryl's hands were shaking. She had not wanted to tell her son that she was seventy-five percent sure that the stranger next to them was his father; she wanted to tell him that she was one-hundred percent positive that it was. "Maybe I shouldn't have said anything, at least not until I know more for certain."

"No, no, that's okay, Mom. I want to know, really. I mean, if it turns out that it's not him, that's okay, too. I mean, I've gone almost fifteen years not knowing the man's name — and survived — it's no big deal."

"Are you sure?" Cheryl asked. "I don't want to get your hopes up or anything — or, my hopes either, for that matter."

"It's your call, Mom. If you want to wait to tell me…"

"No!" Cheryl blurted out. "No. We've both waited a long time for this, and there is absolutely no doubt in my mind that the man I sat next to on Saturday night was the same person I lost my virginity to. His name — your father's name — is, Jason Benton. There, I said it!"

"Jason Benton?" Jimmy allowed the name to roll slowly off his tongue and nodded his head. "I like the sound of that. Hey! Does that mean that I'll have to change my name now to James Benton? That, actually, has a pretty good sound to it, don't you think?"

Cheryl picked up a dish rag off the table and threw it at her son. She laughed and grabbed her coat. "Well, are you coming or not?"

Jimmy pulled his coat back on and laughed back at her. "Sure, where are we going? Oh, wait, don't tell me — we're having supper at the Heavenly Grille Café tonight, aren't we?"

# CHAPTER 10

## - Heaven -
## Martin's Story

"*H* ello, Mr. Martin, sir!" *Andrew Brown shouted happily. Andrew had passed away in December 2011 and was the twin brother to Amos Brown, one of only two living humans who knew the truth about the trio of angels who ran the Heavenly Grille Café. Amos and Amanda Turner, a young woman — full of faith and belief — had been taken in by the angels during the summer of 2011. She had lost everyone close to her, lost her home and job, and had no idea what direction to go, until she stumbled upon the café and its heavenly trio. She and Amos had witnessed Max's transformation from a human to the glorious angel that he was.*

*Martin turned off the huge data screen behind him, with a flick of his wrist. A broad grin spread across his generous lips when he saw Andrew. "Ah, Andrew! You've come for a visit. It's so good to see you again. I hear that you and your parents have been taking in more and more animals, until the animals choose what families they wish to spend eternity with — I'm sure that has been keeping all of you busy."*

*Andrew nodded. "Oh, yessir, those critters do keep us busy. There are so many of them that died without ever having a family or home of their own. They just can't seem to get enough hugs and cuddles. Amanda's dog, Sam, comes to visit every day, too. I have a feeling he's keeping an eye on things – making sure that we don't make any mistakes, you know?"*

*"Yes, Sam does hold a special place in his heart for these animals – especially the ones that suffered at the hands of man while they lived on earth. He's a very special dog, indeed."*

*Andrew bent his head and grinned. When he looked up, he had a smile of accomplishment across his face. "You know what else, Mr. Martin? I can hear all their thoughts now, too. It's amazing the things they have to say."*

*"I knew you would be able to, Andrew. You have a special connection to animals, and they can sense that. They don't allow everyone to hear their thoughts, so you must be mighty special in their eyes." Martin smiled. "Is there anything else on your mind today, Andrew?"*

*"Well, sir...I just wanted to let you know that I went to Amos in a dream last night. I've been trying, ever since he was here for that short amount of time – you know – when he died on the operating table?"*

*"Yes, I remember that visit well," Martin nodded. "I know he wanted to remain here in Heaven with his family, but you have to admit, his life took a drastic change when he returned, now didn't it!"*

*Amos Brown was the older twin, by two minutes. He suffered a major heart attack late in 2013 and died on the operating table. During the time that the doctors worked to revive him, Amos was transported to Heaven and allowed to spend precious moments with his family. When the doctors got his heart beating again, Amos returned to his earthly life and met the woman he would marry, Izzie Ghent.*

*"It sure did!" Andrew shook his head. "I never would have thought my brother would get married so late in life. I think he lucked out with Miss Izzie. They seem to be getting along good and doing lots of traveling."*

*Martin already knew that everything was good in the life of Amos and Izzie Brown, but he encouraged Andrew to continue talking. "So, you had a good visit with your brother in his dreams, did you?"*

"I did, yessir. As happy as Amos is with Miss Izzie, I think he really misses Mr. Max and the others. He said the old café was bought by some mechanic. Of course, the building doesn't have the halo above it, like it used to, and the owner painted the building red and yellow. Yessir, Amos misses that place, but he said he and Miss Izzie might be making a trip to Rome, Georgia a little later to visit everyone."

"Well, you know the café cannot remain in one location for more than five years. There's still a chance that some of the old truckers will find them at their new location, but Max will deal with that when and if he has to."

"Well," Andrew said. "I didn't mean to interfere with your work, Mr. Martin. I told Amos I would stop by and tell you hello. He wanted me to thank you again for giving him the opportunity to visit with us, even if it was such a short visit."

"If you talk to him again, Andrew, please tell him that he is more than welcome. It's probably not necessary, but you might want to remind him again how important it is to keep the angels' secret. He should not even tell Miss Izzie the truth about them."

"You don't have to worry about Amos saying anything. That is one secret he will carry to his grave, and I'm pretty sure Miss Amanda will, too."

"Oh, I don't worry about Amanda keeping the secret. She may want to tell that new husband of hers, Tyler Foster, the truth one day, but, she won't. She will leave it up to Max. If Max feels it is safe to disclose their true identities to anyone, I trust his decision to do so."

There was a moment of silence between the two men. Just as Andrew was about to leave, he turned and asked something that had been on his mind. "It's really none of my business, Mr. Martin, but, just how long have you and Mr. Max known each other?"

Martin threw back his head and clapped his hands. "It might be easier to figure out how long we HAVEN'T known each other, Andrew! As a matter of fact – and, not many people know this – but, Max and I fought in the Colosseum together."

*"No! No way! You were a gladiator, Mr. Martin?"* Andrew
was more than a little surprised.

Martin stood erect and lifted his head high. *"Don't let my
scrawny build fool you, dear boy. The Emperor certainly did
not expect me to survive very long, but with Max's help, I
lasted much longer than anyone ever thought I would."*

Andrew shook his head. *"I can't believe it — you and Mr.
Max — gladiators."* His mood sobered when he continued. *"I
can't begin to imagine what life for the two of you must have
been like."*

Martin draped an arm over the younger man's broad
shoulders and laughed. *"Come on, Andrew. I need to take a
break. I'll walk back with you and tell you about mine and
Max's days together. I don't get to tell the story often."*

During the next couple of hours, Martin educated Andrew
on what life was like for him and Max in ancient Rome. He
described a few of the different categories of Gladiators: the
andabatae, who fought with helmets that had no eye-holes; the
bestiarius who fought against beasts; the cestus who was a
boxer or fist-fighter; the crupellarii who were slave gladiators
equipped with a continuous shell of iron; the equites who were
usually equipped with horses and heavy armor; the tertiaries
who often served as a substitute if an advertised gladiator was
unable to fight; and, the velites who were referred to as
skirmishers and fought on foot, holding a spear with an
attached thong for throwing.

*"I never realized there were so many different kinds of
gladiators,"* Andrew mused. *"What kind exactly were the two
of you?"*

*"I usually fell into the tertiaries category,"* Martin
explained. *"In some of the games, there were often three men
matched against one another. The first two would battle, one
would die, and the winner would be required to fight the third
man. I was usually that third man, which is probably the only
thing that kept me living as long as I did. The winner was
usually so tired by the time he got to me, and I was very quick
on my feet, so it made it easy for me to win. The times they used
me as a substitute, though, were the times I did not think I*

*would survive to see another fight."*

*"What about Mr. Max? He's so big and strong. Was he always that way?"*

*Martin nodded profusely. "Oh, my, yes! Max was even bigger and stronger as a gladiator than he is as an angel on earth — if you can imagine that. Maximus was a bestiary; he fought only against the meanest and hungriest animals they could find."*

*"If y'all were in such different categories, how did you become such good friends?"*

*"We actually met when we were both ordered to bury the mound of dead bodies left over from two days of entertainment for the elite Romans. The regular slaves usually carried out this task, but for some reason, Max had earned the ire of one of the lanistas — today, you would probably refer to him as a pimp for the slave gladiators. This man pointed out Max and me to be the ones to bury thirty of our comrades. I had almost lost my own fight that day and could hardly drag myself to a standing position. The lanista was ready to strike me dead, I believe, when Maximus pulled me up and marched me alongside him. We did our best to look out for the other from that point on."*

*Andrew cleared his throat. "This might not be an appropriate question, Mr. Martin, but...how exactly did the two of you die? You don't have to answer that if you don't want to, just tell me to quit being nosey and mind my own business..."*

*Martin sighed and stopped walking. "No, I don't mind answering your questions, Andrew. It's just that it's been a long, long time since anyone has asked me about these things. It truly does seem like it was a life time ago. There was so much pain and agony, but somehow, Maximus and I found moments of light and hope. We both shared a strong belief and faith in God, and that's probably what got us through that time — that, and having each other to fall back on. No, I don't mind your questions." He took a deep breath before continuing, "Actually, I died first. In fact, I guess you could say that I died in Max's place."*

*"I don't understand," Andrew spoke softly.*

"Well, Max was supposed to open the day's events. He usually did that – opened the events – unless the showings were not as impressive as the Emperor expected them to be; in those cases, he would always save Max's performance for last. But, on the day I died, Max became extremely ill – probably with what we know as pneumonia these days. He was unable to perform, so I was brought in to substitute. The trouble was, that Max was supposed to be the finale performance that day, and I had already fought two battles of my own; I barely scraped by winning the last one. My lanista ordered me to fill in as a substitute for Maximus. Mind you now, I had absolutely no experience fighting animals like Max did. They threw me in the ring and I immediately tripped over my own two feet. The audience roared with laughter. All I had to fight the animals with was a lone spear. Maximus usually killed the animals with his bare hands; needless to say, I did not possess the physical strength and fortitude to do that, so they, also, provided me with a knife. I never got the chance to use the knife. They released not only one lion for me to fight, but two lions. Trust me, dear friend, I never stood a chance, but I gave it all I had to give. One lion attacked me from the front, and the other pounced from the rear."

"What a horrible way to die..." Andrew was quiet and solemn.

Martin decided to lighten the mood. "Oh, goodness, yes – those creatures ripped me to shreds, but, with me weighing in at only one-hundred thirty pounds, they barely got enough to whet their appetites. My lanista rushed into the ring to help secure the beasts, and, as fate would have it, those lions turned on him and completed their meal." Martin clapped his hands and smiled. "Forgive me, I should not be clapping over the death of any man, but, lanistas were NOT very charitable or honorable people. They cared only for themselves and treated all gladiators as nothing more than garbage. Needless to say, you won't find any of them sharing Heaven with us! Oh, dear, I shall have to ask God for forgiveness, again, for the feelings I continue to have toward that man."

"Wow, that is some story, Mr. Martin. I have to admit, I've

*always wondered what your past was — you know, just common curiosity on my part — but, I still cannot imagine you as a gladiator, no, sirree."*

"Well, Andrew, whatever you do, do not repeat that story to Bertie. She has asked me dozens of times to tell her my story, or tried to get it out of Max, but Max always tells her that it is my story to tell. I will tell her one of these days, but not yet. Quite frankly, I enjoy teasing her, knowing that I know something that she is so curious about!"

"What about Mr. Max? How did his end come about?"

Martin grasped his hands behind his back and continued on their walk. "Maximus was the best gladiator of our time. He could have been placed into any category and been the best, but the lanistas kept him as a bestiarius for another ten years. He had earned retirement and was only one fight away from that happening; however, his lanista wanted to impress the crowd, so he surprised Max by turning four lions loose on him. He usually only had to fight two at a time; once, he had to fight three, but this last time, it was four. He had killed three of them, but was bleeding profusely from a bite to his stomach. The smell of his blood gave the fourth lion what it needed to claim victory. They stalked each other and just as Max lifted his knife, blood gushed from his wound and he glanced down. The remaining lion took advantage and went in for the kill. He grabbed Max by the throat and dragged him around the arena like a rag doll. Naturally, the crowd loved it. The more they clapped and roared encouragement, the more the lion shook Max's body. They had to kill the lion in order to get it to release its hold on Max."

A tear escaped from Andrew's eye. He wiped it away. "I didn't think there was supposed to be any tears in Heaven, but I just feel so bad for Mr. Max. I had no idea..."

Martin wiped Andrew's cheek. "You think that was a tear of sadness, Andrew, but it wasn't. Just because we are in Heaven does not mean that we do not feel empathy for whatever someone has had to endure in their life time."

"I didn't know there was a difference," Andrew smiled.

Martin shrugged. "Eh...it's a thin line, I'm sure. That's

*enough of rehashing the past. Look! We're at your home and I do believe I see your mother waving to us from the porch."*

*Andrew looked toward his mansion and waved back at his mother. He took Martin's hand and said, "Thank you for sharing your story with me."*

*Martin nodded. "The pleasure was all mine, Andrew, but remember what I said!"*

*Andrew laughed and hugged Martin farewell. "I won't forget, Mr. Martin – Bertie won't hear it from me!"*

*"For there is not a just man on earth who does good and does not sin." Ecclesiastes 7:10 (NKJV)*

# CHAPTER 11

## Mid-Week Surprises

The next couple of days were fairly uneventful for everyone. The angels continued to help and pray for those in need; Cheryl and Jimmy ate at least one meal daily at the Heavenly Grille, hoping to run into Jason Benton; PJ awoke from her coma with short-term memory loss; Kirk Blankenship checked the paper every day to see if the police had any updates on the murder of the homeless man, Norman Weissman; Officer O'Brady somehow managed to come across Skipper every day during his routine beat, and did his best to engage the older man in conversation; Jason was in a mellow mood and did his best to avoid his fellow, homeless comrades and Doug whenever food was delivered to the group; Joe Sanders and Bernard Cartwright had become closer friends since Norman's death, and talked with each other about the possibility of returning to their families one day; Ernest Blankenship did his best to avoid any contact or conversation with his wife, Rae, while feeling the distance between him and his son growing wider every day; and, Stella continued to work up the courage to do what the young punk had ordered her to do.

Jason's sour mood was lifting, so he was among the four remaining homeless men who sat around their camp fire, trying to keep warm, and waiting for Doug to deliver their late-night meal and coffee. Joe and Bernard sat shoulder-to-shoulder on one side of the fire, while Jason and Skipper sat on the other side, careful to keep at least ten feet between them.

Jason used a long limb to stir the fire. He shivered involuntarily and said, "This feels like the coldest night we've had in January." He rubbed his bare hands together, trying to maintain circulation in them.

Skipper took a long drag off his cigarette, tossed it into the flames, and stood up. He didn't say anything to anyone as he walked over to his duffel bag and rummaged inside for something. He walked back over to the group and tossed a pair of gloves at Jason's feet. "They're old, but should be better than nothing, I guess."

Jason picked up the gloves and stood up. He handed the gloves back to Skipper. "No thanks, I'm good."

Skipper exhaled deeply and stood staring at the younger Veteran. "They're just an old pair of gloves, kid. I don't need them. I have another pair. Take them. Your hands are turning blue."

Jason wanted to say no; it was hard for him to accept help of any kind from anyone. It had not always been that way for him—only since the incident with Dante, had he began to distance himself from humanity. He chewed at his lower lip and stared Skipper in the eye. "Thanks. I'll be sure to get them back to you..."

Skipper shook his head and sat back down. "Forget it, kid. I expect I'll be long gone by then."

Jason put the gloves on and rubbed his hands together before sitting back down in front of the fire.

"So, you're planning on leaving our merry band, are you?" Bernard addressed Skipper. "It seems like our numbers are dwindling at quite a rapid pace."

Skipper nodded. "That's the plan. I might give it another

couple of weeks before I move on."

"Well," Joe said. "We hate to see you leave, Skipper, but we certainly understand the need to move on. I've been thinking more and more about that myself lately."

"Really?" Bernard asked. "Does that mean that you are considering what we've been talking about the last few days? Returning home to your family?"

Joe grinned and nodded. "Yeah, I'm thinking that might be the best thing for me to do. Hell, I'll be 61 years old in a few months, and I miss my kids. I talked to my former next door neighbor a few weeks ago, and he told me that my daughter was pregnant with my first grandchild. Besides, how long can we keep living like this before..." His voice cracked and he shook his head.

"Before we end up like Norman?" Jason asked. "That's what you're thinking, isn't it, Joe?"

Joe nodded. "Let's not forget PJ either."

Jason sighed. "Yeah, she finally woke up, but she doesn't remember any of us. She doesn't remember Norman, or that she was hit by a car. It's funny how that works—short-term memory loss. I mean, how can you not remember something that happened two days ago, but you can remember certain days from thirty or forty years ago?"

"It's different with everyone who suffers from it," Bernard explained. "Since PJ's loss is due to head trauma, it could be days, weeks, or months before her memories return to her. There's also the chance that she might never fully remember everything. The brain is a fairly resilient organ, but damage recovery will vary among individuals."

Skipper had lit another cigarette and was half-way listening to the group's conversation. He had no vested interest in PJ, but he wished her no ill-will either, and hoped for a full recovery for her. He leaned back on his elbows and stared at Bernard. "You sound like you know what you're talking about. What were you in your other life, a doctor or something?"

"Not exactly," Bernard shrugged. "I am a retired

pharmacist and have discussed psychopharmaceutic drugs with many patients. Drugs like Ritalin for people who suffered from deficit hyperactivity disorder, and, Aricept and Exelon, which are believed to help some Alzheimer patients with their short-term memory loss. I could go on, but I don't want to bore all of you. That was a long time ago...in another life time."

Joe was grinning from ear to ear. "Well, I'll be dang— what do you know; this old, former football coach has been keeping company with someone like you. Why haven't you ever told me what you did in the past, Moe?"

Bernard smiled back at the man who had, indeed, become a good friend to him. "Maybe because you never asked, my friend."

"Well, suck my toes and give me goosebumps!" Joe laughed out loud. "A pharmacist? Really?"

"Really," Bernard nodded.

"I guess all we need now is a bag of marshmallows and someone to lead us in singing Kumbaya," Skipper managed a grin of his own.

"Oh, I love marshmallows!" Joe laughed. "Which reminds me...who has a watch? Isn't it time for our friend Doug?"

Skipper glanced down at the old wristwatch that had embraced his weathered wrist for so many decades. "Should be any time now."

The next events occurred simultaneously.

Doug walked through the front clearing, wearing a grin and carrying three bags of food and coffee. "Hey, fellas..." was all he got out. He stopped short and stared toward the clearing closest to the concrete overpass.

The four men around the campfire ceased their conversations and three of them turned to see what had captured Doug's attention. Three uniformed policemen, guns drawn, were storming toward them. One of them was Officer Thomas O'Brady, who had taken a friend's night shift so that the younger cop could be with his wife who was giving birth to their first child.

"Nobody move!" Officer O'Brady shouted his order.

Skipper had his back to whoever had come up behind them, but he immediately recognized O'Brady's voice. He began to push himself up from his sitting position.

"I said, NOBODY move!" the officer shouted again.

Skipper sat back down.

The two other officers quickly made their way to the men sitting around the campfire. They motioned for Doug to merge with them.

Doug moved forward and sat the bags of food on the ground. "What's going on, officers?"

"Quiet!" one of the officers ordered. "No talking." He looked toward Officer O'Brady and said, "Bring her over here."

The group was so caught off guard by the arrival of the police that none of them noticed the old woman who had followed behind the officers.

Doug saw her first. "Stella! Stella, are you okay? What's going on?"

One of the officers kicked Doug behind his knee caps which caused him to fall to the ground. "I said, NO TALKING! We'll ask the questions." He motioned for Officer O'Brady to bring Stella closer. "Okay, ma'am, don't be afraid. Come closer and tell us if any of these men is the one you say killed Norman Weissman."

Norman was no longer a John Doe. His dentures had played an important part in helping the police to track down his true identity. His sister, Lynn, had been notified of his death, and his niece would be laying claim to his body and returning him home for a proper burial.

Stella stepped forward and was almost unrecognizable to her former group of homeless friends. She cleaned up rather well for an old bag lady; she looked almost presentable. She shuffled around Officer O'Brady and stood directly behind Skipper. She looked each of the men squarely in the eye before stopping at Skipper. She pointed her bony finger at him. "That one—he's the one who slammed poor Norman's head against that concrete wall over there, and all because poor Norman had stolen a piece of cake from him. He's the one!"

Officer O'Brady moved to the left side of Stella and looked down at the man sitting on the ground. "Stand up!" he ordered.

Skipper kept his groans to himself as his old bones grimaced beneath the cold ground when he pushed himself to a standing position. He brushed the dirt off his jeans and turned to face Stella and Officer O'Brady. He was almost two inches taller than most of the men there, and he slowly straightened himself to his full height. "Anything you say, Officer," he replied.

Thomas O'Brady paled visibly when he saw Skipper, but he was careful not to give any indication of recognition. Instead, he motioned to one of the other officers to cuff Skipper, while he read him his Miranda rights. When he had finished, he instructed the third officer to get everyone's name and contact information.

When all that had been accomplished, the three officers led Skipper away, and Stella crawled back inside her makeshift tent—but, not before she grabbed most of the food and coffee from the bags that Doug had dropped on the ground.

# CHAPTER 12

## Changes in the Air

The morning crowd at the Heavenly Grille Café on the morning of Thursday, January 28, filled every table in the room. There were a few vacant seats available at the counter when Jason opened the door and looked upward when the angel chimes sounded.

Doug met him and shook hands. He smiled at Jason's reaction to the chimes. "Those were Bertie's idea, but with as many people that come in out and of that door, they can become a little distracting and irritating at times."

Jason shook his head. "Naw, I kinda like the way they sound."

Doug thought that Jason looked uncomfortable in the crowded room, so he placed a hand on his shoulder and ushered him toward the counter section. "Come this way. Joe and Bernard are already here. I'm glad the three of you took me up on the offer to stay in the spare apartment last night."

Jason exhaled and shook his head. "Well, it was pretty cold out last night, and I think that after what happened with Skipper, we all needed a temporary change of scenery." He took a seat next to Joe at the counter. "Morning, fellas."

Joe and Bernard stopped eating long enough to shake hands with Jason.

"I hope we didn't wake you," Bernard grinned, "But, we could smell this awesome food from upstairs, and couldn't wait any longer."

"Yeah," Joe laughed, getting back to the huge bowl of cheese and bacon grits. "You've gotta try some of these grits, kid. You're gonna love 'em!"

Jason picked up the cup of hot coffee that Doug had sat before him on the counter, and took a long sip. He turned to glance out the café's huge front window, to the wooded area across the street. "What about Stella? Has anyone seen her this morning? I can't believe she wouldn't take the opportunity to get in out of the cold last night. There was plenty of floor space in the apartment."

Doug shook his head. "No, I went over early this morning with some food and coffee, but she was nowhere to be found. I'm guessing, maybe, she didn't want a confrontation with any of us."

Jason sat his cup down and rubbed his face between his palms. He closed his eyes for a minute and sighed. "I can't believe what she said...I *don't* believe what she said. There's got to be something we can do for Skipper."

"Well," Joe said. "He *was* missing from the group when we all woke up from Stella's screaming that night."

Jason stared at Joe and said, "If you remember, Joe, I was missing from the group that night, too."

"But you would never do anything to hurt poor Norman," Joe denied.

"And you think Skipper would?" Jason asked.

"No, of course not," Bernard chimed in. "None of us believe that Skipper had anything to do with Norman's death, and especially not over a piece of cake, like Stella said. No...no, Stella is lying, but the question is, *why*? What does she stand to gain from all this."

"Well, she looked like she was all rested and cleaned up," Joe added. "She didn't look like she's been sleeping out in the cold for the past few days. She would need money to stay at a motel, and I don't think Stella has any money."

"I think there's probably a lot that we don't know about Stella," Jason said. "Hell, we don't know a lot about Skipper either, but I'd be willing to bet my life that he would never do what she said he did. I'm pretty sure he's more the type who would walk away from trouble first."

"Why do you say that, Jason?" Doug asked.

Jason lifted the coffee cup again and looked Doug directly in the eyes. "Because he's seen too much death in his life time…because he's been a part of too much death in his life time." He shook his head adamantly. "No. Skipper had nothing to do with what happened to Norman. I'm sure of that."

"How can we help him?" Joe asked. "We probably don't have a hundred dollars between us right now."

Jason stood up abruptly and turned to leave.

Doug moved quickly to his side. "Don't leave, Jason. Please, have something to eat first."

"I'm not hungry," Jason replied.

Doug pulled a key from his pants pocket and handed it to Jason. "Take this, please. It's a spare key to the apartment upstairs. I've given Joe and Bernard one, too. The three of you are free to stay there until this cold weather passes, or as long as you need to."

Jason stared at the key. He wanted to take it, but he did not want to feel obligated or committed to anyone for anything. He reached out reluctantly and took the key. "Thanks. I'll take it until we have found a way to help Skipper. That might be easier to do with clear minds and warmer hands."

"So, where are you going now?" Doug asked.

Jason sighed and shrugged. "I'm going to try to find Stella. She has the answers—I'm sure of that. I don't know why she said what she did, but I intend to find out."

Doug sighed. He was relieved to know that the three men would have a warm place to sleep for as long as they chose to stay. "Wait here, okay. Let me, at least, get you a couple of biscuits to go. We'll be waiting for you later today. I hope you can find her."

Jason watched Doug rush back into the kitchen. "*Oh, I will find her…I will,*" he thought.

On the other side of town, inside their 5,000 square foot mini-mansion, Rae Blankenship was reprimanding their cook about her tasteless food. She pushed her plate away in disgust. "This tastes like cardboard. Where in the world did you learn to cook, Prissy? I swear, the only thing worse than your cooking is your miserable attempt at housekeeping." She pushed the plate of scrambled eggs and bacon away from her.

Priscilla Carson had been Ernest Blankenship's housekeeper for eighteen years. Elizabeth Blankenship had befriended her one cold day in 1998 by offering her a ride home. Elizabeth had seen the old, black woman struggling with two bags of groceries, outside a neighborhood grocery store. This was a couple of years before Ernest Blankenship acquired his first car dealership, and before they could really afford hired help. However, Elizabeth took money from her own meager paycheck to pay Prissy a small salary and a room of her own in their small house. Prissy had been almost sixty then, and she counted her blessings and thanked God that Elizabeth Blankenship had found her when she did. She knew she was too old to still be working, but she had no family and no place to go. When Elizabeth passed away, Ernest assured her that she would have a home with them for as long as she wanted to stay.

Prissy shuffled to the breakfast table and removed the plate of uneaten food. "Mr. Ernest can't be having no salt in his eggs. His blood pressure is way too high, as it is." She scraped the food off the plate, and into the garbage disposal. "I would be glad to make you something else, Mrs. Blankenship."

Rae smoothed her hair and stood up. "Don't bother. I have errands to run. I'm sure I can find something more edible in town. By the way, please make sure I have fresh sheets on my bed today."

"But I just changed them yesterday, ma'am..."

Rae placed her hands on her hips and looked at the old woman with disgust. "And, you will change them *again* today, Prissy. Are we clear on that?"

Prissy began to rinse the dishes before placing them in the dishwasher. "Yes, ma'am. I will change your sheets again today."

Ernest Blankenship entered the kitchen from the back staircase and inhaled the aroma of the cooked bacon. "My, something sure smells good, Prissy!" He nodded at Rae. "Good morning, dear."

Rae looked at him for a long minute. She didn't want to discuss their private business in front of Prissy, but she was more than eager to find out why he had slept in one of the guest rooms, for the third consecutive night. "Good morning, Ernest. I trust you slept well?"

Ernest looked at her, smiled, and lifted his brows. "Why, yes, I did — I slept like a baby. Thank you for asking." He sat down at the large table in the kitchen; he much preferred to eat in the kitchen than in the huge formal dining room. He and Elizabeth had always shared breakfast together in the kitchen with Prissy. He opened up the newspaper and accepted the mug of hot coffee Prissy offered. Ernest glanced toward his wife. "You're all dressed up, dear. Going somewhere, are we?"

Rae looked stunning in her black leggings and long, gold silk shirt. A black belt accentuated her still, tiny waist. Her long auburn hair was up in a tidy bun and her green eyes sparkled. If only her balding, fat husband knew what errand she really had to run — but, no, she had made every effort to keep her many affairs discreet and brief. "I have several errands to run, so I will be out most of the day. Will I see you for dinner tonight?"

Ernest looked up at her and secretly chided himself again for having married so quickly after Elizabeth passed away. If he had it all to do over again, he would have handled things so differently; but, he had made a commitment to this woman, and he would keep it. He knew he would have to get over the feelings of disappointment he was currently experiencing and do whatever he could to make the most of this marriage. He did not believe in divorce. He stood up and walked over to his wife. He took her in his arms and kissed the top of her head. "Yes, of course, you will." He looked over at Prissy and smiled. "Maybe Prissy can make us an extra-special dinner tonight."

Prissy grinned and nodded.

Rae stiffened against her husband's soft and flabby stomach. "Why don't I have something special catered in for us tonight? There's a fabulous new five-star restaurant downtown that I've been dying to try."

"Would you rather I take you out to dinner?" Ernest offered.

Rae shook her head and looked up at him, a coy smile on her lips. "Oh, no...I'll have it catered. Maybe we could even have the meal...in our room tonight, in front of the fire place?"

Skipper lay stretched out on the single cot in his cell. His left knee was bent and the palms of his hands cupped the back of his neck. His eyes were closed when he heard heavy footsteps approaching. He sighed when the steps stopped at his cell. He had a fairly good idea who it was before he cocked open one eye. He rolled his head to the left and said, "I'd invite you in, but the place is a mess." He rolled his head back to the center and stared at the ceiling. When it was obvious that his visitor wasn't going to leave, he sat up on the cot and pushed himself to a standing position.

"Good morning, Skipper," Officer O'Brady smiled and removed his hat. "I just wanted to stop by and see how you were doing, and to let you know that we ran your fingerprints early this morning."

"Let me guess," Skipper stretched and walked over to his cell door. "You found out everything you ever wanted to know about me, but were afraid to ask."

Thomas O'Brady grabbed a hold of the bars and stared directly into Skipper's face. "I did, yes. For instance, I know that your real name is Gordon Whiting and that you come from a small town in upstate New York."

"I was born there, yes," Skipper grinned. "But, I don't consider it home by any means. I left there when I was seventeen and have only been back twice since then."

"We talked to your brother, too."

Skipper stiffened. "There was no need to drag him into any of this. Besides, the last I heard, he's not well, so let's just leave him out of this, alright?"

"That's your call, Skipper. He did ask me to tell you that he has been worried about you, and that he was glad to hear that you're still alive."

Skipper was quiet for a moment. "I haven't checked in with him in almost a year now. Did he sound okay to you?"

Thomas nodded. "He did, yes. His voice was strong, and he sounded very relieved to know that you were okay."

"Did you tell him that you arrested me?"

"I did. He seemed very surprised."

"Yeah, well...like I said, leave him out of this."

Officer O'Brady had his own quiet moment before clearing his throat. "For the record, Skipper. I don't believe you are guilty of what Mrs. Sieber has accused you of, but, unless you talk to me, or to someone else, there's no way to clear you of this crime."

"It's her word against mine, right?" Skipper grinned. "Two homeless people — who are you going to believe?"

Thomas shook his head. "It's not that easy. She puts you at the scene, Skipper. She identified you as the person who forcefully pushed Norman Weissman against a concrete wall, for stealing your food."

"She's lying," Skipper snapped. "Don't tell me you believe anything she said. I don't know why she's lying, but she is; for some reason, she's decided to mark me."

"Who do you think *is* responsible for Mr. Weissman's death? Do you think it was Stella?"

Skipper's laugh was more of a crackle. "Really? Is that the best you can come up with—Stella?"

The officer shook his head. "No, of course not. The old woman barely has the physical strength to push herself up, much less, push a man the size of Norman against a concrete wall hard enough to crack his skull."

"You have no physical evidence connecting me to Norman's death," Skipper stated matter-of-factly. "You can keep me locked up in here as long as you want, but no jury is going to convict me without more evidence to go on than some old bag lady's warped testimony. I'll take my chances in court."

"Do you have an attorney?"

"Nope. I'll let the wonderful city of Rome and its judicial system appoint one for me."

"Oh, before I forget about it, one of the officers will be bringing your notebook to you later today, the one with your poems in it."

"That's great, thanks."

Thomas started to leave, but stopped and looked back at Skipper. "We've talked to everyone who stayed at the camp site with you—except for one person—Peggy Jensen. Her doctor said her short-term memory is gone—could be temporary, or could be permanent, so there's no need to interview her until that situation improves. Is there anyone who can vouch for you, Skipper...anyone who can verify that you weren't at the camp ground when this all went down?"

Skipper turned and walked back to his cot and sat down. "Seems to me that there are three people who know, for sure, the truth of what happened that night—me, Stella, and Norman. Norman's dead, and I'm locked up in here, so if I were a betting man, I would say that your best bet would be to talk to Stella again—find out why she's lying—or who she's lying for might be a better way to approach things."

"Oh, I intend to do that," Officer O'Brady said. "I actually went back to the camp site early this morning, before my shift started, but nobody was there. It looks like everyone has cleared out for good."

Skipper lay back down on his cot and stretched out again. "Well, I can't say that I blame them. I was a hop, skip, and jump away from moving on myself." He closed his eyes and sighed deeply. He was more worried about his predicament than he dared to let on. *"I sure didn't think a jail cell would be my final stopping point...my final chapter."*

# CHAPTER 13

## The Week After

During the next week, Kirk Blankenship had tracked down Stella and given her the five hundred dollars he had promised her. She, in turn, promised him that she would leave town that very night. She lied; instead, the stubborn streak in her won out. She was determined that no punk kid was going to run her out of town. She took his money, paid in advance for a month at a skank motel on the outskirts of town, and proceeded to continue living her life the way *she* chose to—not the way some rich, punky teenager told her to live it. She felt no remorse for the lies she told the police, and later provided them with a video-taped recording of what she had seen. She had managed to stay under their radar since the night she led the police to the camp site.

Joe Sanders had used the café's phone to call his oldest daughter, who was almost nine months pregnant with his first grandchild. He had not been sure what kind of reception he would receive, especially since he had not made any contact with his family since he had left home four years ago. His daughter, Mandy, cried when she heard her father's voice, and Joe cried along with her. She begged him to come home so that her child would grow up knowing his grandfather. Joe had promised her that he would find a way to be there for the baby's birth.

Cheryl had stopped at the Heavenly Grille every morning for breakfast, after dropping Jimmy off at school. She was there again on Thursday, February 4, talking to Doug and Bertie and sipping on a cup of hot coffee when the object of her determination finally walked through the door at the right time.

Doug smiled and nodded when Joe, Bernard, and Jason walked through the front door and began to make their way to the counter for breakfast. He waited until Cheryl had sat her cup on the counter before he took her hands into his own. He stared into her eyes and grinned. "Don't look now, but Jason is coming your way."

"Oh, no..." Cheryl gasped, jerking her hands away and smoothing her long hair behind her ears. She looked nervously at Doug and looked as though she was about to hyperventilate. "How do I look? Do I look okay? What do I say to him? Do I..."

"Too late for questions," Doug whispered and looked beyond her. "Good morning, fellas! I hope all of you brought your appetites with you this morning. Max is whipping up the best country omelets you'll find this side of Dixie. There's plenty of room at the counter; have a seat." He motioned Joe and Bernard to the two farther seats down from Cheryl. "Here you go, Jason. There's one seat left. I'm sure this beautiful young lady won't mind if you sit next to her. Will you...Cheryl?"

Cheryl's eyes opened wide with fear but she continued to stare straight ahead, looking at Doug. She shook her head in response to his question.

"Thanks," Jason said. "Omelets sound good, but I could sure use a cup of strong coffee, Doug."

"Us, too!" Joe laughed. "I like omelets, but I was really hoping for some of Max's buttermilk pancakes."

"He didn't forget you," Doug laughed back. "He has a special stack of them with your name on them, Joe." He looked at Cheryl. "I think the pancakes are your son's favorite breakfast food, too, isn't that right, Cheryl?"

Cheryl still couldn't find her voice, so she simply nodded in affirmation and gulped down her coffee. She loosened the scarf at her neck and began to take off the denim jacket she wore; it had suddenly warmed up considerably in the café.

Jason finally glanced over to look at the person he had sat down next to. He had not noticed the long, auburn hair until the woman began to remove her jacket. His heart gave a quick flutter and he held his breath for a brief moment. When it became obvious that her arm was stuck in the sleeve of the jacket, he stood up and moved to stand behind her. "Here, let me help you with that." He still had not seen the woman's face, but his heart suddenly began to beat a little faster.

Cheryl was staring a hole through Doug, who had moved down the line and deliberately focused his attention on Joe and Bernard.

"That should do it," Jason spoke hoarsely. He couldn't explain why his palms were sweating or why his heart seemed to beat as loudly as an entire drum line that consisted of snare drums, tenor drums, bass drums, and cymbals. His hand grazed the woman's tiny hand as he pulled the jacket sleeve off her arm. That moment—and that touch—was absolutely electrifying. He pulled back at the same time she did.

Cheryl finally turned her stool to face him. She gulped loudly—at least it seemed loud in her own head—and, smiled timidly. "Thank you."

Doug moved back toward the couple and said. "Have the two of you met yet?" He held back a grin when both of them shook their heads, unable to stop staring at the other. "Cheryl Crennan, meet Jason Benton."

Cheryl's focus never wandered from the light blue eyes that she thought she would never see again in this life time.

She held out her hand awkwardly, hoping that Jason would take it. "It's very nice to meet you, Jason." She sighed with relief when he took her offered hand and held it longer than any introductory-meeting required.

Jason shook his head and smiled, and did not immediately release her hand. He spoke low enough so that the other men couldn't hear him. "It's very nice to meet you, Cheryl Crennan…again."

The café had thinned out considerably by eleven-thirty. Joe and Bernard had finished their meals an hour before and had gone into the kitchen and back yard, respectively, to help Max with some small chores. It was the only way they had agreed to live in the apartment—in exchange for helping around the café.

Cheryl and Jason were still sitting next to each other at the counter. They had been talking and catching up on each other's lives for the past two hours, and neither of them wanted to be the first to end their time together.

Jason was the first to make a move to end things. "Cheryl, I have some things I have to do today. I wish I could stay and talk to you some more. I know there's a lot more to catch up on, and I'd like to hear about everything, but…"

Cheryl placed a hand on his arm. "You're right, Jason. There is an awful lot we need to catch up on, but I'd rather not do it here, and, you said you have things to do, so…"

"I want to see you again, Cheryl."

"I want that, too," Cheryl smiled. "Listen, if you're not busy tonight, would you like to come over to our house around sevenish, maybe? I could order a pizza. There's, uh, someone I'd like you to meet."

Jason grinned back at her. "Yeah, I heard Doug mention that you had a son. I think I could make that work. I should be finished with what I need to do by six o'clock. Where do you live?"

Cheryl blushed. "Jason, I know your situation. I know you don't have a car. Why don't I pick you up here around six? Jimmy has basketball practice after school and I usually pick him up around six-thirty. Would that be okay with you?"

"I really don't mind walking," Jason stared back at her. "But, sure, that would be great. I'll be waiting in the parking lot for you."

"It's a date!" Cheryl beamed. She waved good-bye and hurried out the front door.

Jason rubbed the back of his neck and felt his skin heat up. "*A date, huh? Yeah...I remember our last date...*"

Jason spent the rest of the day doing what he had done every day for the past week. He walked into town and searched all the places he thought Stella might be hiding out; he didn't think, like so many others, that she had left town. He stopped by the Rome Police Department to speak with the arresting officer, Thomas O'Brady, and for the first time since Skipper's arrest, found him. Officer O'Brady was headed inside the police station when Jason spotted him.

He yelled out to get the officer's attention. "Officer O'Brady? Could you hold up, please?"

Thomas watched a man wearing a worn, brown, leather jacket run across the street toward the police parking lot. Something about him was vaguely familiar. He instinctively placed his right hand atop the gun in his holster. "That's me—something I can do for you?"

Jason slowed down as he approached the officer. It dawned on him that the night of Skipper's arrest was not the first time he had seen this particular officer. O'Brady had been the officer in the park who had approached him when the three teenagers were ready to cause problems for him. "Yes, sir." He held out his hand. "I'm Jason Benton. I was with the group—the homeless group—the night you arrested our friend, Skipper. I was hoping you might be able to tell me what happened to him, where he's being held."

O'Brady accepted the man's firm and steady handshake. He nodded. "I remember you. I'm really sorry about your friend."

Jason hid his surprise that a cop would say something like that. "Have you seen him? Do you know where he's being held? Can he have visitors? We're all pretty worried about him."

"They transferred him, over the weekend, to the county jail over on New Calhoun Highway. He can have visitors, but he would first have to agree to add you to the list. Each inmate is allowed one or two visits a week, for up to an hour each time. Inmates with special privileges are allowed additional visits, but I think you know as well as I do—that probably won't apply to Skipper."

Jason shrugged. "No, something tells me that Skipper isn't the type that would receive any special privileges. So, he would have to add me to his list, huh?"

Thomas nodded. "Yep, and I'll be honest with you. I've talked to him several times, and I don't think he's interested in adding anyone to that list—not even his own brother."

"He has a brother?" Jason asked, incredulously.

"He does, indeed."

"He never talked about any family," Jason shook his head. "To tell you the truth, I figured he had probably outlived anyone in his family. He's never talked about being married or having kids, but then again, he never talked about much of anything."

Officer O'Brady was quiet for a moment. "Something tells me that you and old Skipper have something in common. You're a Veteran, too, aren't you?"

"What's that got to do with anything?" Jason grew defensive.

Thomas pointed at him and grinned. "That right there—that defensive attitude that seems to comes out of nowhere—and, the way you carry yourself. I'm right, aren't I? I know that Skipper was in Nam. What war claimed your soul?"

"I joined the Army in 2007, served two, back-to-back tours in Iraq. I got out about six years ago."

"Have you been homeless ever since?"

Jason began to feel uneasy with the officer's line of questioning. "Hey, I just wanted to find out some information about a friend. I'm guessing that he couldn't post bail?"

Officer O'Brady shook his head. "The judge denied him bail, even though he had the cash to pay for it himself, believe it or not. Our county prosecutor has deemed Skipper to be an imminent flight risk."

"Is there any way to get a message to him? Just to let him know that we want to do anything we can to help? Maybe you could ask him to add me to his visitors' list?"

"I can do that," the officer replied. "I need to finish some paperwork before my shift ends for the day, but I can make a stop at the jail on my way home. They'll let me talk to him."

Jason held out his hand again. "Thank you. Thank you very much." He turned to leave, but the officer's booming voice stopped him.

"How do I get in touch with you, Jason Benton?"

Jason chewed his bottom lip for a moment or two before responding. "There's a café across the street from where Norman Weissman was killed. It's called the Heavenly Grille Café. If I'm not there, you can leave a message for me there. Thank you again, Officer O'Brady."

Thomas nodded, turned, and headed inside the police station.

Jason looked at the time that flashed across the street on a bank's marquee. If he left now, he should be able to make it back to the café just in time for Cheryl to pick him up for their date.

*"It's not really a date,"* he told himself. *"It's just two people getting together to rehash old memories of their awkward teenage years."* He zipped up his jacket and pulled out the old pair

of gloves that Skipper had given him the night of his arrest. *"I wonder what her son is like..."*

Cheryl's cell phone rang just as she closed the kitchen door on her way to pick Jason up from the café. She saw that the call was from Jimmy. "Hey there, kiddo. I'm leaving now."

"I'm glad I caught you before you left, Mom. Listen, practice is going to run over about a half hour to forty-five minutes, so don't worry about picking me up. The coach goes right by our neighborhood on his way home and he said he would drop me off."

"Are you sure?" Cheryl asked. "I mean, I don't mind waiting for you to finish practice."

"No, it's cool, Mom. Don't worry. I should be home no later than eight, okay?"

"Well," Cheryl sighed. "Okay, then, but try not to be too late. I have a surprise for you."

"Aww, Mom. You know how I hate surprises."

Cheryl laughed and said. "Hurry home, kiddo. I love you."

"Love you too, Mom."

Cheryl hopped in her Beetle Bug, turned on the heater, and headed toward the Heavenly Grille. She was both nervous and excited about tonight. She was nervous that Jason Benton would turn and walk out on them once he found out the truth about Jimmy; but, she was, also, very excited knowing that she would be spending the evening with the only man who had ever made her toes curl!

# CHAPTER 14

## Jimmy Meets His Dad

Kirk and his friends had been riding around since school let out a couple of hours earlier. Kirk was restless, and he didn't want his friends knowing how worried he was about the old woman he had paid to tell the cops her story. He didn't trust her to leave town as she had promised she would do. He was relieved when he read in the paper that another homeless man had been arrested for the murder of Norman Weissman, but, he didn't like knowing that his future—or lack of one—might rest in the hands of an old drunk woman with a sour attitude. He was almost 17 years old, and although his friends might think he had everything under control, he actually felt insecure and scared of what might happen to him if the truth ever came out.

"*I should have killed the old woman, too,*" he thought as he drove along back roads, glancing into the woods, and praying all the while that he would not see the old woman lurking behind the bushes. "*The paper said her name was Stella Sieber. Maybe I could hire someone to track her down...to make sure she really left town. What's to stop her from coming back and demanding more money? Yeah, I should have killed her all right.*"

"Yo, Kirk!" yelled Michael Bozeman from the back seat. "Slow down, buddy! You took that last curve on two wheels!"

Kristy unfastened her seat belt and snuggled as close to Kirk as the front seats allowed. "No, no! Do it again, baby! That was so much fun!" She threw back her head and laughed out loud. "Man, this is some really good boom! Where did you find it, David?"

David Mizen smiled back at her from the back seat. "There's a new supplier in town. He deals some good stuff, but you get what you pay for—this stuff cost me almost twice as much as what I used to get off that redneck kid from the south side of town."

Kirk was within a couple of miles of the Heavenly Grille Café when Kristy stuck out her bottom lip and whined. "I'm really hungry, Kirkie. Let's stop some place and get something to eat. Please!"

"Hey, this place looks familiar," Michael's speech was a little slurred. "Isn't this the place where you…"

Kirk stared in the rear-view mirror into Michael's frozen face. "Shut up, Mike. Not another word from you."

"What's he talking about, baby?" Kristy grinned, looking back and forth among the three young men.

"Nothing," Kirk replied, tight-lipped. "There's a café up ahead. We'll stop and grab some burgers and fries." He looked into the mirror and stared hard into Michael's chagrined expression.

"S-O-R-R-Y…" Michael mouthed back at him and gave him a thumbs-up gesture. "Yeah, I could use some food, too. I'm starving!" He shrugged and punched David playfully on the shoulder, while holding his finger up to his lips and shaking his head in a giddy fashion.

Kirk swerved sharply to the left and barreled into the parking lot of the Heavenly Grille, just as Cheryl and Jason were about to pull out onto the highway.

Cheryl's hand flew to her heart and she gasped. "Oh, my goodness! We almost didn't even make it out of the parking lot." She looked over at Jason, who was holding onto the door handle to keep from rolling onto her lap. "I'm so sorry. That car came out of nowhere."

Jason looked out the back window and watched the teenagers jump from the black Toyota Land Cruiser. He recognized the four teenagers as being the same ones who approached him in the park more than a week ago. "Crazy teenagers," he said. "They don't care about anyone but themselves."

"That's true of most of them," Cheryl agreed, "But, they're not all like that."

Jason grinned. "Oh, that's right. You have a teenage-son, don't you? Well, of course, that doesn't apply to any kid of yours."

Cheryl smiled back at him. "I'm not saying that just because he's my son. Really, I'm not. Jimmy is a good kid." She glanced into her rear-view mirror. "I think I recognize those kids that almost crashed into us. I can't be sure, but I think they might be the ones that Jimmy hung out with for a while." She shook her head. "Maybe not—I'm just glad it didn't take him long to figure out that they were bad news."

"That's a good thing," Jason nodded. "I'm looking forward to meeting him. We're picking him up from basketball practice, right?"

"Oh, I forgot to tell you. No, he called just as I was leaving home tonight to say that practice was running late. His coach is bringing him home later."

"Does that mean I won't get to meet him?"

Cheryl shook her head. "No, of course not. You'll get to meet him. In fact..." she took a deep breath and decided she may as well spit it out now. "It's very, very important that you meet him."

"Why do you say that?" Jason quickly became suspicious of her evasive explanation.

Cheryl took another deep breath and kept her eyes on the road. "Jason, I don't know if you remember that one night we spent together or not..."

"Of course, I remember it," he injected. "I don't think anyone ever forgets their first time."

Cheryl gasped. "What? You mean it was *your* first time, too?"

Jason rubbed the back of his neck. "You mean, you couldn't tell?"

"Honestly, Jason, I really don't remember much about that night. I mean, I was really wasted. It was the first time I'd ever been drunk, and the first time I'd ever...well, you know...but, no, I had no idea it was your first time, too."

"We were both pretty wasted that night," Jason agreed. "But, I still remember what happened between us. Your eyes—those haunting, green eyes—I think I dreamed about them more than once while I was in Iraq."

"Wow, I never would have thought that our one time would be that important to you. I mean, we didn't even know each other's name, for goodness sake."

"There have been a lot of women since that first time, Cheryl, but—no—I never forgot you. My only regret is that I didn't at least find out your name, and tried to stay in touch."

"I really thought I would have seen you again, maybe at school, or the Sonic. I did look for you. I found those guys you were with, but I really didn't want anything to do with any of them, so I didn't ask them about you; but, I never forgot you either." Cheryl kept her eyes on the road. She decided it might be best to tell Jason the truth after they got to her place—rather than when they were in a moving vehicle. "Let's talk about this more when we get to my place, okay?"

Jason nodded. "Okay." An odd feeling was beginning to nag at him; he was suddenly worried that it might have been a mistake to accept Cheryl's invitation.

Thomas O'Brady had been off-shift for two hours when he finally sat down and stared at the Plexiglas before him, waiting for the prison staff to bring in Gordon Whiting. He watched as Skipper nodded at him and sat down on the other side of the Plexiglas that separated them. Thomas picked up the phone and waited for Skipper to do the same. He thought, for a moment, that Skipper's slight hesitation meant that he might not pick up the phone on his side, but, he did.

"Officer O'Brady," Skipper grinned. "What brings you by this fine establishment? I've already told the detectives all I know about Norman Weissman."

"I'm not here about Norman. How are you doing, Skipper?"

"I'm right as rain, Officer. They feed us three meals a day, totaling 2,500 calories—which is a lot more than I am used to eating. I get to exercise an hour a day, and I have access to some of the most outdated books you could ever hope to find; and, best of all, I am able to shower every day. Now that I think about it, I'm surprised you don't find more homeless people committing crimes just so they can have access to all these amenities."

O'Brady grinned back at the old man. "If the homeless knew all that, then I am sure we would see an increase in our inmate population. Have you heard anything from your appointed counsel yet?"

"No, from what I understand, there's a backlog of prisoners requiring counsel, so it could be another couple of weeks before anyone gets to my case."

Thomas nodded and pursed his lips together. "I want you to know that we're still investigating the case."

"You mean you're not one hundred percent sure that an old drunkard bag lady was telling you the truth? Why, Officer O'Brady, you surprise me." One side of Skipper's mouth turned up in a half-grin. "My thought is that whoever is responsible for Norman's death had a hand in the story that Stella dreamed up. She won't shake down easy, either. She's one tough, old hag."

"She might be, but we'll find her and go over her story again. She seems to be hiding out somewhere, though. Your other friends haven't seen her either."

"They're not my friends," Skipper quickly inserted. "We shared a camp fire, that's all."

"So, I suppose that means you're not interested in any visits from them?"

Skipper's eyebrows raised in surprise. "Why would any of them want to visit me?" He seemed genuinely surprised.

"I ran into one of them—your fellow Veteran—today. He said his name was Jason Benton."

"He told you he was a Veteran?"

O'Brady shook his head. "No, but I could tell. Anyway, he wanted me to check with you about adding his name to your visitors' list. He wanted you to know that they were all thinking about you. He seems like a pretty decent fellow."

"Is that so?" Skipper sounded unconvinced. "Well, like I said—they're not my friends." He started to hang up the phone, but stopped when the officer held up a hand and shook his head. He put the phone back to his ear. "Something else you wanted to talk about, Officer O'Brady?"

"Sit back down for a minute, Skipper…please. Your brother contacted the police station again to check on your situation."

"My brother is in no condition to be travelling here to visit me in jail, Officer. If you talk to him again, tell him not to worry. He's almost five years older than me, and he doesn't need to be travelling in this weather. Tell him I'll write him soon."

"He wants to hire a criminal lawyer for you, Skipper."

Skipper shook his head. "Your department saw what my financial situation was when you arrested me and checked into my background. I'm sure you know, as well as they do, that I could very well afford my own lawyer if I wanted to throw my money away on one. No, that money will not be used to get me out of this. Any decent, court-appointed attorney should be able to do that."

"You're willing to chance that, are you?" Thomas grinned.

Skipper returned the grin. "I'm seventy-six years old. It doesn't really matter that much to me what the outcome of this might be."

"You sound like you've given up, and, that doesn't jive with my original impression of you."

"I've never given up on anything," Skipper stared back with a hard gleam in his eye. "It's just that, sometimes, you have to wonder if the last chapter of your life might end before the final page is ever turned."

"I'm not sure I know what that means," Thomas laughed.

Skipper shrugged and started to hang up his phone again, but he stopped and stared at the officer one last time. "Tell Jason I'll add him to the list. Thanks for stopping by." He hung up the phone, turned, and left the room.


It was dark by the time Cheryl and Jason arrived at her house at six-thirty. Once inside, Cheryl put on a pot of coffee and ordered two large, meat-lovers pizzas to be delivered. She had brought a large picture album into the kitchen, and she and Jason were flipping through it. Most of the pictures were of Jimmy, from birth until the present time.

"He's a good-looking kid," Jason commented. "You said that the two of you just moved here a few months ago, right?"

Cheryl closed the picture album and nodded. "Yeah, we lived in Hogansville until then. My grandmother lived there, and Jimmy and I stayed with her from the time he was born until she died in 2014. My Dad sold the house then, and Jimmy and I moved into a small apartment."

"Hogansville, huh?" Jason scratched his head. "You must have moved there, from Columbus, right after you and I hooked up then, right? Sounds like we both left Columbus about the same time."

"You left, too?" Cheryl asked. "I mean, I didn't know who to ask or where to look for you..."

"Why would you want to?"

Cheryl blew out a deep breath. "Jason, there's something you should know..."

The kitchen door flew open and Jimmy bounded in. His cheeks were red from the cold wind, but his green eyes twinkled when he saw his mom sitting at the kitchen table with a man. "Hey, Mom! Coach decided not to keep us late after all. They're expecting an ice storm tonight, so he let us go on time." He shuffled out of his jacket and ran his fingers through his hair. He moved to the kitchen table and offered his hand to the man who had stood up and was staring at him.

Jimmy grinned and looked back and forth between his mom and the man. It didn't take long for him to connect the dots. He took the man's hand in his own and pulled him into a tight embrace. "Hey! I've waited a long time to meet you...DAD!"

Jason's jaw dropped opened and he turned his head sharply to stare at Cheryl.

The doorbell rang.

Cheryl looked helplessly at Jason and cringed. "Pizza's here..."

# CHAPTER 15

## Doug Visits PJ

Floyd Medical Center provided more indigent and charity care than any other medical facility in Northwest Georgia. It provided indigent and charity care services to 49,013 patients in 2015, and the new year already seemed on track to service that same amount, if not more.

Patients recovering from stroke, traumatic injury, or surgery, and requiring intensive rehabilitation, were eligible to receive care through the medical facility's Inpatient Rehabilitation program. The Rehab Center was located on the sixth floor, and, this is where Doug found PJ at six-thirty.

"Hello, PJ! You weren't in your room and one of the nurses said I might find you up here." He grinned widely. "Just look at you—you look wonderful—you've come a long way in just a few days."

A nurse helped PJ back into her wheel chair and nodded at Doug. "She seems determined to get back on her feet. She's a real fighter, this one is." She wheeled PJ closer to where the handsome man with the shocking green eyes smiled back at her. "I was just getting ready to take her back to her room."

"May I?" Doug asked. "I mean, if it's allowed."

"Of course it is. I recognize you as one of Miss Jensen's regular visitors. It's fine, as long as it's okay with her, of course."

PJ looked up at the nurse who had been so kind to her over the past couple of weeks. "Yes, it's okay with me. Hello, Doug. Thank you for visiting me — again."

"I'll see you tomorrow afternoon, Peggy," the nurse smiled when Doug's hand brushed hers as they exchanged their positions behind the wheel chair. A sense of peace and tranquility filled her entire being, and she suddenly felt like she could easily work another double shift if she had to.

"I'll take good care of her," Doug nodded. "Thank you for all you've done to get her to this point."

Doug wheeled PJ to the elevator and waited for it to open. "Are you hungry, PJ? We could make a quick detour to the snack shop if you'd like."

"No thank you, Doug. I still have some of the cake left that you brought yesterday. I thought I would finish it up tonight. There's a vending machine on my floor if you'd like to get us a cup of coffee, though."

"I can do that," Doug smiled down at her. "It looks like you're making really good progress with the rehab they're providing you."

PJ nodded. "I still can't believe they are going out of their way to help me like this. I mean, they have to know that there's no way I can pay for any of this."

"Don't worry about any of that, PJ," Doug explained how the hospital's indigent and charity care functions operated.

"I don't feel right, though," PJ shook her head. "I mean, taking charity like that. I may be homeless, but I still have my pride. I'll just have to find a way to pay them back, somehow."

"All you have to focus on is getting back to your old self, PJ. That's all. Everything else will work itself out. I have to ask, though...have you had any breakthrough in your memory?"

"You mean, do I remember what happened to me?"

Doug nodded. "Yes...or, anything prior to that?"

PJ sighed. "The police have been here three times already. They were asking me all kinds of questions about some man named..." she waved her hands in frustration.

"Norman?" Doug assisted. "Norman Weissman."

"Yes, that's the one," PJ nodded her head up and down. "I told them I didn't know anyone by that name. I didn't know you either when you first came to visit me."

"What's the very last thing that you do remember, PJ— before waking up here in the hospital?"

PJ took another deep breath and waited for the door of the empty elevator to close before she looked up at the kind, white man who had been a regular visitor to her at the hospital. "Well, let's see...I know it's February 2016 now, but the last thing I remember is leaving my home and family in Selma, Alabama...five years ago. I had an awful fight with my mother and my sisters about—well—about the male company I preferred to keep. You see, Doug, I've always felt more comfortable dating white men, and that is just something that nobody in my family could accept. That's why I never married, never had any children of my own. When they gave me an ultimatum concerning my last fella, I chose him over them, and I left Selma. Three months after I left, the man left me for a younger, white woman. I was too embarrassed to go back home and have all my family say *I told you so!* So, I took to the streets and lived my life the way *I* wanted to live it. Everything after that is just a blur, but I'm guessing that I must still be living my life as a homeless person."

Doug grinned. He had never heard so many words come out of PJ's mouth at one time. "Five years is a long time to live on the streets, PJ."

"How exactly did you come to know me, Doug?"

Doug wasn't sure how much information to reveal to PJ. The doctors had been adamant that her memory be allowed to return on its own, if it ever did. "I work in a café located across the street from an area that some homeless people gather, PJ."

"So, I was part of that homeless group then?"

Doug nodded. "Yes, you were."

"This fella that the police keep asking me about— Norman—he lives there, too?"

Doug was beginning to feel out of his element. He wasn't quite sure where to draw the line on how much information to share, but he decided to take it one step further. "He did, yes."

"Did?" PJ queried. "Are you saying he doesn't live there anymore? Did he do something wrong? Is that why the police were asking about him?"

The elevator doors opened and Doug wheeled PJ to her room. He pulled back the covers on her bed and lifted her onto it. He smiled down at her when she closed her eyes and exhaled deeply. "You're tired, PJ, so I'm going to leave now and let you get some rest. You worked hard today, so, get some sleep. I'll stop by again tomorrow and we can talk some more, okay?"

"Well, I am a little tired," PJ smiled. She touched his hand, and like the nurse on the sixth floor, she felt a sudden rush of adrenaline course through her battered body. "Thank you again for coming to visit with me, Doug. You're the only person who has come."

"Something tells me you will have other visitors very, very soon, PJ," Doug held her frail hand between his two larger ones. "I'll say a special prayer for you tonight."


The loud group of teenagers that had burst through the café's front door a half-hour ago was quickly getting on Bertie's last angelic nerve. She carried a stack of dirty dishes into the kitchen and dropped them noisily into the sink.

Max glanced at her over his shoulder. He had been listening in on the conversations between Bertie and Kirk's little group, and he knew that Bertie's tongue had to be sore from her having bitten it so many times in an effort to keep from saying something ungodly to the rowdy group of teenagers. "Just remember, Bertie," he grinned. "Patience is a virtue."

"Oh, Hells-Bells!" she grumbled as she walked up behind Max and punched him hard against his right shoulder. There was no doubt that it hurt her more than it did him. "They're nothing but a bunch of spoiled, rich kids. I'd like to find a long switch, turn all four of them over my knee, and give them a good switching."

"That's not allowed anymore," Max laughed at her apparent angst. "Parents can't even do it, without risk of being reported to that child welfare agency."

"That's a damn shame, too!" Bertie hissed.

Max shook his finger at her. "Watch the language, Bertie. You've been doing so good lately. I would hate for Martin to chastise you when we visit Home on Sunday."

"Yeah, yeah...I'm working on that...besides, Martin doesn't scare me none," Bertie sighed. "Seriously, though, Max—those kids out there all deserve to be locked in their rooms and the keys thrown away. I've never seen a ruder bunch of teenagers. Did you hear them? *Demanding* that cheeseburgers and fries be added to the menu!"

"I heard them; but, they didn't seem to turn their noses up at the food you delivered to their table. It would appear that buttermilk fried chicken and loaded mashed potatoes are a satisfactory substitute for burger and fries."

"Yeah," Bertie sighed again. "That did shut them up for a while. Did you hear them talking about Jimmy Crennan?"

Max nodded. "I didn't like the sound of that conversation. I was hoping that Jimmy wasn't part of their group any longer."

"I don't think he is, but, I don't think their leader —that snotty one with the attitude—feels the same way, though. I think he's bad news, and I think he wants to drag Jimmy down with him."

"Jimmy's a smart kid, Bertie. We have to trust and believe that he will make smart decisions, especially about any involvement with that group out there. Remember, we cannot interfere with anything that's about to unfold."

"Yeah, yeah, I know," Bertie punched him again for good measure. "But, that doesn't mean that I don't want to drag *Kirkie* by the ear, drop his drawers, and blister his bottom with a switch until he can't sit on it for a week!"

Max laughed out loud. "Is that really how you disciplined your own children, Bertie?"

Bertie placed her hands on her well-padded hips and stared up at the former gladiator. "It most certainly is! And, it's the way my mama and daddy disciplined me and my brothers and sisters, too. We all turned out pretty darn good, if you ask me!"

"I don't know," Max shook his head. "I bet that switch hurt like all get out."

"Yep, it sure did," Bertie grinned. "Hey, what about you? It's so hard to imagine you as a child, but, what was life like for you as a kid?"

Max closed his eyes and allowed a flood of memories to rush in. "Life was very different for children of commoners, Bertie. Our parents trained us on everything we needed to know in order to survive in our world. You have to understand…they were more concerned with our moral development than they were with our intellectual development."

"So, they didn't care if you got an education then, huh?" Bertie nodded. "I didn't get that either—I never even finished ninth grade."

"Our parents felt that the most important virtues for any child were reverence for the gods, respect for the law, unquestioning and instant obedience to authority, truthfulness, and self-reliance."

"Sounds like a pretty boring childhood, Maximus."

Max laughed out loud. "Not really. It was all we knew — all we expected. We were taught at an early age to speak

Latin and to learn your basic reading, writing, and arithmetic. At age seven, boys went on to a regular teacher, but the girls remained with their mothers, as their constant companion."

"Why?"

"Well," Max explained, "The girl's formal education was cut short because she usually married early and it was important for her to learn everything her mother could teach her about home management—to spin, weave and sew."

"Not to mention—to cook, clean, and serve the men, right, Max?" Bertie snorted.

"It was a woman's place back then, Bertie. The boys whose fathers were farmers, like my own father was, were taught to plow, plant, and reap. When we reached the age of majority, we discarded our crimson-bordered toga of a child and replaced it with the pure white toga of a man."

"The girls, too?" Bertie asked.

Max shook his head. "No, there was no special ceremony to mark a girl's passing into womanhood."

"So, how old was...what did you call it...the age of majority?"

"It varied," Max continued to explain as he turned to cut four large pieces of the Mississippi Mud Pie he had made for the day's dessert. "It depended on his physical and intellectual development, somewhat on his father's decision, and even more, perhaps, on the time in which he lived. As a general rule, a man's toga was assumed somewhere between ages 14 to 17. I was 16 when I switched togas. Shortly after that, my parents were killed by the king's soldiers and my brothers and sisters and I were sold as slaves. I never saw any of them again—not on earth, that is."

Bertie grew quiet, which was totally uncharacteristic of her. "Wow, I'm really sorry, Max. I never knew that about you. I mean, I knew you were a slave and a gladiator, but, I didn't know you became one at such a young age."

✧

Max placed the four pieces of pie on a tray and pushed it toward Bertie. "It was a life time ago, my friend. That's enough of history lessons for the day. Why don't you deliver this to your table of terror...maybe chocolate will tame the savage beasts."

"Hmmph!" Bertie grunted. "I like my idea of using a switch on all of them better!"

# CHAPTER 16

## - Heaven -
## Norman Talks to Martin

*M*artin grinned as he checked off a block on Bertie's weekly critique sheet. "So much better this week, Bertie...so much better — only one curse word." He looked up from the sheet and shook his head. "However, the week is not yet over."

He sensed a slight movement behind him and spun around quickly to see Norman Weissman standing alongside Andrew Brown. He smiled at them and waved them forward. "Hello, gentleman. Come, come! What can I do for you both on this glorious day?"

Andrew placed a hand on Norman's shoulder. "Hello, Mr. Martin. I ran into Norman on my way to the Rainbow Bridge, and he had some questions that I think you might be better suited to answer for him."

Norman waved a hand in greeting. "Hello, there. I'm still not sure of the protocol expected here in Heaven. I mean, I didn't know if I needed to make an appointment to talk to someone or not."

Martin motioned them both forward and embraced them in a tight hug. "Oh, Norman...you must know that there is no *protocol in Heaven. You answer to one person, and one person only, but we are all here to assist you in answering any questions you might have."*

*"I told him you were the expert on just about everything that goes on here," Andrew laughed. "Well, Mr. Norman, you're in good hands now, so I'd best be on my way. There are hundreds of cats and dogs waiting at the Rainbow Bridge for me."*

*Norman shook his head and smiled. "Everyone on earth talks about that bridge, but, I wasn't really sure if it was real, or whether it was just something that humans wanted or needed to believe was real. My own parents always told us that our pets didn't have souls, so that meant they did not go to Heaven. That was the primary reason I never became a pet owner in my adult life. I hated the thought of loving something so much, watching it die, and then knowing that death was the end of that relationship...that we would never meet again."*

*Martin shook his head and exhaled softly. "There will always be those people who believe that, I'm afraid; but, just imagine their surprise when – or if – they get here, and find all their beloved pets waiting patiently for them. Oh, the look on their faces is absolutely priceless! Biblically, the life of an animal is not valued as highly as that of a human being, who was created in the image of God. However, God created every living thing on earth, so why would he not give every living species a soul that might be reborn after death?"*

*"I haven't been a believer for very long," Norman said, "But, I don't remember reading anything in the Bible that proved that our pets would make it to Heaven after they died."*

*"That is true," Martin agreed. "No, the Bible is, indeed, silent when it comes to educating us on any kind of afterlife for animals. However, we believers know about God's promise to those fortunate enough to inherit His kingdom. When you get a chance, be sure to study 1 Corinthians, Chapter 2, verse 9. It is a key verse for any unbeliever: But as it is written: Eye has not seen, nor ear heard, nor have entered into the heart of man the things which God has prepared for those who love Him." Martin shrugged. "I suppose there's only one way to find out for sure, and, that is to make it to Heaven yourself and find out first-hand!"*

Andrew hugged Norman. "I'd best be on my way now. It was very nice to meet you, Norman. Feel free to stop my family's mansion anytime. We have lots and lots of animals looking to adopt a heavenly family."

Norman laughed. "It was good to meet you, too, Andrew, and I will definitely be stopping by soon. It's nice to know that the animals are the ones adopting their families now, instead of the other way around."

"Yes," Martin smiled. "Our Father does have a good sense of humor, doesn't He?" He hugged Andrew again. "Come visit again soon, Andrew; and, please tell your parents hello for me."

"I'll do that Mr. Martin! I'll be seeing you again real soon."

Martin watched while Andrew quickly faded into the distance. He turned to Norman and locked elbows with him. "Come walk with me for a while, Norman. Andrew said you had some questions you needed answered. I will do my best to answer them for you."

"Thank you," Norman smiled up at the tall, skinny black man whom everyone seemed to turn to for answers. "I wasn't sure if we were supposed to question anything once we got here or not."

"Nonsense!" Martin guffawed. "However is anyone to learn what they need to know if they don't first ask a question?"

The two continued walking along a golden-brick path, their elbows still locked together. A slight breeze stirred the thousands of golden daffodils that lined the path on both sides.

A warmth came over Norman and he closed his eyes. "That breeze — I feel it every once in a while — it seems to come out of nowhere. I mean, there's no real weather here, so what is it?"

"You mean you haven't guessed that yet?" Martin's eyebrows raised in surprise.

Norman shook his head. "No. All I know is that every time it happens, my breath ceases for a moment and I feel like I'm the only one in existence…I don't really know quite how to explain it, other than to say that time seems to — stop — until the breeze passes by."

"Yes, I like that!" Martin laughed. "That's a very good way to explain it, Norman. However, my friend, you need to know that every time you feel that breeze? Well…that is your Heavenly Father walking alongside you…"

*Norman gasped. "Oh...oh!"*

*"If you think that took the wind out of your sails, just wait until He speaks to you!"*

*Norman was unable to speak for the next several minutes, so the two continued to walk along the serene path until they came to a golden bench situated between two of the hugest weeping willow trees that Norman had ever seen.*

*Martin guided Norman to the bench. He sat down and patted the spot next to him. "Have a seat, Norman, and let's talk about the questions you have."*

*"Well..." Norman sighed. "My questions really seem pretty insignificant...especially, after what you just told me."*

*"Don't be silly, there is no such thing as an insignificant question. Go ahead, question number one is?"*

*Norman took a deep breath and looked around him, waiting for another unexpected breeze to surround him. When it didn't come, he took another deep breath and looked directly into Martin's warm, brown eyes. Those eyes seemed to be smiling at him in anticipation. "Okay, here goes. The first question is simple, really. Everything I learned from the Bible convinced me that my former sexual orientation was a...sin. So, if that is true, why and how am I here?"*

*"It is not my place, nor anyone else's place to judge you for the life style you chose to live before you became a Christian, Norman. That is between you and God, only. Trust me, you will be having this conversation with Him one day. We have watched from Heaven while man has rewritten the law, but one thing is for certain – man will never, ever be able to rewrite the word of God; and, God's word is undeniable. Homosexuality is, indeed, a sin; however, there is only one sin that is truly unforgivable. You will understand this better when you study Matthew 12:31-32, which explains to us what the one, unforgivable sin is – blasphemy of the Holy Spirit."*

*"So, God forgives me for the way I chose to live my life back then?"*

*"Indeed, He does. It doesn't matter what sin you committed – we are all sinners; however, the grace of God runs so much wider and deeper than any of us will ever know or understand. His grace*

*is our salvation."*

Norman shook his head and closed his eyes. *"I read all this in the Bible, but, I guess I truly did not believe it was really possible. So...there are sinners in Heaven?"*

Martin waved his long index finger. *"There are* repented *sinners in Heaven, my friend...*repented *being the key word. We all sin. It is virtually impossible to live a full life on earth and not sin, but we are all forgiven for those sins, provided we ask for that forgiveness and believe that He will grant it. My goodness, sin seems to be EVERYWHERE, doesn't it?"* Martin waited a few moments for everything he had said to sink in before he continued. *"Alright, so, on to question number two."*

Norman shuffled his bare feet against the softest grass he had ever walked upon. *"What about the person who took my life? Will he end up in Heaven? Will I come face-to-face with him again one day?"*

*"Murder is one of the worst sins, in my humble opinion,"* Martin began. *If you know your Bible, then you know that there is abundant scriptural support for the death penalty. Exodus 21:12-14, for instance: He who strikes a man so that he dies shall surely be put to death. However, if he did not lie in wait, but God delivered him into his hand, then I will appoint for you a place where he may flee. But if a man acts with premeditation against his neighbor, to kill him by treachery, you shall take him from my altar, that he may die."*

*"So...does that mean that the person who killed me won't make it to Heaven?"*

*"I did not say that, Norman. It is true, that in that particular scripture, God commands that anyone who kills another person on purpose should be put to death."*

Norman nodded. *"Okay, so if the person who killed me didn't do it on purpose, there's a good chance that we'll meet again in Heaven one day?"*

*"That depends entirely on that person's relationship with God when he dies. On earth, of course, it is up to society to enforce God's law. God does not put that person to death; he expects the people to do the right thing by carrying out His law. There is no refuge for a murderer; however, our God is a fair God, and be*

*assured, that He differentiates between murder and accidental killing – or, manslaughter – as society refers to it. "*

*Norman grew quiet again. "I don't think that the person who killed me intended for me to die, Martin."*

*"Why do you think that, Norman?"*

*"Because of the look I saw in his eye before I fell to the ground. I knew, then, that it was an accident that could not be undone. I think he was scared when my head hit that wall – and, that really did hurt, by the way."*

*"I'm sure it did, my friend. It hurts even more, doesn't it, when the person who kills you is someone you consider a friend."*

*"What do you mean, Martin? I didn't know the person who killed me."*

*Martin knew the truth, but he also knew that Norman had to come to his own conclusions about what happened. "Really? You didn't? But, I thought that Skipper was a part of your little group that camped in the thicket across from the Heavenly Grille Café."*

*"What has Skipper got to do with any of this?" Norman was stunned and confused. "Are you telling me that everyone believes that Skipper had something to do with my death?"*

*Martin nodded. "The man has been arrested for your murder, yes. Apparently, there was a witness to the crime. She said she saw everything that happened and felt it was her civic duty to report the truth to the police. I believe her name was...Stella Seiber."*

*Norman was shaking his head adamantly from side to side. "Oh, no...that's not what happened at all! Skipper had nothing to do with any of this. He wasn't even in the camp when it happened. His sleeping bag was empty when I woke up to take care of business, if you know what I mean. I saw the bag of food that Doug had left on top of his sleeping bag, and I just knew that there was another piece of that fantastic buttermilk cake inside the bag. I hate to say it, but I took that piece of cake. I took food from another homeless person. I'm so ashamed, but – no – Skipper did not kill me. It was a young kid – a teenager. I had never seen him before, but there were three others with him. They were just messing around, pushing me between them. My dang feet got tangled up on the last push and I fell hard against that concrete wall. Oh, no, Martin – we have to do something to make this right. Skipper did nothing wrong!"*

*"There's nothing we can do about it, Norman, so please calm down and relax. We cannot interfere with anything that may transpire on earth. It may all work out in the end. Who knows, maybe your death will simply be added to all the other unsolved murder cases of Floyd County, Georgia."*

*"I wouldn't think that Rome, Georgia would have that many unsolved cases,"* Norman answered back, trying not to let his frustration get the best of him.

*"Oh, there's a few, alright,"* Martin said. *"Like the case of a 30-year old mother of four who was last seen leaving a tavern around nine o'clock in the evening of May 7, 1982. Her skeletal remains were found within a mile of that tavern about six months later. Ten years later, there was a man reported as missing; his body was discovered a month later – police thought it might be a case of where a prostitute lured him in and her pimp or boyfriend killed him, but they could never prove anything concrete. I remember another one that happened in February of 1980. The nearly obliterated skeletal remains of a 58-year old man that went missing were found inside a burned building. The police thought that whoever killed him piled tires on top of him and burned them. Again, lots of suspects, but the police were unable to gather enough physical evidence to convict anyone. Well-intentioned Christians often tell family members, in these situations, that God works in mysterious ways."*

*"I've heard that expression more times than I can remember,"* Norman nodded.

Martin's hands flew up in exasperation. *"As if God was actually responsible for allowing the murder to occur in the first place! God gave man free will and made him responsible for the execution of judgment, so He certainly is not at fault for man's failure to obey His law. It is man's failure to execute judgment that results in the continuing growth of criminal behavior."*

*"Geez, my death seems sort of ordinary and boring compared to all that,"* Norman mused.

*"The number of solved crimes – the percentage of solved crimes that actually lead to an arrest – in America, has dropped substantially in the past 50 years, from around 90% in 1965 to*

*around 64% in 2012. This means that more than 211,000 homicides committed since 1980 remain unsolved." Martin placed his hands upon his knees and pushed up off the bench. "My, my, this is such depressing conversation, my friend. Please don't dwell too much on what happened, or what may happen. It is out of your control. Everything will work out according to God's plan."*

*"I know you're right, Martin, but I still feel badly for Skipper. He doesn't deserve this."*

*"Nobody deserves to be accused of a crime they did not commit, Norman. We just have to have comfort and faith that whatever happens will be as it is meant to be. Even we angels don't know the outcome of every situation — and, this is one of those situations. It will certainly be interesting to see how it all unfolds."*

*Norman stood up and sighed. "I understand, Martin. It is what it is."*

*Martin nodded. "Yes, it is! I like that — it is what it is!"*

**"For what happens to the sons of men also happens to animals; one thing befalls them: as one dies, so dies the other. Surely, they all have one breath; man has no advantage over animals, for all is vanity. All go to one place; all are from the dust, and all return to dust. Who knows the spirit of the sons of men, which goes upward and the spirit of the animal, which goes down to the earth?" Ecclesiastes 3:19-21 (NKJV)**

# CHAPTER 17

## The Morning After the Revelation

Jason woke up before dawn on Friday, February 5. Sleep had not come easy to him the night before; the revelation that he was a father to a fourteen-year old boy/man had kept sleep at bay for most of the night. He sat up on the pull-out sofa that had been turned into a bed for him the night before. An ice storm had indeed hit their area, and Cheryl had insisted that he stay with them. Jason did not want her driving under icy conditions, so he had reluctantly agreed. He threw the covers off and reached for his jeans and shirt that he had draped over the recliner. He was buttoning his shirt when Jimmy walked into the room.

"Good morning," Jimmy spoke quietly. "Mom's still sleeping, but, I couldn't sleep, so thought I'd get up and put on the coffee. I figured you both would need a cup this morning."

Jason began gathering up the blankets and converting the bed back into a sofa. "Thanks, I could use a cup of coffee. I didn't get much sleep last night either." He finished his small chore and followed Jimmy into the kitchen.

Jimmy turned on the overhead light above the kitchen

sink and began the menial process of making a pot of coffee. He was both nervous and excited and wasn't sure which emotion would prevail. "Do you like it strong or on the weaker side? Mom doesn't like strong coffee, but I can add more to the pot if you do."

Jason smiled at the young man moving nervously around the kitchen. He could only imagine the thoughts and questions that he must be trying hard to suppress. "Make it the way your mom likes it. Anything is fine with me."

"Okay."

Jason waited for Jimmy to complete the short task of coffee making. "Can we sit, Jimmy, and talk some more about—well—about the fact that I just found out that I'm a father. I'm still having trouble processing that thought—no offense to you—and I'm sure you must have questions, too."

Jimmy grinned and his green eyes twinkled. "None taken. Yeah, I guess we did kind of spring that on you last night, huh? I'm sorry about that. I figured mom must've already told you about me."

"No," Jason shook his head. "We hadn't gotten that far into conversation by the time you burst into the kitchen and..."

"Told you that you were my Dad?" Jimmy grinned again. "Yeah, that was a bummer, I'm sure. I mean, mom has told me the story of how you two hooked up and all, and that she never even knew your name. I think she's been in her own state of shock since she recognized you at that diner."

Jason ran his hands threw his short hair and smiled back. "I wouldn't say it was a bummer, but—yes—it most certainly was a shock. I mean, I absolutely had no idea that the one and only time we were together would have resulted in...you!"

Cheryl had awoken and had been standing outside the kitchen door, listening to Jimmy and Jason's conversation. She cleared her throat and walked slowly into the kitchen, tightening the belt on her robe around her. "Good morning, everyone. I thought I would be the first one up and would make us some coffee." She inhaled the rich aroma that filled the kitchen. "But, I see someone beat me to it. That smells so good." She walked over to the kitchen sink and leaned over to kiss Jimmy on the cheek. "Good boy!" She pulled three cups from the cupboard and turned around to see Jason's eyes boring into her own. "How do you take yours, Jason?"

Jason stood up and walked over to where the petite redhead stood staring up at him. He reached over for one of the mugs and grinned down at her. "Black is fine. Why don't you have a seat? I'll get the coffee." He looked over at Jimmy who was grinning sheepishly at Cheryl. "You, too, Jimmy. The three of us have a lot to talk about this morning."


The city of Rome, Georgia—like most southern states experiencing severe, cold weather—had virtually shut down this Friday morning. The weathermen were saying that the severe weather would last throughout the day, but that warmer weather should melt most of the ice by Saturday afternoon. All schools and city offices were closed for the day.

Bertie looked out the café's windows at seven o'clock and stared into the empty parking lot. "I don't think we're going to get much business today, handsome," she remarked as Doug came through the front door.

Joe and Bernard were right behind Doug and were careful to wipe their feet on the doormat shaped like angel wings. "You've got us, Miss Bertie!" Joe laughed.

"Well, get yourselves on in here then and let me get you fellas something to eat," Bertie fussed and shivered at the cold wind that followed them inside the cozily warm café. "I'll probably go stir-crazy today if nobody comes in to eat all that food Max is preparing. You would think he was expecting an army!"

Joe and Bernard found their regular seats at the counter,

and Doug began pouring cups of hot coffee for all of them. Doug looked at Jason's empty seat. "Is Jason still upstairs?"

"No," Joe shook his head as he poured sugar and cream into his mug. "Matter of fact, he didn't come home at all last night."

"Oh, no!" Bertie cried out. "You mean he slept out in this ice storm last night? How could you let him do that?" She turned and punched Doug on the arm.

Bernard took a slow sip of the hot coffee and smiled back at Bertie. "In case you haven't noticed, Miss Bertie, our Jason is a grown man and doesn't need us to keep tabs on him. He did mention to me yesterday that he was having dinner with a friend last night. My guess would be that the weather turned bad before they finished dinner, and—who knows—maybe he spent the night with his friend?"

"I wasn't aware that Jason had any friends in Rome," Doug injected. "I mean, other than you guys."

"Hmmm," Bernard sighed. "I'm not even sure that Joe and I would fall into that category. Jason and Skipper are both confirmed loners. I get the impression that neither of them makes friends easily."

"Well, I'm worried about him," Bertie sighed as she punched Doug again—for good measure—on her way into the kitchen.

Bernard smiled at Doug and shook his head. "She does that quite a lot, doesn't she—the punching of the shoulder, I mean?"

Doug grinned back. "She does, indeed. It's sort of like her calling card, you could say." He sat down on Jason's empty stool. "I hope Jason is okay, though. I mean, he doesn't have a phone or any way to let us know if he needed help."

"I wouldn't worry too much about Jason," Joe laughed out loud. "I saw him get into a Beetle Bug yesterday with that cute little thing who's been eating here lately—pretty little redhead."

"Cheryl Crennan?" Doug asked. "Hmmm—that's interesting."

Bernard's eyebrows lifted as he watched Doug's reaction to the news about Jason's friend. "You don't seem all that surprised, Doug. Something you want to share with the rest of us?"

Doug shook his head. "No, it's not my place to say anything; but, I'm glad you told me that, Joe. I'm not so worried about him now."

Bernard smiled. "Sounds like there is a good story in there somewhere—maybe Jason will tell it to us upon his return to this fine establishment."

Bertie was fussing around in the kitchen, pulling dishes from the cupboards, and grumbling to herself.

"Okay, Bertie," Max sighed. "What's going on with you this morning?"

"Have you not looked outside at that empty parking lot, Maximus? Just look at all this food you've cooked up, and there's obviously not going to be enough customers to eat it all today. I hate to see food wasted, that's all."

"Oh, ye of little faith, my sweet angel," Max laughed out loud. "Surely you don't think a little ice storm is going to keep people away, do you? Just think of all the power outages there must be around the city this morning."

Bertie pursed her lips together and nodded. "You're right! Power outages mean that folks won't have a way to cook, or even to keep their houses warm. Yep, you're right, Max! They'll all be pouring in here any minute now, won't they?"

Max nodded and returned his attention to the huge pot of cheese grits that were bubbling on the stove top. He grinned when the angel chimes at the café's front door began to jingle—more than once. "I would venture to say that they have, indeed, arrived, Bertie! You had best get a move on it, my friend!"

✧

"I can't believe we lost power!" Cheryl said as they pulled into the parking lot of the Heavenly Grille. "I definitely need more than one cup of coffee. Thank goodness the café seems to be up and running."

Jimmy sat in the back seat and unhooked his seat belt. He leaned forward, an arm on each of his parent's headrest. "I know we all still have a lot to talk about, but it's really hard to discuss something as important as all this on an empty stomach."

"You're right about that, Jimmy," Jason grinned back at the handsome young man he had helped produce. "We do still have a lot to sort through."

Cheryl hopped out of the car and laughed. "Well, the two of you can stay here and talk all you want, but I am starving and intend to eat my weight in whatever Max has cooked up this morning. Feel free to join me after you finish your talk!" She slammed her door shut and ran up the steps and wiped her feet on the angel wings mat. She sighed contentedly when the angel chimes sounded. She saw Doug wave at her from behind the counter and quickly made her way to an empty counter seat

"Good morning, Cheryl," Doug reached for an empty mug and poured her a cup of coffee. "Is Jimmy with you? I heard all the schools were closed this morning."

"He should be in any minute now," Cheryl nodded. "Thanks for the coffee, Doug. We lost power after only one pot of coffee, and trust me—one pot is never enough—especially on days like this."

Bernard cleared his throat and extended his hand. "Pardon me miss, but I am Bernard Cartwright and this gentleman beside me is Joe Sanders. We are—comrades, you might say—of Jason Benton."

Cheryl accepted the man's hand and smiled back at him. "You're friends of Jason's? How nice! He should be coming inside any second now, with my son, Jimmy."

"Ohhh…" Joe grinned as he shook hands with the pretty redhead. "I see…"

The angel chimes sounded again and Jason and Jimmy walked through the door. Jason was about three inches taller than Jimmy and outweighed him by thirty pounds, but the familial resemblance was undeniable when they stood side by side, and smiled identical smiles at the woman waiting for them at the counter.

Bertie stopped what she was doing in the kitchen and punched Max hard against his shoulder. "Well, I'll be damned! Would you look at what just walked in!"

Max shook his head and chose to ignore her foul language. Instead, he grinned back at her and whispered, "This day is off to a miraculous start—yes it is."

The phone in the kitchen rang just then and Max wiped his hands on his apron. "Good morning, Heavenly Grille Café, this is Max." He listened to whoever was on the other end of the line and finally said. "Yes, he is; and, yes, I will most certainly pass the message on to him. Thank you for calling, Officer O'Brady."

Bertie waited for Max to hang up the phone and wash his hands before she punched him against the back of his shoulder. "Well? Who was that—Officer O'Brady?"

Max grinned down at his spunky, angelic co-hort and grinned. "He asked us to deliver a message to Jason; evidently, Jason gave him our number to use as a contact number. He said to tell Jason that Skipper added him to his visitors' list."

Bertie performed a little spin around the kitchen and gave Max another punch. "Hot damn! You keep cooking, big fella—I'll go deliver the message to Jason." She spun around again and repeated her previous expression of excitement.

Max shook his head and smiled as she bounced from the kitchen. "I didn't think we would make it through the week with only one curse word...oh well, I suppose we can start fresh again on Sunday."

# CHAPTER 18

## The Demons Inside Kirk

Kirk had tossed and turned the night before, getting little to no sleep. He had received a text message an hour earlier from David telling him there was no school and that they should take advantage of the unexpected long weekend. Kirk had not answered him yet. Dreams about the homeless man and the old bag lady had kept him awake most of the night. The sound of the old man's head hitting hard against the concrete wall resounded inside his own head—over and over—keeping sleep at bay. The dreams had started on the day Kirk had found the old woman and paid her the five hundred dollars to leave town, and had escalated in detail every night since.

"What the hell..." he mumbled as he threw back the covers and walked to look out of his upstairs bedroom window. Everything was iced over, but he saw several neighbors moving about outside. He noticed that his father's Mercedes was parked in the driveway; the Land Cruiser and his step-mother's BMW claimed the available parking spaces inside their four-car garage, next to his mother's pride and joy—a 1969 Mustang convertible. The garage also housed a 1970 Plymouth Barracuda with a 7-liter Hemi block capable of 425 horsepower. This classic muscle car could still hit 60 in 5.6 seconds and could burn rubber without much effort at all. Only a few hundred of them had been made, and none of them had the same trim, color or transmission—which made each of them a valuable collectible in its own right—and only a dozen or so of the hundred convertibles had the Hemi setup. Kirk had heard his father tell friends that the car was valued anywhere between $49,000 to $2 million. Needless to say, his father had never allowed him to take that beauty for a spin.

Kirk made his way downstairs and was relieved to find only his father in the kitchen. "Where's Prissy? I'm hungry."

Ernest looked up from his coffee and newspaper. "I told her to sleep in. You're more than capable of fixing your own breakfast."

Kirk's upper lip lifted into a half-snarl. "I don't know why you keep that old hag around anyway. She can't cook worth a flip, she never cleans my room..."

Ernest sat his cup down on the table and folded his hands into a fist. "You should stop while you still can, Kirk. I will not have you showing disrespect to Prissy."

"Whatever..." Kirk reached for a box of cereal and a bowl. He brought them and a gallon of milk to the table and flopped down.

"You'll probably need a spoon," Ernest said. He watched while his son got back up, jerked open a drawer, and brought a spoon back to the table. He wished he knew how to reach Kirk—how to help his son with the anger that was so evident in his every move and action. "There's no school today." He waited for a response—any response—but it was obvious to him that there would not be one. "There are power outages all over town. I think it would be a good idea if you stayed home until some of the ice melts. The roads are dangerous."

Kirk shoved too much cereal into his mouth and allowed some of the excess milk to dribble down his chin. He wiped it away with the back of his hand and waited until he was able to swallow the food before he replied. "Why do you even care?"

"What? What do mean by that, son? Of course I care about you driving on icy roads."

Kirk shrugged. "It would sure make life a lot easier for you, though, wouldn't it, Dad? I mean, with me out of the way, you and your little sugar-mama could have the house all to yourself, travel all over the world looking for ways for her to spend all your money."

Ernest pushed up and away from the table. "That's enough, Kirk. I don't know what's happened to you since your mother passed away, but, I do not like the person you have become. You will show respect to Prissy, and you will show respect to Rae. She certainly cannot ever replace your mother—nobody could ever do that—but, she is a member of this family and I expect you to treat her with the respect and dignity that she deserves."

"You really don't see it, do you, Dad?"

Ernest put on his overcoat and gloves before turning back to face his son. "See what, Kirk?"

"Yes, Kirk...what exactly doesn't your father see?" Rae entered the kitchen slowly from the back stair case. She tied the belt around her satin robe and walked over to husband. She reached under his coat, wrapped her arms around him, and stood on her tip-toes to receive a kiss from him. She ran her fingers across his lips and whispered, "You were amazing last night, Ernest."

Ernest sighed and shook his head. "I've got to go. Please try not to kill each other while I'm gone...and, don't disturb Prissy today. I'm worried about her; she doesn't look well this morning."

When the kitchen door closed, Rae turned to face Kirk. She planted her hands on her still-shapely hips and tossed her long auburn hair out of her face. "So, Kirk, tell me...what were you trying to tell your father about me?"

Kirk began shoveling cereal into his mouth once again.

He stared back at his step-mother with all the resentment and contempt that had been building up inside him during the past four years. He stood up, grabbed his empty bowl, and walked over to the kitchen sink. He dropped the bowl into the sink and smiled when it broke into several pieces. He looked back at the woman he blamed for ruining his life, and pointed his finger at her. "You're a gold-digging bitch, that's what I think you are. You saw a man who had just lost his wife, a man who was worth a lot of money, and you played him like the fool that he was—the fool that he is. You don't love him; you love his money. I don't have to tell him all that, though. If you think he hasn't already figured that out for himself, then you're more a fool than he is, and the two of you deserve each other. Now, get out of my way!" Kirk pushed roughly past Rae and rushed up the back stairs, taking them two at a time.

Rae tightened the belt around her tiny waist and tried to calm her rapid breathing. She had not wanted the boy to see how much he really frightened her. It was important that she appear strong and in control, so she only admitted it to herself—how terrified she was of the loose cannon that Kirk Blankenship had become lately.

She looked around the kitchen, at the dirty cups and glasses on the kitchen table, the broken bowl inside the sink—she took a deep breath and threw her shoulders back as she marched purposefully toward Prissy's room. She opened the door, without knocking, and saw the old woman's frail body huddled beneath the blankets. She walked over to the bed and turned on the lamp that sat on the night stand. When the light failed to awaken Prissy, Rae shook her shoulders roughly. "Get up, Prissy! You have work to do—the kitchen is a complete mess, and I'm hungry. Get up now!"

David Mizen received the phone call from Kirk around ten o'clock. He knew that Kirk had been anxious and nervous since the incident with the homeless man, so he had not been completely surprised when Kirk called to tell him about his plan. David called Michael and told him to come to his house immediately. Michael was a follower and always did what Kirk and David told him to do. He had left the note for his parents, just as David had left one for his. Each had told their respective parents that they were spending the weekend at Kirk's house since there was nothing else to do in an ice storm. Kirk had left a similar note in his room stating that he was hanging out at David's house—that he needed some time to cool off and think about things. All three boys knew that their parents would not question the validity of those notes, since they all often spent the weekends at one another's homes. They had the weekend to devise a plan that would ensure that the truth about what happened the night the homeless man died would never be revealed.

Kirk pulled up in front of David's house and found his two friends waiting outside for him, sharing a joint and sliding back and forth on the icy driveway. He honked his horn impatiently and waited for them to jump inside the Land Cruiser—David in the front seat, and Michael in the back. They each had a small back pack that they tossed onto the back floorboard.

"So, we're going to the lake house, huh?" Michael grinned. "That's cool—I always liked that place. I've missed going there."

Kirk had not been at his father's secluded lake house since his mother had passed away. It was full of memories of her, and neither he nor his father had wanted to visit or disturb the house in the past four years. It was the one place his step-mother did not know about, and it was the last place his father would ever think to go, so Kirk knew it would be a safe place to carry out his plan. The demons from his many dreams had convinced him over the past several nights that he could not trust the old bag lady not to say anything to the cops, or not to come back demanding more money. He knew he had to find her and ensure her total silence once and for all—he just had not worked out exactly how to make it happen.

"David told you what we're going there for, right?" Kirk turned around and stared at Michael.

Michael nodded. "Yeah, he told me. I have no problem with the plan. You're right; we can't take any chances on that old hag changing her story to the cops. Do you have any idea where she's at?"

Kirk nodded. "I hired someone to look for her. She lied to me—she never left town like she was supposed to. She's holed up in a motel on the outskirts of town."

"So that's where we're going?" David asked. "We're just gonna grab her and take her to the lake house?"

"If she's there, yeah, that's exactly what we're going to do," Kirk snapped. "If she's not, then we wait for the old bitch to come back. It's really cold outside today; I doubt she'll be gone long if she's not there."

The three friends rode in silence on their way to the Roadside Inn. The inn consisted of eight individual, one-story rooms next to a biker's bar called the Pickled Possum. The rooms were usually rented out by the hour, but Stella had paid a month in advance for room number 8—the room farthest away from the crowded bar.

Kirk parked at the opposite end, nearer the bar area. He rolled down his window and lit a joint. He took three tokes off it before passing it to David.

David took two tokes and passed it back to Michael. He exhaled deeply and stared at his best friend. They had known each other since kindergarten and David considered Kirk to be like a brother to him. "I'm sure you've thought this through, Kirk, but…"

"But, what?" Kirk snapped. "What? It has to be done—it's the only way to make sure that the truth never comes out. I can't go through the rest of my life looking over my shoulder."

"Haven't you forgotten something, Kirk?" David was tense, anticipating what they were about to do.

"What do you mean?" Kirk smirked. "We take care of the old lady, and our troubles go away. That's it."

Michael laughed from the back seat. "Man, even I know what he's talking about, Kirk. He means that the old lady isn't the only one who can tell the cops the truth about what happened."

Kirk was quiet for a moment. He knew that David and Michael could be trusted completely; they had both taken turns pushing the old man around, so they had just as much to lose as he did if the truth ever came out. In the midst of all the dreams, all his insecurity about being able to trust the old lady to leave town, he had forgotten that there was, indeed, one other person who knew the truth about what happened that night. "Dammit!" he pounded both hands repeatedly upon the steering wheel.

"Yeah," David sighed. "Jimmy Crennan is definitely another loose end, alright."

"So, what do we do about him?" Michael asked. "I mean, can you really trust him not to say anything? He's not one of us."

The door to room number 8 opened just then, and Kirk watched the old lady look from side to side before she locked the door behind her. He waited until she zipped her coat — it looked new — and wrapped a scarf around her neck. She pulled on gloves and began walking towards town.

"No," Kirk finally responded. "I don't think we can trust him."

"So, what?" David laughed. "You thinking that we grab him and the old lady and take them both to the lake house?"

Kirk nodded. "That's exactly what I'm thinking."

"Well, the old lady is easy," Michael inserted. "But, Crennan? Man, he's a big kid — strong — he won't be so easy."

Kirk looked back at Michael with exasperation. "There's three of us, you idiot, and only one of him. I think we can handle it." He waited until the old woman was about a half mile ahead of them before he started the car and rolled slowly out of the parking lot.

The half-baked plan he had concocted earlier that morning was actually going to happen. All he had to do now, was to ensure that nothing — or no one — interfered with that plan.

*"It will work,"* he thought. *"It has to work..."*

# CHAPTER 19

## Skipper 's Private Agony

It was almost noon and the Heavenly Grille was packed to the brim. People were sitting inside their heated cars, outside, waiting for a table to become available. Bertie was in her element, serving up hot breakfasts for those whose homes were still without power. Doug stayed busy keeping their coffee cups filled, and bussing the tables.

Cheryl and Jimmy still sat at the counter alongside Jason. Joe and Bernard had given up their seats a half-hour earlier and left the restaurant to renew their search for Stella. Max had provided plenty of food and hot coffee for them to take with them, on what had turned into a daily search for the woman who had condemned Skipper to what might be a life behind bars.

Cheryl looked around the crowded café and shook her head. "Okay, I am officially beginning to feel guilty for taking up space on this stool for so long. Just look at all those people in the parking lot, waiting to come inside. We should be getting back home." She pushed off the stool and reached for her jacket that was draped on the stool.

Jason beat her to it and helped her put it on. "Yeah, I

can't believe we've been sitting here for so long. It seems like only a few minutes, but it's been hours." He turned Cheryl around to face him and stared down into the same green eyes that had captivated him so many years ago. "The roads are better now, but there will probably still be some icy paths, so be careful driving home, okay?"

Jimmy looked at both of them—his *parents!* "You're not coming home with us? Why? I mean…we all still have so much to talk about, right?"

Jason moved toward Jimmy and held him at arm's length; a huge grin spread across his face and he nodded. "You're right, Jimmy. We do still have a lot to talk about. I mean, I certainly don't know where we go from here, but what I do know is that you both are very important to me. I want to get to know you both, but…"

"We can talk about all that later—maybe, back at the house," Cheryl interrupted. "I could come pick you up later this evening and you could have dinner with us…no, wait, I'm sorry. I'm scheduled to work tonight."

"He could still come to the house," Jimmy grinned. "He could hang out with me until you get home."

"I'm working until midnight, kiddo."

"Then he could spend the night again!" Jimmy grinned.

Jason pulled Jimmy—his *son*—in for a quick hug. "Let's play it by ear, okay. There's someone I need to go see today, and I'm not sure how long it will take for me to get there and back here again. I have your home number, Jimmy. I'll call you when I get back later today, okay?"

"That sounds like a plan," Cheryl agreed. "Come on, Jimmy. Jason has things to do, and I need your help with a few things at home. I'm taking advantage of no school today and using your muscle to get some things moved around." She turned back toward Jason and smiled up at him. "I know this is a lot of information for you to absorb in such a short time, Jason. You are certainly under no obligation to even keep in touch with either of us if you don't want to. We are not here to cramp your life style in any way, and we didn't tell you the truth because we needed or expected anything from you in return." She took another deep breath and looked at her son. "I just thought…well, since the opportunity did present itself so unexpectedly…I just thought it was the right thing to do—for you—and Jimmy. You each have the right to know about the other one. I don't expect to fit into that equation, so please don't think…"

Jason bent down and silenced her with a kiss. He had not planned to do that and the act took him as off guard as it had Cheryl. "You talk too much," he whispered.

Jimmy jumped into the air with both fists raised in victory. "YESSSS!" he shouted.

A guard stopped by the old man's cell and stared at the long form lying so still beneath the solitary blanket. He stared hard to see if the old man was breathing, and sighed when he finally heard a soft snore. His good friend, Tom O'Brady, had asked him to keep an eye on the old man; Tom had confided that he thought Skipper had gotten a raw deal and was going to be used as a scapegoat for closing a murder case on another homeless person.

Skipper had his back to his caged door, but had sensed someone there—someone staring at him. He continued to feign sleep for a couple more minutes, but when it was obvious that the person was still there, he pulled the cover off him and turned over on his other side. A young guard, probably in his mid-to-late thirties, was standing there, staring at him. He was holding a folded blanket. "Something I can do for you, officer?" Skipper threw his long legs over the side of the cot and sat up. He was fully clothed in a prison jumpsuit. He walked slowly forward and stopped at his cell door.

"My name is Pete. I promised Officer O'Brady that I would do what I could to keep an eye on you. He seems to think you're pretty special."

"He seems like a decent enough guy—for a cop," Skipper offered a half-grin. "They returned us all to our cells after breakfast this morning; said there was an ice storm last night, so there would be no work details today. Has that changed?'

Pete shook his head. "No, it's still too cold for anyone to be outside. There are power outages all over town."

"But not here in the Floyd County jail," Skipper stood up. "Did you need something—Pete?"

Pete glanced down at the blanket he held. "We have several generators in case the power goes out here. Step back, please." He waited until Skipper had returned to his cot before speaking into the walkie-talkie he held. "Unlock 17." He waited until he heard the lock unclick, before he slid open the barred door. He dropped the blanket onto the floor. "Warden's orders—the older inmates get an extra blanket today." He slid the door back and spoke into the walkie-talkie again. "Close 17."

Skipper heard the lock engage once again and walked to pick up the blanket. "Thanks, I guess I do fall into that category."

Pete looked back at Skipper as he turned to leave. "We got a call earlier this morning. You have a visitor coming in around two o'clock."

"Really?" Skipper was surprised. "I can't imagine who that might be."

Pete took out a note pad and glanced at it. "Jason Benton. Officer O'Brady said you approved him to be added to your visitor's list. Try to stay warm."

"Are you kidding?" Skipper shrugged. "This place feels like a sauna compared to what I'm used to. Thanks for the extra blanket."

Pete returned the shrug. "Just doing my job."

Skipper watched the young man walk away and shivered as a sudden feeling of melancholy washed over him. He sat back down on his cot and reached under the thin mattress for his old weathered note book. He pressed his back against the cold, concrete wall and wrapped the extra blanket around his legs. He opened the notebook and flipped through the pages—pages that told stories of a life that only a select group of men and women could ever relate to. Each poem had been written about a specific event, or a specific person—events and people that Skipper would never forget—no matter how many years separated him from them. There would never be enough time to elapse that would allow him the luxury to forget. He looked at the titles of some of the poems: "The Eagle Never Even Cried"—written to reflect the lack of respect and appreciation the Vietnam Veterans experienced upon their return from war; "Bastard Son"—written to reflect his own status of feeling like America's bastard son; "I Remember When You Fell"—written in honor of one of his platoon leaders who was killed on the battlefield; "Queen of Battle"—written to reflect the Army's Queen, the Infantry; "Dead Survivors"—written to reflect the guilt the survivors felt for having survived when so many others had not; "Angels on the Battlefield"—written to reflect the hope that even the atheists felt when they lay upon the ground and looked up into the cloud formations above them, convinced that the images they saw were angels sent to watch over and protect them; and, so many more titles.

Skipper continued to flip through the notebook, and stopped at one that reflected his general mood every day since his last day of battle. It confirmed his belief that life was a journey for everyone; a journey that ended way too soon for some, or tolerated way too long for others. Life's journey was full of uncertainty—of not knowing if each day would be the last—the uncertainty of not knowing when, or how, we will die. It was titled, "The Script's Final Page".

*With graying hair and a wrinkled brow*
*I realize that yesterday is no part of now;*
*One must view life as a theatrical stage*
*Where the script is near written, except one final page.*

*Friends become fewer while the graveyards flourish*
*It seems death is a fuel that life needs to nourish;*
*Death in itself is not an evil tone*
*The evil is when one must die all alone.*

*I feel no serenity in the views I once cherished*
*Only the agony of truth that unity has perished;*
*The depth of one's thoughts becomes deeper with age*
*With their meaning all written on the script's final page.*

*The time that we borrow to keep up life's pace*
*Must all be repaid at the end of our race;*
*Life's not a gift, it's a chore we must heed*
*Our conscience must guide us until our soul's finally freed.*

*Most of us beg forgiveness for mistakes that we make*
*And feel fully justified when we wrongfully take;*
*Together we shall all meet at the center of stage*
*When the truth is all written on the script's final page.*

Skipper closed the notebook and pulled the extra blanket up and wrapped it around his shoulders. He closed his eyes and allowed a solitary tear to roll down his weathered cheek. He would never understand—no matter how many years he continued to walk this earth—why he survived four tours in Vietnam, and so many others did not. He had never been a religious person, so he had never questioned a God he wasn't sure really existed; however, if it was true that God had saved his life for some special purpose, he still had not discovered what that reason might have been. He did not feel like he had accomplished anything in this lifetime. His bitterness about the war and how America had treated the Vietnam Veterans had festered like a slow-growing cancer inside him all these years. He had never been able to let go of that bitterness and resentment.

"So how about it, God?" he looked upward toward the

cracked and peeling ceiling. "Why have you saved me to continue living in this hell on earth? What purpose did you have in mind for me? You must be pretty disappointed. I've made it seventy-six years on my own, and I don't need you now, so how about it...get out of my head and let me just die in peace. Peace — that's all I ask of you — if you even exist. I just want to die in peace..."

Skipper lay on his back and stretched out his full length upon the cot. He tucked the notebook under the flat pillow and sighed. He closed his eyes and whispered, "Forget it...you might exist for some people, but...not for me."

He fell into a long, deep sleep and allowed the nightmares to, once again, march in — dreams of piercing bullets and exploding bombs, screaming soldiers, scattered body parts, innocent women and children killed — because the next thing Skipper heard was Officer Pete at his cell door.

"Wake up, Skipper. Your visitor is here to see you."

# CHAPTER 20

## The Lake House

Ernest Blankenship purchased the small, run-down fishing lodge in Cave Spring, Georgia – located about 20 miles southwest of Rome – for his wife, Elizabeth – in 1997, a year after he opened his first car dealership. He had paid cash for the six-bedroom, five-bath wooden lodge, complete with a 6,000 square foot unfinished basement. The lodge was situated on almost nine acres of woods – mostly tall pines – on the outskirts of the quaint and picturesque square located in the heart of Cave Spring.

It was almost two o'clock when the Land Cruiser pulled up to the iron gate that blocked entry onto the lake house property. Kirk put the car in park and jumped out. He had not been here since before his mother died, so he had to pull some overgrown vines away to reveal the padlock that secured the gate. He retrieved his keys from his jacket pocket and used a small, universal padlock key to open the gate. He looked back at his friends and ordered, "Check the old woman and make sure she hasn't loosened the duct tape." He looked around in all directions and felt more confident than ever that his plan would work. A body could be hidden in these woods and never be discovered.

It had been even easier than he thought—kidnapping the old lady and stuffing her into the trunk space. Kirk had allowed her a half-mile head start before he began following her along the deserted roadway. He watched her limping silhouette as she shuffled down the road; and, he waited until there were no cars or people in sight before he finally pulled up alongside her.

Stella had been taken by surprise when the dark SUV pulled up beside her. She stopped walking and tried to steady her breathing, which became more labored with every inch that the darkened driver's window lowered. She recognized Kirk immediately and began her pitiful version of the 50-yard dash. "Help!" she yelled, knowing full-well that even if anyone heard her on this side of town, they most likely would not come to her aid. "Stay away from me!" she screamed. "Help me!" she croaked again when she saw the passenger door open. The SUV continued, at a slow pace, moving alongside her, while the young man who jumped out of the car sprinted easily and effortlessly toward her.

Stella reached inside her bag for the small can of pepper spray she had purchased recently. She waved it in front of the young man and yelled again. "You stay away from me!" She tried to pump the spray in his direction, but nothing happened.

David laughed when he reached her and knocked the pepper spray from her bony fingers. "Don't make this hard on yourself, old woman. We just want to take a ride and have a talk with you—that's all."

"No! That ain't all!" Stella choked. "Y'all are gonna kill me—just like you did poor Norman. I told y'all I wasn't going to say anything. Now, get away!"

David never hesitated—he drew back his clenched fist and sucker-punched the old woman, knocking her out cold. He could have sworn he heard a bone crack in her jaw, and felt a momentary stab of regret. He hadn't meant to hurt her. He caught her before she hit the ground and dragged her to the back of the SUV. "Damn!" he grimaced. "She's heavier than she looks—a little help would be nice."

Michael had taped Stella's hands behind her back with duct tape—that good, 'ole southern remedy for any given situation—and, placed a large piece across her dry and cracked lips. He watched now as Kirk shoved open the creaking gate and jumped back inside the Land Cruiser. He peaked over his seat, into the trunk space. "Naw, she's still out. She hasn't moved a muscle."

"She's not dead, is she?" David asked nervously from the front seat. He still felt guilty for having hit the old woman so hard.

"Naw, she's not dead," Michael grinned. "At least, not yet." He giggled the laugh of someone who has smoked way too much weed in his short life span. Unlike David, he felt absolutely no remorse at what they had done, or at what might have to be done in the future.

Kirk drove the SUV down the long, curving graveled driveway. He inhaled sharply when the lake house first came into view. So many suppressed memories rushed in—happy memories of the times he had spent with his parents at this secluded hideaway. He glanced to the left and stared at the long dock—situated about a quarter-mile away from the lodge—that had provided his family so many happy times on their own, private lake. His father had taught him how to fish, and his mother had taught him how to swim in that lake.

He followed the driveway around to the back of the lodge where an enormous patio overlooked the three-acre, private lake. The patio was bare except for two concrete picnic-style tables and benches. "Wait here, until I check inside," Kirk ordered his friends. "Don't take your eyes off that old woman either."

David offered a thumbs-up for confirmation. He looked back at Michael, who had lit up yet another joint and was on his way to his own, private temporary oblivion. "Another one, Mike? Really?"

Michael giggled and held the joint toward David. "Hell, yeah! This is good stuff — want some?"

Stella uttered a small groan from the trunk area and Michael giggled again. "See! I told you she wasn't dead." He got on his knees and peeked over the back seat into the trunk space again. He held the joint out to Stella. "Hey, old lady — how about you — you want a hit?" He giggled again and flopped back onto his seat. "Never mind," he laughed out loud. "You already took a pretty good hit, didn't you?"

David groaned and opened the passenger door. He walked around to the back of the SUV and opened the tailgate. The first thing he noticed was the huge red mark on the old woman's lower left jaw. He grimaced at the dried blood at the corner of her mouth when he pulled the duct tape off. "Are you okay?" he asked. "I'm sorry — I didn't mean to hit you so hard."

Stella lay on her right side, unable to manage a sitting position with her hands secured behind her. She lifted her head slightly and spat a wad of bloody phlegm at David's feet. "Go to hell," she managed to croak.

David helped her to a sitting position. "There's no place for you to run, so be smart, okay? Just do what you're told and you just might get out of this alive." Kirk had not revealed the entire plan to him, but he felt sure that his best friend just wanted to scare the old woman enough to make sure she left town for good.

Stella stared at the young man and confirmed to herself that he was indeed part of the group that had killed poor Norman. She turned when someone giggled behind her, and recognized the other young man as being part of that same group. "All of you are gonna burn in hell for what you did to Norman — burn in hell, I say!"

Kirk heard their voices from his position inside the basement. He glanced quickly out the sliding glass door and saw the old woman sitting on the tailgate, her feet dangling a good eighteen inches from the ground — one of her shoes was missing. He turned back around and removed the small flashlight from his back pocket. He found his way to the kitchen, where the fuse box was mounted inside a large food pantry, and flipped several switches. He was relieved to see that the power outages in Rome had not affected the lake house. The basement immediately became flooded with light, and Kirk's brain became flooded with more memories.

He allowed himself a few minutes to take it all in as he moved around the basement that had been converted into a massive game room. Three comfortable sofas and four recliners were scattered throughout the room, all of them situated for easy viewing of the wall-mounted 65" flat-screen television. The focal point of the luxurious basement was the large, commercial-size pool table located in the very center of the room. There was a wet bar at each end of the remodeled basement and two enormous stone fireplaces at each corner of the oversized sliding glass doors. Another door at the left corner of the room opened to a master suite that was complete with a king-sized bed and full bathroom—to include, an 8-person, Jacuzzi. The Jacuzzi was empty now, but Kirk remembered so many good times, relaxing in it after a day of outdoor activities with family and friends.

The three friends spent the next three hours getting Stella situated in the basement suite and going over the rest of Kirk's plan. When Kirk felt that everyone knew how it was all going to go down, and knew their respective parts in the plan, he told them to wait for him in the car. He checked the long chain that had been secured to Stella's left ankle and stared at her as she sat in the middle of the large bed. "That chain is long enough for you to make it to the bathroom. There's water and sandwiches in the small fridge next to the Jacuzzi. Don't look for any way to escape, because there isn't one. We'll be back soon, and I better not find this room in a mess. Do you understand, old woman?"

Stella curled her swollen upper lip at him and snarled. "Burn in hell!" She refused to show him how scared she really was. The thought had not escaped her that *she* might now be the one to die under "mysterious" circumstances.

Kirk shrugged and walked away. He looked back at her and said, "Too late—I'm already there." He closed the bedroom door and locked the glass doors behind him. "Yeah, it's too late to turn back now..."

Jason had been prepared to walk the seven miles to the county jail if he had do; however, he had reluctantly accepted a ride from one of the café's regular customers, who gladly agreed to drop him off on his way home.

"Thank you for the ride, Mr. Zimmerman," Jason nodded as he closed the passenger door and pulled up the zipper of his worn, weathered jacket. He pulled on the gloves that Skipper had given him and waved good-bye to the old man who Doug had asked to give him a ride. "Drive safe now— these roads are still icy."

"Oh, I'll be just fine, young fella," Mr. Zimmerman grinned back at the younger man. "I wish I could hang around and give you a ride back to the café, but I gotta get home and take this vegetable soup, that Mr. Max made, to the missus—she was too sick to get outside today in this weather."

"Not a problem," Jason waved again and watched the old 1969 Dodge pick-up continue its slow putter down the main road, back toward town. He turned and stared at the large detention facility that stood before him.

The Floyd County Jail was built in 1982 and renovated in 1996; it was the largest county-owned building in Floyd County. The Detention Division was 256,000 square feet and housed 828 beds. It served Floyd County, the city of Rome, and Cave Spring, Georgia pre-trial detainees, as well as county-sentenced and state-sentenced inmates. The 828-bed population was at almost-full capacity on almost any given day.

Jason took a deep breath and moved forward. "You shouldn't be in here, Skipper," he muttered beneath his breath.

Jason showed his military identification and was verified on Skipper's visitor's list. He went through the required electronic surveillance equipment and emptied his pockets; his personal items were kept in a basket for him to retrieve upon his departure. A clerk provided him with a brochure that explained the jail's new video visitation process; she offered a brief explanation of the new system and said that it might be something he would want to consider before his next visit—especially if he visited during another ice storm. She explained that more than half of all jail visits were now done via video visits. Jason nodded with feigned interest and waited behind the Plexiglas.

At thirty-one years of age, this was the first time that Jason had ever been inside a jail, even as a visitor. He shook his head at the reason he was here now. He glanced up when a door opened on the other side of the Plexiglas and a staffer motioned Skipper inside. The staffer closed the door and Skipper nodded at Jason before he took a seat at the table.

"Hi," Jason said and lifted his hand in a wave. He actually blushed when Skipper picked up the phone and motioned for him to do the same on his side of the glass. "Oh," Jason smiled, as he picked up the phone and spoke into it. "Sorry, I didn't know how all this worked..."

Skipper allowed a half-smile to escape. "Let me guess—this is your first time inside a jail, isn't it?"

Jason nodded. "I'm guessing it isn't your first time?"

"You've got that right. I've seen my share."

"I bet you've never been inside one—accused of murder—have you?" Jason was more than a little curious about the man who was such an enigma to them all.

"How can you be so sure of that?" Skipper looked serious, until another small smile broke across his face. "No, Jason. I've never been accused of murder. That's a first—even for me."

"Nobody believes that you did it, you know."

Skipper looked around the tiny visitation room and shrugged. "Well, it's obvious that *someone* believes it, else, I wouldn't be here. Although, I have to admit, it's a lot warmer in here than it is outside. I heard there was an ice storm last night."

"Yeah, the temp really dropped."

"Are the others all okay?" Skipper wasn't sure why he needed to know the answer to that question.

Jason nodded. "Yeah, everyone's okay for now. PJ is still in the hospital, but she's getting stronger every day. Doug—the fella from the café—goes to see her several times a week. The owner of the café offered a room for me, Joe, and Bernard to sleep in until the weather warms up; they're good people—the ones who run the café."

Skipper nodded his head slowly. "And what about our good friend, Stella?"

"We've all been looking for her—ever since she told the police what she did about you. We haven't been able to find her anywhere, but we're not giving up. I don't know why she said what she did, Skipper, but she framed you. We all know that, and we're going to do what we can to find her and prove it."

"We'll see how that turns out, I guess." Skipper stared hard at Jason. "I still don't get it, though. Why do you and the others even care? We're nothing to one another."

"That's where you're wrong, Skipper. You and I share a special bond, and the others certainly don't want to see an innocent man go to prison for something he didn't do. No, we think that Stella knows the truth about what really happened to Norman. For your sake—and Norman's—we all want the real truth to come out."

Skipper drew his brows together. "You think that you and I share a special bond?"

"We do share a special bond—as Veterans—if nothing else."

Skipper nodded. "And you think that connects us, do you? You think that the wars we fought were similar?"

"No," Jason shook his head. "No—I know that we fought in two very different wars, that we were treated very differently by our people and our government when we returned home—I know all that. All I'm saying is that the bond we share is evident in the pain and bitterness of it all, the friends we lost in those wars, the nightmares and the guilt we feel for having survived those wars—when so many others didn't make it back home. You can deny it all you want, but any Veteran who has experienced that kind of loss...yes, there is a bond."

Two minutes elapsed without either man saying a word. They simply stared at each other through the Plexiglas until something happened—a mental connection and acknowledgement was made—because, in those two minutes, both men knew that there truly was a special bond between them. It was a bond that no amount of time would ever eradicate or diminish.

Jason was the first to break the silence. He grinned at his fellow Veteran and asked, "So—how are they treating you in here?"

"Well," Skipper sighed. "From what I hear from some of the other inmates, it's a good thing that we're in here now, as opposed to what it was like just a few short years ago. I heard that they forced the inmates to wear the same clothes—underwear included—for a full week, that the A/C was turned off during the hottest part of the day, that they were forced to eat rotten and rancid food...so, all in all, I would have to say they are treating me like a king in here. Being old seems to have some advantages, too—I even got an extra blanket to keep me warm this morning."

Jason was shocked at hearing so many words spurt from Skipper's mouth; it was the most he had ever heard the old man say at one time. "Wow—that makes being homeless sound like a walk in the park." He smiled and shook his head. "Seriously, though, is there anything I can do for you on the outside? Anyone I can contact for you? Have you talked to an attorney yet?"

Skipper shook his head. "No—no—and, no—to all your questions. My court-appointed attorney should be in next week to meet with me. I'll see what he thinks about the situation. In the meantime, I'm eating three squares a day: usually, oatmeal for breakfast, spaghetti for lunch, and a mystery chicken casserole for dinner. I don't have a cell mate at the present time, so I have my privacy. I'm keeping warm and am off the streets during an ice storm. Life is good."

The door opened and a guard stepped inside. "Wrap it up—two minutes."

"Wow, they don't give us very long to visit, do they? If it's okay with you, Skipper, I'd like to come back. Joe and Bernard would like to visit, too."

Skipper shook his head. "From what I understand, they use their own discretion for the time allowed for visitation— anywhere from fifteen minutes to an hour for each visit. I'm pretty sure they limit the number of what they refer to as *significant relationship* visitors, to two. But, you can come back any time to visit, Jason—anytime. Hey, I heard that they even have video visitations now. I could visit with you from the convenience of my cell, without you having to travel all the way here. I know you don't have transportation."

"I may check into that process, but it's not like I have a computer handy," Jason grinned. He stopped and thought about Cheryl and Jimmy. "But, I do have some friends that might have one I can borrow. That would be a great way to visit with you, to keep you posted on what's going on. I'll do that, okay?"

"You've made some friends—that's good," Skipper smiled. "Thanks for coming, Jason. I really didn't think we would have anything to say to each other, but...I was wrong."

Jason nodded. "I'll be in touch. Take care of yourself, Skipper."

Both men hung up their phones and Jason waited until

the guard had escorted Skipper from the room. He looked at the clock on the wall—it was almost three o'clock. If he left now, he would still have a couple of hours of daylight left in which he could search for Stella, before he walked to the Crennan home. He had hoped to see Cheryl before she left for work at five o'clock, but he doubted that would happen now. She had told him that Jimmy would be there, but if he wasn't, she told him where to find the spare key.

Jason sighed deeply, sat back down on the chair, and lowered his head into his hands. "You shouldn't be in here, Skipper..."

# CHAPTER 21

## Sticking to the Plan

It was four-thirty by the time Kirk and his motley crew had left Walmart, stocked with enough food and toiletries to last them a couple of weeks. He pulled out of the Walmart parking lot and drove toward the south end of town where some of the older homes were located—to where Jimmy Crennan lived with his hot-looking mother. He reached Maple Crest Circle and pulled over to the side, three houses down from the Crennan's cottage. He shut off the SUV's engine and stared at the house. He nodded his head and said, "His mother's at home—that's her Beetle Bug in the drive-way."

David's eyes squinted; he had recently received a prescription for glasses, but simple vanity prevented him from wearing them—a slight eye infection had prevented him from being immediately able to get contacts. "Yeah, that's her car alright. I thought she would be at work. We can't do this if she's home, Kirk." When his friend didn't respond, he repeated, "Kirk? We've got to wait till he's alone—right?"

Kirk continued to focus his attention on the Crennan

166

home. He had Stella secured now; Jimmy Crennan was his
only loose end. His first instinct was to carry out their
plan—now—and not take any chances of Jimmy developing
a conscience and spilling everything to his mother, or to the
cops. On the other hand, he didn't want to act too hastily
either—he was beginning to think that they might need to
take more time to review the plan and how to best carry it
out. He had to make sure that nothing could be traced back
to him and his friends.

Michael giggled restlessly from the back seat. He leaned
forward on both of the front seats and grinned. "Naw, I say
we go ahead and do it now. You can tell the kid's the type
that isn't going to be able to let this go—no matter how
much you threaten to hurt that pretty mama of his. He's one
of those losers who always feel they have to do the *right*
thing. You'll regret it, man, I'm telling you—do it now—
don't wait."

David looked at Michael and rolled his eyes. "Shut up,
Mike. You don't know that. The kid's kept his mouth shut
so far." He looked over at his best friend, who was still
staring blankly ahead. "It's your decision, Kirk. You know
that we'll do whatever you want us to. We have just as
much to lose in all this as you do, but...hell, we've already
kidnapped one person. Do we really want to make it two?
And who's going to babysit them after we lock them up at
the lake house? I mean, all three of us are supposed to be
back at school next week. You can't just lock them both up
at the lake house and not check on them. Kirk?"

Kirk's head snapped to the right. "You're giving me a
headache, David. Shut up and let me think for a minute, will
you? We talked about this back at the lake house—or have
you already forgotten the plan?"

David held up both hands in resignation. "No, I haven't
forgotten the plan. Hey, take your time. We've got all
weekend, right? I mean, nobody will be expecting any of us
back home until late Sunday night."

"We may have until Sunday night," Michael shrugged

and giggled. "But, pretty boy Crennan doesn't have that long. I say we do what we said—stick to the plan—take turns staying out of school next week, so that someone is there with them at all times. That way, we've got almost a full week to decide, for sure, what to do with the old lady and Crennan—like, how and where to dispose of the bodies…"

Kirk banged both fists—hard—against the steering wheel and glared at his two best friends. "Will you both SHUT UP! I can't think…"

Michael giggled again and pointed toward the Crennan cottage. "Hey, lookie there…isn't that pretty boy's hot and sassy mama? Ummm—she does look fine."

Kirk turned his attention back to the Crennan home, where Jimmy's mom was now backing down the short driveway and headed in their direction. "Quick! Everyone get down!"

The three young men stay crouched low in their seats for about thirty seconds before Kirk rose up and watched the retreating Beetle Bug in his rear-view mirror. He had made up his mind in that short, thirty seconds. "We're sticking to the plan—let's go."


Jason had spent almost three hours, after he left the Detention Center, walking the streets and alleys of downtown Rome. He talked to at least a dozen homeless people, and described Stella to all of them. Most of them knew who he was talking about them, but none of them admitted to knowing where she might be. It was almost dark—around five-thirty—when Jason blew warm air into his cupped, gloved hands, and was ready to give up for the day.

A scraping sound in a dark alley on his left caused him to turn back around. He watched while an old man scooted backwards, on his knees, out of a large furniture box. It was evident to Jason that arthritis had claimed root to most portions of the old man's body. "Excuse me?" Jason advanced slowly toward the old man.

The old man turned and stared back at Jason with cataract-filled eyes, and he picked absently at the large growth on the tip of his swollen, Rosacea-infected nose. "What? What do you want? I ain't got nothin', so you best just leave me be, young fella." He couldn't have straightened his bent back if he had wanted to—he leaned most of his 120-pound frame on the old cane that wobbled dangerously against the icy pavement. He lifted his cane, in apparent warning, and immediately began to fall forward. "Go on, now—leave me be!"

Jason moved quickly when the cane lifted and the old man started to fall. "Whoa! I gotcha!" He flinched when he felt fragile, skeletal arms through the thin, worn jacket that the old man wore. "I'm not going to hurt you, old man. I'm just looking for someone. Maybe you've seen her?"

The old man righted himself and used his free hand to pull his knit cap over his cold, reddened ears. He grinned at the young man who had kept him from falling; he had no teeth left in his mouth, so he gummed his lips several times before responding. "Thanks." He tried to stand a little taller, but failed miserably. "So, who is it you might be looking for—a woman, you say?"

Jason released the old man's arm and waited to make sure that he could remain upright on his own. "Yes, sir. Her name is Stella, and she's been living on the streets for a while now. She's old—in her eighties, I think—gray, stringy hair, dull eyes, not many teeth, kind of short, and probably doesn't weigh more than 120 pounds, at the most."

The old man squinted and stared hard at Jason. His vision may have been cloudy, but he could tell that this young man meant him no harm. "You just described more than half of the homeless people in this city."

Jason smiled and scratched his head. "Yeah, I guess I did, didn't I?" He shrugged and grinned again. "I've been looking for her for a couple of weeks now. She used to bed down in the woods near the overpass, just outside of town."

The old man hesitated briefly before nodding his head. "I know Stella."

Jason's head jerked quickly to the left and he stared hard at the old man. "Really? You know Stella? Have you seen her around here? Do you know where I can find her?"

The old man gummed his jaws together in an up-and-down motion, never taking his eyes off the younger man. He finally nodded and said, "Matter of fact, I do—but, first, you've got to tell me why you want to find her—'cause, if you're aiming to hurt her any, then..."

Jason held both hands up and shook his head adamantly from side to side. "No, no—I don't want to hurt her; nobody wants to hurt her. It's just that she might have information that could help another friend of ours—a homeless Veteran that shared our camp."

"You ain't talking 'bout that Vet they arrested for killing old Norman, are you? There's been a lot of talk on the street about that killing. What's Stella got to do with any of this?"

Jason nodded. "Yes, sir; that's the Veteran I'm talking about. He's a friend of mine—a friend of Stella's; and, she might be the only person who can help him get out of this mess."

"Stella talked some about that killing," the old man said. "She said she had to lay low for a little while—until it all blowed over."

"Do you know where she's staying?" Jason was trying not to get his hopes up, but was having a hard time containing his excitement.

"Yep, I do know where she's at," the old man nodded his bobbling head. "What's that information worth to you?"

"Oh, man," Jason shook his head. "Hey, I don't have any money; if I did, I'd give it all to you." He took his backpack off and unzipped it. He had two meatloaf sandwiches and a piece of vanilla-crème pound cake that Max had insisted he take with him when he left the café earlier that day. "I've got some food, though."

The old man licked his lips. "When you only get to eat a couple times a week, food is more important than money, young fella." He held out his free hand for the offered food. He lifted it to his cancer-riddled nose and inhaled its enticing aromas. "Oh, this smells sooooo good!"

Jason followed the old man back to his card board box and watched him crawl slowly inside it. He fought impatience while the old man unwrapped one of the sandwiches and savored that first bite. He managed to hold his impatience at bay until the old man finally swallowed what he had eaten. "So? Stella? You said you knew where I can find her?"

"I can't remember the last time I tasted anything so good," the old man closed his eyes in ecstasy. He took another, smaller, bite of the juicy, meatloaf sandwich and chewed it slowly—not that he had any choice in the matter—sans teeth. He pointed a long, bony finger at Jason and nodded. "I like you, and if you promise that you won't hurt Stella, then I'll tell you where you can find her."

"I would never do anything to hurt Stella," Jason quickly replied. "Never, I promise."

"I believe you—I do. Well then, okay. Stella came into a little money, so she's taken herself off the streets for a while. If she told me the truth—and I have no reason to believe she would lie to me—then you should be able to still find her at the Roadway Inn."

"Where is that?"

"It's a run-down motel on your way out of town. Just ask anyone where to find the Pickled Possum and you'll find the motel right next to it."

"And, you think Stella might still be there?"

"Let's see, what's today?"

"It's Friday," Jason offered. "Friday, February 5th."

"Then she should still be there," the old man nodded. "I saw her on Wednesday, and she said she thought she might stay there for another couple of weeks before maybe moving on. I think she might be waiting for the weather to warm up a little."

Jason bent down and kissed the top of the old man's head. "Thank you, so much!" He grabbed his back pack and took off at a run, in the direction of Cheryl's house. If he ran, he thought he could make it there in about thirty minutes. He could use her phone and contact the officer he had met earlier — Officer O'Brady — and tell him what he had learned about Stella.

The old man watched Jason dash away. He sighed deeply and closed his eyes, almost as if in prayer. "No…thank *you*," he spoke softly and took another, mouth-watering bite of his sandwich. He would sleep good tonight — his rumbling stomach would not keep him awake.

Jimmy sat stoically at the kitchen table, surrounded by three people he had hoped he would never have to speak to again. Kirk sat on one side of him, and David on the other. A giggling Michael stood directly behind him.

It had been almost five o'clock when his mom left for work. He had been sitting on the sofa, his back to the kitchen door, when she had come up behind him, removed his ear plugs, and kissed him good-bye. He had grinned and flippantly wiped the kiss away before telling her bye, and immediately returned his attention to the downloaded music of Mo Pitney.

He never heard the door close when his mother left. He, also, never heard the door open again ten minutes later. By the time he sensed someone else in the room with him, it was too late. The sound of Mo Pitney quickly faded away the moment he felt the cold steel of the knife against his throat — Kirk's knife.

Kirk had instructed Jimmy to move into the kitchen and sit at the table. Jimmy slid his cell phone into the pocket of his jeans, leaving the earphone attachment dangling from his waist. He pulled the kitchen chair out and stared at Kirk. "What's going on? What are y'all doing here?"

Kirk had taken a few minutes to share the purpose of their visit with Jimmy.

David glanced nervously at Kirk. "Come on, man. If we're going to do this, let's do it before someone comes."

"His mom won't be back for hours," Kirk replied impatiently. He returned the knife to his ankle holster. "Relax, David. We can't leave until Jimmy-Boy here writes the note we told him to."

"I'm not writing any note," Jimmy said. He grimaced when Michael slapped him hard against the back of his head.

"Oh, you're going to write the note," Kirk smirked. He pushed away from the table and stood up. He walked into the small family room and picked up a picture of Cheryl and Jimmy that stood on the mantle over the small fireplace. "Because, if you don't, then you won't be the only one leaving here with us tonight. It might be nice to have a little female companionship—don't you agree, fellas?" He turned to look back at his two best friends.

Michael made an obscene grinding motion with his hips and laughed. "Oh, yeah, *nice!*"

Jimmy pushed his chair back and tried to rise up, but Michael pushed him—hard—back into his seat.

David closed his eyes for a second and shook his head. He looked pleadingly at Jimmy. "Please, kid—write the damn note." His voice was almost a whisper. "You have no idea what he's capable of doing to your mom. Hurry—write the note, and make it sound good, okay?"

There was something about the pleading desperation in David's voice that chilled Jimmy to the bone. He had not hung around these three friends for very long, but what little time he had spent with them, made him wonder how far Kirk Blankenship might really take things. He looked at David and nodded. "Okay."

Kirk brought the framed picture into the kitchen and walked to the kitchen table. He propped one leg up on his empty chair and looked at Michael. "Find some pen and paper."

"There's a pad in the drawer over there, by the back door," Jimmy said. He suddenly wanted to get as far away from his home as quickly as possible. He didn't expect his mom home until after midnight, but with the weather being as bad as it was, it wouldn't surprise him if she wasn't sent home earlier. He could not take any chances of Kirk and his gang being here when she got home. He knew that Jason might stop by, too, and he didn't want to risk his father getting hurt—not when they had just found each other.

"Go ahead and write what I told you to," Kirk instructed. "And, for your mom's sake—make it convincing. I don't want anyone looking for you—at least, not before Monday. Now, WRITE!"

Jimmy scribbled the message that he had previously been instructed to write. He told his mom that he hoped she didn't mind, but that he had been invited to spend the weekend at a friend's house—he didn't say what friend— and, that he would be home before dark, Sunday night. He handed the note to Kirk for inspection.

Kirk read it and looked at Jimmy with suspicion. "What's with the XOXOXXX at the bottom?"

Jimmy never faltered in his response. "It's just something we always put at the end of any note we write to each other."

Michael laughed and made smooching noises. "Yeah, dude, it's like hugs and kisses, you know?"

Kirk hesitated but finally nodded. "Okay, that should do it. Let's get moving."

Everyone bundled themselves back into their jackets and hurried out the kitchen door. Nobody thought to lock the door behind them, and nobody noticed Jimmy's cell phone lying on the kitchen chair that he had pushed flush to the table.

The Land Cruiser backed slowly out of the driveway. Jimmy sat in the back seat next to Michael. He didn't know where they were going, but he shivered involuntarily at the thought that he might never return to the small cottage that he and his mom called home. *"I love you, Mom..."* he thought as the house faded into the background and the dark night claimed victory over the diminishing day.

Jimmy's cell phone rang before the Land Cruiser made it to the first stop sign. When he didn't answer, Cheryl left a message for him. *"Hey, kiddo! It's me. Well, this was a wasted trip in to town. It looks like everyone has decided to stay home tonight, so the boss is going to close up early. I should be home by eight at the latest. I'll stop and pick up something to eat, so save your appetite, okay? I love you, kiddo — see ya soon!"*

# CHAPTER 22

## A Secret Code

It may not have been busy at the pancake house where Cheryl worked, but every booth, table, and counter seat was filled at the Heavenly Grille. Bertie was in her glory, bustling about, punching shoulders, making recommendations, shooting the breeze, and reminding everyone to be sure to help fill up the jar on the counter, next to the cash register.

The café always had a jar on the counter, asking for donations for some good cause or a local resident who may have fallen on hard times. A jar for P.J. had been put out the day she was hit by a car, and had been emptied, daily – the money set aside for PJ's medical expenses. The truckers who visited the café regularly were especially generous with their donations. In the two weeks since PJ had been hit, the café had collected over $2,500.

Joe and Bernard were helping Doug by cleaning off the tables so that those customers waiting in the parking lot could quickly fill vacated seats. They were working side by side when Doug walked over to them. "I haven't seen Jason since he left here earlier today – have either of you heard from him?"

Joe shook his head. "Not me — sorry, Doug."

Bernard filled his tray with empty dishes and wiped the table clean. He looked over at Doug and asked, "Wasn't he supposed to visit Skipper today?"

Doug nodded. "Yes, that's where he was headed when he left here. One of our regular customers — Mr. Zimmerman — offered to drop him off at the Detention Center, but I thought for sure he would be back here by now. It's already dark outside."

Joe did his signature end-zone wiggle and grinned. "Maybe he had a *date!*"

"Yes, that could be where he's at," Bernard agreed. "He and Miss Crennan seem to have hit it off with each other, wouldn't you say?"

"I thought of that," Doug replied. He looked out the large front, glass window at the crowded parking lot. "He didn't say anything about going over there tonight, though." He shook his head and smiled. "I'm probably worrying over nothing. I'm sure he's fine."

"Well, it's only six-thirty," Bernard returned Doug's smile. "I'm sure that Jason will find some way to get a message to us if he doesn't plan on returning to the café tonight."

Doug looked over at Bertie, who was standing by the kitchen door talking to Max. He knew that the two of them had probably heard his conversation with Joe and Bernard. He couldn't quite decipher the expression on Bertie's face, so he excused himself and moved swiftly toward the kitchen. "What?" he asked when he reached Bertie and Max.

"I'm not sure," Max's smooth baritone whispered in reply. "Something is happening — right now — but, for some reason, I'm not getting a good reading on what it might be."

"Or who it might be happening to," Bertie chimed in. "Since Jason isn't here, I'm guessing it might involve him. You really haven't heard anything from him since he visited Skipper this afternoon?"

Doug shook his head. "Not a word."

The three angels bent their heads in a quick, silent prayer. "Amen..." Doug whispered.

Ernest Blankenship parked his car in the driveway and entered the kitchen via the garage entry. The first thing he saw was Prissy, leaning on the kitchen counter, loading dishes into the dishwasher. "Prissy!" he spoke loudly.

The old woman's hearing wasn't what it used to be, so she had not heard him drive up or enter the kitchen; but, his loud voice startled her so much that she dropped the china plate she had been holding between her bony fingers. The plate broke into a dozen pieces as it hit the hard, Italian white Carrara marble flooring. Her hand flew to her heart and she gasped. "Oh, sweet, Jesus! I didn't hear you come in, Mr. Blankenship, sir. You done scared me to death, yes sir, you did..."

Ernest stopped her as she started to get down on her knees to pick up the broken china. "I'm so sorry, Prissy. I never meant to scare you. Come on now, get up — leave that mess to me — I'll take care of it. What I want to know is why you are out of bed? You promised me when I left this morning that you would rest today."

Prissy shook her head and held onto the arm he offered. "Yes, sir, but..."

"I don't want to hear any more about this, Prissy. I insist you go to your room, and I don't want to see you lifting your hand to do anything until you're feeling better and have your strength back. Elizabeth would never forgive me for letting something happen to you. Go on now, do as I say."

Prissy sighed and nodded. "I am a bit tired, yes I am. Okay, then," she began moving slowly toward her room down the small hallway. "But you let me know if you need anything, Mr. B., okay?"

Ernest pointed toward her room. "Go, Prissy — rest!"

He waited until he heard her bedroom door shut before

he took off his coat and hung it on one of the hooks beside the kitchen door. He rolled up the sleeves of his white, Maison Margiela shirt and walked back over to the kitchen sink. He was down on his knees, picking up large chunks of glass, when the kitchen door opened. He assumed it would, most likely, be Kirk coming home from whatever activity he had found to do since there was no school today. He tried, but failed, to hide his disappointment when he saw that it was his wife, Rae, coming in. He had not even noticed that her car wasn't in the garage when he arrived home.

Rae had been so sure that she would make it home from her afternoon tryst with her latest boy-toy, before her husband did, so she was more than a little surprised to find Ernest's car in the driveway and him kneeling on the kitchen floor. She recognized the look of undisguised dismay on his face when he first saw her. "For goodness sake, Ernest! Whatever are you doing on your knees?"

Ernest didn't offer an immediate response; instead, he returned his attention to the broken glass.

"That's my good china!" Rae shrieked. "You broke my good china!" She moved quickly toward him.

"Stay back, Rae!" he ordered. He knew he sounded gruffer than he intended to sound. "It can be replaced, don't worry. It was accident."

Rae placed her hands on her hips and looked around the untidy kitchen. "Where's Prissy? She's slacking off again, isn't she?" She removed her fur coat and let it drop to the floor. "I'm going to give her a good piece of my mind," she threatened as she walked around her husband.

Ernest stood up and dropped the broken glass into the trash receptacle. "Sit down, Rae," he spoke more softly this time. "Prissy isn't well. I told you this morning that she wasn't feeling well and that she needed to rest."

Rae dropped into a chair and crossed her arms over her chest. "If she gets any more rest, she'll be dead," she murmured beneath her breath.

Ernest pretended not to hear his wife's retort about

Prissy. "I didn't see Kirk's car. Do you know where he is?"

Rae rolled her eyes and sighed. "He left a note for you in his room. Prissy put it there, on the kitchen table, but—no—I do not know where your son is today." She grabbed the note and held it out toward her husband. "He's almost 17 years old, and he doesn't make any effort whatsoever to inform his wicked stepmother of his daily schedule." She knew she was being too snippy with her husband and that she needed to do whatever was necessary to remain in his good graces; but, she had been unceremoniously dumped by the young, virile man she had spent the afternoon with, and she was not happy at having to find a suitable replacement for him.

Ernest washed his hands and folded the dish rag neatly. It had been a long day, and he wasn't in the mood to argue with his wife. He took the note from her and said, "A simple *NO* would have sufficed."

Rae sighed deeply and turned to walk up the back stairs that lead to their master suite and four other bedrooms. "I need a long bath." She caressed his arm as she passed by him. "If you care to join me, I might consider forgiving you for breaking my good china."

Ernest didn't respond. Instead, he sat down at the kitchen table and opened the sealed note his son had left for him. The note simply stated that Kirk would be staying with his friend David for the long weekend. Ernest lowered his head into his hands for a moment before taking out his cell phone. He wasn't surprised when his son failed to answer his call, but he left a message for him anyway. "Hi, Kirk—it's Dad. I got your note. I was hoping the two of us could have done something together this weekend. We haven't been up to the lake house in years, and, well—I don't know—I guess I just thought that maybe it was time we opened it up again. Okay, then—well, maybe another weekend. Stay safe this weekend, son. Call me if you need anything. I love you…"

Rae stood at the top of stairs, eavesdropping on her

husband's call to his son. She tucked her thick, auburn hair behind her ears and thought, *"Lake house? You've never mentioned a lake house — maybe I should check this out. It wouldn't do for there to be any secrets between us, husband dear. After all, what's yours will be all mine, in the end."*

Cheryl retrieved two large pizza boxes from the back seat and made her way to the side door that led into her small, cozy kitchen. It was 7:15 and most of the lights were on in the kitchen and family room. She knew that Jason had planned on stopping by tonight to spend some time with Jimmy, and she hoped she wouldn't be interfering with their time together. She had not expected to get off work as early as she did.

She pushed open the kitchen door and yelled out, "Jimmy! I'm home, and I have food!" The first thing she noticed was how quiet the house seemed — not at all what she had expected. "Jimmy?"

She heard the flushing sound of the toilet from down the hall and turned to see Jason coming toward her. "Jason — hi! I was hoping you would make it tonight. Listen, it's still so cold outside, so if you want to bunk down on the sofa again tonight, it will be fine..." She stopped when she suddenly realized that the two of them were alone in the house. If her son had been here, there would definitely have been more noise in the house. "Where's Jimmy?" She shivered involuntarily.

"Hello to you, too," Jason smiled. "Sorry, I needed to use your facilities, and nobody was here when I arrived."

"Jimmy wasn't here?"

"No," Jason shook his head. "The back door was unlocked when I got here, and the lights were on in the kitchen and living room. I didn't look at it," he pointed to the note on the table, "But, it looks like he might have left you a note. Maybe he had an errand to run. I hope you don't mind that I let myself in?"

"No, of course not." Cheryl pulled back the kitchen chair and gasped when Jimmy's cell phone clattered to the floor. "That's his phone," she said, a perplexed expression filling her face. "He never goes anywhere without that phone. It's usually attached to his ear." She inserted the ear piece into her own ear. Mo Pitney's song, 'Let Me Tell You About Country' was playing. She sat down at the table and read the note her son had left for her.

Jason watched while the blood seemed to slowly drain from Cheryl's ruddy cheeks. "What's the matter, Cheryl? You look like you've seen a ghost."

Cheryl held out the note for him, but was unable to speak.

"Okay, now you're scaring me," Jason said as he took the note and read it. "I don't get it. What's wrong? He says he's hanging out with his friends for the weekend. Is this something out of the norm for him?"

Cheryl released a long breath and shook her head. "He doesn't really have any friends that he would want to spend the entire weekend with, and, besides—he knew that you might be coming over tonight. He was so excited for the two of you to have some alone time together."

"That's okay, we can do it another time." Jason was still confused as to why this information would appear to be so upsetting to her. "It's no big deal, really."

Cheryl was shaking her head. A single tear finally broke free and eased slowly down her cheek. "You don't understand, Jason. Something is wrong—something is terribly, terribly wrong."

Jason stood behind her, helpless to understand what she was talking about. He placed his hands on her shoulders and leaned forward. "No, I don't understand. Please...tell me what's wrong."

Cheryl pointed at the XOXOXXX that took the place of her son's signature. "It's that."

"Doesn't that mean something like hugs and kisses?" Jason's grip on her shoulders loosened a little.

Cheryl shook her head. "No...not for us, it doesn't. It's a code, Jason—a code that Jimmy and I concocted a few years ago. The three Xs at the end—that's the secret code we agreed upon—a code to let the other one know that something was wrong—that the other one of us needed help."

She held out the cell phone. "The code would have been enough, but he left his cell phone—what teenager goes anywhere without his or her cell phone. It was sort of *hidden* on the seat of this chair—the chair was pushed under the table." She looked up at Jason and trembled. "He would NEVER go anywhere without this phone."

"Damn," Jason responded, almost to himself. He forgot all about the need to call Officer O'Brady and provide the information regarding Stella's whereabouts. He flopped down in the chair next to Cheryl and stared into her desperate, pleading eyes. "Damn..."

# CHAPTER 23

## Settling In

The first thing that Jimmy noticed when they pulled around to the back of the house, was that there were lights were on in the basement. He wondered—hoped— if someone else might be there, or if Kirk was throwing one of his infamous parties. There were no other cars at the house, but it was still fairly early for a party to begin. Nobody offered him any explanations as to why they were at the house—nor, did he bother to ask.

Jimmy had remained quiet and did everything he was ordered to do; he helped unload a large amount of food, mostly snacks, from the Land Cruiser. He helped load the cabinets and refrigerator with enough snacks to last at least a couple of weeks; the volume of food and toiletries gave Jimmy more reason for concern that this might be more than just a weekend getaway for the three friends.

It was almost eight-thirty by the time Kirk locked the Land Cruiser and told everyone to get inside. The night sky was clear, full of stars and a full moon, but the temperature had begun to drop noticeably by seven-thirty, and Jimmy's thin jacket did little-to-nothing to keep him warm. He stood by one of the lit fireplaces and rubbed his hands together. "What's the matter, little boy?" Michael giggled. "You're not cold are you? 'Cause we wouldn't want you to freeze to death...at least, not just yet." He giggled again, grabbed a beer from the refrigerator and flopped down on one of the luxurious, leather sofas. "You may as well take a load off, kid — you're going to be here for a while."

Jimmy looked back and forth among the three older boys. "Is this about what happened to that homeless man? If it is, I told all of you that I wouldn't say anything — and, I haven't."

"Not even to your pretty mama?" Kirk sneered. "Please tell me that you have, so that I'll have a good excuse to go snatch her, too."

"My mom doesn't know anything about what happened that night," Jimmy's voice dropped to almost a whisper.

"What's that? Speak up, pretty boy — I'm not sure Kirk heard you," Michael grinned and propped both feet up on the heavy, wooden coffee table.

Jimmy cast a quick glance at David, who had not spoken a single word since they left the Crennan cottage.

David was quick to look away, but not quick enough for Kirk not to notice.

"What are you looking at David for?" he asked in a low growl. "What? Do you think he's going to help you get out of this? Well, he's not. We're all in this together." Kirk turned his back to all of them and stared out of the massive sliding glass door, into the black night. The water from the lake shimmered beneath the moonlight, and Kirk allowed an old memory of his mom — standing at this very door, looking out at that very lake under the moonlight — to interrupt his thoughts for a quick moment. He turned slowly back around and glared at David. "Isn't that right, David?"

David held Kirk's glare. "I told you that we were all in this together, and that we would have your back, no matter what you decided to do to them."

Jimmy's head snapped around. "Them? You've got me—I told you to leave my mom out of this!"

Michael jumped up from the sofa and ordered, "Get over here, Crennan, and sit down and shut up."

"You said *them*," he stared at David. "Who did you mean?"

Kirk walked slowly toward Jimmy. "Do as Michael said—sit down and shut up. Relax, it's not your precious mommy David was talking about." He nodded at David and said, "You may as well bring her out; with any luck, maybe she had a heart attack and died while we were gone."

Jimmy sat down on the sofa next to Michael. His brain was doing double-time trying to figure out who else might be in the house with them. He watched David make his way to a closed door in the far corner of the room. He had not noticed the door before, but now he saw the dim light coming from beneath it.

David entered the master suite and closed the door behind him.

"Who's in there?" Jimmy asked. "Who else have you dragged into this mess?"

"I wouldn't call it a mess," Kirk grinned. "But, we do have all the major participants here now. I'm sure you'll recognize the rest of our little party when you see her, Crennan."

Jimmy heard something heavy being dragged across the floor and jerked his head back toward the room that David had entered. He stood up from the couch, but Michael pushed him back down.

"Nobody said that you could get up, Crennan," Michael giggled. He shrugged when Kirk gave him the evil eye. "What? There's nothing wrong in having a little fun, is there? You're way too serious these days, Kirkie."

Kirk shook his head and pointed his finger at Michael. "Don't ever call me that again."

"Oops—my bad!" Michael whispered, holding his index

finger to his puckered lips. "I forgot—that was your mama's nickname for you—sorry, man."

Jimmy was straining his neck to see over the high-back sofa, but it only took him a few seconds to recognize Stella when she walked into the light.

David cupped the old woman's elbow, to assist her into the main room.

"Don't touch me!" Stella growled in her shrill, raspy voice. "Haven't you done enough already?"

David released her elbow but stayed a couple of steps behind her, close enough to catch her if she fell.

"Oh, hell!" Michael giggled again. "Look—she didn't die while we were gone." He let out an exaggerated, insincere sigh.

"It's going to take more than a bunch of snotty-nosed, rich kids to kill me!" Stella's cracked voice didn't match her feigned bravado.

"Sit down, old lady," Kirk instructed. "Next to him," he motioned to the sofa that Jimmy occupied.

Jimmy saw the bruise that had formed quickly on the old woman's face. "What did you do to her?" His voice shook with anger more than fear.

Michael jumped up off the sofa so that Stella could sit next to Jimmy.

Stella dragged the long chain with her and sank into the plush sofa. She turned and stared hard at Jimmy. "Who are you? I don't remember you being there the night these three killed poor Norman."

Kirk took three steps forward and glared at the old woman. "Oh, he was there alright. Jimmy-boy was our lookout guy, you might say."

Stella continued to stare at Jimmy. "You're younger than them." She nodded slowly and squinted her eyes, almost as if she were remembering that night all over again. "Yeah, there was a fourth one, but you were too far away. I couldn't make out your face."

Jimmy shook his head and glared at Kirk. "What are you

doing, Kirk? Why is she here? Why am I here? What are you going to do to us?" For the first time since they arrived at the lake house, he was beginning to think that he might be there longer than just the weekend. For the first time, he was beginning to think that he might not be leaving the lake house alive.

Kirk propped a leg on top of the coffee table and removed his knife from the sheath attached to his ankle. He dropped his foot to the floor. His move toward them was slow and deliberate. He watched Jimmy and the old woman closely and smiled. It was not a friendly smile. "Yeah...about that..."

Thomas O'Brady pulled into the Heavenly Grille Café parking lot at 9:00; the flashing neon marque indicated that the café was open until 11:00. It had been a long day, and he had stayed late to complete a week's worth of paper work. He could have done it at home, but he never liked to take his work home with him. He always did his best to keep his work life and home life separate; he felt that he owed that to his wife and children.

His wife had been in bed all day with the flu, and her sister had·been with her, taking care of the 6-year old twin boys, who both looked like miniature versions of their father. He had called home before he left and offered to stop and pick up some vegetable soup from the café that everyone at work had been talking about. He knew that his boys would be in bed asleep, but he thought the soup might help his wife, Dottie, feel better.

A lot of the late-night customers had placed orders to go, so there were a few empty tables when Thomas walked through the front door. He looked above his head and smiled when he heard the angel chimes sound.

Max saw the policeman enter the café and grinned down at Bertie, who was standing beside him. "Hey, look, Bertie—fresh bait!" He laughed out loud and took the anticipated punch to his shoulder. "He doesn't look familiar to me."

Bertie stood on her tip toes and peered through the serving hatch. "Hmmm...nope, I don't believe I've seen him in here before. A cop, huh?" She punched Max again and grinned. "What kind of trouble have you gotten yourself in now, big fella?"

Doug greeted the police officer and offered him the corner booth. "I'll bring you some coffee, Officer. Someone will be right over to take your order."

"Thank you," Thomas replied, removing his hat and placing it next to him on the comfortable bench seat. He looked around at the scattering of people, all of whom seemed extremely serious about the food they were eating. He didn't see any menus on the tables, but the enticing aromas quickly engulfed him—reminding him, that he had not eaten anything since breakfast. He saw a short, energetic woman coming toward him. He tried not to laugh at the bouncing halo headband that bobbled furiously with each step she took.

"Well, hello there!" Bertie grinned. "I haven't seen you in here before, Officer. The name is Bertie. What would yours be?"

Thomas would have sworn that he was talking to the late actress, Shirley Booth. The resemblance between the character, "Hazel," she played, and this spunky waitress was simply uncanny. He grinned and started to stand up for a proper introduction.

Bertie pushed him back down. "There's no need for chivalry here, but I do appreciate the effort, believe me. I swear, the young men of today—you would think hell would freeze over before they opened a door for a lady, wouldn't you?" She leaned down and punched him on his right shoulder. She looked at his name tag. "O'Brady, huh? You got a first name, Officer O'Brady?"

Thomas rubbed the back of his head and grinned again. He liked this woman, and he immediately felt right at home at the Heavenly Grille Café. "Yes, ma'am—it's Thomas."

"Tom, huh?" Bertie punched him again.

He rubbed his shoulder and shook his head. "No, ma'am—I prefer to go by Thomas—not Tom. I never cared much for having people's given names shortened." He grinned at her again. "So, is Bertie short for something else?"

Bertie raised her brows and nodded. "It is, but we won't get in to that right now." She sensed Doug behind her. "Here's Doug—that's short for Douglas—with your coffee, but I'll get the rest of your order for you."

Thomas shrugged. "Okay...do you have a menu? I was hoping to take some vegetable soup home to my wife. She's down with the flu and some folks at work said this place had the best vegetable soup they've ever tasted."

Doug placed the large coffee mug on the table and provided a small metal pitcher filled with cream, and another small metal bowl filled with sugar cubes. Angel wings were etched into each bowl. "It's fresh—just made it. Enjoy your meal, officer." He turned to leave but leaned down and whispered into Bertie's ear, "Be nice, or Max will have him arrest you!"

Bertie reached behind her and swatted Doug on what most women agreed was his best feature; she couldn't have reached his broad shoulder at this angle if she had wanted to. She turned back to the police officer and rested one hand on her ample hip. "Vegetable soup is a staple here, especially in the winter time, so that's an easy one; but, I don't think soup is going to cut it for you. A man your size needs some real food. About a menu—we don't fool with them. I can usually look at someone and tell what they need or want to eat."

"Is that so?" Thomas shook his head and smiled. "What do you think I need or want?"

"Well, you're in luck, because Max made his famous stuffed cabbage today."

"Stuffed cabbage?"

"Don't tell me you've never had stuffed cabbage before?" Bertie punched him again on the shoulder. "Trust me, if you love cabbage, sausage, ground beef, tomatoes, and sauerkraut, then you're going to love Max's stuffed cabbage. The rolls are pretty big, but I think you should be able to eat about three of them. They come with loaded mashed potatoes and stir-fried green beans with bacon and onion in them. Oh, and today's dessert is Max's famous, seven-layer coconut-crème cake—first time he's made it since we opened this location. You'll think you've died and gone to Heaven when you taste it." She raised her brows in query. "Sound good to you?"

Thomas's mouth was watering just hearing about the meal. "Yes, ma'am—it all sounds fine; but, if you could make all that to go, I'd appreciate it. I'd like to get that soup home to my wife before she turns in for the night."

The ringing of his cell phone interrupted his conversation with the waitress. It was dispatch saying he had an important phone call. They patched the call through to him just as Bertie turned to leave.

"Yes—this is Officer O'Brady," Thomas began the conversation. "Who? Oh, yes—I do remember you, Mr. Benton—Jason, isn't it?"

Bertie made a sharp, 180-degree turn and went back to the officer's table. "Is that Jason Benton?"

Thomas was surprised and confused. He held up his index finger to silence Bertie and continued listening to what Jason Benton was telling him. He nodded after a couple of minutes and said, "I've got your location, yes. I have to make a quick stop first, but I should be able to get there within the hour. Yes—remain where you are. I will come to you. Good-bye."

Bertie exhibited much more patience than anyone would have thought she could, but she was about to burst. "We have a Jason Benton who lives in the apartment above the café. Nice-looking fella, in his early thirties, good manners…is that who you were talking to?"

"I'm not sure if we're talking about the same person or not, ma'am—Bertie—but, yes, your description does match that of the man I was talking to."

"We've been waiting for him to show back up here today, but nobody has heard from him since after breakfast. Is he alright?"

"He sounded fine," Thomas reported as he took out a pad and wrote down the address Jason had provided him. "He's at a friend's house and has some information he wanted to give me about a case…"

"You're talking about Skipper's case, aren't you?" Bertie asked excitedly. "That must mean that y'all are still looking into it then, that you're not convinced that Skipper did what that old biddy accused him of doing."

"I'm really not at liberty to discuss any of this with you—Bertie. I really need to get that soup home to my wife…"

Doug came walking toward them with three bags in his hands. "Here you go, Officer O'Brady. Please tell Jason that we're here if he needs us."

It did not escape Thomas that he had not shared his name, or his food order, with the young man who placed the bags of food on the table. He also wondered how the man called Doug knew about his call with Jason—he had been too far away to hear anything—but, he was in a hurry now, and didn't have the luxury of time to ask those questions. He reached into his back pocket for his wallet, but stopped when Bertie punched him on the shoulder for good measure.

"Your money is no good here. Now, go on—scoot! Go take care of your wife and go talk with our Jason. You tell him he needs to get back here and update us on what's going on, you hear me?"

"Yes, ma'am," Thomas smiled. "Thank you for the food. I'll be sure to pass along your message to Mr. Benton."

The angel chimes sounded again on his way out the

door, and he was still shaking his head in wonder when he pulled out of the parking lot. "No, that wasn't strange..." he exhaled and lifted the corner of his mouth in a half-smile. "Not strange at all."

# CHAPTER 24

## Missing Person Report

A car pulled into the Crennan driveway at 9:45; its headlights shone brightly into the kitchen where Cheryl and Jason still sat at the kitchen table.

Cheryl jumped up. "That must be him—the police officer you talked to." She jerked open the kitchen door before Thomas had a chance to knock on it. Cheryl's look of dismay was evident when she saw a man in street clothes smiling down at her. "Oh, I thought you were someone else. May I help you?"

Jason came to stand behind her and placed his hands on her shoulders; he gave them a gentle squeeze. "Cheryl, this is Officer Thomas O'Brady. He's off duty but offered to come over and talk to you about Jimmy. Officer O'Brady, this is Cheryl Crennan."

"Oh," Cheryl nodded. "Please, come inside Officer O'Brady. I thought they would send a real cop."

"Well," Thomas grinned as he stepped inside and looked around the small but homey kitchen. "I am a real cop, Mrs. Crennan. Our Dispatch operator patched Mr. Benton's call through to me when I was on my way home this evening. I took some food home to my wife, and changed clothes, while I was there; but, if you would rather talk to a *real* cop—one in uniform—I would be happy to have someone come out." He winked at Jason and smiled again.

'It's *Miss*, and I'm so sorry," Cheryl shook her head. "I didn't mean that you weren't a real copy; I guess I was just expecting someone in uniform. If you're off duty, then why are you here? They could have sent someone else, couldn't they?"

"They could have, Cheryl, but I specifically asked for Officer O'Brady when I called. Let's all sit down at the table," Jason offered. He guided Cheryl back to her seat. "We have a fresh pot of coffee made, Officer O'Brady. Would you like a cup?"

"No, thanks," Thomas shook his head. "It will keep me up all night and I'm off work for the rest of the weekend. I have rambunctious 6-year old twin boys to keep out of my wife's hair while she recuperates from the flu."

"You have sons?" Cheryl asked as she sat down and picked up Jimmy's cell phone and the note he left her. "Then you won't think I'm crazy to think that something has happened to my son, Jimmy." She waited for the officer to sit down and then passed him the note. "I found that on the table when I got home from work, almost two hours ago now.

Jason sat down next to Cheryl and waited for the officer to read the note. He had no doubt that O'Brady would have the same initial reaction that he had when he first read the note.

Thomas shook his head and stared at Cheryl. "You're obviously reading more into this note than what I am seeing, Miss Crennan. It sounds as though your son is staying with friends for the weekend. It says that he will be home on Sunday night."

Cheryl was shaking her head adamantly from side to side. "No, no—you don't understand. See the bottom of the note, where he has the XOXOXXX ? That's a code that the two of us came up with a few years ago."

"What kind of a code?" Thomas asked.

"A sort of secret warning code," Cheryl explained. "It was our way to let the other know that something was wrong." Cheryl handed Jimmy's cell phone to the officer. "Plus, Jimmy would never, ever leave this house without his cell phone."

"Most teenagers wouldn't," the officer agreed. "Still…anyone reading this would assume that it is what it appears to be—your son is spending the weekend with friends."

"You're not going to help me, are you?" Cheryl pushed up from the table. "Fine, then, please leave so that I can go look for my son myself!"

Thomas stood up and touched her shoulder. "I didn't say that I wasn't going to help you."

Jason ran his fingers over his buzz-cut head and exhaled. "Isn't there something that says we have to wait 24-to-48 hours before filing a missing person report? I mean, that's why I called you instead of reporting it right away. I thought there might be something you could do while we're waiting for enough time to lapse."

Thomas shook his head. "No, that whole 24-to-48 hour thing only happens on television and the movies. There is no waiting period required before filing a missing person report. No, as soon as you suspect a child or adult is missing, it should be reported to the police. I will call this report in myself before I leave here tonight."

Cheryl lunged toward the officer and wrapped her arms tightly around his waist. "Oh, thank you, thank you, thank you!" she cried against his shirt.

Thomas held Cheryl out at arms' length. "No thanks is necessary, Miss Crennan. I will need to keep the note, and Jimmy's cell phone. Maybe you could look through it and see if you recognize any names or numbers on it, so that we can follow up with some of his friends. I'll need a recent photo of him, also. If you could tell me what he was wearing when you last saw him, give me his height, weight, any identifiable birthmarks—that sort of thing."

Cheryl wiped away a tear from the corner of her eye and looked up at the kind officer with the red hair and green eyes. "Let me check his room. I know what he had on when I left for work, but he could have changed clothes. I have a good picture of him in my room. I'll be right back."

Jason waited until he knew that Cheryl was out of earshot. "I'm really sorry to have bothered you, but I didn't think it would be looked in to until after Sunday if we called it in to the police department."

"I'm glad you called," Thomas said. "May I ask what your involvement is with this family, Mr. Benton?"

Jason rubbed the back of his neck. "Well, long-story-short, I just found out a few days ago that Jimmy Crennan is my son."

"Really?" Thomas sat back down. "You had no idea?"

"Nope," Jason joined him at the table. "Trust me, it came as a total shock to me; but, Jimmy—he's a really good kid. He and his mom are really tight, too. If she said that he left her a warning code, then I have to believe that something isn't right."

Thomas nodded. "You said on the phone that you, also, had some information about Gordon Whiting's case."

Jason looked puzzled for a minute before he realized who the officer was talking about. "You mean, Skipper?" He looked past the officer and could see Cheryl moving about in her bedroom. "Yeah, I do. I was looking for Stella again in town earlier today, and I came across another homeless man who—how do I say this—shared a cardboard box with Stella at one time. He traded some information for food, and told me that Stella told him she was staying at some motel on the outskirt of town—near a bar called—the Pickled Possum."

"That's a bad side of town," O'Brady nodded. "The Roadway Inn—we get a couple of calls every weekend about fighting or shots fired at the Pickled Possum. So, the old man thinks Ms. Seiber might be staying at the Roadway, huh?"

"That's what he said," Jason confirmed. "I thought it might be worth a shot—that, maybe, you could check it out? I would have done it myself, but it's hard for me to get around with no car."

"It's an ongoing investigation, Mr. Benton, so you really need to stay out of it. If I can't get there myself this weekend, I'll have one of the other officers working the case to check it out. We really do need to talk to Ms. Seiber again. We have her taped recording of the events that happened the night that Norman Weissman was killed, but there are some parts of her story that we need to double check. Thank you for the information."

"Skipper's a decent guy," Jason added. "I admit, I don't know him all that well, but, I don't think he's the type of man who would kill anyone—especially another homeless person."

"Well, you and I both know that Mr. Whiting has indeed killed before, don't we?"

Jason's head snapped up and he stared hard at the officer. "That's true, but we both know that it only happened on a battlefield, too."

"I hope you're right about him," Thomas said. "I want to believe that, but, I still have to prove it, don't I...and, Stella Seiber may be the answer to that problem."

"Can I call you again—to see what you found out—about Stella?" Jason offered his hand to the officer.

Thomas shook Jason's hand and nodded. "You can call me anytime, Mr. Benton. I may not be able to tell you everything that's going on, but I will tell you whatever I can."

"Thank you for that," Jason sighed.

Cheryl ran back into the kitchen, holding a framed picture of Jimmy that she had taken during Christmas vacation. "He didn't take any of his clothes with him! None of his clothes are missing. His toothbrush is still in the bathroom. He didn't take *anything*!"

Skipper had been awake for an hour on Saturday morning, when he heard the intercom announce "CHOW TIME." He had been re-writing a poem he had started a couple of days ago. It was yet untitled, but read:

*As a six-year old, I still remember*
*When our soldiers came home from World War II;*
*They survived that hell, but our nation thanked them well*
*God bless the Red, White, and Blue.*

*I wanted to be a soldier, too.*

*The Korean War came along and took our boys again*
*Still too young, I watched them go on through;*
*They, too, served in hell, but our brave boys did well*
*God bless them, and our flag, too.*

*I still wanted to be a soldier, too.*

*My time finally came with the Vietnam War*
*A long-awaited time to fulfill my dreams to go;*
*We were marched, from home, straight to Satan's Dome*
*For whatever reason now, we may never know.*

*I am now a soldier and still proud to go.*

*I felt the presence of an angel on the battlefield*
*That would guide my torn, weary body home;*
*After ten years of war, we needed no more*
*On those fields where the gallant roam.*

*I wondered if a soldier could ever go back home.*

*Our flag still stands and is proudly flown*
*Amongst the dissenters and the brave;*

*When the winds diminished, the war was finally finished*
*While America turned its back on those who gave.*

*I don't want to be a soldier anymore.*

Skipper lay back down on his bunk and closed his eyes. He had been six years old when he saw his first soldier in uniform walking down the street he lived on in Ogdensburg, New York. He remembered how totally in awe he had been of the young soldier, and he knew in that very instant, that he would one day join the Army and be a solider himself. The happiest times of his life had been the twenty years he had proudly served his country—even though, he still felt that his country had betrayed him and all the other Vietnam Veterans who had left their homes and families to serve and protect the United States of America.

He opened his eyes when he heard his cell door automatically slide open. He got up and watched the line of men leaving their cells and moving down the hall toward the cafeteria. He had learned during one of his earlier jail sentences why the men always formed individual groups before entering the cafeteria—groups were usually broken down into blacks, Hispanics, Asians, and whites. The groups tended to stick to their own races because of "controlled movement"; once a prisoner got his tray of food, he was required to sit at the next available open table, wherever an open seat was available.

Skipper could have cared less what group he ate breakfast with—he didn't like any of them—so it really didn't matter who he had to sit next to. Unfortunately for him, it did matter to the leaders of the individual groups.

A hard-muscled black man spat on Skipper as he tried to get in line. It reminded Skipper of all the times he had been spat upon, while in uniform, upon returning from one of his tours in Vietnam. He turned to look at the black man. "That was a mistake."

The big black man went by the name of King Daddy.

Skipper had heard others refer to him as this and thought that it might, one day, make a good title for another poem. King Daddy was at least fifty years younger than he was, but Skipper didn't think the age difference would stop the younger man from retaliation; he didn't look like the type that would take any back-talk from an old, white man.

"What you say, 'ole geezer?" King Daddy snarled. "Git yoself in the back of da line, with the rest of yo white trash. You don't belong to this here group. Go on now, before I shank you."

A guard appeared at the front of the group. "Quiet! No talking in line."

King Daddy bumped Skipper in the shoulder before he moved forward. "I'll be watchin' you."

"Hope you enjoy the view," Skipper whispered as he made his way to the back of the line.

There was one table set aside for misfits—usually consisting of older men who didn't fit into their respective groups. Skipper could have cared less which group he sat with, but he found himself sitting at the last available table, surrounded by four other men who aged from sixty years and up.

He placed his tray on the table and sat down. He stirred the watery oatmeal—it was cold, again—and took a bite. There was no sugar in it, and he didn't dare pour any of the two cartons of skimmed milk into it; it was watered down enough as it was. His three pieces of toast were cold, so the two squares of margarine they were given didn't melt on them. He spread the two packages of grape jelly evenly over his toast. He pushed the oatmeal away and peeled an orange; the prisoners were given one piece of fruit with breakfast—nobody said it had to be fresh fruit. The inside of the orange was so dry that there wasn't even a hint of juice in it, but Skipper ate it anyway.

An old Mexican named Chico sat across from Skipper and rolled his eyes in both directions to make sure nobody was watching. "If you ain't gonna eat that oatmeal, I'd be happy to take it off your hands."

Skipper nodded his head and the old man pulled the bowl onto his plate. He watched the old man lift the bowl to his thin, cracked lips and drink it down in a matter of seconds. He noticed that the other prisoners, sitting around the tables scattered throughout the room, all stared down at their food—seemingly careful not to make eye contact with him.

Skipper had finished the cup of diluted coffee and drank both containers of milk, as well as all his toast and the orange—all, within ten minutes. It wasn't much, but he didn't need much to sustain himself; he was certainly use to eating much less than this for breakfast. The misfit table was the last table, farthest away from the serving line and the guard who stood watch at the door. Skipper sat on the outside end of the table, with his back to the serving line and the other groups of prisoners. His left hand lay on top of the table, and he held his empty, plastic coffee mug in his right hand.

He never saw it coming, and he never felt any pain when King Daddy drove the shank deep into the top of his left hand.

There was very little blood.

"Stay outta my line, Geezer," King Daddy whispered as he ripped the shank out of Skipper's hand, and blood spurt across the table, spraying Chico's pudgy face.

# CHAPTER 25

## Saturday Morning Cartoons

Jimmy was awake but kept his eyes closed, and listened to the sounds of—*cartoons*—playing in the background. Homer and Marge Simpson were shouting at the top of their lungs for their three kids—Homer, Lisa, and Maggie—to get their butts out of bed and get ready for school.

The wood floor that he had been forced to sleep on was cold and hard, and the thin blanket they had thrown over him had done little to keep him warm during the night. If he hadn't been lying in front of one of the huge fireplaces, Jimmy thought he might have frozen to death. He tried to turn from his curled position onto his back, but the sound of the heavy chain dropping against the wood floor made him stop abruptly.

"You may as well open your eyes—I know you're awake."

Jimmy recognized David's voice and actually felt relieved to hear it. Maybe Kirk and Michael had left during the night, leaving David in charge. He pushed himself to a sitting position and saw David sitting on the couch with a heavy, wool blanket wrapped around him. "It's really cold in here," he shivered involuntarily.

"Yeah, I know. Kirk and Mike are checking the furnace. The pilot light probably went out during the night. This place hasn't been used in a long time."

"Where are we?" Jimmy pulled the thin blanket tighter around his shoulders.

David walked across the room to a small utility closet in the tiny kitchen/bar area. He pulled a heavy, Army-wool blanket from the shelf and brought it to Jimmy. "Here — take this. I would've given it to you last night if I knew the furnace was going to shut off."

"Thanks," Jimmy shivered again as he double-wrapped himself in the large blanket. He stood up and sat down on the rock ledge next to the fireplace. "I don't know what's going on here, David, but..."

David held up his hand to silence him. He looked nervously around the room. "They can come back at any time, so trust me — you don't want to be asking a bunch of questions when they do."

"Okay, no questions, but..."

"What part of *no questions* don't you understand, kid? You have no idea what Kirk is capable of doing. Ever since his mother died, he's become a totally different person. I really thought he was just bringing you and the old woman up here to scare you a little — to make sure you knew that he meant business about keeping your mouths shut."

"So...you don't think he's just trying to scare us anymore? What else would he do to us?"

"Don't you get it, kid?" David paced around the basement area, checking the small staircase that led to the upper level periodically to make sure the others weren't coming back down. "Kirk is like — I don't know — paranoid or something. He's afraid that you and the old woman — knowing what you know — will jeopardize the plans he has for his future."

"We both promised not to say anything," Jimmy began. "I can't vouch for the old woman, but I've kept my mouth shut, and I have no intentions of talking to anyone about what happened. I'm not exactly proud of the part I had in it."

David shook his head and walked into the kitchen area. He grabbed two bottles of orange juice from the refrigerator and offered one to Jimmy. He sat down next to him on the hearth. "I don't think your promises mean anything to him anymore..."

"Well, well! Isn't this cozy?" Kirk's sarcastic tone carried downward from his position at the top of the staircase. "Why don't you offer him a Danish while you're at it, David?"

David jumped up quickly and moved away from Jimmy. "He just woke up. I thought he might be thirsty."

Kirk stared back and forth between David and Jimmy. He had not heard any of their conversation, but the sight of the two of them sitting next to each other on the hearth unnerved him. He couldn't afford for David to become caring and sensitive toward his prisoners. "Yeah, whatever, now get away from him and go check on the old woman."

"I checked on her about thirty minutes ago, before Jimmy woke up. She's sound asleep." David tried to keep his tone even and sure.

"Check on her again," Kirk ordered. "Michael had to drive into town to find a part we need for the furnace."

"Sure, okay..." David walked across the room and entered the master suite. He closed the door behind him.

Kirk walked down the stairs and poured himself a cup of coffee. He actually hated the bitter taste, but thought it made him appear to be more grown-up—more in control of the situation. "There's another half-bath past the kitchen, Crennan, if you need to take a piss or wipe away your tears."

Jimmy almost declined the offer, but had second thoughts. Maybe he could find a weapon of some sort in the bathroom. "Thanks. Over there?" He headed toward the kitchen.

"Yeah, but leave the door open," Kirk instructed. "Hey, don't think that I haven't noticed that you forgot to bring any clothes with you. Was that on purpose? Did you think it might be a signal for your mom, or something?"

"No—it wasn't on purpose," Jimmy said as he dragged the long chain with him, and walked past Kirk; the half-bath was almost the size of the Crennan's entire kitchen. He glanced around quickly at the double sink, a corner shower stall, a commode, and two dressing tables; he didn't see anything that could be used as a weapon. "She won't even notice that I didn't take a change of clothes, trust me." He really did have to use the rest room, so he unzipped his jeans and proceeded to take care of business. When he finished, he dragged the chain to the sink and washed his hands. Plush, monogramed towels lined both sides of the sinks, and he quickly wiped his hands on them—they were dusty, like they had been hanging there for a long time. Another quick glance around the bathroom re-confirmed his initial thought that there was nothing that would be useful as a weapon.

Kirk had thrown more wood on the fire while Jimmy had been in the bathroom. He glanced up when David exited the master suite. "Is she still alive?"

"She's breathing," David replied, "But the cut on her arm looks like it might be getting infected. I took the bandage off to look at it; it's all red and puffy."

Kirk had not intended on hurting anyone with his knife the night before—he only meant to scare his two prisoners—but, the old woman had freaked out when she saw it and lunged at him. He had attempted to push her away from him, and cut her on her forearm when David and Michael jumped in to drag her off him. "Serves the old bitch right," he murmured.

"Where's the kid? You didn't..." David whispered feverishly just before Jimmy walked out from the half-bath.

Kirk stared at David and shook his head. "I'm beginning to think I've had you pegged all wrong. I thought you had more balls than this. What are you going to do when it comes time to do what has to be done? Tell me, David!"

David pursed his lips together and clenched his teeth. "I've told you before that I will do whatever it takes— whatever you feel we need to do."

"Well, if that's true, then I suggest you stop trying to be best friends with Jimmy-Boy here, and quit worrying about that old hag in there. Trust me, if she could have gotten that knife away from me last night, none of us might be here this morning. That old woman is crazy as hell."

"I don't think she's crazy," Jimmy injected, as he stepped from the bathroom into the kitchen area. "I think she's just scared, that's all."

"Nobody asked you!" Kirk yelled. "Now, go sit back down and finish watching your damn cartoons!"


Thomas O'Brady couldn't get Jimmy Crennan or Stella Seiber off his mind. He had tossed and turned the night before, and finally went to sleep on the couch so that Dottie might get some much-needed rest. By ten o'clock, he had fed and dressed his twin Tasmanian devils and had them busy building a super hero out of their Lego blocks; he figured that would give him at least an hour to go over his notes. He had called in a missing person report on Jimmy Crennan the night before, but he had kept the new information about Stella to himself. He wanted to personally check out the Roadway Inn to see if she was, indeed, living there. He had called his sister-in-law and pleaded with her to babysit the boys for a few hours while he checked out a lead on his case.

Thomas glanced at his watch. His sister-in-law should be arriving at any moment and he needed to check on his wife.

Dottie beat him to it. She had pulled on a robe and was standing behind him when he placed his notes on the coffee table and stood up. "Good morning, handsome. Thank you so much for the vegetable soup you brought home last night. I don't know what they put in it, but it must have contained a miracle cure, because I feel more like myself this morning than I have in over a week. Where did you find vegetable soup so late at night?"

Thomas walked behind the couch and embraced the love of his life. He kissed the top of her head and held her at an arm's distance to get a better look at her. "Well, I do believe I see some color in those beautiful cheeks." He kissed her cheek and led her to the sofa. "Have a seat, Babe. The boys are playing with their blocks and Belinda is on her way over to watch them for a few hours—I hope you're not mad that I called her again."

"You're supposed to be off work this weekend, Thomas," Dottie sighed. "If you're not careful and don't slow down a little, you're going to be the one laid up for a week." She sat down on the couch. "So, where *did* you find that delicious soup?"

"Oh, it's a new café that opened up at the edge of town, by the overpass. I think it's called the Heavenly Grille Café. I'll have to take you and the boys there when you get well. The food is the best I've ever tasted."

"Better than mine?" Dottie teased. She knew better than anyone how much her husband loved and appreciated a good meal.

"Don't shoot the messenger!" Thomas teased back. "Seriously, though, you've got to try it, and you've got to meet the waitress who works there. Her name is Bertie and she is really something."

"Oh, should I be jealous?"

Thomas laughed out loud. "I'll let you be the judge of that when you meet her." He began gathering up his notes and placing them in his satchel. "I promise—I won't be gone long. I should be home by two o'clock, at the latest."

"What are you working on that's taking you away from us today?"

"A missing 14-year old boy—I called it in last night, but I promised the mother that I would check back in with her

208

today. I, also, have to follow up on a lead I received last night—it has to do with the murder of that homeless man a couple of weeks ago."

Dottie nodded. "I remember that one, but, I thought you said it was pretty much an open and shut case. Something about a witness that came forward and identified the murderer, right?"

"That's the one, yes," Thomas replied, "But, I can't shake the feeling that we've locked up the wrong person for that murder. I've talked to the suspect several times; he's another homeless man, but, he's also a decorated Vietnam Veteran."

"Oh, really? You didn't tell me that," Dottie tucked her legs beneath her and took a sip of the coffee left over in her husband's mug. "What makes you think he's innocent?"

"You would have to meet him, Dottie. Once you met him, and talked to him for a bit, I think you would agree with me. I've been doing some research on Vietnam Vets ever since I first met Skipper—his real name is Gordon Whiting—and, he's homeless by choice. I wouldn't be surprised if he doesn't have more money stashed away than you and I will ever make in this life time."

"You know, I remember a research paper I worked on back in college; it was about the Vietnam War, and, there were some pretty depressing statistics to wade through."

Thomas nodded. "Indeed." He pulled out one of the papers on which he had scribbled some notes. "Like these…let's see…there were 2,709,918 Americans who served in Vietnam, and, there are less than 850,000 estimated to be alive today; the youngest one would be around 54 years old; 390 of these Veterans die every single day; there were 7,484 women who served in Nam—of course, almost 84% of them were nurses—but, they were still there; there were 47,378 hostile deaths, 10,800 non-hostile deaths; the average age of the soldiers that died hostile deaths was only 23 years old—there were actually five killed in Nam who were only 16 years old!"

"Oh, my goodness!" Dottie laughed softly. "You have

been doing some research, haven't you, Thomas?"

Thomas grinned. "I couldn't help it. The more I talked to Skipper, the more I felt the need to understand him. Part of me acknowledges that it's probably because I never got to know my own father who died in Vietnam. Anyway, Skipper writes the most poignant poetry you've ever read..." His cell phone beeped and he grinned again. "Officer O'Brady, here."

Dottie watched the transformation on her husband's face—from one of pure joy as he talked about Skipper's poetry, to one of shock, disbelief, and anger—in that order. She waited until he ended the call before asking, "Thomas, what's wrong?"

"That was Madge from Dispatch. She called to tell me that Skipper was stabbed, during breakfast, at the prison this morning."

"Oh, no...honey, I'm so sorry. Go on—leave now—you don't have to wait for Belinda. I'll be fine until she gets here."

Thomas appeared to be torn, as he struggled with his decision. He finally nodded, grabbed his badge and gun, kissed his wife, and was out the door within thirty seconds.

# CHAPTER 26

## PJ Has a Breakthrough

Doug followed slowly behind Joe and Bernard as they made their way through the hospital parking lot and entered the main lobby to Floyd Medical Center.

"I hate hospitals," Joe shuddered. "Every time, when one of my players got hurt and I had to visit them in the hospital, I felt like death was following me around every corner." He shuddered again.

"Well, it's just the opposite for me," Bernard laughed good-naturedly. "I actually worked as a pharmacist *inside* one of our local hospitals. I always thought the reason my wife wanted me to own my own pharmacy was because it would mean more money available to her and the kids to blow and buy all those meaningless items they were always buying—I think that's why I stayed put, working in the hospital. It was more to aggravate my wife than it was anything else; but, I have to agree with you, Joe. There were many days when the smell of death would be so overwhelming that I thought it was going to tap me on the shoulder and say, '*Okay, you're next!*'."

Doug motioned them to the elevators and shook his

head. "Well, I'm sure that PJ will be glad to see you both, and thankful for the sacrifice you both are making by entering this building of doom and death."

"Do we sound that bad?" Joe grinned as the doors closed and the elevator advanced one floor. He gasped and held his breath when the doors opened and an orderly stood on the other side, beside a gurney. All Joe saw was the still form beneath a white sheet. He quickly pushed the CLOSE button and yelled, "Sorry, you'll have to catch the next one—we're in a real hurry!"

The door closed and Bernard looked down at his friend. "I cannot believe you just did that, Joe."

Doug smiled at them both and nodded. "There was plenty of room, Joe, and we're not exactly in all that big of a hurry."

Joe's eyes grew wide and he shook his head feverishly from side to side. "Didn't you see what he was pushing? It was a dead body! I don't know about you two, but I sure didn't want to be riding with Death in this closed elevator!"

"Oh, for goodness sake," Bernard sighed. "That, most certainly, was not a dead body! They wouldn't take the visitors' elevator to transport a dead body."

"They wouldn't?" Joe queried. "Are you sure about that? Because I sure as heck didn't see any breathing going on under that sheet!"

Doug laid a calming hand upon Joe's right shoulder. "It's true, Joe. The orderly would have used a service elevator to transport the body to the hospital's morgue. The patient may have been given a sedative, prior to testing, maybe."

Doug's touch had once again done its job. Joe felt his previous queasiness and nervousness dissipate as quickly as it had come upon him. He closed his eyes and exhaled slowly. "You're right—of course, you're right, Doug." He opened his eyes again when the door opened at PJ's floor. "Hey, did you tell PJ we were coming with you today?"

"No, I didn't," Doug winked. "I wanted it to be a surprise—not that she's going to remember who the two of you are, but you never know when a breakthrough will happen for her. I've talked about the two of you with her on my other visits, so she knows that all of you lived as a group at the camp ground for a while."

"Maybe we shouldn't have come," Joe whispered as they stood outside of PJ's room. "What if we screw things up with her memory or something?"

Bernard rolled his eyes and pushed his way in front of them through the open door. "Oh, for heaven's sake..."

PJ's roommate had been released earlier that morning, so she was alone in her hospital room. She was sitting in a chair that had been placed in front of the window. Her lunch tray had been placed on a rolling table in front of the chair and she was finishing her Jell-O when the door opened and a tall man walked through. Something about him seemed vaguely familiar; that vague memory brought a small smile to her face. "Hello..." she spoke softly. She let out a small sigh of relief when she saw Doug enter third, behind another man who, also, seemed vaguely familiar to her.

Doug moved around Joe and Bernard and crossed the room to where PJ sat in front of the window. He bent down and kissed the top of her head. "I hope we haven't interrupted your lunch, PJ. I've brought a couple of friends with me today. Do you recognize either of them?"

Bernard approached PJ first, bent down and took her left hand into his own. He kissed the top of her hand and smiled at her. "I'm so glad that you're healing, PJ. You may not remember me, but, my name is Bernard — Bernard Cartwright. We shared many camp fires together, you and I."

PJ allowed the tall, white man to kiss her hand. Something told her that this was probably the first time in her life that any man had actually kissed her hand. It was something she had only seen in old movies. "Hello, Bernard," she shook her head. "No, I'm sorry; I don't think I do remember you."

"Hey, he is pretty forgettable!" Joe laughed, as he made his way toward her. He performed his signature side-to-side, end zone dance before he stopped in front of her. "But, I'm sure you remember me, right, PJ?"

PJ gasped loudly and her hand flew to cover her mouth. She stared wide-eyed at Doug and pointed to Joe. A tear trickled down from the outside corner of her eye. She pointed at Joe and nodded. "Joe? Your name is Joe, isn't it?"

Saturday at lunch time was always an extra-busy time at the café. Bertie was busier than ever since Doug had taken Joe and Bernard with him to visit PJ at the hospital, but, by one o'clock the crowd had become more than manageable for her. She stood beside Max in the kitchen and sighed. "I think I like this new location, Maximus."

"So, you're not terribly disappointed that we didn't relocate to Rome, Italy, then?"

"I didn't say that!" she punched the seven-foot giant on the back of his left shoulder. "No, I would still like to meet the Pope one day, but, with the way things are going—I may just have to wait for the Rapture before that meeting ever takes place."

"Well, I'm glad that you're not too disappointed, Bertie." Max grinned down at her. "You have to admit, though; even small-town America has enough drama going on to keep things interesting and challenging for us."

"That's for sure!" Bertie grinned as she propped herself on her elbows and stared out at the lunch crowd. "There's definitely no shortage of drama and excitement in Rome, GA. By the way, I've been so busy, I forgot to ask Doug if he had heard anything from Jason this morning."

Max turned off the burner to the frying pan that was full of bubbling, country-fried steak and gravy. "Yes, Jason called Doug just before they left to go visit PJ. I listened in on the conversation."

"I was going to," Bertie nodded, "But, I was too busy

entertaining that little girl who came in with her father — the one who wanted to wear my halo — did you see her?"

"I did, yes," Max answered. "Do you think her father suspects that the child is sick?"

Bertie shook her head. "No, not yet, but, we both know that he's the one who will notice it first, and get her the help she needs — in time."

"He will," Max agreed. "I'm glad, too. So many parents these days are so wrapped up in the busyness of their lives that they can't see what's going on with their family — right before their very eyes."

Bertie stood up straight, stretching to her full 5'2" height. She rolled her shoulders and turned to face the former gladiator. "That's something I don't understand, Max. You know, I was only 26 when I died way back in 1911, but I can't imagine me not knowing what was going on in my children's lives. I mean, we were busy as hell, too — probably even busier than mothers today — but, I think I would have known immediately when something was wrong with one of my kids."

Max crossed his arms across his massive chest. "We've worked together for more than 50 years now, Bertie, and I admit — I know very little of what life was like for you when you were alive."

Bertie glanced through the serving hatch to make sure all her customers were still happy and filling their bellies before she looked back at Max. "Well, I'll admit, my life probably wasn't as exciting as yours. I mean, I certainly didn't spend my day killing lions and spilling guts all over some huge arena, but — it was as exciting as anyone else's life during that time, I suppose. I had to quit school in eighth grade to help my family with the farm, so when my husband married me, he always joked that I was *innocent of book learning*."

"Which means, you didn't finish school?"

"That's right, big fella; but trust me, getting that piece of paper doesn't guarantee that a person will be any smarter than anyone who didn't get it. You wouldn't believe how many college graduates I've met who didn't have the good sense it takes to come in out of the rain. Nope, I don't believe you need a piece of paper to prove that you're smart. I may have been *innocent of book learning*, but I had a helluva lot more common sense than most people I've met!"

Max's loud laugh filled the kitchen. "No doubt, Bertie, no doubt." He reached for a large pot to boil the noodles he needed for his famous macaroni and cheese casserole. "You lived on a farm, didn't you?"

"All my life," Bertie clicked her tongue. "All my life." She closed her eyes for a quick moment and smiled. "It was a hard life, Max, but it was a good life. We didn't have much, so there really wasn't all that much housework for me to do, so half my day would be spent helping my husband on our farm. I was healthy and strong, and we didn't have our kids right away, so there was plenty of time for me to help. I think that's when he became my best friend—you can learn an awful lot about a person when you're stinking sweat beside each other for almost ten hours a day, every day. I remember—I would get up around four o'clock most mornings, dress and tie my hair up in a bun, get the fire started in the kitchen, tend to the garden while the fire was heating up, sweep the floors, and then cook our breakfast."

"What did you like to eat, Bertie?"

"Oh, that's an easy one," Bertie laughed. "No doubt about it—I loved my grits, with scrambled eggs and bacon all mixed up in them. That's the kind of breakfast that would stick to your ribs, you know?"

Max nodded. "That explains why you're always first in line when cheese grits are on the menu!"

"Oh, yeah!" Bertie laughed. "We angels may not *have* to eat, but I won't be one to complain about being able to enjoy eating my grits again! In case I haven't told you before, Maximus, your grits are even better than the ones I use to make for my family."

"That's a real compliment—thank you, Bertie."

Bertie smiled at her thoughts down memory lane. "Well, enough of all that—talking about all that just makes me homesick to see my family again."

"Tomorrow is Sunday, so you won't have to wait much longer, Bertie."

"I know, I can't wait," she laughed and punched him on the shoulder again. "So, back to what we were talking about—what did Jason say to Doug when he called this morning? Have they heard anything from Jimmy?"

"No, they haven't. Officer O'Brady showed up at Miss Crennan's home last night and took her statement. I believe he filed a missing person report for her. Jason told Doug that it appears that Jimmy may have left behind a secret message for his mother."

"I knew this was coming," Bertie nodded, "But, I have no idea how it's all going to end—do you, Max?"

Max was quiet for what seemed like a very long time to Bertie.

"Maximus? Please don't tell me that this is not going to end well." She watched him intently. "You *do* know how it's going to end, don't you?"

Max nodded. "Yes, I do, Bertie; however, this is one time where I must keep that information to myself; besides, the ending that I know about could very well change at the drop of a hat. We'll just have to be patient and wait it out, like everyone else."

"Well, Hells-Bells! Who do you think I'm going to tell?" Bertie was exasperated.

Max raised his brows and looked down at the spunky angel who had worked by his side for so many years. "Really, Bertie? You have to ask me that?" He raised his hand when he saw the impending objection on her face. "No! Just accept that this is one time where it is better for you not to know how things will play out."

"You won't even give me a *hint*?" Bertie was flabbergasted. "Hell, we're angels, Max! Where's the trust?"

"Bertie," Max spoke slowly. "You know as well as I do

why it took you over 50 years to earn your wings—not to mention, the number of times you've been placed on probation."

"There's a big difference between cussing and keeping secrets," Bertie continued to object.

"Not for you," Max pointed his finger at her and smiled. "You're not good at keeping secrets and you're not good at controlling your foul language—although, I will be the first to admit, that I have seen definite progress on your part lately regarding the latter."

Bertie started to reply with a foul comment about his opinion, but the ringing of the angel chimes above the café's entrance stopped her. She shook her finger in his face and said, "You're just lucky that I have work to do, big fella!"

Max smiled as she stomped off to wait on the new customers. He shook his head and sighed. "Oh, I bet your husband had his hands full with you, Bertie..."

PJ thoroughly enjoyed her visit with Joe, Bernard, and Doug. Her doctor had been called in and told of her memory breakthrough. She was confused that she remembered almost everything about Joe Sanders, but nothing concrete about Bernard. Her doctor told her that it was completely normal, and that every patient was different. He told her that it was very possible that her memories would return in spurts rather than gushing back in their entirety.

Doug, Joe, and Bernard had waited outside PJ's room while she talked to her doctor, but, returned to her the moment the doctor left and informed them they could continue their visit.

Doug approached PJ's bed and sat down in the chair beside her. He took her hands into his own and smiled. "What did the doctor say, PJ?"

PJ felt the calming sensation course through her body when Doug took her hands into his own. She closed her eyes and enjoyed the feeling of peace that came over her. When she opened her eyes, she smiled at Joe and said. "I remember everything about you, Joe. The doctor said that it was common for some people to do that." She looked at Bernard and lowered her eyes. "I'm sorry, Bernard, but I still don't remember you. You seem familiar to me, but..."

"Don't be silly," Bernard shook his head. "I'll be the first to admit that this big oaf is much more memorable than I could ever hope to be."

Joe grinned and did his side-to-side victory dance again.

"See?" PJ pointed. "That's what did it—that dance! Something clicked inside my head when I saw you do that, and...well, I just remembered everything about you, Joe."

"I am pretty unforgettable," Joe grinned again. "I'm very happy for you, PJ—very happy for whatever part I may have had in some of your memories returning to you."

"I hate to cut our visit short, PJ," Doug said, "But, I left Bertie and Max alone with the lunch crowd, so I should probably get back soon to help them out."

"That's okay," PJ smiled. "I'm so glad all of you came to visit. Would you mind asking the nurse if there's someone who could take me downstairs. It would be good to see something other than these four walls and the rehab room for a change."

"I'll go ask," Bernard offered. He spoke to someone at the nurse's station and came back to PJ's room with a wheel chair. "Put your robe on, my lady." He bowed. "Your chariot awaits! The nurse will send someone down to the main waiting room in fifteen minutes to help you get back to your room."

PJ laughed with her three friends during their short trip on the elevator. Their laughter stopped short, however, when Joe accidentally hit the wrong button and they exited the elevator on the same floor on which the emergency room was located. They all stopped laughing when they saw the busy doctors and nurses moving from room to room.

"Oh, dear," Peggy whispered. "I think we got off on the wrong floor."

"Not a problem, my dear," Bernard whispered back. He passed a room that had a police officer stationed outside the open door. "I'll just turn your chariot around and get us away from this place."

PJ nodded and turned to look inside the room where the police officer stood guard. A nurse was standing in front of a patient who was sitting up on the side of the bed. She appeared to be working on one of his hands. The man looked up and saw PJ staring at him. He nodded and she gasped. "Oh, my goodness..." she was trembling noticeably.

Bernard stopped the wheelchair and Doug bent down to take her hands into his own once again. "What's the matter, PJ?" Doug asked.

"What's wrong with her?" Joe was worried. "She's shaking all over. PJ? Tell us, what's wrong?"

PJ shook her head and pointed to the man sitting on the bed. "What is Skipper doing here?"

# CHAPTER 27

## - Heaven -
## Bertie Chills Out

*B* ertie sat in the old rocker that had sat on the front porch of
her heavenly "mansion" for more than 100 years. There was
nothing stately about the mansion that she had selected to live in.
It was a Daniel Boone-type log home – much bigger than the home
she had shared with her husband and children when she died in
1911 – but still very simplistic in style. She knew that her
husband, Harold, would love it whenever he joined her in Heaven,
which had occurred much later than Bertie had ever anticipated –
he had outlived both their children when he died in his sleep at the
age of 81.

Bertie was only 26 years old when she was run over by one of
the first automobiles sold in her rural county. Harold had been ten
years her senior when she married him, and had remained a single
father to their two children, Joshua and Marilyn, until they had
grown up, married, and made him a grandfather, seven times over.

Bertie's closed eyelids lifted when she heard the squeaky screen
door open. "Hey, there, 'ole man! It's about time you came
outside." She jumped up and embraced Harold, who now looked
like a healthy, robust 60-year old. She punched him on his
shoulder and laughed out loud. "I swear, I never get tired of

*looking at you, but for the life of me, I still say it's not fair."*

*Harold hugged his wife and grinned down at her. "What's not fair, Bertie?"*

*Bertie pushed away and placed her hands on her hips. "The fact that I died in my prime at 26; and, yet, my heavenly body is holed up in this plump 40-something body – while, YOU, die an old man at 81, and now have the body of someone twenty years younger. I think God likes playing jokes, that's what I think. I mean, Hells-Bells – you were 36 when I died, and you really don't look like you aged much more than that now. I think you actually look better now than you did at 36!"*

*Harold laughed and pulled her back to him. He kissed the top of her head and said, "I would love you no matter how old you were, Bertie, and, no matter what body you were in; but, you're right, it is interesting how the Lord decides what our heavenly bodies will look like. So...how was your week on earth? Anything new happening with the murder investigation you told me about a couple of weeks ago?"*

*"Oh, hell, yeah!" Bertie nodded.*

***"B-E-R-T-I-E!!"***

*"Crap..." Bertie slapped the heel of her palm against her forehead. "Sorry, Lord! You know I've been doing a lot better, but I do slip up every now and then." She grabbed her husband's hand and dragged him into the yard and through their front gate. "I would say that I'm only human, but even that's not true anymore, so I don't think He will accept that excuse," she whispered in Harold's ear. "Come on, we'll talk on the way. It's been too long since I've been to the Golden Falls, and I could use a refurbishing of the soul!"*

*Harold walked a few feet behind and remained on the golden-brick path, and watched Bertie as she ran through the aromatic fields that were home to hundreds upon hundreds of flowers, bushes, and trees. There was no sadness in Heaven, but Harold often became contemplative whenever he thought of all the years he and Bertie missed out on together – the years he had been a single father raising a six- and a four-year old after his wife had been tragically killed. He tried not to think of all that Bertie had missed out on after having died at such a young age; she had not seen her son graduate from medical school and become a well-respected cardiologist, and she had not been able to enjoy watching her seven grandchildren grow up and become happy, well-adjusted adults in their own right.*

*Bertie looked back at her husband and quickly identified the reason for the longing look in his eyes. "You're thinking about all the things I didn't get to experience, aren't you, 'ole man?"*

*Harold smiled and nodded. "I am, yes. But, I guess I should, also, look at it as a blessing that you didn't live long enough to see both your children pass away, as well as two of your grandchildren. It's not a natural occurrence — parents should never have to outlive their children or grandchildren." He looked down at the ground and kicked at a small stone. "I think you're right," he looked up and smiled again. "The Golden Falls are what we both need right now."*

*Bertie hooked her arm through his offered bent elbow and punched him with her free arm. "God's plan is different for all of us, Harold. I've been in Heaven for — what — almost 105 years now, and I still don't understand how or why life happens to us the way it does. What I have learned is that it's not for us to worry about; we have to reach a point where we finally just go with the flow and trust that everything that happens, or happened, to us, was all part of a well-laid out plan." She sighed and shrugged. "I am glad that He took me, though, before I had to see my kids and grandkids die. I don't think I could have survived that, Harold." She stopped walking and looked up at him. "I think God probably took me first because He knew that I couldn't handle what you had to handle."*

*"Maybe you're right," Harold nodded. He saw the golden glow in the bend of the road up ahead and exhaled deeply. "I have a surprise for you today, Bertie; I had a feeling you might need a visit to the Golden Falls today."*

*"A surprise? What might that be, 'ole man?" Bertie punched him again for good measure.*

*"You'll see," Harold replied. "You'll see…"*

*Bertie's brows drew together. "You know that I'm not big on surprises, Harold. What's going on?"*

*Harold stopped and pushed Bertie gently ahead of him. "You'll enjoy this one, trust me. Go on ahead of me — I'll catch up." He waited until she had gone around the bend in the road; he waited until he heard her scream of joy before he walked closer to the Golden Falls. When he came around the bend, he smiled and sighed when he saw the two women hugging each other — his wife, and the daughter she had not seen since 1911. That was another perplexity about Heaven that he did not understand — why some family members were immediately reunited, while it took years before others might be reunited. He assumed that this, too, was all part of God's ultimate plan. Who knows — maybe God was rewarding his Bertie for going more than a week without using a cuss word!*

Max and Martin embraced each other while they watched Bertie and Marilyn's reunion take place on the huge screen that Martin controlled.

"Will you look at that," Martin wiped a joyful tear from the corner of his eye. "I was beginning to think that this reunion wouldn't take place until the Rapture or the Millennium!"

"I know what you mean, my friend," Max shook his head. "I'll be hearing about this, on earth, for a long time to come." He closed his eyes in prayer and whispered, "Thank you, Jesus..."

"Her husband died in 1956, but her daughter, Marilyn passed away about 10 years before that," Martin explained. "They didn't know a lot about the type of cancer she had back in the 40's, so there was no treatment for it. She suffered for a very long time before she passed. It's probably a good thing that Bertie did not have to witness her child's demise in that way."

Max nodded. "Yes, cancer is a terrible disease. We've seen so much death on earth because of it. Anyway, mother and daughter have finally been reunited. I'm very happy for Bertie."

"So am I...so am I," Martin nodded. "She never updated Harold about the murder investigation involving Gordon Whiting. I've been busier than usual this past week, so I have to be honest — I have not kept up with his particular situation."

"Well, Gordon — or, Skipper — as we all refer to him, is still in jail. In fact, he ended up at the emergency room yesterday around lunch time."

*"Oh, no!" Martin exclaimed. "Is he alright — well, of course, he's alright — that's not what I meant — I would know if he wasn't alright. What happened to him that he ended up at the hospital?"*

*"A prisoner who calls himself 'King Daddy' stabbed him in the hand during breakfast call yesterday morning. Skipper never said anything to the guards; he just wrapped his hand in a towel when he got back to his cell. By the time lunch rolled around, an infection had already set into the wound — I believe the doctors called it cellulitis — I'm pretty sure that's what Doug told us. The wound, more or less, developed an abscess, and streaks of red were traveling up Skipper's forearm. The warden decided that the wound needed to be treated in a real hospital setting, so they transferred Skipper to Floyd Medical Center for some intravenous antibiotics. The hospital recommended he stay overnight for observation."*

*"King Daddy? Who calls himself that?" Martin puckered his thick lips and shook his head. "So, Skipper's wound is not life threatening?"*

*"No, it's not. They mostly wanted to keep him overnight to make sure that the abscess would not require emergency drainage." Max pointed to the screen behind them. "I'm surprised you didn't see what happened while he was at the emergency room yesterday."*

*"What do you mean?" Martin was perplexed. "If something bad had happened, I would have known right away."*

*Max laughed and dropped an arm over his friend's shoulder. "Oh, it was most certainly nothing bad." He turned Martin around and laughed again. "What do you say we take a long walk and catch up on some things?"*

*Two earth hours later, Martin and Max sat side-by-side on top of a beautiful hill that overlooked the valley where the Rainbow Bridge sat. They watched, for several minutes, while pets and their former owners were once again reunited.*

*"I could watch these reunions for the rest of time," Max sighed. "I never tire of watching them, and I will never understand how some people on earth believe that these animals have no feelings. The look of joy and happiness on their furry faces is undeniable."*

*"I agree," Martin nodded. "Speaking of joy and happiness — I*

*would imagine that your Skipper falls into that category right about now."*

Max shook his head. *"To tell you the truth, old friend, I honestly don't think Skipper is capable of happiness. I wonder if he's ever known real happiness in his life time."*

*"Whatever do you mean, Maximus? Of course, the man must have known happiness at some point in his life – don't you think?"*

Max watched the dogs and cats reuniting with their owners for a few more minutes before responding. *"I'm not sure I can say that he has, Martin. Look at his history – his mother left home when he was only four years old and his brother, Charles, was nine. Their father wasn't home much, so they were left in the care of an aunt who used them as child labor to help run her bar. His brother joined the Army the day he turned 18, but returned home less than a year later, suffering from severe depression and withdrawal from society, so Skipper took care of him, too. He quit school in the ninth grade, and joined the Army himself the day he turned 18. He married, briefly, when he was 20, but his wife slept with every friend he had; they divorced before he left for his first tour in Vietnam..."*

*"They never had any children together, did they?"* Martin interrupted.

*"No, they didn't, and that was probably a blessing, because Skipper became even more of a recluse after four tours in Vietnam. He bounced around from woman to woman, from city to city, and never went home again. He sold everything he had in 1996 and has been homeless, by choice, for the past 20 years. So – no – I truly do not believe that Gordon Whiting has known much happiness in his life time."* Max exhaled and shook his head. *"It's very sad to think that anyone could go an entire life time and not experience the love of a good woman, a family, a life..."*

*"But, it has all been by choice, is that not correct?"* Martin asked. *"He has willingly chosen a life of solitude?"*

*"He has,"* Max closed his eyes. *"Maybe there's a chance that will change now that PJ's memory has returned. She will be able to clear Skipper's name and I assume he will be released from jail soon."*

*"Well, I will most definitely keep him in prayer, Maximus. I*

*will, also, pray that the man will be able to find peace with his life on earth."*

*Max shook his head slowly. "Unfortunately, my old friend, that may not happen for Skipper; he may very well have to wait until his end to find that peace."*

*"Is he a believer?"*

*Max looked over at his friend and shrugged. "You know, I'm not entirely sure about that. I'll have to discuss that with Doug when we get back; he might know."*

*"Did Doug come Home for a visit today?" Martin stood up and stretched his long arms high above his head. He inhaled the purest quality of air anyone could ever hope to experience, and slowly released it. "I think he was probably overdue for some rest and relaxation."*

*The two angels turned back toward the path that would return them to Martin's work area. Martin turned quickly when he felt a hard punch to the back of his shoulder. "Oh, no," he sighed. "Is your visit with your family over already?"*

*Bertie pushed herself between the two black men and wrapped an arm around each of their waists. "Oh, don't pretend you don't know what surprise Harold had for me today, you old fart!"*

*"B-E-R-T-I-E!!"*

*"Well, damn!" Bertie whispered. "When did the word fart become a cuss word!"*

*Max shook his head. "Whatever are we going to do with you, Bertie?"*

*Bertie laughed out loud. "Hey, I'm a work in progress – our Lord knows and accepts that about me!" She ran ahead of them when she saw Doug walking toward them. "Hey, handsome! You're not going to believe what happened to me today!"*

**"But of that day and hour no one knows, not even the angels in heaven, nor the Son, but only the Father. Take heed, watch and pray; for you do not know when the time is." Mark 13:32-33 (NKJV)**

# CHAPTER 28

## Monday Morning Rolls Around

Kirk pulled into the school parking lot and swerved sharply into the first parking space he spotted. He ignored the loud honking from the driver of the car that had seen the space first.

"You were pretty quiet on the ride in," Michael said. He leaned across his seat and grabbed his backpack from the floorboard. "Are you having second thoughts about leaving David with them? I mean, since it's the first day any of us will be alone with them?"

Kirk rubbed his middle fingers against the bridge of his nose and closed his eyes. He hadn't slept much over the weekend, and he was tired. He wouldn't admit it to his friends, but he had begun questioning the decisions he had made; however, he also knew that he had already taken things too far to turn back now. He looked over at Michael and snarled, "No."

Michael grinned and held up both hands. "Okay, okay. I was just wondering. You, uh...you don't think he'll turn soft on us, do you?"

"What do you mean, Mike?"

"Come on, Kirk. You know what I mean. You've seen how he looks at the two of them. You can tell he feels sorry for the kid and he feels even worse for the way he beat up the old hag. I'm not convinced he has the balls to go through with our plan." He looked out the window and watched the students hustling to get inside before the final bell rang. "You know you're thinking the same thing."

"David will do whatever I tell him to do," Kirk scolded. "And so will you. So, go on to class. Skip the last class if you can, and get your ass back out to the lake house to relieve David. He'll need to get home and check in with his parents. You've got your excuse for tonight covered with your parents?"

Michael snorted and opened the car door. "You know as well as I do, that my parents could give a rat's ass about my plans. I doubt if they even noticed that I wasn't there all weekend."

"Yeah, you're probably right," Kirk replied. "They both probably stayed drunk and high all weekend."

Michael lit a cigarette and leaned back inside the vehicle. "No, they'll never be nominated for parents of the year, that's for sure. That's why it will be easy for me to be the one to stay at the lake house if either you or David can't make it. But you know, don't you, that we can't keep this up for too long. You need to make a decision this week about what you're going to do with the two of them. Think about it, buddy." He closed the door, snubbed out his cigarette, and took his time entering the school building after the last bell sounded.

Kirk exhaled deeply and leaned his head back against the head rest. "What the hell have I gotten myself in to..."

Rae Blankenship stood at the kitchen window and watched her husband back out of the driveway. She wiped his wet kiss off her cheek and said, "Good riddance." She turned around sharply when she heard the shuffling of feet. "Priscilla! What have I told you about sneaking up on people?"

Prissy stared hard at her employer's wife. She shook her head and started to walk away. "I heard what you said about Mr. B. I heard you..."

Rae started to go after the old woman, but quickly changed her mind. She doubted, very seriously, if her husband would take his maid's word over that of his own wife; besides, she could always resort to her powers of sexual persuasion if she had to. She knew that she could control her husband with those powers, even though he had successfully managed to avoid them over the past few days. She poured another cup of coffee and returned to the laptop she had brought downstairs with her. "Let's see now...how do I look up the Floyd County Property Appraiser site?" She was determined to find out what she could about the mysterious lake house. "Oh, yes, there you are!" She skimmed over several entries until she stopped at an entry for a piece of lake-front property in Cave Spring, Georgia; the deeded owner of the property was Elizabeth Blankenship. "Well, that explains why I didn't know about this piece of property," she pursed her pouty lips together. "He put it in his wife's name, but...she's dead now, isn't she, so the property would go to the estate of Ernest Blankenship." She studied the entry about the lake house and smiled. "Maybe I should have a look at that property for myself...before I decide whether or not if it's worth the effort of having to seduce my husband to have it put in my name."

Priscilla had been watching and listening to her husband's new wife, through the crack in her bedroom door. "We'll just see about that, missy, yes we will..."


Bertie punched Doug on the shoulder when the angel chimes sounded and Jason and Cheryl walked through the door. "Look at that poor woman—she looks like she hasn't slept all weekend."

Bertie rushed over to the couple and put an arm around Cheryl. "We heard about Jimmy, and we want you to know that both of you are in our constant prayer. I just know he'll be home soon—safe and sound—and will probably have one helluva story to tell us all."

Cheryl smiled back. "I hope you're right about that, Bertie." Her smile faded as she allowed Jason to guide her towards a table in the far, back corner.

Bertie shook her head and looked up at Doug. "Where could he be, handsome? That boy just isn't the type to disappear like that and not let his mama know where he's at. He loves her too much. He knows that she would be so worried about him."

"I don't know, Bertie," Doug sighed. "I was hoping he would have returned home by the time we all got back from Home last night."

"Well, you go fetch them both some coffee, and I'll get them something to eat. Maybe today will bring them some good news."

Jason exhaled deeply as he sat down beside Cheryl. It had been a long weekend for them both, but he had not left her side. He had slept on the couch for the past three nights and been there with her each time the phone rang, and it wasn't Jimmy. "Hey, I'm glad I was able to talk you into leaving the house for a little while," he reached for her hand and clasped it securely within his own. "You've got your cell with you. Officer O'Brady will call if he hears anything."

"But what if Jimmy comes back and I'm not there? What if he's hurt and needs me..." Cheryl closed her eyes and shook her head. "No...no...he's okay. I would know if he wasn't okay." She looked over at Jason and laid her head against his left arm. "Thank you so much for staying with me, Jason."

"I wouldn't be anywhere else right now," Jason smiled. "Hey, here comes Doug with some coffee. I want you to try to eat something, too, okay?"

Cheryl nodded. "I will." She smiled up at Doug when he placed two steaming mugs of coffee on their table. "Thank you, Doug. I could really use a cup right about now."

"Has there been any more news about Jimmy?" Doug asked. He knew that Max and Bertie would be listening in on the conversation. Bertie had told him that Max knew more about the situation than he was willing to reveal to them, so that meant that he would have to find out answers for himself. "Is there anything we can do to help find him?"

Cheryl shook her head. "No, but thank you so much for wanting to do that. I honestly don't think the police have taken it seriously…until today. I waited until I knew school had started before I called to see if Jimmy was there. He wasn't, so the first thing I did was to call and tell Officer O'Brady. As it turns out, he was already at the school, waiting for it to open, so he knew a few minutes before I did that Jimmy had not reported for class. He thinks his department will act more quickly on it now that it looks like it wasn't just Jimmy getting away from home for the weekend."

Jason took a sip of the energy-boosting coffee and stared at Doug. "Officer O'Brady, also, said that he would be checking out the lead I gave him regarding Stella Sieber. He has a few officers delegated to riding the streets, searching for Jimmy, but he wanted to follow up on that lead personally."

"I guess you heard the news about PJ and Skipper?" Doug grinned.

Jason returned the grinned and nodded. "Yep, best news ever. Officer O'Brady said it looks like PJ's testimony about what happened that night is enough to clear Skipper of any crime. That's why he's so intent on finding Stella, and to find out why she lied. He's sure that she knows more about what happened than she's telling the police."

Bertie marched toward them with plates balanced on both arms. "Make yourself useful, handsome, and take some of these." She smiled at Cheryl and said, "You need to eat, to keep your strength up, young lady."

"Yes ma'am," Cheryl smiled back. "I didn't think I would be able to eat anything, but, this all smells so good. Thank you, Bertie." She reached first for the plate of fried potatoes, smothered with Max's famous sausage gravy. "Especially this one!"

"Thanks, Bertie," Jason looked at the two café employees, who had quickly become so much more than that to all of them since Norman was killed. "We'll be heading over to the police station after we finish here. I have a feeling they'll be sick of us before the day is over, but Cheryl wants to make sure that they're taking all this more seriously now."

"I don't blame her one bit," Bertie clucked. "Not one bit. You give them hell, young lady, and don't let them give you the runaround, you here?"

Cheryl swallowed the large bite of savory potatoes and nodded. "I intend to do just that, Bertie."


Thomas closed the door to the small office of the Roadway Inn and looked up and down the street. He had questioned the manager and found out that only one of the eight rooms at the inn was currently filled. The manager had winked when he informed the officer that most of his customers rented his rooms by the hour. Thomas held the key to Room Number 8 in his hands and took a deep breath. He knocked on the door. "This is the police—open up!" He put his ear to the door, but did not hear any movement coming from within. He put on a pair of vinyl gloves and used the key to unlock the door and opened it to a darkened, musty room that reeked of stale cigarette smoke. He flipped on the wall switch and took in the unmade bed, the towels on the floor, an empty pizza box on the small table, and an ash tray filled with cigarette stubs.

He walked through the room and looked into the bathroom. The sinks were dry, as were the discarded towels. He turned and looked at the disheveled bed. There was a hairbrush on the nightstand; he instinctively bagged it as evidence and sat down on the lumpy mattress. He could hear the loud music already coming from the Pickled Possum, and it was barely ten o'clock in the morning. He stood up to leave and the toe of his shoe got hooked on the handle of a bag that had been shoved under the bed. He pulled the bag out and unzipped it. The rank smell from the clothes inside the bag almost made him gag, but he was sure the clothes belonged to Stella. He found a knotted sock in the bottom of the bag; when he loosened the knot, he counted out almost four hundred dollars in cash. "How did you come on this kind of money, Stella?" One last look around the room convinced him that Stella Seiber had not been in this room in the past twenty-four hours. He returned the money to the sock and re-knotted it, zipped the bag, and locked the door behind him. He tossed the bag into into the back seat of his car, and returned the key to the manager. He looked toward the Pickled Possum and rubbed the back of his head. "Where are you, Stella?"

He locked the police cruiser and walked the few hundred feet it took to reach the Pickled Possum. He didn't expect to get any useful information from anyone inside, especially at this hour of the morning, so he was excited when the bartender told him that he had last seen Stella walking toward town on Friday morning.

"Friday, huh—the same day that Jimmy Crennan was last seen," he was talking to himself as he began walking down the same road Stella would have taken toward town. "Nah, there couldn't be any connection between those two. There's no way that Jimmy would have known the likes of Stella Seiber." He had walked about a half mile when he spotted it—a woman's shoe. "Well, I'll be damned," he whispered. The shoe could have belonged to anyone, but he dropped it into an evidence bag just the same. He spent another few minutes searching the woods on both sides of the road; he half expected to find Stella's dead body in one of the ditches. When he didn't find any sign of Stella, he walked back to the spot where he had found the shoe. "It probably isn't even be her shoe," he spoke out loud, "But, then again—there's a fifty-fifty chance it could be."

He turned to his left and glanced down into a small ditch. "What is that?" he wondered as he made his way down the small incline. He picked up the small, metal can. "Pepper spray." He dropped it into an evidence bag, too, and turned to walk back to his car. That is when he spotted the imprint of a shoe—a much larger shoe than any Stella might have worn. He pulled his phone from his pocket and took several pictures of the area. The imprint was faint and smudged, but, Thomas thought that there might be enough of it for the forensic inspectors to use as—what—evidence?

David stood outside the lake house, staring off into the distance. He wished he was anywhere but here, standing guard over two people that probably wouldn't live to see the week's end, if Kirk had his way. He sighed and rubbed the back of his neck. "What the hell have I let Kirk talk me into?" He paced the length of the back porch and stopped again to look out over the 3-acre lake. "This isn't right," he shook his head. "I can't let this happen, but I can't really do anything to stop it either."

He paced for another ten minutes before the frigid cold finally forced him inside. The old woman and Jimmy were both sitting on one of the large sofas—as far away from each other as possible—pretending to watch television. David stared at them for a long time, taking in the clothes they had both had on since Friday. "There's a washer and dryer upstairs. If y'all want to give me your clothes, I'll wash them for you." He fumbled through his backpack and pulled out two pairs of sweats. "Here, you can put these on while I take your clothes upstairs."

"I ain't taking my clothes off in front of you!" Stella yelled. "You're crazy as hell if you think I'm gonna let you see me naked!"

David tossed the sweats onto the couch. "Trust me, old lady, seeing your naked body is about the last thing on my bucket list. Go on into the bedroom and change—don't forget your underwear and socks, too." His gaze moved slowly over both of them, and stopped suddenly when he stared at their socks and shoes.

Their socks and shoes...

David's head snapped back up and his panicked voice creaked when he jumped toward Stella and roughly shook her shoulders. "Where's your other shoe, old lady? Where is it?"

# CHAPTER 29

## Ernest Has Second Thoughts

Ernest Blankenship sat in his glass-encased office, located on the second level of his largest car dealership. He had not been able to focus on work the entire day; if he was honest with himself, it had been several months since work had claimed his full attention. Another review of the last quarterly sales sheets, this morning, had only reinforced that fact.

He stood up and paced the circular office. He watched while his salespersons, dressed professionally in business suits, greeted customers from all walks of life. He looked down at his own three-piece suit and shook his head. He closed his eyes and briefly remembered the early years—the poverty years—that he and his first wife, Elizabeth, had made it through. Those were what he laughingly referred to as his blue-jean years.

Ernest had left the small television in the office playing while he sorted through the quarterly reports; background noise always helped him focus on the task at hand. He walked over to it now and turned the volume up to listen to a report by a local newscaster.

*"This is Paul Wilshire reporting. We are interrupting your regular-scheduled program to bring you some important news about a recent murder involving a homeless man, Norman Weissman. Another homeless man—a decorated Vietnam Veteran—Gordon Whiting, was charged with the January 22, 2016 murder of Mr. Weissman. Mr. Whiting has done little to cooperate with the police involving this case; however, another homeless person in their group—a woman by the name of Peggy Jensen—has come forward to clear Mr. Whiting of this murder charge. Ms. Jensen was severely injured when she was hit by a car on January 23, 2016; as a result of that accident, her memory was affected. That all changed yesterday when Ms. Jensen spotted Mr. Whiting at the Floyd Memorial Hospital, and her memories of that night resurfaced. The police are not releasing any information provided by Ms. Jensen—all they are saying, at present, is that all charges against Mr. Whiting have been dropped, and he will be free to go once he is released from the hospital. We will continue to update you on this story as we receive further information from our local police department."*

Ernest smiled and closed his eyes. "Well, thank, God for that. I remember reading about you, Mr. Whiting." He sighed and shook his head. "It's good to hear some good news for a change."

He didn't hear the door to his office open.

"What do you mean, Ernest?" Rae Blankenship closed the door behind her and waited for her husband to assist her with her fur coat. She glanced at the television. "What was that all about?"

Ernest hung her coat up on the iron coat rack that stood next to the television. "Nothing you would be interested in hearing about, Rae?"

"Well, if it was something you considered to be good news, then I most certainly would be interested, dear." She sat down on the leather sofa that faced his desk, and crossed her shapely legs. She may have been forty-nine, but she worked hard and extensively to maintain the body of someone much, much younger. Good familial genes, also, played an important part in her success along those lines.

Ernest sighed and sat back down at his desk. "What brings you by, Rae? Shouldn't you be at some yoga or Rhumba class?"

Rae flinched at the bitterness she detected in his voice. "Well, I certainly don't know what has you in such a sour mood today, Ernest, but whatever it is, there's no reason why you should be taking it out on me. I was in the neighborhood and I haven't had lunch yet, so I thought I would stop by to see if you wanted to join me."

Ernest stared at the beautiful woman before him and understood why he had jumped into marriage so quickly with her. He, also, was not a fool. He knew that his money was probably the only attraction that Rae Sanchez had initially felt for him. He sighed again and shook his head. "No, I'm sorry, I can't. I'm in the middle of quarterly reports. Sales are down…"

Rae jumped up and approached his desk. "Sales are down? How can that be? What's wrong? Are we in trouble?"

"No, Rae—*we* are not in trouble. We took a large cut in profits this quarter, but things should turn around once warmer weather arrives. Don't worry, dear, your life style will not have to change."

"You must think of me as being very materialistic, Ernest. You do, don't you?"

He thought about lying—about placating her enough for her to leave so that he could get back to work. He changed his mind. He stood up and walked around his desk to where she still stood. The closer he got, the more determined he became to say what was really on his mind.

Rae saw something in her husband's eyes that she didn't recognize—it appeared to be determination. She truly never thought he had enough backbone to become determined about anything. "What are you looking at me like that for, Ernest?"

Ernest sat on the corner of his desk and lifted his wife's

chin so that they were eye-to-eye. "To answer your question, Rae—yes—I do. You are one of the most materialistic people I've ever had the misfortune to know." He removed his finger from her chin but continued to meet her challenged stare-down. "We made a mistake—no, let me rephrase that—I made a mistake when I asked you to marry me four years ago." He saw that she was about to interrupt him, but he held up his index finger and shook his head. "No—let me finish—and, then you can talk."

"Ernest…"

His normally friendly, placid eyes turned the color of cold steel. "I made a mistake, Rae. My wife—my beautiful, loving wife, Elizabeth—had only been dead a few months. I was a single father, with no clue on how to raise my son alone. I didn't want to be alone. I didn't think Elizabeth would have wanted me to be alone." He took a deep breath and shook his head again. "I screwed up, Rae. The day I married you was the day I began to lose my son. He has never forgiven me for trying to replace the mother he loved so very much. He was a good kid back then—kind, loving, compassionate. That all changed within a few months of mine and your marriage. I should have had it annulled as soon as I saw the change in him, but I was in denial, I guess. I convinced myself that things would get better."

"I don't believe it!" Rae spun around and grabbed her fur coat. "You're blaming me for the mean and psychotic creature that you call a son? Well, you're crazier than I ever thought you could be, Ernest. I had nothing to do with creating the monster that walks all over you, steals money from you, take advantage of you—who cares about nothing or no one except himself. He's YOUR son, not mine, and if he hasn't turned into the fine upstanding citizen that you had hoped he would become, then it most certainly is not my fault. And another thing, if you think the last four years have been a walk in the park for me, then you're more of a pea-brained idiot than I first thought you to be…" Her hand flew to her mouth to try to stop any more scathing words to escape. She moved quickly toward him and tried to touch him. "Oh, Ernest, I'm so sorry—I didn't mean any of that..."

Ernest took her coat from her and helped her put it on. He turned her around to face him, and smiled for the first time since she had entered his office. "I think we've both said exactly what needed to be said, Rae—and, it's been long overdue. I need you to leave now. We will talk more about what happens next, later."

"What do you mean—*what happens next!*" She stiffened her back and squinted her eyes as she stared back at her primary source of revenue. "If you think you can get rid of me so easily, Ernest Blankenship, then you have another thought coming. Trust me, I will take you for every cent I can get, and I know a very good attorney."

Ernest sighed. "I'm sure you know a lot of attorneys, Rae—not to mention, a lot of pool boys, massage therapists, personal trainers—the list is long. Did you honestly think you were being discreet all those times?"

"*Oh, no...*" Rae's mind was racing. "*He couldn't possibly know about the affairs. No way! The man is too stupid...*" She opened the door to leave, but turned back around and glared at her husband. "It won't be easy to get rid of me, Ernest. You may want to rethink things before you come home tonight." She turned and slammed the door shut.

Ernest stood at the glass windows and watched while his wife shoved people out of her way in her attempt to rush from the building. He closed his eyes and bent his head backwards. "Thank you, God, for giving me the strength to do that..."


PJ finished her daily physical therapy session and was returning to her room when she decided to take a detour to the second floor. She knew that Skipper was being released at the end of the day, and she wanted a chance to say good-bye to him.

PJ was surprised to find that there was still a guard

posted outside Skipper's room. She rolled her wheelchair up to him and asked. "Excuse me, is it possible for me to see him?"

The officer nodded and opened the door to Skipper's room.

PJ rolled in and found Skipper sitting on the edge of his bed. His left hand was bandaged and positioned in a sling to keep it mobilized. "Hi," PJ spoke softly. "I was hoping to see you before you left."

Skipper slid off the bed and rolled his shoulders. "Come on in, PJ," he nodded to the police officer, who closed the door behind her.

"Why are the cops still outside your door, Skipper? I thought you were free to go now — that you were cleared of all charges."

Skipper offered a half-smile. "I have been, but, evidently, the police department must feel bad for locking up the wrong man, so they left one of their own behind, to give me a ride to wherever it is I want to go. Officer O'Brady wants to do that, but just in case he doesn't get back in time, another officer will drop me off."

"And, where do you want to go, Skipper?"

Skipper sat down in one of the visitor's chairs and lowered his elbows to his knees. He clasped his hands together beneath his chin and stared at PJ. "It doesn't really matter, now does it? I'll probably have him drop me off at the old camp site."

"You're going back there?"

"Why not?" Skipper shrugged. "It's as good a place as any. I'll probably stay a few more days before deciding where to move on to next."

"Have you ever thought about going home?"

Skipper's face went blank as he stared back at her. "I have no home, PJ. I left all that behind a long time ago. There's really nothing to go back to."

"But, I heard someone say that you had a brother who is still living. Why don't you go back to him?"

"Charles?" Skipper shook his head. "No, my days of taking care of Charles are long over. One of the biggest favors I ever did for him was leaving when I did—forcing him to live again and take control of his own life."

"Why did you have to take care of him? Was he sick or something?"

Skipper didn't like talking about his personal business or life with anyone, but he didn't feel threatened by PJ. There was nothing she could do about any of it, and he didn't think she was the type of person to judge him for leaving his brother to finally fend for himself. "Some people might call it a sickness, I don't know. Personally, I think my brother is just a very weak example of a man."

"What do you mean?"

"It's a long story, PJ, but—long-story short—Charles is about five years older than me. He joined the army when he was eighteen, during the Korean War. He was only over there for a few months when something happened to him— something he has never been able to come to terms with."

"What? What happened to your brother?"

"He killed someone."

"But it was war—a lot of people were killed."

Skipper shook his head. "No, you don't understand. It was his first battle and—truth be told—he was scared out of his wits. He had no business having access to a gun and being in battle; he should have been working in S-4 ordering supplies for the troops. I don't have specifics about what happened; all I know is that Charles tripped and fell, and his gun went off." Skipper smiled at the puzzled look on PJ's face. "His gun went off and he killed one of the men in his troop—friendly fire, they called it."

"Oh, no..." PJ shook her head. "That must have been a lot for an 18-year old to handle."

"Even harder for Charles because, like I said, he never should have been a combat soldier—that wasn't his calling. They didn't call it PTSD back in the fifties, but I'm pretty sure that's what my brother suffers from—something a lot of soldiers battle every day."

"So…you took care of him?"

Skipper nodded. "I did—until I joined the Army when I was eighteen. I never went home again after that. Well, that's not exactly true. I went home a couple of times—for funerals—but, Charles had married and had someone to look after him by then, so I didn't feel bad about leaving for good twenty years ago."

"That's a long time, Skipper. Doug said that your brother has been calling—that he wanted to come see you when you were in jail."

Skipper grinned. "Well, maybe I can high-tail it out of this town before that happens." He shook his head. "No, PJ, I am no longer my brother's keeper, and I sure as hell don't need for him—or anyone else—to be mine."

# CHAPTER 30

## Shift Change

Jimmy had to admit that it felt good to have clean underwear on. He had been in the same clothes since early Friday morning, and he had no doubt that his drawers were standing at attention by the time David had tossed them into the washing machine. David's sweats had been too short for him and were super baggy on the old lady, but at least he had not had to see the old woman in her birthday suit.

He had tried several times during the day to engage David in conversation. He knew that, if he was going to get out of this predicament, David was his best resource to make that happen. Unfortunately, David seemed as though he was in a world all his own. He had brought them breakfast and lunch, and given them plenty of water to drink, but, his actions were almost robotic.

Jimmy glanced at the large elk clock on the wall close to the sliding glass doors. It was five o'clock and the sun would be setting in about half an hour, at best. The old woman was in the bedroom, lying down, so Jimmy thought he would try talking to David again. "So, what happens now, David?"

David continued staring off into space.

"David? Hey!" Jimmy yelled to get the boy's attention. "David!'"

David turned slowly toward Jimmy. "What do you want, Crennan? I've told you not to talk to me, or ask any questions."

"So, you don't know what happens next, do you?"

David shook his head. "Not true—I do know what the plan is, and trust me, you really don't want to know."

"Why is Kirk doing this? I told him I wouldn't say anything to anyone—and I haven't—not even to my mom, and we tell each other everything."

"Haven't you figured it out by now, Crennan? Kirk is C-R-A-Z-Y, and I, for one, do not ever intend to get on his bad side. If he says we have to take care of things, then that's what we'll do."

"So, what? The plan is to kill us—me and the old woman?"

David nodded. "Initially, it was just the old woman. Kirk said he didn't trust her to keep her mouth shut, or to not come back later, demanding more money from him. He didn't want to have to keep looking over his shoulder for the rest of his life."

"You said, initially, it was just the old woman? Why did he change his mind about me? Did I do something to make him not trust me?"

David stared at Jimmy and smiled. "You're cut from a different mold, Jimmy. You're not like the rest of us. We've had everything handed to us—born with a silver spoon in our mouths, as they say—but, not you. Kirk knows you well enough to know that you have a conscience. My guess, is that he thought your conscience would lead you to tell the truth to somebody down the line."

Jimmy didn't respond.

David shrugged. "Looks like he was probably right about you. Hey, it's nothing personal."

"Nothing personal?" Jimmy stood up and the heavy

chain on his ankle clanked against the wood flooring. "You guys want to kill me and want me to believe it's nothing personal? Man, you're just as crazy as Kirk and Mike are."

The glass doors slid open and one of the subjects of their conversation popped in. "Did I hear my name?" Mike grinned and took a toke off the joint he held between his thumb and index finger.

David jumped up. "It's about time you got here." He began gathering up his bag and putting on a heavy jacket. "It'll take me at an hour to get home in late afternoon traffic, and I don't need my mom asking me a bunch of questions about what I've been doing all weekend and what took me so long to get home from school."

Michael shrugged and grinned. "Like she really cares? Who are you trying to fool, David? Your parents probably don't even realize that you haven't been home all weekend."

"Oh, and you think yours does?" David screamed back. "Yours have probably been passed out since Friday and don't even realize what day of the week it is—much less, where their kids are. Your sister's probably been whoring around all weekend and your kid brother stays at his friends' homes more than he does his own."

Mike pointed his finger at David and approached him slowly. "Cool it, David. I know you're a little antsy, but it would be in your best interest to shut your damn mouth about my family. I can say what I want about them, but you need to shut up."

Stella stumbled out of the bedroom, scratching her crotch and dragging her chain behind her. "Who the hell can sleep with all this racket going on?" She scratched her crotch area again and snarled. "What did you wash my underwear in— lye soap?"

David shot the old woman an invitation from his middle finger and looked down at Michael when he brushed against him at the door. "They're all yours. I'll be back Wednesday after school." He jumped in Michael's car and sprayed gravel as he sped away from the lake house. He would drop Mike's car off at the Bozeman home and walk the half-mile to his own home; chances were that Mike's parents would see their son's car in the driveway and assume he was locked in his room, as usual.

Michael watched David speed away and did his best to keep a worried expression off his face. He didn't want Jimmy and the old hag knowing how worried he was about David's role in all this. He didn't think David had the balls that it was going to take, to do what had to be done. Personally, he was looking forward to it. He had seen people die in movies, but this would be his first experience at watching someone die close up—well, his second experience—he kept forgetting that he had seen the homeless man die after his head cracked open against the concrete wall—but, that really had been an accident.

He stepped onto the back porch and brought in several pieces of firewood. He dropped them onto the hearth. "Make yourself useful, Crennan, and put another log on the fire—I think there's one of your country songs with those words." He giggled and looked over at Stella. "What about you, old woman? Can you do anything useful? Do you know how to cook, at least?"

Stella spat on the wooden floor. "It'll be a cold day in hell before I cook anything for the likes of you." She spat another wad of green phlegm on the floor.

Michael walked slowly toward her until he was within a couple of feet. He stared hard at her and said, "Clean it up."

"Like hell I will!" Stella bellowed. "Clean it your damn self!"

Mike never hesitated. He turned sideways and delivered a karate kick to her stomach.

Stella groaned and went down on her knees. She was gasping for air when Jimmy rushed over to her.

"Stay back, Crennan, unless you want some of what she just got." Mike grabbed Stella by what little hair she had left on her head and jerked her head as far back as it would go. "Take off your shirt, old lady, and clean that crap up."

Stella shook her head and spit dribbled from the corner of her mouth. "No, you can't make me do that." She had finally caught her breath, but still held onto her stomach.

Mike kneeled down and pulled tighter on her hair. He grinned at her and whispered, "Unless you want me to take that shirt off for you, I suggest you do it NOW." He released her hair and waited for her to stand up. "Don't ever spit on that floor, or anything else, again." He turned and walked into the kitchen area. "Get over here, Crennan—give the old hag a little *privacy* while she cleans up her mess."

Stella removed her clean, flannel shirt and used the hem of it to clean up the two large wads of phlegm. The look of her own bodily fluids almost caused her to gag, but she managed to keep control of her weak stomach. She held the shirt out to Michael. "This needs to be washed again."

Michael grimaced at the sight of the old woman's sagging skin and breasts; she had not been wearing a bra when they took her. "Yeah…that's not going to happen on my shift, old lady, so you better hope it dries up quick. Now put that shirt on so we don't have to look at your shriveled-up old body anymore."

Stella saw the look of embarrassment on the kid they called Jimmy. She remembered that he had not been part of the three who were pushing old Norman around. He had been their lookout. She shrank bank when the younger kid moved toward her, offering his help. She almost spit another wad out, but stopped herself in mid-hack. She rubbed the hem of her shirt against her worn-out pants and slowly put it back on. She took her time buttoning the shirt up and never took her eyes off Jimmy. "I don't need your help. You ain't no better than the rest of your friends, and I hope you all burn in hell."

Jimmy flinched and moved away from Stella. He had a feeling it was going to be a long, long night with Michael at the helm.

✧

The dinner crowd had thinned out, and there were only about three tables with customers when Jason and Cheryl entered the Heavenly Grille. Bertie was quick to greet and seat them at the counter; she knew that Doug wanted to talk to Jason about Skipper.

She placed an arm around Cheryl and squeezed her tight. "How are you doing, hon? I know all this has got to be so hard on you, but you have to have faith that Jimmy is going to be okay."

Cheryl's religious upbringing had been nil-to-none; however, when she moved in with her grandmother, that all changed. Her grandmother had not been ashamed to take an unmarried, pregnant teenager with her to church every Sunday. Cheryl had felt uncomfortable and on display the first couple of weeks she went, but it had not taken her long to warm up to the wonderful folks in Hogansville, Georgia. They had all taken her under their wing and helped her find her way through the Bible and to a Lord she had never heard anything about. Cheryl was baptized at the same time Jimmy was—when he was just six months old. She sighed and closed her eyes. "I'm doing my very best, Bertie, but— it's really, really hard. I keep asking myself why God would allow this to happen. I mean, Jimmy and I—we've never hurt anyone."

Jason had been raised in a large family, and all his family was still alive, but none of them had any strong religious beliefs. His parents had never forced or encouraged their children to attend church; they left that decision up to their children—so that they could make up their own minds about God and Heaven. Jason was still in limbo—he wasn't sure what he believed at this point.

Doug was behind the counter and poured four cups of black coffee. "God did not allow this to happen, Cheryl." His voice was low and soothing.

Cheryl looked up at him and smiled. "I know that, really I do, but…it's just so unfair that this has happened to my Jimmy. I mean, where is he? Is he hurt? Did someone take him—which is what I'm inclined to believe. I think the police have finally come around to that way of thinking, too." She took a long sip of coffee. "They began interviewing a lot of the students at his school today—they got through with all of those in his class, but they said they didn't get any good leads from any of them."

"He didn't have any other friends?" Bertie asked. "If memory serves me, that first morning the two of you came in here, didn't he have to go outside to take a call from a friend?'

Cheryl's brows raised in surprise. "Wow, Bertie! You remember that little detail, do you?"

"I have a memory like an elephant," Bertie nodded. "It's a gift. Isn't that right, handsome?" She reached across the counter and punched Doug on the shoulder.

Doug rubbed his arm and grinned. "It's true. Our Bertie never forgets a face, a name, or a place; and, it's obvious that she must never forget a phone call either." He moved away quickly when Bertie moved to punch him again.

Cheryl smiled and sipped at her coffee. She was quiet for a moment before looking back up at her friends. "I had almost forgotten about that group of older boys he hung out with for a few months—he stopped seeing them—oh, I can't remember when, but it hasn't been that long ago. For the life of me, I can't remember any of their names now."

"They were older?" Jason asked. "Did they go to Jimmy's school?"

"Yes, to both questions," Cheryl answered back. "What was that boy's name? I remember I only met him one time, and there was something about him that—well, that probably isn't important...anyway, I'll be sure to mention it to Officer O'Brady—to make sure they talk to some of the older students. Maybe someone will remember seeing Jimmy with those friends he hung out with, and know who they are."

Doug wanted to say something, but one look at Bertie, and he was silently reminded that it was not their place to interfere with anything that might transpire. "Maybe you'll think of the name later," he suggested. He grunted when Bertie punched him on her way into the kitchen.

"I'll be back with some food for you both," she yelled over her shoulder. She looked at Max when she got inside the kitchen. "Did you hear that? Our handsome angel almost interfered, didn't he? Now, if that had been me, I probably would have already heard about it from Martin, or someone in even higher authority."

"Calm down, Bertie," Max smiled as he began filling two plates with the dinner special: 15-bean soup, seasoned with ham hocks, onions, and smoked sausage, piled atop rice, and accompanied by pole beans and his famous baked macaroni and cheese with four cheeses and bacon. It was a stick-to-your-ribs kind of dinner that was sure to get anyone through the cold night ahead. "Doug could have provided the boy's name, but he knew better."

"Do you think that boy could have anything to do with Jimmy's disappearance, Max? Or is that something else you're not allowed to share with us about these whole shenanigans?" Bertie pouted a little.

Max pushed the plates toward her. "Those folks are tired and hungry, Bertie. Go feed them so that they'll have the strength to endure whatever may come."

# CHAPTER 31

## One Man Alone

Cheryl and Jason did not leave the café until almost ten o'clock.

Bertie watched the door close behind the tired couple and looked over at Doug. "That poor girl is absolutely exhausted. I hope she's able to get some sleep tonight."

Doug removed some plates from the counter and shook his head. "I don't think she'll have another sound night's sleep until her son is home again." He took the dishes into the kitchen and nodded at Max. "There's no one else out there, Max. It's been a slow night."

"Yes, it has," Max smiled. "It's another cold night. Most people probably decided it wasn't worth the effort to get out in this cold—not even to sample my 15-bean soup. It really is good; have you tried it? Or—maybe you know of someone else who could use a bowl of hot soup to get them through the night?"

"You sensed him, too, didn't you?" Doug stared into the dining room, through the large glass windows, and into the dark night that caressed the old camp site across the street. "Skipper?"

"I did," Max nodded and reached for a quart-sized, TO

GO, container. "He's been over there for a few hours now." He filled the bottom of the container with rice, followed by heaping ladles of the steaming bean soup.

"They were supposed to release him before five o'clock today," Doug said. "I offered to pick him up and take him wherever he needed to go, but he refused. He said he had a ride, but I'm wondering if he didn't end up walking the entire way from the hospital."

"Yes, you weren't the only one who offered to give him a ride." Max put a lid on the container and reached for two smaller ones for the pole beans and macaroni and cheese. "Officer O'Brady visited him at the hospital—brought his personal belongings, from the jail."

Doug shook his head. "I've never met a more stubborn human being than Skipper. I wonder if he's ever allowed anyone to help him."

"I can answer that," Max sighed. "No, he hasn't. He hasn't felt like he belonged anywhere or to anyone his entire life."

"That is so sad," Doug rubbed the bridge of his nose. "I'll bag the food up and walk over there. Maybe he'll feel like talking tonight."

Max released a small laugh. "I have no doubt he'll accept the food, but I wouldn't get my hopes up for any deep or lengthy conversation with Gordon Whiting."


Jimmy had watched Michael all night—smoking one joint after another, drinking one beer after another. It was a little past midnight and the lake house was eerily quiet, but the sounds of nature outside were in full orchestra. He had lived in Georgia—mostly rural areas—his entire life and he recognized the sounds in the woods outside the glass doors to be a mixture of cave crickets, katydids, catbirds, white-tail deer, and bobcats.

The old woman had retreated to the bedroom an hour earlier after searching the cabinet and refrigerator for some real food. She had to settle for a jar of peanut butter and saltines. Since they had no access to silverware, Jimmy assumed she would use her fingers to spread the peanut butter on the crackers. She had glanced down at Mike, who was passed out in one of the huge recliners, and whispered to Jimmy as she shuffled past him, "You should kill him in his sleep."

Jimmy waited until the old woman had closed the bedroom door. "Psst...hey, Mike...are you awake?" Jimmy whispered loudly from his spot across the room. The low flames from the fire place provided the only light in the large game room. He stood up slowly and carefully, and the sight of his looming shadow scared him back to a sitting position. "Geez," he gasped. "That must be what it means to be afraid of your own shadow." He waited a few moments and stood back up. He held his chain up high so that it didn't drag against the wood floor, and took tiny, quiet steps toward the recliner.

Jimmy stopped when he reached the recliner, and looked around the room for anything he might be able to use as a weapon. He didn't want to hurt anyone, but then again, he didn't want to die either. He was so worried about his mom and what she might be going through—missing him and frightened about what could have happened to him. He had to get back to her.

Jimmy had watched Kirk, on Friday, as he thoroughly cleared the basement rooms of any objects that could be used as a weapon. He knew that all sharp items had been placed in the kitchen pantry, and secured with a padlock—a padlock very similar to the one that secured the chain to Jimmy's and the old woman's ankles. He knew that his three former friends all had their own keys to those padlocks.

Where were Mike's keys?

Jimmy backed slowly away from the recliner and inched his way into the kitchen. He didn't see the keys anywhere. It was possible that Mike had placed them in his pants pocket, but Jimmy had been watching when Mike arrived earlier, and he didn't remember seeing him with his keys. "Well, I'm no Dick Tracy," Jimmy spoke out loud. "But, that could mean that he left the keys in his car, or in his coat pocket— maybe." He took a deep breath and moved over to the wall hooks that currently held only two jackets—his own and Mike's.

*"Please be in there,"* he prayed silently. He really didn't expect to feel anything when he searched the first pocket— and, he didn't. He took a deep breath, closed his eyes, and offered another quick, silent prayer before sticking his hands into the second pocket. His fingers felt the cool ridges of several keys on a large keyring. Jimmy opened his eyes and willed himself to breathe—just breathe. He shook his head and pulled his top lip down with his teeth. "Thank you, God..."

A loud snore from across the room startled Jimmy so much that he immediately dropped the keys onto the stone hearth. He thought the clattering sound was surely loud enough to wake the dead—and most certainly—Mike. He was wrong. Mike was so strung out on pot and booze that he was in a deep, drug-and-alcohol induced sleep. Jimmy froze and waited for what seemed like an eternity before he had the nerve to turn around and glance back at Mike—to assure himself that the sound of the keys had not awakened him. He leaned over slowly and retrieved the keys. He moved them, one by one, slowly around the key ring, and finally found one small enough that it had to be the one that would unlock the padlock.

He sat down on the hearth, inserted the key into the padlock at his ankle, held his breath, and turned the key slowly. He thought the sound of the click releasing the lock would surely wake Mike, but the loud sound he was certain it made had only been in his head. He blew out three quick breaths when he released the chain from around his ankle. He looked around for his shoes, but David had locked them away when he discovered the old woman's missing shoe. It had taken a while, but David eventually convinced himself that the missing shoe had to still be in the trunk of Kirk's car—something he intended to verify when he saw Kirk.

Jimmy peered at the set of keys and quickly identified the key to Jimmy's Toyota Tundra pick-up truck. "Who needs shoes, anyway?" he asked himself as he moved toward the sliding glass doors. "Well, look at that," another sigh escaped him. "Mike left the door unlocked..."

The loud clank of chain against floor echoed throughout the room when Stella shuffled back into the room. "What the hell are you doing?" she barked.

Mike snorted loudly in his sleep and he turned on his side, but he didn't wake up.

Jimmy closed his eyes and pursed his lips together. He brought his finger to his lips to silence the old woman, but doubted she could see that small gesture from across the darkened room. He moved quickly to where Stella stood outside the bedroom door and grabbed her shoulder. "Hush! I found the key. Come on, let's get out of here!" He bent down to unlock the padlock at the old woman's ankle.

Stella held onto the boy's shoulder to steady herself. She had resigned herself that she would, most likely, die in this place, and she was quickly taken aback at the prospect for escape. "Okay, okay—but, hurry! He could wake up at any time."

"He's totally drunk—passed out cold," Jimmy said as the lock fell away from Stella's swollen ankle.

"Take it from someone who knows, kid—he could wake up at any time—nobody is ever that drunk." She moved away from Jimmy and made her way to the sliding door. She slid it open and shivered. "We're gonna freeze our asses off out there."

Jimmy moved quickly to her side and glanced down at their shoeless feet. He dangled the key ring in front of her and glanced back at Mike, who was still oblivious to what was happening while he slept. "Lucky for us—we have the key to his truck, too. Come on..." He grabbed his light jacket off the hook, and handed Mike's to Stella.

Once outside, Stella rushed quickly to the pick-up truck and hopped into the front passenger seat. Jimmy put the vehicle in neutral, and pushed it a hundred feet away from the lake house before he hopped in, put it in gear, and drove away slowly, headlights off.

"I gotta hand it to you, kid," Stella said between coughing fits. "You surprised me—and there ain't much out there that surprises old Stella anymore." She coughed again and stared ahead at the long, gravel drive-way. "You do know how to drive, don't you?"

Jimmy grinned and stared into the darkness ahead of them. "Yes ma'am, I do—my mom taught me." He slowed when they reached the huge, iron gate. "I forgot about the gate; it needs a key, too—I saw Kirk unlock it when we first got here." He could only hope that the padlock key would open the gate, also. He cut the engine off, removed the key ring, and rushed to the front gate. The lights from the truck allowed him to quickly find the padlock key. He inserted it and, once again, uttered another quick, silent prayer.

The key fit.

Jimmy laughed out loud and pumped his fist into the night air. He pushed the gate open and hopped back into the truck. "It worked!" he grinned at the old woman across the seat from him. "It really worked!"

He started the truck back up and put it in gear. They cleared the gate and Jimmy wasn't the least bit concerned about shutting it behind them. "We're out of here..." he sighed.

The oncoming headlights blinded him and he shook his head in denial when the old woman began screaming. The single-lane road that lead to the lake house drive-way was surrounded on both sides by tall pines and massive shrubs; both cars would never fit on that narrow road—there was nowhere for Jimmy to pull off—to go around the black Land Cruiser that blocked their path.

❖

Doug flipped over the CLOSED sign as he walked out the café's front door, carrying two large sacks of food and coffee for Skipper. He was going to do his best to talk Skipper into coming back and sharing the upstairs bedroom with Bernard. The temperature was supposed to drop below freezing again tonight, and he couldn't bear the thought of Skipper sleeping on the cold, frozen ground — especially with the infection in his hand still at risk.

He walked quickly across the street, through the bushes, and into the campground. There was a small fire burning, and Doug sighed with relief when he saw Skipper sitting close to the fire, leaning over it for warmth. His back was to Doug, and his backpack pressed against his lower back — Doug assumed it was for support.

Doug saw the collapsed boxes that used to be home for Norman, Joe, and Bernard. The winds had destroyed the makeshift tents. The site looked exactly like what it was — deserted, except for one man alone — Skipper.

Doug cleared his throat and walked closer. "Hi, Skipper. I thought you might be hungry. Max made some soup that you're going to love, but it's bean soup, so it's probably a good thing that you're here by yourself tonight..." It was apparent to him that his feeble attempt at humor was not having any impact on the lone Veteran. "Skipper?"

Doug cleared his throat again when he reached Skipper's side, and sat the bags down beside him. "It's really cold out tonight, Skipper. I was hoping I might talk you into coming back to the café with me. You can share the room with Bernard. Jason is staying with Cheryl, and Joe went home — he's so excited about becoming a grandfather. Did you know about that, Skipper?" Doug had never expected any lengthy conversation from Skipper, but he thought his words might at least generate a grunt, at the very least.

Something was wrong. Skipper should have said something to him by now, or at least acknowledged him. It was mere seconds before he was convinced that something really was wrong — very wrong. "Skipper?"

Neither he nor Max had picked up on anything like he now suspected.

He walked slowly and stopped in front of Skipper, who sat cross-legged, elbows on his upper legs, hands clasped and propped under his chin. His head and shoulders were bent forward. Doug kneeled down slowly and laid his hand upon the old Veteran's shoulder. "Skipper?"

Skipper's notebook of poems dropped from his lap and Skipper fell over on his side, onto the cold ground.

The slightly bluish tint of his lips should have been more than enough to convince the angel that the homeless Veteran who had served his country so well, and so hard, had finally gone home. "Oh, no...Skipper," Doug bowed his head in prayer He raised his head when he heard the angel chimes sound from across the street.

Bertie and Max held each other and looked upward into a night filled with total darkness, except for one lone star, directly above them.

"Welcome home, Skipper," Max choked. "Welcome home..."

# CHAPTER 32

## No Chance for Escape

Dottie O'Brady climbed out of bed and put her robe on. She checked on the twins before she made her way down the dark hallway that led to the downstairs. The light coming from the study convinced her that she had been right—her husband had waited until she fell asleep before getting out of bed and going back to work. She stood in the doorway to the study and crossed her arms. "Thomas O'Brady, you promised you would wait until tomorrow to sort through your notes."

Thomas made an attempt to look chagrined. "Sorry, love, but something kept nagging at me about Stella Seiber."

Dottie flopped down into the small, well-worn recliner and lifted the latch to prop her feet up. "The old woman, right? The one you went looking for at that nasty bar at the end of town?"

"That's the one," Thomas grinned. "I told you I found a shoe on the road that led back into town. I can't prove that it's Stella's, but something kept nagging at me, so I went back to the Pickled Possum before I came home tonight. I wanted to interview a few other customers—ones that might not have been there early in the morning when I talked to the bartender." He shuffled through his notes until he found what he had been searching for. "Here it is!"

"You didn't tell me you went back to that bar?" Dottie stretched out in the recliner and reached for the crocheted afghan that draped over the back of the chair. "I could smell the smoke on you when you came in this evening."

"I'm not surprised," Thomas replied absently, as he re-read his notes from an interview with one of the bar's regulars. He tapped the paper. "This man—a regular at the bar—told me that he passed Stella on his way to the bar—said she was walking toward town—on Friday afternoon. He said she was a regular at the bar, too, so he knew who she was—didn't know her name—but identified her from the picture I showed him. He said he went inside the bar but had to return after a few minutes to get his wallet from his truck. He said that's when he saw a black SUV pull up beside Stella as she was walking down the road. He saw someone get out of the passenger side, approach Stella, punch her, and then dragged her into the car."

Dottie sat upright. "He saw all this and didn't report it? I don't believe it!"

Thomas shook his head. "You have to consider the source, love. That side of town—and the people you find there—trust me, nobody wants to get involved with anyone else's business."

"But he watched an old woman get punched and dragged into a car, and he didn't think it was worth reporting."

"He said he figured it was someone who Stella stole from or owed money to, and he wasn't about to get involved."

"Well, could he at least give you a description of the car?" Dottie was still angry at the lack of humanity and compassion that some people exhibited.

"The car was too far away, but he said it looked new and expensive. He did say that the person who grabbed

Stella looked young."

"Young?"

Thomas nodded again. "Young—as in—not quite a man yet, teenagers maybe."

"What kind of teenagers can afford new and expensive SUVs?" Dottie grimaced.

Thomas looked back at her and smiled from ear-to-ear. Her last question had released something from his recent memories—a black SUV, full of teenagers, who had tried to pick a fight with a homeless man in a park. "Well, I'll be damned..." His cell phone rang. "O'Brady here." He was quiet while he listened to dispatch tell him about the call that had just come in about Gordon Whiting. "Thank you," he whispered into the phone and hung up.

Dottie was out of the chair the moment she noticed the paling of her husband's skin. "What's wrong, Thomas?"

Tears flowed from Thomas' eyes and he shook his head. It felt like he was losing a father all over again; he never knew the first one, and Skipper was the closest he had ever come to knowing anyone who might have been like his own father. "He's dead...Skipper is dead."

Kirk jumped from the Land Cruiser and reached for the Smith & Wesson, M&P Shield 9mm he carried inside a waistband-concealed carry holster. He had taken the gun from his father's locked gun cabinet when he got home from school, earlier that day. His father had a collection of seventeen handguns and twelve rifles and shotguns, so he doubted that this one gun would be missed anytime soon.

Kirk had spent the entire day at school, thinking about the situation he was in with his two hostages. The more he thought about it, the more convinced he became that killing them both was the only solution to his predicament. The old woman would be easy—nobody would miss her anyway; but, the Crennan boy was a different matter. He had seen the police at school today, interviewing the students in Jimmy's classes. He figured it would only be a matter of time before they got around to talking to other classes, as well.

The three friends had worked out a schedule to get them through one week. David would keep watch over their hostages on Monday; Mike would change shifts with him after school on Monday; and, Kirk would replace Mike on Tuesday morning, early enough for Mike to make an appearance at school. They intended to keep this schedule for a week, but Kirk had not anticipated the immediate response from the police department. Their search for Crennan had mandated that Kirk speed up things—to re-think his initial plans.

"Stop right there, Crennan! Don't you dare take another step—you either, old lady. Turn around, both of you. Start walking back to the house, and don't try anything stupid. I know how to use this gun."

Jimmy took a step forward and tried to reason with Kirk. "You don't have to do this..."

Kirk pulled the trigger and the bullet ripped through Jimmy's left shoulder, missing his heart by only two inches. The bullet entered and exited Jimmy's skin cleanly. There was a lot of blood, but Kirk wasn't lying when he said he knew how to use the gun—he could just as easily have centered his target on the heart.

Jimmy grabbed his shoulder and dropped to his knees. Stella screamed loudly into the empty darkness. There were no other houses around—no chance for anyone to hear her screams, but she kept screaming, nonetheless.

Kirk slowly aimed the gun at Stella. "Shut up, old woman—or you're next!"

Stella either didn't hear Kirk, or she was too scared to care—she continued screaming.

Kirk raised his gun again. His aim was sure and as accurate as he intended it to be. Stella Sieber stared blank-eyed at him and fell like a ragdoll, to the ground. The bullet had found its mark—square and center of her forehead.

Jimmy was losing a lot of blood and was in shock—not so much from his own loss of blood, but from seeing the old woman drop beside him and stare up at him with open, accusatory eyes. He had failed to save them both.

The screaming and gun shots had jolted Mike from his drunken sleep. He came running—huffing and puffing—from the direction of the lake house. He saw Jimmy on his knees, and the old woman lying in a heap at his feet. He saw blood soaking through the back of Jimmy's jacket. He stared wide-eyed with panic at his best friend, who stood in front of them both, holding a pistol. "Damn, Kirk—what did you do, man?"

Kirk took three deep breaths and finally returned the pistol to its hidden carrying case in his waistband. He stared hard at Jimmy, barely glanced at Stella, and then looked back at the person who was supposed to be watching his prisoners. "This is all on you, Mikie—all on you. Put them both in the back of your truck and get back to the house," his voice echoed into the empty night.

Mike ran his fingers through his hair and tried hard to focus on what was happening—what had happened. "But…we had a plan, Kirk. We had a plan."

Kirk jumped back inside his car and rolled down the window. He gunned the engine loudly and yelled back. "The plan just changed!"


It was after midnight when Officer O'Brady followed Doug back to the Heavenly Grille Café. He went inside and Doug poured them both a cup of coffee.

"I can't believe he's really gone," Thomas sat on the stool and lifted the hot coffee to his frozen lips. "I mean, here the man was—accused of a crime he didn't commit, stabbed by some crazy inmate, and, finally cleared of the crime. Justice had been served. He was free to go." He stared at Doug with a dazed look. "He gave me a hard time about giving him a ride from the hospital, but I wouldn't take no for an answer. I dropped him off at the campsite just after dark tonight. He said he was going to work on his poetry. I was worried about him being out in the cold; I even offered him our couch for the night."

"Skipper wasn't one to accept generosity from anyone. Don't blame yourself, Officer. That's why I went over to him tonight—to try to talk him into coming back and staying in the upstairs apartment." Doug walked behind the counter and grabbed Skipper's backpack. He handed it to the officer. "I brought this back with me. I probably should have left it at the campsite and let the police deal with it, but, I don't know...it just didn't seem right to have strangers going through his stuff. You probably talked with him more than anybody else ever has, so I thought you might know what to do with all this—who to give it to."

Thomas opened the backpack and saw the notebook lying on top. He took it out and held it to his chest.

"That fell from his lap," Doug offered. "I didn't see a pen, so I'm guessing, maybe, he was just reading some of his poems."

"I think they were the only thing that ever gave him peace of mind," Thomas smiled. "His poems were a way for him to remember and acknowledge the soldiers he served with—especially the ones who didn't make it back home." He flipped through the pages again. He stopped at the last written page. "This must be a new one—I don't remember seeing it before. I guess he could have written it while he was in jail, or in the hospital, maybe."

"Which one?" Doug asked as he peered over the officer's shoulder.

Thomas pointed to the last, filled page of the notebook. "This one—he titled it, *That One Final Day*." Thomas read the poem to himself and smiled. "Listen to it..."

*Dreams seldom last beyond first light*

*Leaving the horrors of realism to pass in the night;*
*We focus on life as we know it today*
*Knowing we are all destined to that one final day.*

*Depth of one's vision rules all the late years*
*Defining all truths along with the fears;*
*We must brace to the wind while facing the rain*
*Then harness our thoughts into full refrain.*

*Time fades the sight as the mind grows less keen*
*Remembering less each day of the life we have seen;*
*There seems to be less faith when we kneel down to pray*
*As we drift to the downside of that one final day.*

*The progression of time is more difficult to endure*
*A once positive mind becomes less and less sure;*
*Days flash by without the freshness of youth*
*Only to collide with the harshness of truth.*

*We can never recapture the youth that we've spent*
*As our body gains age, a message is sent;*
*Both the rich and the poor shall wither away*
*Then we all become equals on that one final day.*

Thomas closed his eyes and barely managed to hold back the tears. He had grown attached to this lone, brave Veteran over the past few weeks, and he would miss him. He closed the notebook and held it to his chest again. He looked over at Doug and said, "Thank you for this. I have the contact information for Skipper's brother. I'll notify him in the morning."

Doug nodded. "Yeah, he did have an older brother, didn't he?"

"Yes, he did. I don't think they had seen each other in a long, long time. It's too bad that their reunion also has to be their final good-bye."

Doug placed a comforting hand upon the officer's

shoulders. "Our Father always told me that good-byes are not forever — good-byes are not the end — they simply mean I'll miss you...until we meet again."

"*OUR* Father?" Thomas asked.

Doug squeezed the officer's shoulder again. "Yes, *OUR* Father..."

# CHAPTER 33

## Too Late for Regrets

Neither Michael nor Kirk had gotten any sleep. Michael paced back and forth in front of the glass sliding doors, glancing occasionally at what he knew still laid in the bed of his pick-up. He had bitten his nails down to the nubs during the long night. His mind was relatively clear of drugs and alcohol, but he wished that it wasn't. He knew that he could handle everything that had happened much better if he could just dull the finality of it all.

"Will you please sit down!" Kirk yelled. "Go check on Crennan before you leave—make sure the packing is holding in his wound. I wouldn't want him bleeding to death before I can kill him, too."

"You really did it, Kirk," Mike continued his pacing. "I can't believe you really did it. I mean, I guess I thought this was all just fun and games—that you were just trying to scare the two of them—but, man oh man, I never thought you would ever really do it."

"I need you to hold it together, Mikie. I never thought you would be the one to freak out on me." Kirk went into the kitchen and put on a pot of coffee.

"No, man!" Kirk shrieked. "It's not like that, I swear. If anything, man—I'm like in freaking awe of you. That was awesome! You really killed that old hag! BANG! Right square between the eyes, too!"

"Calm down," Kirk sighed deeply. "This isn't one of your stupid video games. It really happened. The old woman is dead."

"Yeah, man, like I know that—she's in the back of my freaking pick-up truck!" Mike shook his head and paced some more. "Hey, she can't stay there, right? I mean, like, I've got to get to school. We have to keep doing this, right—keeping to the schedule?"

Kirk nodded. "Yeah, for now anyway, but things are moving quicker than we first planned." He started to pour himself a cup of coffee, but instead, walked over to the hearth and put on his jacket. "Get the old woman's chain and come with me."

Mike's jacket was still on Stella, so he grabbed Jimmy's lighter-weight one—the one with a blood-stained bullet hole. He gathered up Stella's chain that had been left where it had fallen the night before. "What about Crennan?"

"We'll check on him when we finish what we have to do."

"What do we have to do?" Mike asked as he bumped into Kirk's back on the way out the door. "The sun's barely up, and I need to sneak home and change clothes before I go to school."

"Just bring the chain, Mike—and hurry up," Kirk opened the tailgate to his friend's truck. He dragged Stella's cold, stiff body to the edge of the truck, bent down and threw her over his shoulders.

Mike was still tagging along at Kirk's heels and had to jump back when half of the old woman's body flew over his friend's shoulders. He drew back again when her head bounced off Kirk's back and one of her hands flew out toward him. "Damn!" he hissed. "She is dead, isn't she?"

Kirk sighed but didn't look back at his friend. "Just bring

the chain and follow me."

"Where are we going, Kirk? What are you going to do with her? We don't need the chain to bury her, do we?"

Kirk bit his tongue and didn't respond to Mike's idiotic questioning. Instead, he walked quickly and steadily toward the end of the dock. When he reached the end, he leaned forward and allowed Stella's body to drop hard against the wood decking. He nodded toward some concrete blocks that were stacked near one of the postings. "Grab one of those blocks and bring it over here. Give me the chain."

Reality seeped in quickly—even for Mike. He giggled and hurried to retrieve the concrete block. "Oh, man! This is just like in the movies—I love it! Nobody will ever find her in the bottom of this lake. It's one of the deepest lakes in the county."

Kirk wrapped one end of the chain around Stella's bony ankle and secured it with the padlock. He looped the other end of the chain around the holes in the concrete block, and secured it with another padlock. He stood up and stared down at Stella—at the clean hole in her forehead. Her eyes were still open, staring at him, but he felt *nothing*—no emotion at all when he stared back at her. "I wonder if she spent all of the five hundred dollars I gave her?" He bent down and dragged her body to the very edge of the dock.

"Maybe we should, like, row her out to the middle of the lake and dump her there," Michael suggested.

Kirk looked back at him like he had grown two heads. "I'm not rowing out to the middle of the lake—are you? Do you want to do it?"

Mike backed up and lifted both hands. "No, man—it was just a suggestion."

Kirk used his foot to push Stella over the edge of the dock. It was only a two-foot drop to the water, so there wasn't much of a splash. She didn't weigh enough to drag the concrete block all the way along with her, so he pushed it to the edge to make it easier for momentum to take over. He removed the gun and holster from his waist, and threw them as hard as he could toward the middle of the lake.

"That should keep her down there until the fish get their fill," Mike giggled. "Oh, man — I can't believe we did this. Awesome — totally, awesome! That was a nice gun, though, man — too bad you couldn't have kept it."

The two friends turned and walked back to the lake house. "Go check on Crennan before you leave, Mike. He should be fine; the bleeding stopped last night."

"What are going to do with him, Kirk? You can't shoot him, because you just threw the gun away. Hey — whatever — just make sure you don't do it before I get back here, okay?"

Kirk nodded. "Go on. I'll be here all day and night. David will relieve me in the morning. I'll make final plans by the time we all gather back here on Friday afternoon."

"Okay, okay," Michael giggled again. "Hey, you know the police are looking for Jimmy-Boy, right?"

Kirk shrugged. "So — let them look. They have no reason to connect any of us with him."

Officer O'Brady walked out of the police station and headed for his cruiser. He had Skipper's notebook in his hand and dropped it into the passenger seat. He looked over at it as he buckled up and smiled. "One last ride with me, Skipper, before your brother comes to claim you and all your belongings." He laughed out loud and shook his head. "Well, that sounded a little morbid, didn't it?"

It only took him about fifteen minutes to get to Rome High School. He wanted to follow up on his suspicions about the black SUV that supposedly picked Stella up on Friday afternoon. He remembered the name of the teenager who drove a black SUV — Kirk Blankenship, a rich kid with a bad attitude.

Kirk was reported as absent this Tuesday morning, but Thomas was able to secure the names of some of his closest friends, from his homeroom teacher. He glanced down at his pad—David Mizen, Michael Bozeman, and Kristy Littleton. He stopped at the classroom where David Mizen was supposed to be and knocked softly on the door. The teacher opened it, and he explained that he needed to talk to David.

David walked down the hallway with the officer, already suspecting why he had pulled him from class. *"Be cool, David—just be cool. They don't know anything,"* he told himself.

Thomas led him to a small room that the school had assigned the police to conduct the questioning. He held the door open for him. "Please come inside, David."

David wiped his sweaty hands against his jeans. "What's this about?"

Thomas took note of the nervous gesture, but didn't think much about it. He would have been more surprised if the young man had not been nervous talking to police. "You may have already heard, but the department is interviewing students here about the disappearance of Jimmy Crennan."

David shrugged. "Never heard of him."

"Are you sure about that, David?"

David shifted in his seat and looked at the floor. "Yeah, I'm sure."

"Okay," Thomas nodded. "What about Stella Seiber? Have you ever heard of her?"

"Who?" David was genuinely surprised because he never knew the old woman's name.

"Stella is a homeless woman who was assisting the police in a murder investigation. We need to ask her some more questions, but she seems to have disappeared, too."

David grunted. "I don't know any homeless people." He shifted again in his seat and looked down at the floor.

"Look at me, David."

David tensed at the firmness and authority in the officer's voice. He looked up. "What? I told you I don't know either of those people."

"I don't think you're being honest with me, David."

Thomas leaned back in the chair and continued to study the boy's nervous movements. "You see, one of our officers talked to several of Jimmy's classmates yesterday. One of them told the officer that Jimmy hung out with some older kids for a few months. One of those older kids was you, David."

David's head jerked up. "Well, they're lying. I told you that I don't know this Crennan kid, and I sure don't know any old, scrawny homeless woman."

Thomas was quiet for a few moments before he sat his chair back down on four legs. "I never said anything about Stella Seiber being old and scrawny, David."

Michael had rushed home after he left the lake house, to change clothes before heading to school. His parents had both already left for work, so he was relieved not to have to deal with them. He took a quick shower, dressed, grabbed his backpack and Crennan's jacket—he needed to get rid of that jacket—and broke every speed limit to get to school before his first class ended.

He could not get the image of the old woman out of his head—the small hole in her forehead, her open eyes, her frail body as it rolled off the dock and sank quickly into the lake. He was grinning to himself when he ducked in a side door and tried to remember which class he was supposed to be in that morning. He was running down the hall when a door opened and David walked out. "Hey there, buddy! Man you would not believe what went down last night..."

Mike didn't immediately connect the look of panic on David's face—until a policeman walked out behind him.

Thomas held the door open and nodded. "I know who Kirk Blankenship is, so I'm guessing you might be..." he looked down at his pad. "Michael Bozeman?"

Michael froze and the smile on his face quickly dissipated.

"Michael Bozeman?" Thomas queried again.

Mike pulled his shoulders back and put on his best

tough-guy image. "Yeah, that's me. What's going on?"

"I have some questions for you, Michael. Your friend here, David, has already talked to me. Haven't you, David?"

David's panicked expression returned when he saw Michael glare at him. He shook his head vehemently, from side to side. "I didn't tell him anything, Mike."

Thomas didn't know what these two boys were hiding, but he knew they were hiding something. Maybe a trip to the police station would loosen their tongues. "I think the two of you need to come down to the precinct with me, for more questioning. Your parents do not have to be present, but I'll be glad to contact them, if that will make you both feel more comfortable."

"But, I already talked to you!" David replied weakly. He looked to Mike for silent affirmation of what to do.

Mike shook his head. "Naw, we don't need our parents there; but, why can't you just talk to us here, like they did everyone else yesterday?"

Thomas stared hard at them both and went with his instinct. "Because I think you both might know more than you're willing to tell me here at school. Come on, boys, let's go. I'll drive."

David and Mike walked in front of the officer, exited the building, and stood in the parking lot.

"I need to get something out of my truck," Michael spoke curtly.

"Go ahead, Michael," Thomas nodded. "We'll walk along with you."

Thomas and David stood at the back of the truck while Michael pretended to rummage for something inside the truck. He shoved Crennan's jacket under the driver's seat and began quickly removing the joints from his backpack and shoving them under the seat, too—in case the police asked to search his bag. It didn't occur to him to just leave his bag inside the truck.

Thomas moved closer to the bed of the truck and glanced inside. He noticed small dark streaks of something that ran from the middle of the bed to the end of the tailgate; another dark smudge was on the other side of the streak. He moved around to the back of the truck and opened the tailgate, and rubbed the dark streak with his finger. It was congealed, but he knew it was blood.

"What's this, Michael?" he asked when Mike joined them at the back of the truck.

Michael paled visibly and glanced quickly at David.

David shrugged and looked back at him, wide-eyed and fearful. He still did not know what had happened the night before.

"I went hunting over the weekend," Mike finally answered. "Caught me a six-pointer."

"Really?" Thomas looked at both boys. "A deer, you say?"

Mike nodded. "Yeah—it was a deer—a really big one."

Thomas nodded back at him. "Okay. That should be easy enough for our forensics department to verify. You'll need to hand over your keys, Michael."

"Why?" Mike asked stubbornly. "I told you I killed a freaking deer!"

"It won't take long to confirm that it was a deer. I'll need your keys until the wrecker service brings your truck in for examination."

David rubbed the back of his neck furiously. He didn't say anything to Mike until the officer placed them both in the back seat of the police cruiser. "What happened last night?" he whispered before Thomas opened the driver's door.

Mike looked at him and threatened, "You just keep your mouth shut about everything..."

# CHAPTER 34

## A Mother Knows

Jason stepped out of the shower a little after ten o'clock Tuesday morning. He looked into the mirror, at the stubble that had grown over his face—he had not shaved since Jimmy went missing last Friday. He rubbed his hands over his face and stared into the steamy mirror. "A few more days and you'll have a full-grown beard." His voice sounded weak, even to him. The last few days had been agony for him, so he could only imagine what impact it was all having on Cheryl. He thought she had been holding together extremely well, considering everything that was running through his own mind.

He continued to stare into the mirror and finally shook his head. He closed his eyes and looked upward. "I'm not sure if I believe in you or not, God; but, if there's the slightest chance that you're real, then please help us out here. Don't let this linger. Please help Cheryl get the answers that she needs." He shook his head and kept his eyes closed. "I just don't understand it, God. Why would you give me a son—a family—if you only intended to snatch them away from me? Why?"

Cheryl heard his murmuring and knocked on the bathroom door. "Jason? Are you alright?"

Jason opened his eyes and cleared his throat. He flushed the unused toilet, ran some water under the faucet and yelled out. "Be right there. I didn't know you were up yet—hope I didn't wake you."

Cheryl leaned her head against the door. She thought that his voice sounded funny—it almost had a quiver in it that she had not heard before. "No, I barely slept again last night. I made a pot of coffee, whenever you're ready."

"I'll be out in a few minutes," he yelled back. He took several deep breaths and composed himself as best he could. He had to be strong for Cheryl. He couldn't let her suspect how worried he was that her son—their son—had now been missing for more than seventy-two hours.

He only owned three changes of clothing, and Cheryl had washed all of them for him the night before. He looked down at his faded flannel shirt. "Well, at least you're clean." He rubbed his face again and cast one last look into the mirror. "I'll shave when Jimmy comes home."

Cheryl smiled when he walked into the kitchen. "I can fix you something to eat, if you're hungry."

Jason shook his head. "No, thanks, I'm good—still full from the food Max sent home with us last night. "If he wasn't a man, I think I'd marry him for his cooking."

Cheryl allowed a tiny laugh to escape. She had almost forgotten what it felt like to laugh. "Well, if you don't claim him, I think I will!"

"He does cook up one mean meal, alright," Jason grinned and poured himself a cup of coffee. "Have you ever—I don't know how to explain it—but, have you ever felt *different* whenever you're at the café?"

Cheryl cupped her hand over her mouth in an attempt to stifle a yawn that still managed to escape. "Different?" She paused and thought for a minute. "Well, now that you mention it...yes."

"How?" Jason pushed for more information. He was

curious to see if she had ever experienced the same feelings he had whenever he was around the café or the people who worked there.

Cheryl shrugged. "I'm not sure, exactly, but...well, it's sort of like a feeling of peace that comes over me. Whenever I'm there, I don't have all the negative thoughts about what's happened to Jimmy, as I do whenever I'm here at the house. Does that make sense?"

Jason sat down beside her. "Yeah, it does. There's something else, too."

"What?"

"Have any of them—the workers at the café—have any of them ever...*touched* you?"

Cheryl looked at him and grinned. "Touched me how?"

Jason closed his eyes and shook his head. "No, no—I don't mean like that, silly. I mean, like just laying a hand on your shoulder, or holding your hand..."

"I was just teasing you," Cheryl touched his shoulder. "To answer your question—yes—I've had a strange sensation whenever Bertie has hugged me, pulled me close, or held my hand. It's a very comforting sensation, if you know what I mean."

"Oh, I know exactly what you mean," Jason nodded. "The effect they have is a little puzzling, don't you think? Sometimes, I feel like I'm being—*bewitched!*"

"Ooohh...maybe they're witches!" Cheryl poked fun at him.

Jason was embarrassed at bringing up the subject. "Never mind, you probably think I'm crazy."

Cheryl took his hand into her own and stared deeply into his eyes. "Jason, you are anything but crazy. You're right—I do think there is something very special about that café, and even something more special about Bertie, Max, and Doug." She rubbed a finger over his high cheekbone. "But, I also think there's something even more special about you. You have no idea what your being here with me these past few days has meant to me. It's probably the only thing that has kept me sane and helped me to deal with the waiting."

Jason stared back at her—her face only mere inches from his own. He sighed and leaned forward enough to allow just the slightest touch of their lips. "I've wanted to do that again since I kissed you in the café—to cease your talking—remember?"

"Oh, I definitely remember," Cheryl sighed as she leaned in for another kiss. She would have enjoyed it lasting longer than it did, but the sudden ringing of her cell phone jarred them apart.

She didn't recognize the number, but answered it anyway. Her blood chilled and a stinging sensation began a slow creep down her spine—even before she heard the voice on the other end.

The voice was barely a whisper. "Mom?"

Cheryl stopped breathing and paled visibly.

"What's wrong?" Jason asked, alarm evident in his voice. He leaned in closer to try to listen in on the call.

"Mom? Are you there? I'm at the lake house…"

Cheryl's mouth hung open and she had not been able to utter a single sound before she heard a loud, clunking sound, followed immediately by a dial tone.


It was almost eleven o'clock when Kirk came back inside the lake house. He had been out to the dock several times that morning, not exactly sure of what he expected to find. He, mostly, wanted to reassure himself that Stella's body had not floated to the surface since he and Mike had pushed it into the lake. He had been having second thoughts and doubts about Mike's previous suggestion that they should have rowed the body to the middle of the lake before dumping it.

He flopped down on the couch and turned on the television to drown out the different voices and suggestions he kept hearing inside his own head. He stopped surfing channels when a local news report caught his eye. The reporter was telling his audience about the death of a homeless man—Gordon Whiting—who had only recently been acquitted of the murder of another homeless man, by the name of Norman Weissman. Kirk listened to the end of the report and chewed at his bottom lip. If Gordon Whiting had been acquitted, did that mean the police would continue looking for Weissman's killer? How did they know that Gordon Whiting wasn't the killer? Had the old woman told them the truth before he had gotten the chance to pick her up? Could the police be looking for him right this minute? Was that why David and Mike had not been answering his calls this morning?

Kirk began a rapid pace around the large game room, keeping his head down and trying not to listen to the voices again. Maybe he could plead temporary insanity if they discovered that he had anything to do with Weissman's murder. He felt confident that the old woman's murder would never be tied to him—but, there was still one person who could connect him to the old woman. "Crennan..." How was he going to dispose of Crennan without having it come back on him and his friends?

He looked down at his clothes and saw the dried blood all over his shirt and jeans. He would have to burn them. "I need a shower," he mumbled as he pushed open the door to the master suite. He went over to the bed to make sure Crennan was still breathing, then turned and closed the door to the master bath.

Jimmy had feigned sleep and waited several minutes until he heard the shower running. He tried to push himself to a sitting position, but collapsed against the pillows when his left shoulder betrayed him. He was sore and stiff, and the hole where the bullet went in and exited through his back burned like a forest fire. He looked around the room for the old woman, and it took several minutes before the memories of the night before came flooding back to him. His tears flowed and soaked the pillows, as he remembered that the old woman was dead—she had to be—Kirk had shot her squarely in the forehead. "Dear, God…what did he do?"

He turned his head to the left and saw Kirk's pile of dirty clothing lying in a heap outside the bathroom door. Something black and shiny was poking out of the pants pocket. Jimmy tried to focus on the object—tried to convince himself that it really was what he thought it was—what he *prayed* it was. He rolled over on his right side and was able to push himself up to a sitting position. The pain in his shoulder was unbearable, and for one quick moment, he thought he was going to pass out from it, but he worked through it and began a slow slide off the bed. He grabbed his chain with his good hand before it could clunk to the floor—the motion of that quick movement released a sharp intake of air from his lungs.

He took several short breaths as he made his way across the floor, to the pile of clothing. The closer he got to the clothes, the louder the water from the shower seemed to echo in his head. He felt safe as long as he continued to hear the sound of that running water.

When he finally made it to Kirk's piled clothes, he stopped and leaned his head against the bathroom door. The room felt like it was spinning, and the last thing he needed to do right now was to faint. He took three more giant breaths before kneeling down and using his thumb and index finger to pull the black, shiny object—a cell phone—from Kirk's pants. He held his chain and the cell phone in the same hand and made his way back past the bed, to the far window in the room. "Please let there be a signal," he spoke softly and listened for the sound of the running water. He punched in his mother's cell phone number and held his breath. She answered on the second ring.

"Mom?" He couldn't believe she really answered—that it was really her voice he was hearing. Tears flooded his eyes.

He was so focused on hearing his mom's voice, that he never noticed that the sound of running water had stopped.

"Mom? Are you there? I'm at the lake house…"

Kirk slammed a fist against the right side of Crennan's head. The force of the blow knocked the younger boy hard against the wall—his left arm and shoulder taking the full impact. The cell phone flew from Jimmy's hand, onto the wooden floor, and Kirk rushed to pick it up. He put it to his ear but didn't hear anything, so immediately disconnected the call. He assumed that he had gotten to the phone in the nick of time, before it had a chance to connect with whomever Jimmy Crennan had attempted to call.

His hands were balled into tight fists as he stared down at Jimmy. "That was a dumb move on your part, Crennan. Now, get up," his voice sounded calm, yet ominous. He saw that the bandage on the kid's shoulder was once again soaked with blood. The fall must have opened up the wound again. "I said, get up."

Jimmy struggled to get to his knees, and he was gasping for air. He didn't know which hurt more now—his torn shoulder, or his bashed-in temple. He could already feel his right eye beginning to swell shut. Somehow, he managed to push his weight against the wall and come to a standing position. He shook his head and stared at Kent. "You really killed her, didn't you? You killed that old woman?"

Jimmy only had a towel wrapped around his waist, but held it closed with one hand and moved closer to Jimmy. He was almost as tall as Jimmy so they were virtually eye-to-eye. He had a good twenty pounds on Jimmy and easily grabbed him around the throat with his free hand. "I did, Crennan—and, trust me, *that* should have you very, very worried." He released his hold on Jimmy and walked back toward the bathroom. "Get back in bed—unless you're prepared to die right now."


Ernest Blankenship couldn't explain why he was so restless and uneasy. He looked at his calendar and recognized the date immediately—the anniversary of Elizabeth's death. He looked up at the clock on his office wall for the fifth time in ten minutes. It was only 1:15 and the dealership seemed quieter than usual, almost eerily quiet. Business was slow—even for a Tuesday—but, it was more than that.

He had not slept well and had awakened at 2:00 in the morning. He had returned to his matrimonial bed the night before—having lost the conviction he had found in his earlier confrontation with Rae. He had gotten out of bed, and moved quietly from the room—trying not to awaken his wife, who snored softly and slept with a night mask over her eyes. They had talked about divorce, but she had eventually convinced him that he had not made a mistake in marrying her. He had reluctantly given in to her sultry advances, once again, and—once again—was disappointed in himself. He knew he needed to end the marriage before it was too late; it might very well already be too late for his son—the marriage had already caused so much turmoil between father and son. Ernest feared it could be too late to undo the damage.

He had opened the door to Kirk's room before he headed downstairs. The room was dark, but Ernest saw a dark silhouette of what he assumed to be his son, lying on his side, with his back to the door—the sheets pulled up high toward his head. That's what Ernest thought he saw.

Once he was downstairs, he fixed himself a cup of hot chocolate and took it into his study. He ran his hands over the books on the shelves and stopped when he came to a thick photo album, with a wide brown-velvet covering. He smiled and carried the album to his desk. The photos within the album brought him a sense of peace and tranquility that he had not felt for a long, long time. There were pictures of him and Elizabeth at the justice of the peace, working in their small yard together, playing with one of their many pets, sitting side-by-side in her hospital room the morning she gave birth to their only child, trips to Disney World and

Six Flags, boating trips, and so, so many pictures of their time together at their lake house.

Ernest shook his head as he sat at his office desk and thought about all the pictures he had looked through earlier that morning. The ones of the lake house especially haunted his memories. He closed his eyes and lowered his forehead onto his clasped hands. "Such good times, Elizabeth," he sighed. "We were all so happy then. Kirk was so happy then..."

When he finally opened his eyes, he knew what he had to do—what he needed to do. He punched in his secretary's extension and told her to clear his schedule for the rest of the day. He gathered his heavy coat and hat, walked to his car, and headed in the direction of Cave Spring. Maybe the lake house would bring him the peace that he so desperately needed in his life—especially today—the anniversary of his first wife's death.

# CHAPTER 35

## David Breaks

A lot of times—in a lot of situations—one good break might present itself and prove to be crucial to an ongoing investigation; rarely, however, do two breaks fall, simultaneously, into a cop's lap.

Officer Thomas O'Brady received such a break on Tuesday afternoon, February 9, 2016. He had brought David Mizen and Michael Bozeman in for questioning earlier that morning. The two had been kept separated upon their arrival at the station; Thomas continued his interview with David, and a detective working the case interviewed Michael.

Thomas had picked up quickly on the propagation that David was the weaker of the two friends.

If one of them was going to break, Thomas felt that it would be David. He had asked the detective in charge of Norman Weissman's murder investigation if he could be allowed to interview David again; the detective had agreed.

From 11:00 to 11:30, David had remained stoically quiet, refusing to answer any more of Officer O'Brady's questions.

From 11:30 to 12:00, David accepted a sandwich and soda

from Officer O'Brady. He ate in silence while O'Brady continued to ask him questions.

From 12:00 to 12:30, Officer O'Brady showed David pictures of Norman Weissman, lying in a pool of blood with his skull cracked open. He showed him pictures of Stella Seiber and Jimmy Crennan, both supposedly missing. By 12:30, David acknowledged that he did know Jimmy, but did not know anything about his whereabouts.

From 12:30 to 1:00, Thomas presented a picture of the shoe he had found on the side of the road. He stretched the truth and told David that they had a witness that could put Kirk's SUV at the scene of Stella's disappearance. He told him the witness had identified a younger man—possibly a teenager—he had seen punch Stella and drag her into the vehicle. Thomas had watched the young man's face intently and did not miss the grimace when he mentioned that someone had seen a young man punch the old woman. The last picture he showed David was the imprint of a man's shoe, found at the scene where Stella disappeared. Thomas turned the picture around and around and looked at it with great interest. He looked down at David's shoes. "What do you think we'll find, David, if we compare your shoe print with the one found at the scene?" His questions were primarily generated by sheer instinct at this point.

By 1:30, Thomas had called David's parents into the police station and explained about his interview with David, and the possible outcome of that interview. They immediately contacted their lawyer and instructed their son not to say another word. They left the room to make arrangements for David's release and Thomas moved in with what he hoped would be the deciding factor for David. "You can become a state witness against your friends, David." He was interrupted by a knock on the door and given a report of the blood found in Mike's truck. He looked at David and said, "This might be what they refer to as the nail in your coffin, David. It's the preliminary report on the dark stains found in Michael's truck." He paused for dramatic effect. "It was not animal blood, David—it was human blood."

David looked up; his face was a frantic canvas, mixed with fear, shock, and disbelief. He shook his head. "I don't know anything about that blood, Officer. Honest, I don't. All I know is what Mike said when he first got to school— that I wouldn't believe what went down last night."

"I think you know more than you're telling me, David. You get one chance today to help yourself. I can tell you what I suspect—that you and your friends are involved with the disappearance of two people: Stella Sieber and Jimmy Crennan. I can only demise that since Stella lied about Gordon Whiting being the killer of Norman Weissman, that she knows who really killed Norman. My guess is that you might, also, know something about that killing that you're not telling me."

"What do you mean—one chance to help myself?" David was steadily wiping his sweaty palms against his jeans. His ashen expression indicated that he might faint at any given moment.

Officer O'Brady had been correct—David was the weaker of the two friends. He stood up and gathered up the papers in his file. He looked down at David and said, "Tell me the truth—about everything—and be a witness for the state, against your friends—and, you will get a much lighter sentence than the one that awaits Kirk and Michael. We might not have enough concrete evidence today to arrest you right now, but you can rest assured that we will be watching your every move until we find out everything we need to know. Your every move, David." When it appeared that David wasn't going to volunteer any information, Thomas turned to leave the room. "I'll have your parents come back inside."

The officer was half way out the door when David jumped up and yelled. "No—wait! I…I want to help. I'll tell you everything I know…"

By 2:00, the detective had informed Michael that his

friend had turned state witness against him—that David had told them everything. Michael had giggled, called the detective a liar, and then grown extremely quiet when it dawned on him that the cop wasn't playing him—that David really had spilled the beans. He began screaming that it wasn't him who killed the old lady at the lake house—it was Kirk Blankenship.

By 3:00, the detective had a warrant to search the home and business of Kirk and Rae Blankenship, to include the lake house in Cave Spring, Georgia.


Jason and Cheryl had spent the last few hours sitting in her kitchen, mentally willing her cell phone to ring again. Cheryl had immediately called the police station and asked to speak to Officer O'Brady, but was told he was unavailable to come to the phone. She spoke to another police officer and told him about the phone call from her son. The officer assured her that he would pass the information along to Officer O'Brady. He, also, told her to consider the fact that the call could have been a prank call.

Cheryl stood at the kitchen window and stared outside. It was another bitterly cold day and she shivered when she looked at the coat hooks at the back door and saw Jimmy's heavy, cold-weather jacket hanging there. Only his light-weight jacket was missing; wherever he was, he must be so cold.

Jason came to stand behind her and rested his chin on top of her head, while he wrapped his arms around her.

She sighed and closed her eyes. "It wasn't a prank call, Jason. I know my son's voice. It was Jimmy—I'm sure of it. Why won't the police take this seriously—and, why hasn't Officer O'Brady called me back?"

"He's a good cop, Cheryl, and I'm sure there's a good reason why we haven't heard back from him yet."

She turned to face him. "Do you think it was just my imagination? Do you think I just wanted it to be Jimmy's voice so badly that I convinced myself it was him? And what about the lake house? What did that mean? We've never been to any lake house."

"But, that's what he said, right—that he was at the lake house?" Jason knew it was better to keep her talking than to let her imagination continue to run askew.

"Yeah—he said he was at the lake house—and, then, it sounded like he dropped the phone, maybe, and the call ended." She shook her head and exhaled. "What if whoever took him found him talking on the phone, Jason? What if they..." She couldn't finish that supposition.

Her cell phone rang and Cheryl jumped in Jason's arms. She pushed him away and rushed to the kitchen table where the phone lay. "Hello! Jimmy? Is that you, Jimmy?"

"It's Officer O'Brady, Ms. Crennan. I'm sorry it's taken so long for me to get back to you, but we've had a major breakthrough today. We interviewed two young men who know exactly where Jimmy is. I'm on my way there now, hopefully, to bring this ordeal to an end. I need you to sit tight, for a little while longer. Can you do that for me, Ms. Crennan?"

"You're going to the lake house, aren't you?" Cheryl's voice was beginning to crack.

Thomas cleared his throat. "Excuse me?"

"That's where Jimmy said he was at; he said he was at the lake house, and then he dropped the phone and the call went dead. I called the department, Officer O'Brady—I think the man who took the call thought the call I received was a prank call, so I wasn't sure if he would deliver the message to you or not."

"Oh, he delivered it alright," Thomas answered back. "He delivered it at the perfect moment, too. One of the young men had already confessed to me what he knew. By the time I saw your message and it was presented to the second young man, he told us everything we needed to know. I can tell you that as of 6:00 this morning, your son was very much alive, and if the call came in—what, around

10:30 — then that gives us even more hope that we'll get there in time."

"But where is this lake house?" Cheryl wanted to know. "Can I meet you there?"

"No, you cannot, Ms. Crennan. I need you to stay at home, close to your phone. I'll be honest with you. I don't know what I'll find when I get there. I'm heading out ahead of our back-up team — but, if Jimmy is hurt, then we'll get him to a hospital and let you know where. If he's okay, then I'll need him to go to the police station with me. Again, I'll call and let you know the second I know what's going on — you can meet us there, at the police station."

"But..." Cheryl was desperate to help — to do something besides sit at home and wait for the phone to ring.

Thomas was firm in his reply. "The sooner you allow us to do our job, Ms. Crennan, the sooner we can bring your son home to you. If you try to find the lake house, your life could be in jeopardy, or you could be putting your son's life in further jeopardy, so please...stay home. I promise that I will call you the minute we find Jimmy."

"Okay...okay. Thank you, Officer. I'll be waiting for your call."

"Are you alone, Ms. Crennan?"

"No," Cheryl shook her head and smiled when Jason wrapped his arms around her again. "No, I'm not alone..."


Kirk opened the door to the master bedroom. The lamp on the nightstand was on and provided enough light needed for the dismal, cloudy day outside. It was almost 2:30, but the heavy clouds made it seem closer to 4:30. He placed a bottle of water and some aspirin on the night stand. He almost grimaced when Jimmy turned to look at him, through his swollen, half-closed eye. "Take the aspirin, Crennan. I don't need you dying on me — not yet, at least." He slammed the bedroom door on his way out.

He walked back over to the sofa where he had left his cell

phone and tried to call Michael and David—again. He had been calling and texting them all day, and neither of them had responded to his texts and messages. He knew they were both in school, but, he also knew that they both checked their phones repeatedly throughout the day. He had the strangest sensation, and suspicion, that something was wrong—something was very wrong. He had decided to ride into town and check on them both, personally, if he had not heard from them by 4:30. They would regret it if he had to do that.

He paced the room for several more minutes before deciding to step outside to get some fresh air. The cold, damp air felt good against his clammy skin. It made him feel awake; it made him feel alive. He walked, once again, to the end of the dock and looked into the dark, murky water. Was it his imagination, or did he see the old woman staring up at him—mocking him, even in death?

"You're dead, old woman!" he screamed into the water. "You're dead! You can't come back for more money, and you won't ever be able to tell anyone the truth about what happened that night. You're dead!" His loud voice reverberated around the dock. Something splashed in the water beneath the dock, and Kirk nearly jumped out of his skin.

He turned away from the water—suddenly fearful that he really would see the old woman's reflection—and began walking back to the lake house. He stopped when he heard what sounded like tires on gravel, further up the driveway. "Well, it's about time!" he shouted. He was sure that it would be David, arriving early for his shift.

When he reached the driveway, he began running full-force toward the sound of the approaching vehicle. He intended to give David a piece of his mind for avoiding his phone calls all day. He was approaching a bend in the driveway when he came to a complete halt. He shook his head in denial. "No—no—no..."

The car screeched to an abrupt stop as it came around the

bend, breaking hard to avoid any contact with the young man that stood in the middle of the driveway.

The driver rolled down his window and leaned his head out. "Kirk! What are you doing here?"

Kirk shook his head and started backing away slowly. "What are *you* doing here, Dad?"

# CHAPTER 36

## Charles Meets His Past

Bertie sat beside one of her favorite truckers and listened to his traveling tales. Two other truckers sat across from them, and laughed at Bertie's shocked expression when they explained to her what it meant for a trucker to stop at a "pickle park."

She punched the trucker everyone called Tramp hard against the shoulder. "Get out of here!" she shook her head in disbelief. "*That's* what a pickle park is? Well, I'll be damned!"

She could hear Max's critical murmur, all the way from inside the kitchen where he stood looking out at her and shaking his head. "*You were doing so good, Bertie,*" his voice echoed inside her head. She turned to look back at him and shrugged. "*Sorry!*" she winked at him and returned her attention to the truckers.

"So, Bertie, you really had no idea what that trucker meant when he told you he needed to head on out, so that he could find a pickle park before it got too dark out?" Tramp shook his head and laughed out loud.

Bertie punched him again. "Are you kidding? I figured a

pickle park was just what the name says—a dang 'ole pickle park, where they probably sold gourmet pickles!"

The three truckers all laughed good-naturedly at their favorite waitress's naivety. They thought everyone knew the slang term that truckers used to refer to rest areas that truckers stopped at to meet up with other, same-gender, truckers.

"Oh, they are most definitely a different kind of pickle," Tramp laughed.

"Well, I certainly hope none of you fellas stop at places like that!" Bertie pushed herself up and looked down at the three men who enjoyed teasing her. These three were some of her favorite customers, and it always made her feel better to enjoy a laugh or two with them—even if it was at her own expense. "I hope y'all saved room for dessert."

Tramp rolled his shoulders and looked out the window. "I'll have some, Bertie, but I'll have to make it quick." He nodded toward the outside. "That sky is getting pretty dark out there, and I was hoping to make South Carolina before dark."

"I'll be back in a jiffy, fellas. I'll freshen up those coffees for you, too, because nothing goes better with double-chocolate brownie punch-bowl cake, than a good cup of coffee." She winked at them and turned toward the kitchen.

Max raised his brows at her when she entered the kitchen and shook his head.

Bertie flopped her hand and wrist in his face. "So, I slipped up! It was only one cuss word, and it wasn't even a cuss word, was it? I mean, all I said was *I'll be damned!*" She turned to get bowls from the cupboard and removed the large punchbowl full of double-chocolate brownie cake— chunks of brownies on the bottom followed by layers of Cool Whip, chocolate pudding, and drizzled melted frosting, from the refrigerator. She filled three large bowls full of the decadent dessert. "Never mind, don't answer that. I'm sure I'll get an earful from Martin next Sunday. I'll do better, I promise. I won't say another bad word for the rest of this week!"

Max just shook his head and grinned. "Bertie, my old friend, I have a distinct feeling that it will literally be a cold day in hell before you ever go more than a week without letting at least one bad word slip from your mouth."

"Well, you have to admit, I have gotten better at controlling my tongue, Maximus," she lifted one shoulder and tilted her head in his direction. "Hand me one of those trays, will you?" she pointed to a stack of trays on the back counter. "This dessert of yours weighs more than I do!"

Max handed her a tray and helped her load the desserts on it. "Doug should be back any time now to help you out."

"He went to visit PJ again, huh?"

"Yes, he did," Max nodded. "The police were visiting her again today to get a written statement from her about what she saw the night that Norman was killed. Doug and Bernard, both, wanted to be there with her—for moral support."

"Can she identify who the killer was?" Bertie leaned against the counter top.

"I believe Doug said the police were bringing her some photos to look at, hoping she might be able to identify someone."

"Well, I hope she's able to help bring some closure to all this mess. Have you heard anything else about the Crennan boy?"

Max picked up the tray of desserts and held them out for Bertie. "No, nothing since Jason called Doug earlier this morning about the phone call that Cheryl received. I think all they can do right now is to sit tight and wait for the police to get back to them."

The angel chimes sounded as the front door opened, and a blast of cold air evaporated into the warm, inviting café. Bertie took the tray and turned to leave. "Looks like another hungry customer that's come in from the cold. We'll talk more later, Maximus—you be sure to let me know if you pick up on anything bad, you hear me?"

"I hear you, Bertie," Max grinned. He watched carefully while she placed the desserts on the truckers' table and moved to seat the new customer.

Bertie placed the bowls of punch-bowl cake in front of Tramp and the other two truckers. She leaned over and gave Tramp a final punch on the shoulder. "If you're going to eat punch-bowl cake, then you've got to expect an extra punch to go along with it." She laughed and moved quickly toward the front door. She paused when she looked over the elderly, well-dressed, man waiting to be seated. Something about him was special—but, she didn't know exactly what. She cast a quick glance at Max, who was staring back at her and the customer, and saw him raise his eyebrows in surprise.

"Come on in!" Bertie touched the old man's shoulder—she could feel the frailty of his bones, even beneath the warm, knee-length coat he wore. "Let's get you seated and warmed up. How about a cup of coffee to start things off? We have smothered steak with peppers and onions, seasoned rice, and the best broccoli casserole you've ever tasted. You can have your choice of breads, but I would highly recommend Max's jalapeno cornbread to go with this meal—it sops up the gravy soooo good!"

It wasn't until she was leading him to an empty table, that Bertie noticed—and recognized—the dirty backpack that he carried with him. She looked down at the backpack and waited for the old man to be seated. She nodded at the backpack. "That's Skipper's backpack—might I ask what you're doing with it?"

The old man looked over at the backpack and patted it tenderly. "You knew my brother? I'm so glad. They told me at the police station that I might be able to find a man here, who knew Gordon—they said his name was Bernard Cartwright. Do you happen to know this man or where I might find him?"

Bertie motioned for the old man to scoot over, and quickly sat down beside him. "Yeah, I know Bernard.

You've come at just the right time, too, because he's leaving town tonight—returning home to his family, I heard him say." She stared at Charles for a moment longer. "So, *you're* Skipper's brother, huh? I thought he said you were sickly— too sick to travel?"

The old man removed his hat to reveal a head full of silvery white hair. "Well, I'll be eighty-one this year, so I definitely have my good days and my bad days—it does seem, lately, that the bad have outweighed the good, but...I wanted to come, personally, to claim my brother's body—to return him home for a proper military burial. My name is Charles, and yes...I am Gordon's older brother."

Bertie placed her hand upon the old man's shoulder. "We were all so very shocked, and saddened, about Skipper's— Gordon's—death. It was just so sudden; nobody expected it."

"Well, since there was no evidence of foul play, neither the police—nor I—saw any reason for the need of an autopsy. We will just have to assume that Gordon's heart finally gave out. My biggest regret, though, is that he was alone when he died. Nobody should be all alone when they leave this earth." Charles slumped a little in his seat, but immediately sat upright again. "Forgive me, dear lady..."

Bertie shook her head and smiled at Charles. She looked deeply into his sad eyes and said, "Nobody is ever all alone when they leave this earth."

It took Charles a moment to understand what the waitress was referring to, but when he did, he nodded. "You're talking about God, I presume? Well, unless he changed dramatically since the last time I saw him, I'm almost certain that Gordon had given up on your God—a long, long time ago."

Bertie stared back at the old man. "Something tells me you might have, too?"

It wasn't like Charles to open up to a total stranger like this, but there was something instinctively trustworthy about this woman. He nodded and closed his eyes. "You would be right. Something happened to me many years ago that instilled that doubt deeply inside me."

"What might that be..." Bertie began, but stopped when the angel chimes sounded again at the front door. She turned to look back and saw Doug and Bernard shuffle in. She stood up and said, "Excuse me, but, there's Bernard now. I'll send him over so that the two of you can have a little chat, and I'll get your food ready. I'll have Doug bring you and Bernard some coffee over, okay?"

"That would be nice," Charles smiled. "Thank you, very much." He sighed and took a deep breath. It would be interesting to talk to Bernard — a stranger who probably knew Gordon much better than his own brother ever did.

Bertie rushed over to Doug and Bernard. "Hey there, handsome. Everything go okay with PJ?"

Doug nodded. "It went better than just okay, Bertie. PJ was able to identify the young man who pushed Norman against that concrete wall. His name is Kirk Blankenship. She said there were two or three other boys with him, but she couldn't positively identify any of the others — just Kirk. The police are working on things now to bring Kirk in for questioning." He looked back at Bernard. "Come on over to the counter, Bernard, and I'll get you that coffee I promised you."

"Oh, no you don't!" Bertie punched Doug and grabbed Bernard by the sleeve. She pointed to the old man sitting in the first booth by the door. "See that man sitting there by the door?" She waited for Bernard to nod, and continued. "Well, that's Skipper's brother, and he was hoping to have a chat with you about him."

"With me?" Bernard drew back. "But, I barely knew the man."

"Trust me," Bertie locked elbows with Bernard. "As true as that statement might be, you knew him better than his own brother did!" She looked back at Doug and instructed him to bring two coffees to table #1.

Bertie led Bernard to the table and introduced the two

men. "Coffee's on its way, fellas. I'll go get that food I promised you." She winked at Doug on her way into the kitchen. "Don't keep them waiting, handsome!"

Doug waved at Bertie and nodded. He filled two cups with steaming hot coffee and walked over to the two men, who had quickly fallen into a mutual discussion about Skipper. He sat the coffees on the table and was turning to leave when the hairs on the back of his neck literally stood on end. He held his breath for what seemed like an eternity before turning back to get a better look at Skipper's brother.

"Charles? What's wrong?" Bernard asked with an extremely worried expression covering his face. "You look as though you've seen a ghost."

The look of panic, fear, and disbelief was more than evident on Charles Whiting's wrinkle-lined face. His eyes grew wider and his mouth turned dry as it fell open. He balled his right fist tightly against his upper left chest and began hyperventilating—all this, while never taking his eyes off Doug.

Doug moved in slow motion as he turned completely around to face the old man sitting with Bernard at table #1. His own eyes expressed shock and disbelief, and he shook his head slowly from side to side. "It can't be..."

Charles pointed a bony finger at him and shook his head in adamant denial. He repeated Doug's words, "It can't be..."

Doug began backing away slowly from the table and quickly bumped into Bertie.

"Whoa, handsome—be careful, or you'll be wearing this smothered steak..." she ceased talking when she saw the bewildered and perplexed expression on Doug's face. She looked beyond him at table #1 and saw an identical expression on Charles Whiting's face. "What the hell is going on?"

Doug's rapid breathing eventually slowed, and he whispered as he rushed past her. "Charles Whiting? I knew him only as *Chuck*; he's the man who accidentally killed me in 1953..."

# CHAPTER 37

## Still Waters Don't Run Deep Enough

Kirk's balled fists remained at his side. He stood still and waited for his father to get out of his Mercedes. His rapid, exhaled breaths spurted small streams into the frigid air. "What are you doing here?" He pursed his lips tightly together; they were already tinged a light blue from his short time outside.

Ernest left the car running and closed the driver's door behind him. "What am *I* doing here? What are *you* doing here, Kirk? You're supposed to be in school."

Kirk's mind was running in a thousand different directions. He had to get his father out of here, without him going inside the house, but he had no idea how he was going to accomplish that. "I left early," he mumbled and shoved his hands deep inside his jacket pockets. "I...I couldn't concentrate today..."

Ernest nodded. "I know, son. I was feeling the same way. Today is a hard day for us both, I know. I thought coming to the lake house would help."

Kirk had no idea what his father was talking about; with everything that had transpired over the past several days, he had forgotten that today was the anniversary of his mother's passing. "What?"

Ernest stiffened and stood up straighter. "Did you forget, son—about what today is—the anniversary of your mother's death?"

Kirk was rocking back and forth on the balls of his feet. He bit his bottom lip and said, "I'm surprised you remembered that, Dad."

The steps he took toward his son were slow and deliberate. He stopped when he was within a couple of feet of Kirk. "Of course, I remember it. I loved your mother more than life itself. I thought I would die myself when we lost her—sometimes, I wish I had."

Kirk didn't even try to hold in his anger. "I wish it had been you instead of her!" he yelled, removing his hands from his pockets and balling them into fists once again. "It should have been you!"

Ernest took a step backward. "That's an awful thing to say, son..." He knew his son had become bitter and resentful—especially since the marriage to Rae—but, he never guessed that he held such hatred against him. "Please—let's go inside where it's warmer—let's talk about this."

Kirk panicked. There was no way he could allow his father to enter the lake house; he couldn't let him find Jimmy Crennan. "No!" he yelled as he turned and fled back toward the dock.

"Kirk! Wait!" Ernest chased after his son as fast as his overweight stature would allow. "Come back—please!"

Kirk stopped when he got to the end of the dock. He glanced down into the murky water, expecting once again, to see the old woman's face staring back at him. *"This was a mistake,"* he told himself. *"This is the last place I needed to lead my father to—no—inside the house is the last place..."* He turned around quickly and saw his father stop about twenty feet from him, bent over, huffing and puffing. "Go away, Dad! Leave me alone—I need to be alone!" A lone tear escaped the corner of his eye. "Please...if you still love me, please...just go...leave me alone today, okay?" He took a step backward and teetered close to the edge of the dock.

Ernest thought his son was going over the edge of the dock and, instinctively, rushed forward in an attempt to save him. He reached Kirk quicker than he thought was humanly possible and grabbed for his son's outstretched hand. His hands were sweaty from the effort of his jog to the dock, and they easily lost the grip on Kirk's hand.

Kirk grabbed hold of a corner post and managed to keep himself upright, but his father was not as agile and coordinated. He lost his footing when he lost the grip on Kirk's hand. His feet shot out from under him and he fell backward, hitting his head on the dock before continuing his slide toward the dark, shadowy water beneath them.

The splash was much louder than the splash the old woman had made earlier that morning.

"Kirk! H-E-L-P!" His father screamed from below the dock.

"Oh, no..." Kirk pressed the heels of his hands tightly against his ears, trying to drown out the sound of his father's plea for help. He didn't know what to do—which way to turn—but, he knew he had to get out of there—to erase any evidence that he had been at the lake house. He backed away slowly at first, then turned, and ran full-force toward the lake house.

Ernest was trying to keep his head above the water, but his heavy winter clothing—now water-logged—was pulling him downward like a magnet. "Kirk!" he managed to yell out one more time before beginning to sink. He took a deep breath before his head went under and tried to kick off his shoes. He pushed the shoes off and struggled to shimmy out of his heavy jacket. He had sunk about ten feet, and almost had the jacket completely off, when his foot bumped against something in the water below him. He looked down quickly and stopped kicking, a regrettable action which caused him to immediately begin sinking further.

One arm was still caught in the jacket when he came face-to-face with Stella Seiber.

Jimmy was sitting on the edge of the bed when he heard the glass door slam open. He tried to stand up, but the pounding in his head made the room spin and he sat quickly back down. His right eye was completely swollen shut now, and blood had seeped through his bandaging and soiled the bed sheets. He didn't know why he felt the need to do it, but he quickly covered the sheets with the blanket and tried to stand up again.

He heard the slamming of doors and cabinets. He, also, heard Kirk yelling a stream of profanities that would make any sailor proud. He had not heard any voices other than Kirk's, so he assumed that Kirk was still alone. He pressed his right forearm under his left rib cage and moved slowly toward the open doorway of the bedroom.

Kirk sensed someone watching him and looked up to see Jimmy leaning against the doorway.

"What's going on?" Jimmy asked weakly.

Kirk stopped what he was doing and marched rapidly toward Jimmy. His first instinct was to shove him hard against the door, but he managed to refrain from doing so. Instead, he shook his fist in front of Jimmy's face and yelled; spittle flew from his raging mouth. "It's *your* fault—all of this is *your* fault. None of this would have happened if I could have trusted you to keep your damn mouth shut."

"What do you mean, it's all my fault, Kirk?" Jimmy felt lightheaded and held onto the door frame for support. "I told you all along that I wasn't going to say anything to anyone, and I never told a soul—not even my mom…"

"Oh, you think you're so perfect, don't you, Crennan? Well, it's not fair—it just isn't fair that you still have your mom."

"What!?" Jimmy shook his head. Kirk wasn't making any sense at all. What did their moms have to do with any of this?

"Shut up and get ready. We're leaving here." Kirk turned and continued shoving food and kitchen items into a large shopping bag.

Jimmy watched as Kirk threw several sharp knives into the bag, and his heartbeat rose quickly. "What do you mean, we're leaving here? Where are we going? Why? What are you going to do with me?"

Kirk dragged two bags out the door and threw them into the trunk space of the Land Cruiser. He stormed back inside and grabbed an extra jacket he had brought, off the rack. He walked back across the room and threw it at Jimmy. "Put this on—or don't—I really don't care." He pushed past Jimmy and pulled bandages and aspirin from the bathroom cabinets. He threw them into a smaller backpack and looked quickly around the room. He didn't have time to clean the place, but decided there was no real evidence to prove he had been there.

He straightened the cover on the bed, but never pulled it back to see the blood on the sheets.

Jimmy watched in horrid awe while Kirk moved frantically from room to room. If he had been stronger, he would have argued the point more with Kirk—tried to rationalize the situation with him—but, he felt himself becoming weaker by the minute, and he knew that Kirk was in no mood to listen to anything he had to say. He picked the jacket up off the floor and managed to drape it across his shoulders. "Where are my shoes?" he was afraid to ask, but he wasn't looking forward to walking on the cold ground again in only his socks.

"Move! Get in the car—forget about your damn shoes!" Kirk yelled. He waited for Crennan to finally make it across the game room and out the door, onto the back porch. He fumbled in his jacket for the key to lock the sliding glass door, but remembered his keys were still inside his car. "Oh, to hell with it," he growled as he slammed the door shut.

He forgot to turn off the indoor lights and heating.

"Hurry!" he yelled. He cast a final glance toward the lake and fought against the unexpected remorse that tried to seep into his head. He jerked open the back door. "Get in!"

"Whose car is that" Jimmy asked, nodding toward the Mercedes. "Is someone else here?" He looked around wildly in all directions. "H-E-L-P!" he tried to scream. The effort doubled him over in pain.

Kirk pushed Jimmy hard against the open wound in his back. "Shut up and get in!"

Jimmy had barely gotten his whole body inside before Kirk slammed the door shut and jumped into the front seat. He felt the vibrations of the car when it started, and immediately felt the warm heat from the vents. He lay on his good side and stretched out as much as he could on the back seat.

Kirk saw that Jimmy was lying down on the back seat and nodded eagerly. "Yeah, that's right! That's good—stay down and don't get up until I tell you to." His mind was running in a thousand different directions. He knew, in his heart, that he had screwed things up; he had screwed everything up—and, that nobody could help him now—he had to help himself. Daddy wouldn't be around to help get him out of this mess. He couldn't depend on Mike or David to help him out of it, either. No—there was no one he could turn to for help any more. The only person that he had ever truly felt safe with, and could depend on, had died on this day, four years ago.

There was no turning back now.


There was a fork at the end of the narrow road that led away from the entrance to the lake house. A turn to the right would take Kirk east, back toward Rome. When he reached the end of that road, he still had no idea of what to do, or where to go. He only knew that he couldn't go back to Rome—he could never go back home. He laid his head on the wheel and closed his eyes. When he opened them, he took a deep breath and turned west, toward to Georgia/Alabama state line.

Five minutes after Kirk Blankenship turned west off the narrow road that led to the lake house, Officer Thomas O'Brady made a left turn onto that same road. He stopped when he saw how narrow the road was; it was definitely a one-car-at-a-time road. He glanced down at an aerial map of the wooded area. There was no road sign to identify the road, but if this was the right road, then the lake house should be about a mile down the road, on the left.

Five minutes—if he had arrived at that road only five minutes sooner—Officer O'Brady would have run smack into the black, 2016 Land Cruiser that belonged to Ernest Blankenship.

Kirk had not taken the time to relock the entrance gate, so Thomas got out of his cruiser and pushed the gates open. He looked at his watch—it was 3:15, but the skies were getting so dark that it seemed more like 5:30, the time of day when dusk usually arrived this time of year. He drove slowly down the gravel driveway and couldn't help but notice how beautiful a setting this was. It must be nice to be able to afford a place like this to get away from it all. He doubted he would ever know what that felt like.

Thomas put on his brakes when he came around a small bend in the driveway, and almost hit the Mercedes. He got out of his cruiser to inspect the car—its engine was still running. "Someone must be here," he spoke aloud, the obvious. He looked around the immediate area, but didn't see anyone. He opened the driver's door and turned off the ignition. He walked slowly around the car and saw tire tracks, in the gravel—they appeared to have swerved around the Mercedes, evidently toward the entrance gate, since Thomas didn't see any other vehicles in the driveway. He kneeled down to get a closer look at the tire marks. "Yep...definitely more than one car." He left his cruiser where it was and began a slow walk toward the back porch. He saw lights on inside the house, and immediately drew his gun—more out of reflex than fear. When he reached the door, he saw that it was open about half an inch. Someone had to be inside; after all, there was a running car parked in the driveway. Or, maybe someone else had been there and left in a hurry; after all, there was more than one set of tire tracks. Regardless, all of this rationalizing gave Thomas ample reason, and cause, to enter the property—without waiting for the back-up team to deliver the search warrant.

Thomas eased the door open and stepped inside. He listened for any sounds coming from upstairs, but didn't hear anything. He moved into the kitchen and pushed the door open that led into the small bathroom—nothing or nobody was in there. He backed into the game room and directed his gun to the left, toward a room in the far left corner. A dim light was coming from that room. He listened intently, but didn't hear anything, so he eased himself into a large master bedroom suite. A light was on in the bathroom, but—again—there was nothing or nobody in that room either. He took notice that the shower stall was still wet—someone had taken a shower recently.

When he was certain that he was alone in the house, he returned his gun to its holster and began walking around the large room. He walked around to the left side of the bed and saw a long, heavy chain—a key was still in the padlock. "What the hell?" he said as he lifted the chain. It had to be at least twenty feet in length. He followed the end of it and saw that it was secured to a metal rail beneath the bed. He stood back up and looked more closely at the bed. It looked rumpled, as though someone had made it quickly—maybe, too quickly.

Thomas pulled the left side of the cover back. He didn't know what he expected to see, but something compelled him to move to the other side and pull it back, too. When he did, he saw the large spread of blood on the pillow and sheets. "Oh, Dear, God..." Thomas bowed his head quickly. "Please, no...don't let me be too late."

He made a quick search of the rest of the lake house and

rushed back to his car. He radioed Dispatch—it would seem that he needed back-up quicker than anticipated. He told them that he had arrived upon what could be a possible crime scene. He also gave them the tag number on the Mercedes and asked them to track it. He started to close the door to the cruiser and turn on the heater, while he waited for the forensic team to arrive. The running car still nagged at his brain. Someone still had to be here if that car had been left running. He rubbed the back of his head and got out of his car. Once again, he perused the beautiful setting that surrounded the lake house. His gaze returned, more than once, to the dock, and the still waters of the lake that surrounded it. He felt a slight nudge against his right shoulder and spun around, but nobody was there. "What was that?" he shook his head. Once again, his gaze returned to the dock, and he felt the slight pressure against his shoulder. He couldn't explain it to anyone if he had to, but he knew that something—or someone—was directing him toward the dock.

A tremendous burst of thunder roared above him, and Thomas could have sworn that he felt the vibrations coming up through the ground. "Okay, okay," he grunted as he looked toward the darkening skies. "I can take a hint."

He began walking toward the dock.

There was a small row boat tied to one side of the dock, next to steps leading down into the water—other than that, the area was empty—no other boats or houses, and certainly, no other people were around. Thomas walked to the very edge of the dock and looked out toward the middle of the lake. He looked upward again. "I don't get it. What is it that I'm looking for?"

Another loud burst of thunder sounded, causing him to jump and glance down into the water.

At first, he saw nothing—just black shadows that seemed to move stealthily beneath the water. He shook his head and was ready to turn around and leave, when he saw it.

A hand—fingertips really—that were on top of the water

one second, and slowly sinking the next.

Thomas never hesitated. He threw off his shoes, hat, and jacket, and dove into the frigid lake. It only took him mere seconds to open his eyes and see a man begin a final plunge into a watery grave. He wrapped one strong arm around the man and began kicking his way back to the surface. His head popped above the water and he gasped for air. He looked up at the two feet that separated the water from the dock. He knew that he would never be able to lift a man the size of this one that far from the water onto the dock, so he floated him toward the row boat.

Thomas had seen Ernest Blankenship in several local television commercials, so he had immediately recognized him once they were above water. It took all the strength he had—plus some extra that had miraculously appeared out of nowhere—for Thomas to drag the man toward the front end of the dock and into the rowboat. He knew nobody would ever believe him, but he would tell his wife later that night, about the strong pressure he had felt against his backside and legs—pressure that provided him the extra push he needed in order to save Ernest Blankenship.

He quickly climbed the ladder at the end of the dock and pulled Blankenship from the rowboat. He began CPR on him until the man began coughing up, what seemed like, gallons of lake water. He turned him on his side and said, "Hang tight, buddy. I'll be right back." He rushed back to his car and radioed Dispatch again. "This is O'Brady again—get me an ambulance out here—to the Blankenship lake house—STAT!"

He became aware of just how cold it really was— especially in his wet clothing—when he rushed back to Blankenship. He gathered his shoes, hat, and jacket, and put them all back on over his wet clothing. He grabbed Blankenship under the arms and dragged him back to the police cruiser. He laid him on the back seat, turned the heater on full blast, and pulled an old army blanket from the trunk. He wrapped it securely around Ernest. "You've got to hang on—help is on the way!"

Ernest felt the warmth from the vent and opened his eyes. He reached out for the officer's arm and whispered in a hoarse voice. "Find—my—son..."

Thomas stared back at the man, whose skin was blue from being in the frigid water. He was more than a little amazed that Blankenship had regained consciousness. "I will—I will find Kirk."

Ernest closed his eyes again and whispered something else that Thomas couldn't quite make out.

"What did you say?" he leaned closer to Blankenship.

"Woman—in—lake..."

"Oh, Dear, God..." Thomas shook his head and backed quickly out of the car. "Is there someone else in that lake..." he was talking to himself the entire time he was running back toward the dock. He tossed aside his shoes, hat, and coat—again—and dove back into the frigid water.

# CHAPTER 38

## So Long Bernard

It was almost 4 o'clock when Bertie walked back into the kitchen for the umpteenth time in less than two hours. She placed her hands on her hips and stared up at Max. "I can't believe you didn't warn me about this!"

Max looked down at the feisty angel who had been at his side more than 50 years now; on days like today, it felt more like 500 years. "Bertie, like I've already explained to you four times now—I did not know this was going to happen. Yes, Martin was concerned about the possibility that it could happen, but the odds were against it. You have to remember—Doug has only been dead for what—63 years? He was only 20 years old when he died on July 16, 1953 during the Battle of Pork Chop Hill. We've always known that it was possible that he could run into someone who knew him when he was alive back then."

"But for goodness sake, Maximus! We're not just talking about anyone here—we're talking about the person who killed him!"

"Correction, Bertie—Charles Whiting did not set out that day to kill Doug. It was ruled an accident—death by friendly fire."

"Humph!" Bertie snorted. "I sure as hell don't see anything friendly about getting shot in the back by one of your own men. I don't understand why they call it friendly fire, anyway."

"Today's Army might agree with you on that, Bertie. They might even refer to such a death as 'collateral damage' instead — either way, it usually refers to an accidental death. The term 'friendly fire' actually refers to an attack by a military force. It can be caused by misidentification of the target, inaccuracy, or, even human error — which was the case with Doug and Charles. Charles was young and inexperienced. He was nervous and panicky that day, and literally tripped over his own feet."

"Collateral damage? I think I like the term 'friendly fire' better after all. Yeah, I've heard the story before," Bertie calmed down. "But, how weird is this, really, Max! I mean — to come face-to-face with the person who caused you to die! I wanted to talk to Doug about it, but he was so upset. He never went back out to the table until it was time for him to take Bernard to the bus station."

"Is Charles still here?" Max peered through the serving hatch. He could see table #1 clearly from his vantage point. "His table is empty."

Bertie looked over his shoulder. "He seemed so upset after seeing Doug — so confused — that I told him to go upstairs and rest for a bit. He said he wasn't going to leave until he could talk to '*that young man*' again. He's no spring chicken, you know, and I sure didn't want him keeling over in here, so I talked him into lying down for a while. The upstairs room is empty again now that Bernard is gone."

Max sighed and nodded. "You know, I'm going to miss Bernard. They were all special in their own way, but Bernard was different."

"He was their unofficial leader, I think," Bertie sighed, too. "Do you think he made the right decision about returning home?"

Max shook his head. "That's not for me to say, Bertie."

Bertie placed her hands on her hips again. "I'm not asking for the gospel here, Maximus—just asking for your own general opinion. I know you have one."

Max laughed at Bertie's ability to always bring the obvious to light. "Point taken, my friend. Do I think he made the right decision?" He paused for a moment before nodding. "Yes, I do. He's been talking to his wife and kids ever since Joe left. He initially left because he just got tired of the rat race—of trying to keep up with the Jones', as they say. He thought his wife and kids only wanted him around for the material things he could provide them with, and he got tired of feeling like he was alone in the relationship—like he was the only one putting forth any effort."

"Well...that's all pretty much true, isn't it?"

"Not really," Max shook his head again. "Bernard was just as wrapped up in maintaining his high stature in society, that he lost sight of what was really important—his God and his family."

"That's why he's always thought that he wasn't good enough for God to love, isn't it?" Bertie puckered her lips. "Yep, he let his own shortcomings interfere with his relationship with our Lord."

"Sort of," Max replied. "I think he just forgot, for a few years, that God is a forgiving God. Bernard broke the tenth commandment—thou shall not covet your neighbor's house; you shall not covet your neighbor's wife, nor his male servant, nor his female servant, nor his ox, nor his donkey, nor anything that is your neighbor's."

Bertie couldn't resist. "Come on, Max—do you really think Bernard ever had servants, or an ox, or a bleeping donkey?"

"Bleeping?" Max smiled.

"Hey, I'm trying here," Bertie grinned back. "Just kidding, I know what you mean—he wanted what he thought everyone else had."

"He's back on the right track now, Bertie. He has a long

way to go, but I have a feeling that when he gets home, he's going to get a lot of love and support from his family—something he never expected."

"Well, I'm happy for him," Bertie smiled. She looked over her shoulder when the angel chimes sounded. "It's Doug!" She rushed out to meet the younger angel.

Doug walked into the café slowly and peered over at table #1. He saw Bertie rushing toward him. He tilted his head to the right and asked, "Is he gone?"

Bertie punched him on the shoulder before giving him a tight hug. "No, handsome, he's not gone. He's resting in the upstairs apartment. I don't think he's going to leave here until he talks to you."

Doug ran his long fingers through his thick, black hair. "What am I going to do, Bertie? I tried talking to Max about it before I left to take Bernard to the bus station, but he's leaving it up to me. What do I do? I've never been in a situation like this before."

Bertie punched him again before walking away to check on her customers. "You pray about it, handsome—you pray about it." She winked at him and grinned.

Doug smiled as he watched her walk away. "I knew that…" He waved at Max as he walked through the kitchen on his way out the back door. "I'll be back here for a while, Max."

Max nodded. "Take all the time you need, Doug—take all the time you need."

One of the things Max always included at the Heavenly Grille Café—regardless of its location—was his creation of a small back yard that was conducive to prayer and tranquility. Their newest Rome location was no exception. The café backed up to a natural forest, but Max's creation consisted of several winter sweet plants, all of them about 10 feet high. Their normally dark green leaves turned to yellow-green in the fall, and they were now filled with waxy, yellow-white flowers with purple centers. Max had also planted jasmine, honeysuckle, and Japanese apricot plants. The combined fragrances of all these plants encapsulated the feeling that Max had hoped to attain— *heavenly!*

Doug sat down at the concrete patio table and bowed his head in prayer. "What do you want me to do, Lord? I know I'm not supposed to reveal what I am to anyone on earth, but...this is an old man—and not just any old man. This is the man who took my life. If I were Home, maybe I would know exactly how to handle this situation, but here on earth, I feel like my timing is off. I feel confused and uncertain. I feel worried, Lord. I don't want to disappoint you, but if I pretend like I'm not who Chuck thinks I am, then it is a disservice to him."

Bertie came into the kitchen and placed several orders in front of Max. She glanced out the back door window and nodded. "It's going to be dark soon. How long has he been out there?"

"Not long," Max began humming a hymn that had become a favorite of his during the past thirty years.

"I like that song," Bertie smiled. "I forget what it's called—you haven't sung it in a while."

"It was written and sung by that really country-sounding fella, Bertie—you remember—Buck Owens. It's called 'Bring it to Jesus'".

Bertie smiled again when Max began whistling the tune—off-key, as usual. "You sing a lot better than you can whistle, Maximus."

The two of them sang the song together and when they finished, Bertie closed her eyes and said, "Yep—like the song says—bring it to Jesus and he will show you the light!"

"Amen, Bertie, Amen!" Max nodded toward the back door. "I think Doug has reached a decision on what he needs to do."

Bertie stood on her tip-toes to get a good look outside. "He's going around the side of the café, Max. Oh my, goodness! I think he might be going upstairs..."

✧

Charles had taken the waitress, Bertie, up on her offer to rest in the upstairs apartment. Seeing the face of the young man he had accidentally shot and killed 63 years ago had taken the air out of his sails, for sure. He had recognized Doug at once—he had imprinted that face in his brain many, many years ago. Even though the shooting had been ruled an accident, Chuck Whiting had never been the same again. He had been issued an early release from the Army, due to mental trauma that tormented him on a daily basis. He had never been able to forgive himself for being so clumsy and careless, as to have caused another man his life. He had attended Doug's funeral—from a distance—and watched his parents and sisters cry for the son and brother they had lost too soon in life. No, had never been able to forgive himself, and that inability to forgive himself had affected his entire life, as well as the lives of those people closest to him. He had pulled away from family and friends and lived a virtual life of recluse. He would venture outside to perform his job—which changed from year to year—but, it was 25 years before he began to socialize with other people, and to eventually marry.

He had been looking out the small, upstairs window and had seen the young man sit down at the table in the back yard. He appeared to be praying—a concept that Charles had long ago given up on. He sat back down on the comfortable twin bed and folded his hands on his lap. He didn't know what he was waiting for until he heard footsteps coming up the concrete staircase, outside his door. He took a deep breath when he heard a light tapping on the door, and stood up.

Doug stood outside and smiled at the old man when the door opened. "You deserve some answers to the questions I know you have. I'd like to give you those answers now, Chuck."

Charles gasped loudly and grabbed at his chest when a brilliant, golden hue began to surround the young man who stood outside his door—the same young man he had killed 63 years ago. His mouth fell open and he fell on his knees and lowered his head. "Oh, God, Almighty, in Heaven—what's happening?"

"Please stand up, Chuck—trust me, there's only one person you should ever bow down to, and that is not me." Doug felt good about his decision; he knew it was the right one, even if there would be repercussions from Martin about it. "If you don't invite me in, someone else might see something they shouldn't see." He bent down and took the old man under the elbow, and assisted him to a standing position.

Charles moved aside and allowed the *apparition* to literally float into his room. The young man's feet were a good foot above the ground when he entered the apartment. "Are you a…ghost?"

The golden hue still surrounded Doug, but he floated gently back to the floor. He touched the old man's shoulder and smiled. "Have a seat, Chuck."

Charles moved back to the bed, but never took his eyes off Doug. "You are a ghost, aren't you? You've come back to haunt me—to drive me totally over the edge this time." He closed his eyes. "Go ahead, do what you came to do. I deserve it…"

Doug kneeled down and laid his hands upon the old man's arthritic knees. "Open your eyes—look at me, Chuck."

A powerful sensation came over Charles when the young man touched his knees. He could, quite literally, feel the years and layers of self-deprecation and blame slowly evaporate into the warmness of the small room. His lungs felt full and his heart beat strong—he had not felt this alive in many, many years. He opened his eyes and watched as the golden hue slowly, and gradually, dimmed, until it disappeared altogether. He shook his head and stared at Doug. "You're not a ghost, are you?"

Doug smiled and shook his head. "No, Chuck; I am not a

ghost."

"Then...then, you must be an..." Charles shook his head feverishly from side-to-side. "No, no—that's not possible. There's no such thing."

"It is possible, Chuck. Please—look at me." He smiled when the old man complied. "Thank you, Chuck. I need you to say it for me. Tell me what you think I am."

"Why?" Charles asked. "Why do I need to say it?"

Doug lifted Chuck's chin until they were staring eye-to-eye with each other. "Because, my friend...if you say it, trust me...you will believe it; and, once you believe it, then all the torment you've carried inside you for all these years will vanish forever."

"How can that be possible?"

"Because it is God's will, my friend, it is God's will. The will of God will never take you where the Grace of God will not protect you."

Charles took a deep breath and stared back at Doug for several moments. A small grin finally escaped and he nodded as he took Doug's hands into his own. "You're an angel, aren't you?"

Doug smiled back and nodded. "Yes, Chuck, I am an angel, and there's something you need to hear."

"What's that?"

Doug squeezed Chuck's hands and helped him stand up. They were almost the same height, and Doug could have sworn that the old man stood a little straighter than he had earlier that afternoon. "I forgive you, Chuck. Please do not blame yourself for what happened. It truly was an accident, and it's time for you to forgive yourself. Can you do that?"

Charles shook his head. "I don't know—I don't think I can." He took several deep breaths before adding, "But I'm going to give it one helluva try!"

Doug was grinning widely. "I'm so glad, Chuck."

"Can I ask you something else?" Charles seemed nervous.

"You can ask me anything," Doug continued smiling

back at the old man. "Anything."

"Okay," Charles nodded. "Okay. So—are you the *only* angel here, or is everyone here an angel, too?"

Doug laughed out loud. "Well, allow me to correct myself, my friend—you can ask me *almost* anything!" He laughed again and said, "What do you say we go back downstairs and get you something to eat. You've got a long trip ahead of you tomorrow, and we all want you to get Skipper safely back to where he belongs—to give him the honorable funeral that he deserves."

Charles followed Doug out of the apartment and climbed carefully down the stairs. When they got to the bottom, he stopped and took Doug's arm. "Oh, how I wish Skipper had known the truth about you. It might have made all the difference for him."

Doug leaned down and whispered into the old man's ear. "Well, I'll be going Home on Sunday for a visit. I promise to call you when I get back, and let you know if I see him there."

Charles stopped in his tracks. "It's true, isn't it? There really is a Heaven?"

"Oh, yes, Chuck—there's a Heaven, but let's save that discussion for another time, shall we?"

It was dark outside by the time the two men entered the café. Doug turned back to look up into the dark sky. The threatening clouds that had dominated the afternoon had moved on, and the sky was perfectly clear, except for the half-moon and...one lone star. "I have a feeling I'll see you on Sunday, Skipper." He saluted the lone star and closed the door softly behind him.

# CHAPTER 39

## Good and Bad Reunions

Cheryl had waited at home for as long as she could before she and Jason drove to the police station. It was almost six-thirty and they had been there for two hours, waiting to hear something—anything—from Officer O'Brady.

Cheryl stood up and began pacing the waiting room—again. She had chewed every nail down to the nub. "What's taking so long?" she looked at Jason. "He should have called in by now. This can't be good. Something must be wrong—that's why we haven't heard anything..."

Jason stood up and wrapped his arms around her. "You've got to stop torturing yourself, Cheryl. I'm sure he'll call when he has something definite to tell us. It doesn't mean that something bad has happened."

"Then why hasn't Jimmy called me back?" Cheryl croaked. She allowed herself to be comforted by Jason, and in a different situation and environment, it would have been a very good feeling, indeed. "I can't stand this waiting. I thought it would be easier—go quicker—if we came down here, but now, I'm wondering if we shouldn't have stayed at the house. What if Jimmy came home and I wasn't there?"

Jason shook his head. "Don't do this to yourself. Please, come sit back down. We'll give it another thirty minutes or so, and if Officer O'Brady hasn't called in by then, we'll go back to your place. Okay?"

Cheryl took a deep breath and tried to steady her emotions. She knew she needed to remain calm—for Jimmy, and for whatever else might happen before this awful night finally came to an end. "Okay."

Jason saw the desk sergeant talking on the phone and staring at them. Was he imagining that? He didn't know anymore. He turned away for a moment and led Cheryl back to the hard, wooden bench. When he sat down, he glanced over again at the desk sergeant. *"Okay, that's not my imagination. He's definitely talking to someone about us."* He held his breath when the sergeant came around the counter and walked over to them.

"Miss Crennan?" he spoke quietly. "Officer O'Brady just checked in; he should be here in about 10 minutes and has asked that you wait for him in his office—over here, please." He led them to an empty room. "May I get you some coffee, or water?"

Cheryl shook her head. "No, thank you. Did Officer O'Brady tell you anything? Did he find my son? Is he alright?"

The sergeant's lips pursed. "Please wait here, Miss Crennan—it shouldn't be long. Officer O'Brady will answer your questions then." He closed the door behind him.

Cheryl's eyes showed panic and she grabbed Jason's arm tightly. "This can't be good, Jason. They brought us in here because they have bad news, don't they?"

"We don't know that, Cheryl. Please don't go down that road. We'll have some answers soon."


Rae Blankenship returned home at six-thirty and found Prissy sitting in the darkened kitchen. She flipped on the lights and dropped her fur coat on the kitchen table as she pranced past the maid. "Hang this up, Prissy. Whatever are you doing sitting in the dark, anyway? Are you that dumb that you forgot to turn on some lights?"

Prissy raised her head and threw back her narrow shoulders. She pushed herself up from the kitchen chair and stared at the woman who had made her life miserable for the past four—almost five—years. "I's been trying to reach you, Miz Blankenship."

Rae lifted her nose in the air and turned to go upstairs. "Well, not that I need to explain anything to you, but I had my phone off for a couple of hours. I was at...a gallery opening...and certainly didn't want my cell phone going off during that. What did you want—another day off, perhaps?"

Prissy turned to face her employer's wife—that was how she thought of Rae Blankenship. "No, ma'am, that's not why I's was trying to reach you..."

Rae waited for the old woman to continue, but when she didn't respond quickly enough, she turned and started up the stairs. "Oh, for heaven's sake, Prissy. By the time you get around to telling me whatever it is you want to tell me, it will already be tomorrow. I'm tired. Please fix me a sandwich and some soup and bring it to the master suite. I'm going to soak in the tub for an hour."

"You need to get back down here, Miz Blankenship."

Rae snapped around and walked slowly toward Prissy. "*What* did you say to me, Prissy?"

Prissy did not attempt to hide the contempt from her face. "The hospital—Floyd Medical Center—called an hour or so ago. The police took Mr. B. to the hospital. They said he almost drowned and that you should get there as quick as you can." Prissy squared her shoulders and continued to stare back at Rae. "I waited till you got home so I's could tell you face-to-face. I'll call a cab to come pick me up and take me to the hospital, so I's can be with Mr. B."

Rae was speechless—which had not happened very often in her life time. "What happened?"

"I's don't know all the facts. All I know is the police found him at the lake house — in the lake — in this cold weather. It's a wonder he survived in that icy water." Prissy walked over to the phone and punched in the number for a local cab company — she knew the number by heart. She gave them her address and hung up. "Will I be seeing you at the hospital, Miz Blankenship?"

"Well, it's probably nothing, Prissy. He probably just slipped or something, and couldn't have been in the water for long. The lake house, you said?"

"Yes ma'am. It was a place that Mr. and Mrs. B. spent a lot of time at, whenever they could. They taught Kirk how to fish there. They were all very happy together at the lake house. He probably needed to be there today, especially."

"Why? What's so special about today?"

Prissy turned the collar up on her long, winter coat and turned to face Rae. "Because today is the anniversary of Miz Elizabeth's death. Mr. B. probably needed to get away for a few hours, by himself."

Rae retrieved her coat from the kitchen table and put it on. She grabbed her purse and keys and moved past Prissy. "I could care less how *happy* they all were at the lake house, Prissy. Lock up behind you, and, for Heaven's sake — leave some lights on."


Thomas had to call Dispatch for a third time after he pulled Stella's body from the lake. He had thought that Ernest Blankenship was heavy and hard to pull up the ladder, but after a second dive into the frigid lake, he was praying for more of the "extra" help he had experienced earlier with Blankenship. He managed to drag Stella's body onto the dock, but his energy was almost depleted when he tried to haul up the heavy concrete block that had been attached to her leg chain.

He didn't bother attempting with CPR when he saw the bullet hole in Stella's forehead. "I'm so sorry this happened to you, Stella. What did you get yourself into?"

Back up and forensics made it to the lake house in record time, and immediately went to work taking fingerprints and samples from both inside and outside the lake house. Thomas caught up with the gurney as Ernest Blankenship was being loaded into the ambulance; the man had regained consciousness and was asking for the officer who saved him.

"I'm right here, Mr. Blankenship. Everything is going to be fine; you're going to be fine. They're taking you to the hospital. We'll contact your family and let them know what's going on." He paused but he knew time was of the essence. "Who did this? I don't think you fell into that lake by yourself, and I know the woman we found did not go willingly either. Can you tell me who did this?

Ernest pulled the officer closer and managed two words before he lost consciousness again. *"My son..."*

Thomas immediately called in an APB for Kirk Blankenship, age 16, thought to be driving his father's 2016 black Land Cruiser. He noted that the suspect was thought to be dangerous and, most likely, was armed with a weapon. He also reported that 14-year old Jimmy Crennan might, also, be in the vehicle with Blankenship.

He called the station to report in and was told that Cheryl was waiting for him, and that a bloody jacket had been found in Michael's truck. Thomas clinched his jaws tight and left the forensic team to finish up what they needed to do. He told the detective in charge of Norman Weissman's murder to wrap things up for him.

It had been a long day, and it was proving to be an even longer night.

Kirk had driven mindlessly for hours. He kept turning the day's events over and over inside his head. This was not the plan. This was not the way he had planned for things to end. Yes, he intended to get rid of the old woman, but he had not planned on shooting her. He wished now he had never taken the gun from his father's gun cabinet; if he hadn't taken the gun, everything might have turned out much differently. He tried to formulate another plan as he continued driving, but nothing was taking definitive form. The truth was—he had no plan—no idea of what to do next.

Jimmy tried to suppress the coughing fit that suddenly overtook him, but failed. What had started as a dry cough the day before had now settled deep in his chest. He coughed up a small amount of blood and tried not to panic. He tried to remember what he had read about this symptom, especially when it was accompanied by dizziness and shortness of breath—all of which, he was currently experiencing. He coughed again.

"Quiet back there, Crennan!" Kirk warned. "What's wrong with you, anyway?"

"I need some water...please stop," Jimmy answered back. "I...I'm coughing up blood...dizzy...fever...can't breathe. I think I'm gonna throw up." He pulled the jacket tighter around him. "So...cold..."

Kirk jerked to the side of the road and braked to an immediate stop. He looked in every direction and saw a sign advertising a gas station and fast food restaurant about a mile up the road. "Damn!" he slammed his fists against the driving wheel. He glanced down at the gas gauge and was totally surprised to find it almost empty—he could have sworn that he filled it up the day before, but maybe he hadn't.

There were only a few cars on the road, so Kirk eased back onto the road quickly. It was completely dark outside and there were no street lights on this back road that would take him across the Georgia state line.

If he had checked his rear view mirror a second time after he pulled back onto the road, he might have noticed the police car that followed three cars behind him.

Rae went to the hospital to check on her husband and was told that he was still unconscious; all she could do was to wait for him to wake up. The doctor expected Ernest to make a full recovery, but the first twenty-four hours were still very critical for hypothermia patients. They told her that his outcome would have been very different if he had remained in the water much longer. They gave her the officer's name who had rescued Ernest. She knew that Prissy was in the waiting room in case anything happened, so she told the nurse that she was going to make a quick trip to the police station—to see if she could talk to the detective who had saved her husband.

That was a lie, of course. Rae was more concerned about what had happened to her husband's Mercedes. Was it left at the lake house? Did the police have it? She knew that Ernest often carried large sums of cash in his glove compartment, and she didn't want any greedy police getting their hands on that money—*her* money!

She pulled into the police parking lot and stepped out of her BMW. She locked the doors and walked quickly, to get inside and out of the cold wind. She put her gloves on before she pushed open the glass doors that led into the precinct. "God only know how many perverts have touched these doors," she grimaced. She walked into the waiting area, held her head high, and clutched the top of her fur coat around her throat. She spotted an officer behind the counter and pushed her way to the front of the line—three other people had been in front of her. "Excuse me," she pouted, "But this is an emergency."

The desk sergeant stared her down and said, "Lady, you're in the wrong place to be acting like that. Now, go on back to the end of the line."

"I most certainly will not!" Rae stomped her foot and ignored the teetering laughter behind her. "I am Rae Blankenship, and I insist on speaking to an Officer O'Brady—right now, please!"

The sergeant looked over to the interview room/part-time office, where Officer O'Brady was talking to Cheryl Crennan. "You will have to wait your turn, Ms. Blankenship. Now—get to the back of the line!"

Rae pursed her lips and glared at the desk sergeant. "It's *Mrs*. Blankenship!" she stomped her foot again, but did as she was instructed and moved to the back of the line. She passed by two drunken derelicts sitting on the only bench in the waiting room. "What are *you* looking at?" she hissed as she flaunted past them.

She tapped her foot relentlessly for the next twenty minutes — waiting for her turn in line.

She explained to the desk sergeant why she was there and to whom she needed to speak. She grinded her teeth and clamped her mouth shut when he calmly told her to have a seat on the bench — that Officer O'Brady would speak with her shortly.

She turned around at the exact moment that the interview room door opened and Cheryl walked out, with Jason holding her hand. "Thank you, Officer O'Brady — I'll be waiting for your..."

Someone bumped hard against her, shoving her against Thomas. If Jason had not been holding her hand, she might have fallen. She thought that she had been careless and turned to apologize to whoever she had crashed in to. "Excuse me — I'm so sorry..."

Rae dropped her handbag when the young woman bumped her. "What is wrong with all you people?" she snapped. "For heaven's sake, watch where you're going!"

Cheryl stooped to pick up the woman's handbag and stood back up to give it to her. "I'm really so sorry..." Her breath caught in her throat and time stood still for a full thirty seconds. When the movements and sounds returned to Cheryl's brain, she squeezed Jason's hand so tightly that she felt him flinch.

She and the woman stood staring at each other for what seemed like an eternity. The first thought that came to Cheryl's mind was that they were so eerily similar in appearance. The second thought that came to mind came out in one very weak word.

"*Mother...*"

# CHAPTER 40

## Emotional Endings

It was almost 8 o'clock when the State Trooper radioed his dispatch that he had eyes on the Land Cruiser. He provided them his location and continued to follow Kirk at a safe distance. He followed Kirk for another mile and went past the Land Cruiser after it turned left, into a gas station. He confirmed the plate number and drove another block up the road, before making a U-turn and parking behind an old building that had obviously been vacant for several years. He turned off his lights and positioned himself so that he still had eyes on the Land Cruiser. He requested back-up before pulling his gun and making his way, on foot, back to the gas station. He didn't want to risk having the driver take off if he saw the police vehicle.

He made it to another building and stopped behind a huge oak tree. The streets in this small rural town were dark and empty — the only stores open were the gas station and a fast food restaurant across the street. The Trooper watched the driver exit the car, pump gas, and go inside the station. He took that opportunity to move closer to the vehicle. He was crouched on the passenger side of the Land Cruiser, and raised his head. He looked into the station and saw two or three people waiting in line, ahead of the driver. He rose up a little higher and looked into the front seat—he saw nothing but trash and empty beer bottles on the floorboard. He moved toward the back end of the car and peeked inside the back windows.

"Bingo!" he whispered. He saw a younger boy curled up on his right side in the back seat. *"That must be the Crennan boy,"* he thought. He remembered that the APB had indicated that Kirk Blankenship could be armed and dangerous. The Trooper had a 16-year old son at home, and the last thing he wanted to do tonight was to have to kill Kirk Blankenship; however, another quick look at the boy in the back seat confirmed that he did not have the luxury of waiting for back-up, or the luxury of following the driver until he could be stopped with spike strips.

Jimmy felt on fire with fever. He licked his dry, parched lips. He was so thirsty and the wound in his shoulder was throbbing with pain. He felt sure the wound was probably infected, and he doubted that Kirk had any intentions of getting him any medical help. He lifted his head slightly when he heard Kirk open the driver's door. "Must be getting gas," he murmured. "Get away—I've got to get away..." He opened his one good eye and stared at the back of the front seat. He tried to push himself up, but the pain was too great. He lay on his back and drew his knees up. His head was facing the right passenger window, and when he opened his good eye again, he almost screamed when he saw a man's face peering in at him.

The Trooper raised his index fingers to his lips and shook his head.

Jimmy closed his eyes. He was positive that he was hallucinating. He thought he saw a cop at the window. He almost screamed out again when the left back door jerked open and Kirk threw a bottle of water and a handful of aspirin at him. He glanced up toward the ceiling again, but didn't see anyone at the window this time. *"Yeah...I'm seeing things...*" he thought as he reached for the bottle of water that Kirk had thrown on the floor. He somehow managed to get to a semi-seated position and opened the water. He began guzzling it down as quickly as he could swallow it.

"Slow down, Crennan. If you puke in my car, I'll drag you outside, slit your throat, and dump you on the side of the road. Bet that would just break your sweet mama's heart, wouldn't it?" Kirk got back behind the wheel and closed the door. He started the car and was taking off when the passenger door was jerked open and a State Trooper jumped inside.

"Stop the car, Kirk, get out slowly, and raise your hands," the Trooper was calm; but, he made one mistake when he cast a quick, sideways glance at Jimmy.

Kirk took that opportunity to gun the car full-speed out of the gas station. By the time he passed the Trooper's parked car, he was running at 80 MPH. The passenger door was swinging open, and the Trooper was hanging onto the overhead grab handle with his left hand. He waved his gun at Kirk with his right hand.

Kirk made a sharp 180-degree turn into a cow pasture and the Trooper almost lost his hold on the handle. The gravitational force of the turn threw the Trooper completely off balance, and it was taking all his physical strength to hang on and not fall out of the open passenger door.

The sharp turn forced Jimmy off the back seat onto the floorboard. He landed on his wounded left side. The wound burst open again and was bleeding profusely. *"I'm not going to make it...I'm not going to survive this..."* was his last thought before he passed out.

Kirk continued making sharp curves in the cow pasture, to keep the Trooper off balance. He didn't want to give the Trooper a chance to get a clean shot. He laughed out loud when the Trooper's legs slid out from beneath him when he made the next turn a complete circle.

The Trooper was using all his strength to hang onto the grab handle, but his grip was slipping more and more with each sharp turn the boy took. He lost his final grip when Kirk made the complete circle, and he felt his legs sliding out the door. The force of the gravitational pull was too much this time. His fingers slid away from the grab handle, and the pull of the car carried both of his legs beneath the moving vehicle, just in time for the back wheels to roll over and crush them.

The driver's door finally closed behind him.

Kirk felt the slight thump as the wheels ran over the Trooper. He felt no remorse; instead, he felt like the guy on the movie, *Titanic* — he felt ON TOP OF THE WORLD! "Hell, yes!" he screamed inside the car, as he made one final loop before guiding the car back onto the highway. "Man, that felt good!" he looked in the rearview mirror, but didn't see Jimmy on the back seat. "Oh, no — hell, no!" he screeched the car to a complete stop and jumped out. "You better not have gotten out, Crennan — not after all this, man."

He jerked open the back door, his breath coming hard and fast. He held his breath for a few moments and finally released it when he saw that Jimmy had been thrown to the floor. He leaned into the car and poked Jimmy on his legs. "Get up, Crennan!" He waited another few moments. "Man, you better not be dead — not this way — this would be too easy. Get up!"

Jimmy didn't move.

Kirk walked around to the back of the car and removed a large kitchen knife from one of the bags. If Jimmy wasn't already dead, Kirk knew what he had to do. He closed the trunk door and looked all around him. It was so dark outside, and the only lights he saw were the ones on his car. There did not appear to be anything but pasture land surrounding him. His headlights illuminated the road ahead — a small incline — and, he knew he couldn't be far from the Georgia/Alabama state line. He looked back at Jimmy. The high he had attained from trying to throw the cop from his car was subsiding, and he suddenly felt very tired. It had been a really long day, and so much had happened already. He felt almost like all of this was happening to someone else—like he was watching a movie play out. He looked back down at Jimmy and shook his head. "I really didn't mean for anyone to die—I really didn't. I only meant to scare you and the old woman. I needed you to *think* that I would kill you, but, I really didn't mean to hurt anyone.

Kirk stood in the middle of the road and allowed the tears to come—tears for a cranky, old woman who nobody would ever miss; tears for his father and the years he had wasted hating him since his mother died; tears for including his two best friends in his hair-brained schemes; tears for Jimmy Crennan, who had done absolutely nothing wrong except having gotten involved with him and his friends in the first place; and—finally—tears for the life he knew he would never have.

He closed the back door and fell to his knees. He closed his eyes and pressed the heels of his hands against his ears, and, began rocking back and forth. He still held the knife in his right hand. The tears rushed in like the floodgates of Hell had been opened. He knew he had screwed everything up, and he had hurt so many people along the way. "Mom," he sobbed. "Why did you have to leave me? W-H-Y?"

He felt the slight vibrations while he knelt on the pavement, and sensed swirling lights behind his closed lids. He opened his eyes and saw three police cars coming down the hill in front of him, with their red and blue lights lighting up the dark night. He looked behind him and saw at least three more police cars. He took a deep breath and stared straight ahead.

The police cars all stopped when they got within 50 feet of the Land Cruiser. One officer stepped outside his car, but remained behind his open door. His voice echoed across the lonely pastures and into the empty night. "It's over, Kirk. DROP YOUR WEAPON, SON!"

Tears continued to flow freely down Kirk's cheeks. He could have sworn he heard a lone cow mooing far off in the distance; it sounded more like a plea to him—a plea for help—a plea for release. He shook his head and held onto the side of the car until he was in a standing position. He had messed everything up, and he had lost everyone that he ever cared about. He wasn't stupid; he knew what the future held for him if the police took him. He shook his head again. "I'm so sorry, Dad..." he whispered low. "So, so...sorry..."

Kirk raised the knife high into the air, uttered a war-cry scream, and charged forward.

The sound of gunfire filled the night.


Ernest had awoken on the morning of Wednesday, February 10, to find Prissy sleeping in a corner recliner. His throat was dry and scratchy, and he felt extremely weak. "Prissy..."

The old woman stirred in her light sleep. She opened her eyes and saw her employer staring at her. She pushed the blanket off her lap and got up slowly from the recliner. She walked over to him, smiled, and patted his cheek. "I's been praying for you, Mr. B.—all night long, I's been praying for you." She took his hand into her own. "There's been a lot happening in the past 24 hours, Mr. B."

Ernest nodded and tried to swallow. "Water...please."

Prissy used the remote control to raise the head of his bed. "Yes, sir, I got you some water right here...yes, I do." She poured a glass of water from the pitcher on his night stand, found a straw, and helped him drink. "Just a little now, Mr. B.—we don't want you to get choked. You swallowed enough of that dirty 'ole lake water, you know."

Ernest closed his eyes and allowed the memories to come rushing back to him. He opened his eyes again and stared at Prissy. It did not escape his attention that his wife was not present in the room—nor did he really care. He kept staring at Prissy, trying to interpret the sadness he saw in his eyes. He closed his eyes and a tear rolled down.

Prissy wiped the tear away and squeezed his hand. "He's gone, Mr. B. — our little Kirk has gone to be with his mama in Heaven. He ain't in pain anymore, Mr. B. He's home with our Lord."

His breaths came in sharp, ragged agony. This pain — the pain of losing his son — his only child, was worse than he ever could have imagined. His chest heaved and his body shook as the reality of what Prissy said finally registered. "But, what if that's not where he ended up, Prissy..."

Jason paced back and forth in the Intensive Care waiting room. Cheryl sat on a loveseat, with her knees pulled up to her chest, and her head resting on her knees. They had been there all night, ever since Officer O'Brady called to tell them that Jimmy had been found and was being rushed, by helicopter, to Floyd Medical Center — it was the closest hospital around that was equipped to handle trauma cases like Jason's.

Jimmy had been rushed into surgery to correct the damage from the gun wound, and the subsequent infection that had set in. After three hours of surgery, the doctor spoke to Cheryl and Jason about Jimmy's injury. He told them that if Jimmy had to be shot, he was lucky it had been a handgun, rather than a rifle, since handguns produced much slower velocity projectiles. There did not appear to be any significant tissue damage, but they were more concerned about keeping the infection from spreading. He explained that Jimmy would remain in ICU for 24 to 48 hours before being moved to a private room.

Jason walked over to Cheryl and kneeled down in front of her. "He made it through the surgery. He's one tough kid — he's going to be fine."

Cheryl sighed and raised her head. "I know," she smiled and ran her hands over his buzz-cut. "I've been praying all night, so I know in my heart that he's going to pull through this. I just worry about how it's going to change him. He's been through so much. Officer O'Brady told us what those other two boys confessed...how Jimmy and that old woman were kept chained. He must have felt so alone and afraid."

"He's stronger than you might think," Jason smiled back. "He's luckier than some kids—he had you as a mother."

The elevator doors opened and they both looked over to see Officer O'Brady walking toward them.

Cheryl stood up and walked over to him. When they got closer, she rushed at him and threw her arms around his waist. "I cannot thank you enough for everything you did—for finding my son, in time."

Jason walked over to join them and shook the officer's hand. "She's right—thank you, Officer O'Brady."

Thomas guided them both back to the sofa and said, "Let's sit down. It's been a long, long night, and I'm running on adrenaline right now, but I wanted to stop by to see you both before I headed home. I wanted you to hear some things from me, before the media has a field day with everything."

Cheryl nodded. "Okay—everything happened so fast last night. We really don't know what happened, except for the call that Jimmy was alive—that's really all I remember—that's all I was focused on."

Thomas removed his hat and sat down in the chair next to the love seat. "The other two boys involved in all of this—David Mizen and Michael Bozeman—have both cooperated fully since they heard about Kirk's death. I think they're both in a state of shock right now; they really don't realize how much trouble they are in—this is something that their rich parents won't be able to fix with money either."

Jason put his arm around Cheryl and shook his head. "Forgive me if I don't feel any sympathy for them."

Thomas nodded. "That's completely understandable, Jason. One thing I wanted you both to know is that the county prosecutor has already gotten involved. He intends for both boys to be tried as adults for the parts they played in the murders of Norman Weissman and Stella Seiber, as well as kidnapping charges. David has turned state witness, so he will probably receive a lesser sentence. Michael did lead the police to the gun that was used to kill Stella, so that will help him some, but both boys will be behind bars for a very long time. Their childhood has ended."

Cheryl nodded but saw something else in the officer's eyes—something she couldn't quite identify. "What aren't you saying, Officer O'Brady?"

Thomas cleared his throat. "One thing we didn't know—both boys confirmed that Jimmy was with them the night that Norman Weissman was killed."

"What?" Cheryl exclaimed. "That can't be—not Jimmy!"

"How do you know they aren't lying about that?" Jason asked.

"We'll have to wait until Jimmy wakes up, of course, until we can question him about that night; but, the homeless woman who was hit by a car the day after that murder—Peggy Jensen?"

"PJ?" Jason nodded. "Yeah, she's the one who cleared Skipper of the charges."

"Well, she also saw four young boys who were there that night. The only one she could positively identify was Kirk Blankenship; both David and Michael put Jimmy at the scene, too. So, we will have to talk to him as soon as he wakes up. I've asked the nurse to notify me, personally, when he does wake up. I want to be the one to question him."

Cheryl was in shock. She couldn't believe that Jimmy could have been involved in a murder; he would have come to her and told her about it. She knew it. "Okay, okay," she finally said. "I'm glad it will be you."

Thomas stood up. "You might, also, want to know that Kirk left his father to drown in the lake at their lake house. Ernest Blankenship survived. He's on the second floor now, but should be released to go home tomorrow." He paused again and shuffled uncomfortably.

Cheryl looked up at him. "Let me guess—it's about my

mother?"

Thomas rubbed the back of his head. "You know, I truly believe that the Lord works in mysterious ways. Who would ever have thought that Olivia Rae Blankenship was your mother."

"In title and name only," Cheryl stiffened. "She is one woman who knows nothing about what it takes to be a mother. Last night was the first time I've laid eyes on her since I was 15 years old. She threw me out of the house when she found out I was pregnant. My father helped as much as he could by helping my grandmother support us both. My mother divorced him a month after I left—after that, we both lost complete touch with her—not that either of us really gave a damn about what had happened to her."

"Well, she's gone by several names since you last saw her," Thomas answered back. "It would appear that she's maintained a certain lifestyle these past 15 years by marrying well and divorcing quickly—usually with a substantial settlement. I have no doubt that is exactly what she had in mind when she first met Ernest Blankenship."

"She's a real piece of work, alright," Cheryl smiled. "I hope that life eventually deals her the hand that she deserves."

"Well, that might just happen. It seems that Mr. Blankenship's housekeeper has been keeping a thorough log of Rae's activities over the past four years. She has pawn tickets that your mother kept—it seems that she pawned several expensive pieces of jewelry owned by the first Mrs. Blankenship. That will be the first thing that we investigate—something tells me that we'll be finding a lot more evidence to use against your mother."

"She never even spoke to me," Cheryl said, shaking her head. "Never acknowledged me at all while we were at the station."

Jason wrapped an arm around Cheryl's shoulder and kissed the top of her head. "Don't give your mother a second thought, Cheryl—she's not worth it. I'm just so glad that this whole ordeal is finally over..."

The door to Jimmy's ICU room opened and a nurse came out. She walked over to the couple and smiled. "Your son is awake, and he's asking for you both."

# EPILOGUE

## - Heaven -
## Welcome Home

$M$artin stood at the large screen with Max, Bertie, and Doug. He waved his hand and the images of Jimmy at home with his parents disappeared. He sighed and turned around. "Well, I must say, there is never a dull moment down there, is there?"

Doug shook his head. "Nope, one thing about it — life on earth is never dull. It looks like Jimmy will make a full recovery."

"Yes, he will," Max smiled. "I never doubted that he would tell the truth about what happened that night with Norman. That will side well for him when the authorities make their decision about what to do about his involvement."

Doug nodded and smiled. "Thomas O'Brady told me that, most likely, Jimmy will receive probation for the part he played in all of that. He told the police everything he saw regarding Stella, too."

"You know," Bertie grunted. "I have to admit — she wasn't on my list of favorites, but I hate that she had to die like that." She turned to look at Martin. "I don't suppose she was saved in time, was she?"

Martin shook his head. "No, Bertie. It didn't really matter when or how Stella died. I don't think she ever would have asked

340

*forgiveness for all her sins and accepted God as her Lord and Savior. Some people never do..."*

"That's too bad," Max turned and put an arm around Bertie and Martin. "If people only knew what hell and damnation was like, and that it was real, I think the majority of them would make very different decisions."

"Yes," Martin nodded. "There are many people who think that Heaven doesn't really exist and that they're living in Hell while they're on earth."

"If they only knew – and believed," Doug sighed. "Listen, I hate to leave all of you, but there's someone I need to see while I'm here today." He turned and floated quickly away into the whiteness of Heaven.

"Oh, I bet I know who it is!" Bertie laughed. "I'm sure he'll tell us all about it later tonight." She punched both Max and Martin hard against their shoulders and laughed. "I'll catch both of you later. I have a lot to tell my husband about what went on this week. He enjoys hearing about everything from week to week – he said it's better than any mystery book he's ever read." She didn't wait for their replies – she simply shimmied away.

"She's always so dramatic," Martin said. "I mean, she could have simply floated away, but no, our Bertie has to make a production out of every exit, doesn't she?"

Max laughed. "Bertie will never conform, Martin – she will never be the angel that you want her to be. You'll just have to learn to accept that." He turned back to the screen. "Can you show me what's going on with everyone else, now that things have finally come to a close – for now, at least?"

"Oh, indeed!" Martin waved his hand and the large white screen with scrolling black lettering appeared. "Let's see, now...who first?"

"Peggy Jensen," Max nodded.

Martin flicked his hand again and Peggy's life story appeared before them. "She is healing nicely, and will be transferred to a rehab center. It may be another couple of months before she is able to leave and function on her own. I have, no doubt, that Peggy will return home and make amends with her family. Her mother and sisters have already reached out to her."

*Max nodded. "What about Joe and Bernard?"*

*Martin snapped his fingers and Joe Sander's story appeared. "Joe became a grandfather, for the first time – let's see – oh, yes, it looks like the baby was born at the exact moment that Kirk Blankenship died. He's going to be pitching in to help coach a Little League football team for the kids in his neighborhood. It looks as though the tight end his wife left him for dumped her a few months after she kicked Joe out. She's trying to win Joe's favor back again, but – that may take a lot of work on her part."*

*"And Bernard?"*

*"Ah, yes – our leader of the three stooges," Martin smiled. "It would seem that Bernard completely read his family wrong all those years ago. He thought that they only wanted him for the material things for which he could provide them, but that was all in Bernard's head – it wasn't true. His family has never given up looking for him, and waiting for him to come home to them. Now that he has, things will be very different, I believe. Oh, look! It looks like Bernard even agreed to go to church with his family this morning – now, that is progress!"*

*Max nodded. "I almost hate to ask about Ernest Blankenship."*

*Martin sighed. "That one is heartbreaking. He has lost his only son – and before you even ask – no, Kirk Blankenship will never be reunited with his mother in Heaven. It was too little, too late for him, I'm afraid. Ernest is grieving, as one would expect him to, but he has turned his pain and grief over to God – and, God will get him through this. It may take a while, but Ernest will get through this. He's lucky to have Miss Prissy by his side, too. Now that one! She's a true believer – she will have a great impact on Ernest and his ability to move past all this."*

*"What about the two other boys – David and Michael?"*

*Martin puckered his thick lips and shook his head. "Their fates and destinies are still up in the air, but it will be up to them to come to terms with what they have done. It will be up to them to accept blame and show true remorse. I have a feeling that David will come to terms with everything before Michael does – if, Michael ever does! Regardless, they will both have many years behind bars to think about the consequences of their youth."*

*Max scratched his head in thought. "Oh, yes...and, Officer*

O'Brady?"

"Recently promoted to detective, largely in part to the role he played in all this," Martin nodded. "That is one fine individual, that one is. He has a good heart."

"Yes, he does," Max smiled.

"Oh, and the best part about Thomas? Even he doesn't know it yet, but he will before this time next week." Martin laughed out loud. "I love it – I do! Thomas and his wife, Dottie, will become parents for the second time – with another set of twins!"

Max laughed out loud. "That is wonderful news! It's a good thing he got a promotion out of all this. Oh, I'm curious about Cheryl and Jason, too. I don't suppose you care to share a little of your insight into how that relationship might turn out, would you?"

"Well," Martin wiggled his shoulders. "I don't normally like to spoil the ending for anyone, but – YES – things will turn out marvelously for the two of them. Marriage is on the horizon, as well as permanent jobs for them both. All we have to hope for now is that Cheryl and Jimmy can continue to guide Jason down the religious path he needs to take."

"Somehow," Max grinned, "I don't think that will be a difficult thing for them to do." He sighed and took Martin's hand. "Well, I think I'll be off now, my old friend. I'll catch up with you before we head back to the café."

"Tsk, tsk!" Martin shook his finger at Max. "Aren't you forgetting someone?"

Max went over the list of characters in his head. "No, I don't think so."

"Cheryl's mother, of course!" Martin giggled. "Oh, I've saved the best for last. It's true what they say, you know – what goes around comes around!"

"Meaning?" Max smiled. "You look like you're about to burst."

"Now, don't get me wrong, Max – I will continue to pray for this woman's soul, but a small part of me was hoping that this woman would finally get what she has dished out all these years."

"That's not a very Christian way to feel and think, Martin."

Martin shook his head. "No, of course it isn't, and I will have to ask for forgiveness, I'm sure, but...that woman was caught trying to sell more of Elizabeth Blankenship's jewelry. Ernest reported the jewelry as stolen, and Olivia Rae has been arrested. Her husband has filed for divorce, and she has no money of her own to hire a fancy attorney to get her out of this mess. If the stolen jewelry wasn't bad enough..." Martin laughed out loud. "Well, the night she stormed out of the police station after seeing Cheryl there, she got drunk and propositioned an off-duty police officer." He giggled again. "She was charged with prostitution, no less!"

Max shook his head. "Oh, my goodness. I know exactly what Bertie would say about all that!"

The both felt invisible punches against their shoulders and heard Bertie's raucous laughter. "Heh, heh! Karma's a bitch, ain't it fellas?"

**"B-E-R-T-I-E!!!!"**


Doug wasn't sure if he would see Skipper today or not, but he was hoping he would. He had been ecstatic to find out that Skipper had arrived in Heaven because he wasn't completely sure of what Skipper's religious beliefs had been.

He wandered through several valleys before he finally reached the one he had in mind. He stood at the top of the hill and looked down on the lush, green grass, the blue sky and white clouds, and the flowers and butterflies filling every empty space.

He spotted the lone Veteran at once; Skipper was only about 100 yards ahead of him – walking down the hill, into the valley of soldiers. There were soldiers from almost every war – soldiers who died during World War I in 1917, all the way up to soldiers who had fought the War on ISIL. There were hundreds of thousands of them, and they all lifted their right hands in salute to Skipper as he made his way slowly down the hill.

Skipper stopped in mid-stride and stood motionless, looking down at the sea of soldiers below him. Tears of joy soaked his face when he saw all the young men he had fought with in Vietnam – all of them, healthy and whole again. He walked slowly into their arms and for the first time since his brother returned home –

damaged from the Korean War – he felt loved and accepted for whom he was, and for what he had fought.

Doug joined the band of soldiers and hugged Skipper tight. "Every winner has scars, my friend. God will not look you over for medals or diplomas...but, for scars." Doug hugged Skipper again. "I read that a long time ago, and always thought it especially applied to those of us who died as soldiers. Once a soldier...always a solider. You're just marching with a different Army now."

A gentle breeze began blowing through the valley and every soldier stood still and closed their eyes. They all knew what was coming next, because it had happened to each of them, in turn.

"What is that?" Skipper asked Doug. "That breeze – it feels different from any I've ever felt before."

"Just wait – close your eyes – and listen, my friend," Doug smiled as he closed his own eyes.

Skipper closed his eyes and felt the warmth, love, and joy that surrounded the valley. He felt the breeze as it blew across his face, and he felt two strong arms embrace him – he knew, instinctively, that it was not Doug who hugged him now. Tears flowed freely from his eyes and a huge smile covered his face when he heard his Father speak.

**"WELCOME HOME, MY SON... WELCOME HOME..."**

*"...whereas you do not know what will happen tomorrow. For what is your life? It is even a vapor that appears for a little time and then vanishes away. Instead, you ought to say, "If the Lord wills, we shall live and do this or that." James 4:14:15 (NKJV)*

*THE END...yes, really, this time!*

READERS: Thank you so much for taking the time to read my third book in THE HEAVENLY GRILLE CAFÉ series—STAR-SPANGELED REJECTS. I hope you enjoyed reading it as much as I did writing it. If you did, please consider telling your friends about the series, and posting a short review on Amazon.com or Barnesandnoble.com. Word of mouth is an author's best friend, and your reviews are very much appreciated. — J. T. LIVINGSTON

If you enjoyed the poetry in this final story, feel free to check out the complete book of poetry, entitled, "Eyes of the Eagle", by Edwin C. Livingston, available online at Lulu.com.